RAKES

*2 Glittering
Regency Romances*

THE VIRTUOUS CYPRIAN
by Nicola Cornick

THE UNCONVENTIONAL
MISS DANE
by Francesca Shaw

THE Regency RAKES

THE
Regency
RAKES

by
Nicola Cornick & Francesca Shaw

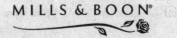
MILLS & BOON®

MILLS & BOON and MILLS & BOON with the Rose Device are registered trademarks of the publisher.

*First published in Great Britain 2002 by
Harlequin Mills & Boon Limited,
Eton House, 18-24 Paradise Road,
Richmond, Surrey TW9 1SR*

THE REGENCY RAKES © Harlequin Books S.A. 2002

The publisher acknowledges the copyright holders of the individual works as follows:

The Virtuous Cyprian © Nicola Cornick 1998
The Unconventional Miss Dane © Francesca Shaw 1997

ISBN 0 263 83664 9

138-1202

*Printed and bound in Spain
by Litografia Rosés S.A., Barcelona*

THE VIRTUOUS CYPRIAN
by
Nicola Cornick

Nicola Cornick became fascinated by history when she was a child and spent hours poring over historical novels and watching costume drama. She still does! She has worked in a variety of jobs, from serving refreshments on a steam train to arranging university graduation ceremonies. When she is not writing she enjoys walking in the English countryside, taking her husband, dog and even her cats with her. Nicola loves to hear from readers and can be contacted via her website at <u>www.nicolacornick.co.uk</u>

Also by Nicola Cornick
in Mills & Boon Historical Romance™

THE NOTORIOUS MARRIAGE
AN UNLIKELY SUITOR ★
THE EARL'S PRIZE
THE RAKE'S BRIDE (within **Regency Brides** short story collection)

★ **The Steepwood Scandal** mini-series

Look for
THE CHAPERON BRIDE
Coming March 2003

Chapter One

Nicholas John Rosslyn Seagrave, eighth Earl of Seagrave and Dillingham, was contemplating matrimony. It was not the abstract state that preoccupied him as he strolled along Bond Street in the afternoon sunshine, but his own approaching nuptials, confirmed that very morning by a notice in the *Gazette*. Miss Louise Elliott, his future Countess, was everything that his pride and lineage demanded: well-bred, accomplished and pretty, albeit in an insipidly pale way. He should have been delighted; instead, he was beset by the habitual boredom which had dogged his heels since his return from the Peninsular Wars several years earlier. All the delights of Town, sampled in full measure, had failed to alleviate this ennui. Now it seemed that his impending marriage could not lift his spirits either.

Some seventy miles away on Seagrave's Suffolk estate, it was also a somnolent summer afternoon, and the Earl's agent, Mr Josselyn, was dozing surreptitiously at his desk in the Dillingham Manor Court. There had been very little business to keep him awake.

A dispute over the enclosure of common land had been resolved with the offender reluctantly agreeing to remove his fence; a violent argument between two of the villagers over the antecedents of a certain horse one had sold the other had led to fines on both sides. The last matter of the afternoon was the transfer of a copyhold tenancy on an estate house to the nephew of the late occupant. Mr Josselyn shuffled his papers, anxious to be away. He cleared his throat.

'Mr Walter Mutch has petitioned that the copyhold tenancy for the house named Cookes in the village of Dillingham be transferred to him, by right of inheritance on behalf of his mother, sister of the previous lessee, Mr George Kellaway...'

The sonorous words echoed in the high rafters. Walter Mutch, a dark young man whom Josselyn privately considered rather wild, got to his feet with a show of respect. Josselyn examined him cynically. Mutch had never been close to his maternal uncle, but had seen his chance quickly enough to claim the house on Kellaway's death. Cookes was a fine property, set back from the village green and with several acres of orchard and gardens attached. Kellaway had been a gentleman of means, but his interests as a scholar and explorer had led him to choose to rent a house rather than maintain his own home during his long absences abroad. He had been a friend and contemporary of the previous Earl of Seagrave, and it had been natural for him to take a house on the estate. The copyhold agreement under which Kellaway had held Cookes was unusual, allowing for the tenancy to be inherited and not to revert to the Manor. Not that Lord Seagrave would care about the disposal of a minor property like Cookes, his agent thought a little sadly. The Earl seldom visited his Suffolk estate, evidently preferring the more sophisticated pleasures of the capital.

Josselyn was suddenly distracted by a movement at the back of the room. The courtroom door swung open, the draught of fresh air setting the dust motes dancing and bringing with it the scents of summer. He frowned. Who could be disturbing the court session at this late stage?

'The petition of Walter Mutch having been given due consideration, this court agrees that the house called Cookes be transferred to his name from this, the fifth day of June in the year of our Lord one thousand eight hundred and sixteen, and in the fifty-sixth year of the reign of our most gracious sovereign King—'

'One moment, sir!'

The clerk's quill spluttered on the parchment at the unexpected interruption and he reached hastily for the sand box to help staunch the flow of ink. Josselyn was dazzled by the sunlight and shaded his eyes impatiently.

'Who wishes to speak? Step forward!'

The door closed behind the newcomer, cutting off the light. A whisper ran round the sparsely populated courtroom.

'Your pardon, sir.' A woman was coming forward to Josselyn's desk, gliding across the wooden floor like a ghost, garbed in unrelieved black and heavily veiled. She moved with youth and grace. He watched her approach incredulously. At the back of the room an older woman, also dressed in black, slid self-consciously into a seat by the door. The newcomer had reached the clerk's table now and was putting back her veil. Josselyn, and every male member of the courtroom below the age of eighty, caught his breath at the daz-

zling fairness that was revealed. Hair the colour of
spun silver curled about a face that could only be described as enchantingly pretty. Eyes of a charming,
limpid cornflower blue met his confidingly. Her nose
was small and straight, her complexion peaches and
spilt cream, and that soft pink, smiling mouth…
Josselyn felt himself go hot under the collar.

'Madam?' All the assurance had gone out of
Josselyn's manner. The whole room appeared to be
holding its breath.

'I ask pardon, sir, for this intrusion.' Her voice was
low, musical and slightly husky. A lady, Josselyn
thought, even more perplexed. He adjusted his spec-
tacles and fixed her with what he hoped was a professional regard.

'In what manner may we serve you, madam?'

Her voice, though quiet, carried to all corners of the
room. 'In this manner, sir. My name is Susanna
Kellaway of Portman Square, London, and I claim the
house of Cookes by right of inheritance as the elder
daughter of the late George Kellaway.'

Mr Josselyn might be a dry-as-dust old lawyer, buried in the country, but even he had heard of Susanna
Kellaway. Who had *not* heard of the scandalous
Susanna Kellaway, one of the most famous courtesans
in London? The outrageous Susanna, who had been
mistress to a whole parade of rich and famous men
and whose career had reached new heights recently in
a highly publicised and disreputable affair with the
Duke of Penscombe? Josselyn found that he was almost gasping for breath. Could this bird of paradise
really be the daughter of the scholarly recluse who had
lived quietly in Dillingham for over thirty years?

Walter Mutch was on his feet, his chair clattering

back. He had always had a hot temper and was several degrees below his late uncle's station in country society. He saw no need to hold his tongue. 'It's a lie!' he shouted hoarsely. 'My uncle never had a child! I protest—' He started forward, only to be restrained by his younger brother.

'There must be some mistake…' Josselyn began hopelessly, and looked up to meet the comprehension and wicked mischief in the lady's eyes, which told him more eloquently than any words that his identification of her had been correct.

'I assure you that there is no mistake, sir,' Susanna Kellaway said, with cool confidence. 'I have here my parents' marriage lines and the record of my birth. As I said, sir, I am the rightful claimant to Cookes!' She placed the papers in front of Josselyn, but they could have been written in Chinese for all the sense he could make of them in his current state of agitation.

The whole courtroom burst into uproar. Mutch was shouting, his brother pulling on his arm to try to quieten him. The clerk was banging his gavel and demanding order, but no one was taking any notice. All occupants of the room had turned to their neighbours and were avidly debating whether George Kellaway had ever had a daughter, and which members of the village could remember. And such a daughter! Josselyn looked hopelessly at the lady in question and saw that she was enjoying his discomfiture. She evidently appreciated both the effect she invariably had on men and also the drama she had caused. She leant across his table and he caught a tantalising hint of expensive perfume.

'My lawyer will be in touch to negotiate the terms of the lease,' she said with a charming smile. 'I bid you good day, sir.' And so saying, she turned on her heel and walked out, leaving Josselyn in the midst of the disarray, contemplating the ruin of his afternoon. He reached instinctively for paper and ink with a hand that shook. Normally he would not trouble Lord Seagrave with estate matters, but in this instance... He shook his head incredulously. He dared not risk leaving his lordship in ignorance of this astounding piece of news. Besides, the situation was too complex for him. He had no notion of how Seagrave would feel at a notorious Cyprian establishing herself on his country estate. Remembering the Cyprian and her melting smile, Josselyn came out in a hot sweat again. No, indeed—Lord Seagrave would have to be told.

'Whatever can have brought you here, Susanna?'

A less thick-skinned woman than Susanna Kellaway might have noticed the lack of enthusiasm in her sister's voice, but she had become inured to snubs over the years. Besides, she knew that Lucille's cool welcome stemmed less from disapproval of her twin than recognition of the fact that Susanna only sought her out when she wanted something. She gave her sister the benefit of her feline smile and waved one white hand in a consciously elegant gesture.

'Why, I came to commiserate with you on the death of our dear father! I assume that you had heard?'

A frown darkened Lucille Kellaway's fine blue eyes. She was sitting in the prescribed manner for her pupils at Miss Pym's School for Young Ladies, Oakham: upright with her hands neatly folded in her lap and her feet neatly aligned and peeping from beneath the hem of her old blue merino gown.

'I collect that you refer to the death of George

Kellaway? Yes, I heard the news from Mrs Markham.'
She sighed. 'I fear that I always think of the Markhams
as our true parents, for all that our father paid for our
upkeep and education!'

Susanna made a pretty moue. In the school's shabby
parlour she looked both golden and exotic, too rich for
her surroundings. 'For my part, I have no filial regard
for either Gilbert Markham or George Kellaway!' she
declared strongly. 'The former left us penniless and
the latter never did anything for us, either living or
dead! First he gave us away as babies, then he refused
to have anything to do with us whilst we were growing
up. When Mr Markham died and we needed him,
where was he?' She answered her own question bitterly. 'Travelling in China! And we were left to make
shift for ourselves! In my opinion, it's a most unnat-
ural father who can treat his children such, dismissing
them without a thought!'

Lucille Kellaway's own opinion was that there was
no point in feeling resentful about their treatment at
the hands of a man neither of them had ever known
and could not regard as a father. George Kellaway,
widowed when his wife had died in childbirth, had
obviously considered himself incapable of raising two
daughters on his own. It was also incompatible with
his lifestyle as an academic and explorer. He was
therefore fortunate that he had a childless cousin,
Gilbert Markham, who was only too pleased to take
on the responsibility for the children's upbringing.
And they had been happy and well-cared for, Lucille
reflected fairly. George Kellaway had provided the
money to see his daughters educated at Miss Pym's
school, and they had spent the holidays at the
Markhams' vicarage near Ipswich.

Their father had never shown any desire to set eyes
on his offspring again, but then he had been forever
travelling in Europe and, when war broke out, further
afield. It would perhaps have been useful to have had
him to turn to on Mr Markham's death, for their adoptive father had left his small competence solely to his
wife and the young daughter the couple had unexpectedly produced in later life. There had not been
sufficient fortune to keep four people, and Markham
had clearly expected Kellaway to support his own
daughters. Lucille shrugged. What point was there
now in regretting the fact that George Kellaway had
been abroad on his cousin's death, and totally unable
to help his children even if he had had the inclination?
He had not even appeared to have a man of business
to whom they could apply. Penniless, they had been
obliged to make their own way in the world—and they
had chosen very different courses.

'Did he leave you anything in his will?' Susanna
asked suddenly, the carelessness of her tone belied by
the sharp cupidity in her eyes.

Lucille raised her finely arched brows. 'His will? I
thought he died intestate—in Tibet, was it not? But
since he had no property—'

Susanna relaxed again, the same little, catlike smile
on her lips. 'Now that is where you are wrong, dear
sis! I have been living in our father's house this week
past! And a sad bore it has been too,' she added, with
a petulant frown.

The entry of the school's housemaid with a pot of
tea prevented Lucille from asking her sister to explain
this extraordinary sentence. The maid cast Susanna
one wary but fascinated look before pinning her gaze
firmly on the floor as Miss Pym had undoubtedly in-

structed her to do. She put the tray before Lucille and backed out, but as she was leaving the room she could not resist another look at the wondrous creature draped over the parlour sofa. Miss Kellaway was so beautiful, she thought wistfully, with her silver gilt curls and warm blue eyes—and that dress of red silk…and the beautiful diamond necklace around her slim throat, a present, no doubt, from the besotted Duke of Penscombe. Fallen woman or not, Susanna Kellaway was much envied at that moment.

'Thank you, Molly,' Lucille said, a hint of amusement in her voice, and the maid was recalled to the present and could only wonder how so luscious a beauty as Miss Kellaway could have a twin sister as plain as Miss Lucille.

The door closed behind her, and Lucille considered her sister thoughtfully, seeing her through Molly's eyes. Susanna had disposed herself artfully on the sofa to display her figure to advantage. Lucille imagined this to be a reflex action of her sister's since there were no gentlemen present to impress, although she expected the drawing and music masters to appear on some spurious excuse at any moment. The dress of clinging red silk which Molly had so admired plunged indecently at the front and was almost as low at the back; completely inappropriate for the daytime, Lucille thought, particularly within the portals of a school full of impressionable young girls. That Susanna had even been allowed over the threshold of such an establishment had amazed Lucille, for Miss Pym had never made any secret of the fact that she deplored the fact that one of her former pupils had become 'a woman of low repute'. Miss Pym clearly felt that Susanna's fall from grace reflected directly on the moral failure of the school.

'You were saying, sister?' she prompted gently.

'Oh, yes, my sojourn in Suffolk!' Susanna stifled a delicate yawn. 'A monstrous tedious place, the country!' She stopped.

Lucille, used to her sister's butterfly mind since childhood, did not display any impatience. 'Did I understand you to be saying that you had been visiting our father's house? I was not aware that he owned—'

'But of course you were! We were born at Cookes! I understand that Mr Kellaway always lived there between his travels!'

Lucille frowned in an attempt to unravel this. 'Of course I knew of Cookes, but I thought it to be leased. Yet you say you have inherited it?'

Susanna smiled patronisingly. 'I have inherited the lease, of course! Old Barnes told me all about it—you remember Mr Markham's lawyer? I kept him on to deal with my business—why, whatever is the matter?'

Lucille had clapped her hand to her mouth in horror. 'Susanna, you do not employ Mr Barnes as your lawyer? Good God, the man's business was composed solely of country doctors and parsons! Surely you shocked him to the core!'

Her sister threw back her head with a gurgle of laughter. 'Which shows how little you know of business, Luce! Barnes was only too happy to take on the work I gave him! What was I saying—oh yes, it was Barnes who read of our father's death and drew to my attention the fact that I had a claim on the copyhold of Cookes. He is nothing if not thorough! And I thought—why not? There might be some financial advantage in it! After all, mine is not a very secure profession!'

Lucille put down the china teapot and passed her sister a cup. 'I see. So you have the right to claim the house and its effects as George Kellaway's eldest child?'

'So Barnes tells me. But there is no inheritance, for he spent all his money on his travels, and the house is full of nothing but books and bizarre artefacts from China!' Susanna looked disgusted. 'It's all of a piece, I suppose! At any rate, you need not envy me my good fortune!' She gave her sister her flashing smile.

Lucille raised her teacup and drank thoughtfully. 'But what are the terms of the lease? I collect our father held the house from the Earl of Seagrave?'

'Lud, who knows?' Susanna shrugged pettishly. 'I leave all that to Barnes, of course! Anyway, it is the dullest place on earth and if it were not for the fact that I may have something to gain, I would not stay there another moment, I assure you!'

She looked a little furtive. 'Actually, Luce, it was that which brought me here. You see, I need to go away for a little and I want you to go to Cookes and pretend to be me.'

Lucille, who had just taken a mouthful of tea, almost choked. She swallowed hard, the tears coming to her eyes. Susanna was watching her with a calculating look which made those limpid blue eyes look suddenly hard. There was a silence, broken only by the distant voices of some of the girls as they played rounders outside. Lucille put her teacup down very carefully.

'I think you must be either mad or in jest to make such a suggestion, Susanna.' Her voice was level and quite definite. 'To what purpose? Such childish tricks were all very well when we were in the schoolroom, but now? I would not even consider it!'

Susanna was now looking as offended as her indolence would allow. 'Upon my word, you have grown most disagreeable since we last met! This is no childish ploy; I was never more in earnest! Do you think I would travel all the way from Suffolk to Oakham for a mere jest...' she gave an exaggerated shudder '...and stay in the most *appalling* inns along the way just for the pleasure of it? Well, I declare! You are the one whose wits are going begging!'

There was some truth in this, Lucille reflected. Susanna could be relied upon never to do anything against her own comfort. She knew she should not give the suggestion a moment's thought, not even discuss it...and yet...

'Why on earth do you need me to consent to so foolish a masquerade?' Her curiosity had got the better of her, for Susanna was looking both dogged and determined, expressions normally alien to her.

'I need you to do it because I *have* to go away,' Susanna said with emphasis. 'Sir Edwin Bolt has invited me to go to Paris with him, and I cannot risk delay. I do not want to let him escape me!' She pulled a dainty face. 'The timing is most unfortunate!'

Something which might have been pity stirred in Lucille. 'Is Sir Edwin so important, then, Susanna? Do you love him?'

Susanna laughed, a bitter sound which matched the scornful sparkle in her eyes. 'Love! Lud, no! But he might be persuaded to marry me! And you know, Luce, we are neither of us young any more. Twenty-seven! I cannot bear to think of it!' Her unsentimental blue gaze considered her sister. 'I suppose you might continue teaching here until you died, but it's different for me. I need to secure my future!'

Lucille swallowed her sister's carelessly hurtful reference to her own prospects. 'I see. But I thought that you had claimed Cookes for that purpose…'

'Exactly!' Susanna rewarded her with a flashing smile, as though she had said something particularly clever. 'I cannot be in two places at once! My best chance lies with Sir Edwin—after all, he might make me a lady!' She did not appear to see the humour in her own remark. 'But at the same time I do not wish to relinquish my claim on Cookes in case there is some money in it for me! It really is so unfair! Why did our father have to die so inconveniently?'

Lucille's lips twitched at this supreme piece of self-centredness. 'I daresay he did not think of it,' she said, with a sarcasm that completely passed her sister by. 'Forgive me if I am being a slowtop, but I do not really understand why you feel you cannot leave Cookes now. Surely there could be no danger in you travelling abroad for a little now that you have secured the lease?'

Susanna pulled a face. 'But I know they want me out of that house! They wish I had never claimed it!' She saw her sister's look of scepticism and hurried on a little defensively, 'Oh you can look like that, Luce, but you didn't see those lawyers! They have been pestering me all week, trying to disprove my claim! I know they don't want me there! Why, they will break the lease if I give them half a chance, and then I may never be able to claim the inheritance I deserve! So I daren't go away without knowing that there's someone to look after my interests, and it's easiest for you just to pretend to be me for a little while! That way it looks

as though I'm really interested in living in the house.
After all,' she added, tactlessly, 'no one even knows
you exist, so they would not suspect!'

Lucille felt as though she was struggling in a quick-
sand. 'But cannot your lawyer represent your interests? After all, he was the one who told you of your
claim to Cookes in the first place. Would he not be
the most appropriate person—'

Susanna was shaking her head stubbornly. 'But my
lawyer is in Holborn! I need someone in Suffolk! I
need *you,* Lucille!'

'But, Susanna,' Lucille said helplessly, 'the deception… It is fraud, after all! And if they were to realise—'

Susanna curled her lip. 'Lud, you always were so
pious, Luce! No one would guess! The only person
you could possibly meet is old Josselyn, the agent, and
even he has probably tired of trying to disprove my
claim and will leave you alone! I thought you might
like a chance to look at Cookes,' she added slyly. 'It
is full of dusty old tomes that would no doubt be fascinating to you. For myself, I cannot bear bookish
things, but I know that you are the most complete
bluestocking.'

There was another silence whilst Lucille struggled
against an inner compulsion. 'It wouldn't work,' she
said, more forcefully this time. 'Why, we do not even
look alike!'

Superficially, this was true. Lucille felt her twin's
gaze skim her with faintly malicious consideration.
She knew what she must look like to Susanna's sophisticated eyes: a country dowd in an old dress, an-
gular where Susanna was generously curved, her silver
fair hair several shades paler and drawn back in a dis-

figuring bun. They had the same sapphire blue eyes, but whilst Susanna made flirtatious use of hers, Lucille's were customarily hidden behind her reading glasses. Lucille's complexion was porcelain pale, without any of the cosmetic aids which Susanna so artfully employed—powder and rouge for the cheeks, carmine for the lips, kohl for the eyes… The effect was spectacular and could only serve to underline the differences between them.

It was three years since Lucille had seen her sister, and she felt that Susanna had not changed in either appearance or attitude. It was typical of Susanna to arrive without warning, demanding that her sister embark on some harebrained escapade just to oblige her. Lucille, forever cast in the role of the sensible twin, had tried to restrain her sister's wilder schemes in their youth, but to little avail. Susanna was headstrong and obstinate, and had not improved with age. Lucille could still remember the horror she had felt when Susanna had announced defiantly that, their adoptive father's death having left them destitute, she would try her luck among the *demi-monde* in London. She had been quite determined and neither her sister's reasoned arguments nor the shocked disgust of their remaining family had swayed her. That had been nine years ago, and who was to say that she had been wrong? Lucille thought, with faint irony. Susanna had never been troubled by the moral dimension of her choice and materialistically she had done very well for herself.

Susanna got to her feet with the fluid grace that was one of her trademarks, and crossed to her sister's side, pulling her to her feet. They regarded their reflections in the parlour mirror, one a pale shadow of the rich colour of the other.

'You could be made to look like me,' Susanna said, slowly. ''Tis only a matter of clothes and cosmetics, and no one at Dillingham has seen me properly—why, I've told you, no one but Seagrave's agents have called in a week! So you see…' she gave Lucille a calculating sideways look '…you need consult nothing but your own inclination! It would not be for long, and I daresay you could do with a holiday from this prison!'

Lucille jumped, shaken, for her sister had hit upon the one truth which Lucille did not wish to acknowledge. Over the past few months, Lucille had been aware of an increasing need to escape the claustrophobic confines and predictable routines of the school. She needed time to read, study, walk and be on her own, but she had had nowhere to go. In some ways the genteel world of the school, the endless classes of little girls, the restricted horizons of all the teachers, was indeed the prison Susanna described.

Susanna was virtually all the family Lucille possessed and Susanna had made it clear long ago that her antecedents were not an asset in her chosen course in life, and she would be obliged to her twin if she did not broadcast their relationship. This suited Lucille, who could see that it would not be to her advantage to claim sistership with one of the most infamous Cyprians in London. The parents of her pupils would be outraged—or believe that she was cast in the same mould. It was a strange twist of fate that had cast two sisters adrift in the world for one to turn into a bluestocking and the other a courtesan.

Lucille sighed. She had no illusions that Susanna wanted to use her, but more than half of her was crying out to her to seize the chance Susanna was offering. The prospect of spending some time in the house where their father had lived and worked held a curious appeal for her. But an impersonation was both fool-hardy and immoral, the voice of her conscience told her severely. But it would not be for long, temptation countered defensively, and she would not really be doing anything wrong…

'How long do you think you would be away for?' she asked cautiously, and was rewarded by a vivid smile from Susanna, who sensed that her battle was already won.

'No more than a week or two,' she said carelessly, resuming her languid pose on the sofa. 'And you would need to do no more than occupy the house. I do not imagine that anyone will call—doubtless it will all be a dead bore, but then you must be accustomed to such tedium far more than I!' Her disparaging look encompassed the faded respectability of the school parlour. 'Lud, how I detest this shabby-genteel place!' With a chameleon change of mood, she smiled on her sister once more. 'Oh, say you will do it, Lucille! You would so enjoy a change of scene!'

Lucille bit her lip at her sister's shamelessness. Unfortunately Susanna was right. Whilst the idea of the impersonation appalled her, the lure of Cookes def-initely held a strange charm.

'All right, Susanna,' she said wryly. 'No doubt I shall live to regret it, but I will help you.'

Susanna glanced at the ugly clock on the parlour mantelpiece. Now that she had got what she wanted she did not wish to linger. 'Lord, I must be going or that old gorgon will be turning me out of doors!' She turned eagerly to her sister and clasped her hands. 'Oh, thank you, Luce! I'll send for you soon!'

She let her sister go and scooped up her fur stole and jewelled reticule. 'You must not worry that you will have to deal with anyone I know,' she added carelessly, with one hand on the doorknob. 'No one of my acquaintance would be seen dead in the country!'

'And the Earl of Seagrave?' Lucille asked suddenly. 'He is the owner of Cookes, is he not? There is no likelihood of him coming down to Suffolk?'

Susanna stared. 'Seagrave? Upon my word, what an extraordinary idea! *He* has no interest in the case, I assure you! Why, Seagrave employs an army of agents and lawyers in order to avoid having to involve himself in his estates!'

Lucille turned away so that her sister could not see her face, and made a business of collecting up the cups and saucers. 'Do you know him, Susanna? What manner of man is he?'

Had Susanna had more interest in the motivation and feelings of others, this enquiry might have struck her as odd coming from her bookish sister. However, she seldom thought beyond her own wishes and needs. She wrinkled up her nose, frowning with the unaccustomed mental effort of trying to sum up someone's character.

'He is a charming man,' she said, at length, 'handsome, rich, generous... Lud, I don't know! He does not belong to my set—he is too high in the instep for me! But you need have no fears, Lucille—as I said, Seagrave don't care a fig about Cookes!'

Lucille stood by the window, watching as her sister ascended elegantly into the waiting carriage. Her thoughts were elsewhere. In her mind's eye she could see another June morning, a year previously, when the bright, fresh day had lured her early from her bed.

Lucille's bedroom was at the back of the school, over-looking a quiet lane and the courtyard of the local coaching inn, The Bell. Lucille had thrown her case-ment window wide, relishing the light breeze on her face, the quiet before the routine of the school day began. She had been leaning on the sill when there was a commotion in the inn yard and a spanking new curricle had driven in, its driver calling for fresh horses.

Lucille had stared transfixed as he had jumped lightly down and engaged the landlord in conversation whilst the grooms ran to change his team. He was tall, with the broad-shouldered and muscular physique of a sportsman; a figure which showed to advantage in the tight buckskins visible beneath his driving coat as he swung round to view the progress of the grooms. The early morning sun burnished his thick dark hair to a rich chestnut and illuminated the hard planes of his face. Lucille had caught her breath and suddenly, as though disturbed by her scrutiny, the man had looked up directly at her. It had been an extraordinary moment. Lucille had stood frozen, the breeze flatten-ing the transparent linen of her nightdress against her body and stirring the tendrils of silver blond hair that were for once loose about her face. It was as though they were only feet apart as the man very deliberately held her gaze for what seemed like forever. Then he grinned, his teeth showing very white in his tanned face, and raised a casual hand in greeting before turn-ing away, and Lucille slammed the casement shut, her face aflame with embarrassment. And it was only later, whilst out in the town, that she had heard that their illustrious visitor had been none other than the Earl of Seagrave…

Lucille found that she was staring blankly out into the empty street. A wave of heat washed over her at the memory of the encounter. Never had the even tempo of her life at the school been so disrupted! Accustomed to seeking a rational explanation to everything that happened to her, Lucille was completely at a loss to explain the startling compulsion that had drawn her eyes to Seagrave in the first place and then held her captive staring in such a shameless manner! And then for him to notice her standing there immodestly in her shift! Well, Lucille thought, tearing her mind away, there was no danger of the experience recurring. Susanna had reassured her of that. Which, a small corner of her mind persisted in telling her quite firmly, was a great pity but perhaps for the best.

The atmosphere in the crowded gaming room was tense. There was no doubt that the Earl of Seagrave had had the run of the cards; several less fortunate players had been forced to retire, their pockets to let, grumbling wryly about his diabolical luck. His dark gaze was intent, a slight frown between his brows as he concentrated on the cards. It was a face of character, perhaps a little too harsh to be classically handsome, the dark, gold-flecked eyes deep and unreadable.

Another hand ended in his favour—and from the doorway, with disastrous clarity, came the stage whisper of some luckless sprig of nobility:

'Lucky at cards, unlucky in love, they say… It's all over the Town that Miss Elliott is about to throw him over…this business of the Cyprian…too blatant, only a week after their betrothal…on my honour, it's true…'

Too late, someone shushed him and he fell suddenly silent. Seagrave turned his head, and the crowd fell back to expose the speaker as one Mr Caversham, very young and cruelly out of his depth.

'Pray continue, Caversham.' All Seagrave's acquaintances recognised the note of steel beneath that silky drawl. His dark eyes were coldly dispassionate as they pinned his victim to the spot. 'Your audience is rapt. Miss Elliott is about to terminate our engagement, you say. Further, I infer that the reason is some…alliance of mine with a certain barque of frailty? Did your informant also vouchsafe the name of this ladybird? I feel sure they must have done, Caversham.'

There was a profound silence as Mr Caversham's mouth opened and closed without a sound. All colour had fled from his face, leaving him looking pitifully young and vulnerable. The Honourable Peter Seagrave, exchanging a watchful look with Lord Robert Verney across the card table, shook his head slightly in answer to Verney's quizzically raised eyebrows. They had seen Seagrave in this mood before and understood something of the devils that drove him. Peter put a tentative hand on his brother's arm and felt the tension in him as taut as a coiled spring.

'Nick, let be! The fellow's a foolish puppy who knows no better—'

Seagrave did not appear to hear him. He shook the restraining hand off his arm and got slowly to his feet. There was a collective intake of breath. Caversham was tall, but Seagrave towered over the younger man. Strong fingers reached for the neckcloth at Caversham's throat, drawing him inexorably closer in the Earl's merciless grasp.

'Do please reconsider your silence, Caversham,' Seagrave said, still in the same, smoothly dangerous tones. 'You possess a certain piece of information which I am anxious for you to disclose.' He gave his victim a slight shake.

Caversham was a fool but he was no coward. His mouth dry, his neckcloth intolerably tight, he managed to gasp, 'It is Susanna Kellaway, my lord! I heard…I heard that she had taken a house on your Suffolk estate… The story is all over Town.'

Seagrave gave him an unpleasant smile. 'True in all particulars! I congratulate you, Caversham!' The young man was released so suddenly that he almost fell over. Loosening his collar with fingers that shook, Caversham watched as Seagrave unhurriedly turned back to the card table, collected the pile of guineas, rouleaus and IOUs and sketched a mocking bow to his companions.

'My apologies, gentlemen. I find some of the company here little to my taste. Peter, do you come with me, or would you prefer to stay?'

There was a bright light of amusement in Peter Seagrave's brown eyes. 'Oh, I'm with you, Nick, all the way!'

The whispers gathered pace as they went down the stairs. 'Can it be true? He did not deny it… So *la belle Susanna* has thrown the Duke over for a mere Earl?'

Seagrave gave no sign that he heard a word as they left the club. His face might have been carved from stone. The brothers went out into the cold morning air, where a hint of dawn already touched the eastern sky. Once out in the street, Seagrave set off for St James's at a brisk pace which demonstrated that he was stone-cold sober. His brother almost had to run to keep up.

Peter, who had been invalided out of the army after Waterloo the previous year, had still not quite recovered from the bullets he had received in the chest and thigh and after a few minutes of this route march he was forced to protest.

'For God's sake, Nick, slow down! Do you want to finish what the French started?'

That won him a glance with a flicker of amusement and although Seagrave did not reply, he slowed his pace to a more moderate rate that enabled his brother to keep up without too much difficulty. Not for the first time, Peter wished that his brother was not so difficult to read, his moods so impenetrable. It had not always been so. Now, for instance, he sensed that Seagrave was blindingly angry, but knew he would say nothing without prompting. Peter sighed and decided to risk it.

'Nick, what's all this about? When that idiot Caversham started talking I thought it was all a hum, but you knew all about it already, didn't you? You *wanted* him to tell everyone about Miss Kellaway!'

There was a silence, then Seagrave sighed. 'Your percipience does you credit, little brother.' There was a mocking edge to his words. He drove his hands deep into his coat pockets. 'Yes, I knew. Josselyn wrote me some garbled letter earlier this week to tell me that Miss Kellaway—' he sounded as though there was a bad taste in his mouth '—had claimed a house in Dillingham. I wanted to see how much of the story had become common knowledge.'

Peter was frowning. 'But if you already knew about the Cyprian, why did you not take action?'

He waited, and heard his brother sigh again. 'I did

not think that it mattered,' Seagrave said, with the weary boredom that was habitual.

'Did not think—?' Peter broke off. He was one of the very few who knew the depth of his brother's disaffection since his return from the wars, his apparent lack of purpose in civilian life. They had shared similar experiences whilst on campaign and Peter could see why Seagrave had been so deeply affected and had found it difficult to settle in a society that seemed to offer only instant, superficial gratification. Peter had the happy temperament to be able to recover from his harrowing experiences, albeit slowly, but Seagrave had always been much deeper, had dwelt more on all that he had experienced. It was as though some part of him had become shut away, unreachable and uninterested.

Nothing could hold his attention for long. He had the entrée into any *ton* function that he chose to honour with his presence. He had women fawning on him and a fortune to spend at the card tables. He could not even be accused of being a bad landlord and neglecting his estates, for he made scrupulously careful arrangements to ensure that all his tenants' needs were met. He just chose never to attend to such matters himself. No wonder then that a letter from Josselyn had met with such indifference.

Seagrave sighed again. 'I see now that I was naive in thinking that it did not affect me.' His tone was coolly reflective. 'It needed only for some busybody to hear the tale—as they have done—for it to be all over Town. And now Miss Elliott is to give me my *congé*! I wish I cared more!'

Peter frowned. He knew that Seagrave had never pretended to have any more regard for Louise Elliott than the mutual respect one would expect to have for one's future wife, and he also knew that this had nothing to do with the exquisite actress which his brother currently had in keeping in a discreet villa in Chelsea. But even if his feelings were not engaged, the match with Louise was worth preserving if possible.

'Go and see the Elliotts tomorrow,' he urged. 'I am sure all can be put to rights. Louise is a sensible girl and will understand the truth of the matter.'

Seagrave's mouth twisted with wry amusement. 'Just so, Peter. I am persuaded you are correct. My future wife is indeed the sort of cold-blooded young woman who could easily ignore the fact that I had a Cyprian in keeping. What she is less likely to forgive, however, is the public humiliation that will reflect on her now that this story is known. And in order to avoid future misunderstandings, I reluctantly feel it is my duty to travel to Dillingham and ascertain exactly what the situation is.' His voice hardened. 'I am sure that, with the right inducement, Miss Kellaway can be impelled to see sense.'

Peter had never met Susanna Kellaway but suddenly, hearing the underlying anger in his brother's voice, he found himself feeling very sorry for her indeed. A thought occurred to him.

'I say, Nick, do you know Miss Kellaway at all?'

'Not in the sense you mean,' Seagrave said dryly. 'I've met her, of course.' His tone was unpleasant. 'A cheap little piece with a commercial mind—and the commodity she sells is herself.' He hesitated. 'Do you remember Miranda Lethbridge?'

'Cousin Sally Lethbridge's girl?' Peter frowned. 'Yes, of course—she was about fifteen when I went away in '12. Why do you ask?'

'Miranda made her come out a couple of years ago.' Seagrave sounded amused. 'You may remember her as a child in pinafores, Peter, but she had improved dramatically and there were plenty who fell at her feet.' The amusement fled from his tone. 'Amongst them was Justin Tatton, whom you may remember served with me in Spain. He was bowled over by Miranda and she was equally smitten. We all thought they'd make a match of it.' Seagrave's voice was suddenly savage. 'Miss Kellaway had other ideas, however. This was before Penscombe swam into view, and though Justin has no title, he was rich... Anyway, she made a dead set at him, and in a weak moment he succumbed.' Seagrave shrugged, a little uncomfortably. 'God knows, I am in no position to judge another man, but the unutterable folly... Justin said later that it had been a moment of madness, that after a single night he felt nothing but disgust and repulsion. But the damage was done. He begged Susanna Kellaway to tell no one, but she was furious that she could not hold him, and she made very sure that Miranda heard—and in the worst terms possible. Naturally the poor girl was devastated. She refused to even speak to Justin, and last year she made that hasty marriage to Wareham...' Seagrave shook his head.

'I am not a sentimentalist,' he added with a touch of humour, 'but I deplore the way Miss Kellaway takes whatever she wants with no concern for the destruction she causes! Even in my worst excesses I was never so careless of the feelings of others, and God knows, I have done some damnably stupid things in my time!'

Peter was silent. When Seagrave had first returned home from the Peninsula he had been possessed by a spirit of wildness which Peter suspected was the result of escaping the war with his life intact. He knew that as one of Wellington's most promising officers, his brother had been sent on some secret and highly dangerous missions and had brushed with death on more than one occasion. He had fought with the Portuguese militia, the *ordenanca*, as well as covering himself with glory in a more orthodox manner on the battlefield of Talavera. Seagrave's reaction to civilian life had been a very public and unrestrained year of hellraising that blazed a trail through the *ton* until it had burned itself out and he had changed into the deeply world-weary individual he was now.

Seagrave looked up to where the crescent moon was perched above the rooftops, fading from the summer sky as dawn approached. He sighed. 'No, with Miss Kellaway it is one excess after another! There will always be some poor fool who is besotted and will fall victim to an experienced woman preying on impressionable young men for their fortunes!'

Peter grimaced. 'I wonder what she wants with you, Nick,' he mused. 'You could scarcely be described as an inexperienced youth!'

His brother gave him a cynical glance. 'Come on, Peter, you're not an innocent either! She wants money—in one form or another! It's what she always wants! And I'm damned if she'll get any out of me!'

The reception which Seagrave met with the following morning at Lord Elliott's house in Grosvenor Street was not auspicious. The butler had at first tried to turn him away with the news that Miss Elliott was not at home, but Seagrave greeted this information with well-bred disbelief. The butler, flustered, could

not stand his ground and could only protest as the Earl
swept past him into the drawing-room, where he found
both Lady Elliott and her daughter. Seagrave's intended, a plumply pretty blonde with pale, slightly
protruberant blue eyes, looked up from her embroidery
frame at his entrance and uttered a small shriek.

'You!' she gasped, in tones of outrage. 'Seagrave!
How *could* you! Oh, I wish I were dead!' She burst
into noisy tears.

Lady Elliott was made of sterner stuff. She swelled
with indignation. 'I am astounded that you see fit to
show your face here, my lord! To come from the arms
of that creature to my own, sweet, innocent Louise! It
defies belief! The notice terminating the engagement
has already been sent to the *Gazette*!'

Louise sobbed all the louder. Seagrave, who had as
yet uttered not one word, found that there was no necessity for him to do so. His sense of humour, long
buried, began to reassert itself. Giving the outraged
matron and her snivelling daughter the full benefit of
a wicked smile, he executed an immaculate bow,
turned on his heel and left the room.

It was late when the stage pulled into the yard of
the Lamb and Flag in Felixstowe and decanted its occupants onto the cobbles. Lucille Kellaway, stiff and
sore from the discomforts of her journey, picked up
her shabby portmanteau and looked about her. There
was no sign of her sister Susanna, despite the agreement that the two had to meet there.

Lucille had found the journey from Oakham fascinating. She had travelled so little that each new view
was a delight to her and each new acquaintance was
a pleasure to meet. She now knew all about Miss

Grafton, a governess about to take up a new position with a family in Ipswich, and Mr Burrows, a lawyer visiting a client in Orford. She had looked out of the coach window and admired the well-kept farmland that stretched as far and as flat as the eye could see, and had glimpsed the sea as they drew into the town.

She struggled towards the inn door, her heavy case weighing her down. The smell of roast meat wafted enticingly from the kitchen and light spilled from the taproom onto the cobbles, accompanied by the sound of male voices and laughter. Lucille shrank. Although not of a timid disposition, she was too shy to march into the public bar and demand attention. The landlady found her cowering in the passageway.

'I am looking for Miss Kellaway,' Lucille said, a little shyly, and immediately saw an expression of mingled prurience, curiosity and disgust flit across the good lady's features.

'Miss Kellaway and the gentleman are in the private parlour,' the landlady said, tight-lipped, nodding in the direction of a closed door at the end of the passage. She marched off to the kitchen, leaving Lucille alone.

Lucille knocked a little hesitantly on the door of the parlour. She could hear the intimate murmur of voices, but no one answered her. She pushed the door open and recoiled, almost turning on her heel to run away. Susanna was reclining on the parlour sofa in much the same pose as she had held at the school, but with shocking differences. Her emerald green silk dress was cut very low and it had fallen off one shoulder completely, exposing one of Susanna's plump breasts. A portly, florid man with thinning sandy hair was leaning over her, fondling her with impatient hands whilst his mouth trailed wet kisses over her shoulder. He looked up, met Lucille's horrified gaze and straightened up, an unpleasantly challenging look in his eyes.

'Egad, what's this! My good woman—'

Susanna pushed him away much as one might repel a fractious child. She hoisted her dress back up without the least embarrassment.

'This is my sister, Eddie.' She turned to Lucille, a frown marring her brow. 'You're monstrously late, Lucille! I had quite given up hope of you! We sail with the tide tomorrow morning, so there isn't much time.' She did not ask whether Lucille had had a good journey, or if she was hungry, nor did she invite her to sit down.

'Now, my carriage will take you to Dillingham in the morning. I have left Felicity there—my housekeeper, Felicity Appleton,' she added irritably, seeing Lucille's look of incomprehension. 'She will help you choose your clothes appropriately. I have left a large wardrobe at Dillingham, but Eddie will buy me more in Paris, won't you, darling?' She touched his hand and fluttered her lashes at him.

The gentleman, whom Lucille assumed to be Sir Edwin Bolt, had been scrutinising her through his quizzing glass these few minutes past with what Lucille considered a most ill-bred regard. Now he guffawed.

'Take more than a parcel of clothes, Susie m'dear! Why, the girl's as strait-laced as a nun, and as cold, I'll wager!'

Lucille flushed and Susanna gave a flounce. 'Well, she need not meet anyone in Dillingham! I am not asking her to *be* me!' She saw his sulky, mulish expression and her tone softened. 'But I do see what you mean, my love!' She giggled girlishly. 'I fear that my prim little twin will never thrill to a man's touch! The delights of love are not for her!'

Lucille was beginning to feel rather sick. An insight into Susanna's relationship with her lover was something that repelled rather than interested her. Sir Edwin, mollified, had started to paw Susanna's shoulder again as though he could not keep away from her. His hot, blue gaze roved lustfully over her opulent curves. The dress slipped a little.

'Send the girl away so we may pick up where we left off,' he muttered, pressing avid, open-mouthed kisses on Susanna's white skin. Lucille looked away, her face flaming.

'If that is all—' she said, with constraint.

Susanna had tilted her head back to facilitate the progress of Sir Edwin's lips down her neck. He was already pulling at her dress again. She waved her sister away. 'Very well, Luce—' she sounded like someone dismissing her servant '—you may go now. Unless you wish to join us, that is!'

Sir Edwin looked up, a lascivious look suddenly in his eye. 'Now there's an idea! Introduce the priggish virgin to fleshly delights, eh? What do you say, Miss Kellaway? Why, we could show you a thing or two…'

Their mocking laughter followed Lucille from the room. She closed the door with exaggerated care and leant against the wall of the passage for a moment to recover herself. Her whole body was one burning blush, her mind revolted, a sick taste in her mouth. That Susanna should have sold herself for that, and not even appear to care… The stone wall was cool beneath her fingers and Lucille was glad of its chill and the darkness that surrounded her. As she straightened up, however, she realised to her horror that she was not alone. At the end of the passageway, hidden from view, two men were talking.

'…travel on to Dillingham tomorrow. Do you go to the Yoxleys' for a while?'

It was a mellow voice, the cadences smooth and pleasing to the ear. Lucille paused, her attention arrested despite herself. The other man's voice was less distinguishable.

'…a sen'night, perhaps…join you at the Court… A Seagrave…back at Dillingham, Nick…'

From being overheated, Lucille suddenly found herself icily chill. Surely she could not have misheard? Had the man not mentioned the names of Seagrave and Dillingham? She dropped her portmanteau from nerveless fingers.

The voices cut off abruptly at the crash. Lucille bent clumsily to pick her case up again, only to find that when she stood up her way was blocked by the tall figure of a man. The light was behind him and she could not see his face, but in the claustrophobically small passage, his physical presence was overwhelming.

'Can I be of assistance, ma'am? Are you unwell?' His voice was very pleasing to the ear, smooth and mellifluous, Lucille thought again, confused. His hand had taken her elbow in a steadying grip which nevertheless felt as though it burned through the fabric of her dress. She had not heard him speak on that infamous occasion when they had seen each other in Oakham, but she knew instinctively who he was.

'No…' Lucille's voice came out as a thread of a whisper. She looked up into the dark face, into fierce, gold-flecked eyes, and felt quite dizzy. 'I thank you, sir, I am quite well… Excuse me.'

She had pushed past his astonished figure and was already halfway up the stairs before she realised that she had no notion of where she was going. She paused in dread, hoping that the gentleman would not follow her; a moment later, to her inexpressible relief, she heard a door close softly below. She sat down heavily on her portmanteau and almost cried. Had she been able to return to Oakham at that very moment she would not have hesitated. But Miss Pym had closed the school for the summer, and had gone to visit her good friend Fanny Burney for a few weeks. Lucille realised that she had nowhere to go except Cookes. She leant her head against the wall and closed her eyes.

'Whatever is it, miss? You look proper moped and no mistake!' The landlady's judgmental tone had softened as she considered the shabby, huddled figure. This one was no Cyprian like that painted hussy downstairs! 'Come along, miss,' she added encouragingly. 'I'll show you to your room. Everything will look better in the morning!'

Chapter Two

'Miss Kellaway.' The voice was soft and smooth as warm honey. It spoke in Lucille's ear.

Lucille had been at Cookes for ten days and thought that she had stumbled into paradise. The house, converted from a charming jumble of medieval cottages, was crammed full of books, treatises and journals enough to keep her occupied for weeks. Her previous reading had been restricted to the books available from Miss Pym's limited collection and from the Oakham subscription library. At Cookes she could read until the print blurred and her head ached. And then there was the garden—a wilderness where one could wander for hours amidst the rioting roses, or sit in the cool shade of the orchard. It had all been like a blissful dream, a thousand miles away from the petty cares of the school regime and uninterrupted by callers from the outside world.

Lucille's conscience, originally troubled by the impersonation of Susanna, had grown quiescent as nobody disturbed her peace. The memory of that dreadful night in the inn at Felixstowe had faded away. She now thought it quite possible that she had misheard the snatches of conversation that had led her to believe that the Earl of Seagrave would be in Dillingham, and mistakenly believed him to be the gentleman who had offered her his help. Certainly she had seen neither hide nor hair of him since her arrival.

The other legacy of that evening had been the slow realisation of what an impersonation of Susanna might mean—the memory of the landlady's prurient scorn and Sir Edwin's lustful advances still made her shiver. That someone might think she was Susanna, and as such was fair game for such treatment, made her feel ill. In her innocence she had not even considered it before—ignorance, not innocence, she now chided herself bitterly. But while nobody called and she had no wish to go out, it was a matter that could be put to one side, if not ignored.

The warm, southern aspect of Cookes's drawing-room, with its delightful views across the lawn to the fishpond, had lulled Lucille into a sleepy state of relaxation that afternoon. Her copy of Walter Scott's *Waverley* had slid from her hand as her head rested against the panelling and her eyes closed irresistibly in the sunshine. She had removed her reading glasses, which rested on the window-seat beside her, and had drifted into a light doze.

The voice spoke again, this time with an inflection of impatience.

'Miss Kellaway?'

Lucille opened her eyes slowly, and thought that she was probably still dreaming. Eyes of the darkest bitter chocolate flecked with gold were about three inches away from her own. His face was all planes and angles, she thought, bemused, except for his mouth which, though firm, was sensuously curved and quite

delicious… Her gaze lingered, transfixed, and then one
of the pins holding her unaccustomed Grecian knot
dug into her head painfully, and she realised she was
awake.

With growing horror, Lucille removed her gaze
hastily from the man's mouth and met the distinctly
speculative look in those dark eyes. They were not
friendly but piercingly appraising. He had been leaning on the seat beside her and now straightened up,
moving away from her, and Lucille found to her relief
that she could breathe again. She struggled upright,
aware that the charming gown of rose pink crêpe—
one of Susanna's more restrained dresses—had slipped
off her shoulder as she dozed, and was revealing the
upper curves of her breasts in a manner to which she
was completely unaccustomed. The gentleman, on the
other hand, was clearly the sort of man who was used
to seeing women in *déshabillé*. Certainly he was not
in the least embarrassed by her obvious discomposure
and his gaze lingered with blatant consideration in a
way she found completely disconcerting.

'Miss Kellaway?' he said for a third time, with the
same deceptive gentleness. 'We have met before, but
may I perhaps remind you? I am Nicholas, Earl of
Seagrave and as such—' his voice became heavily
ironic '—your landlord.'

Lucille already knew. She had recognised him almost at once. He was just as she remembered, only
more so. He had a tall, athletic figure, immaculately
clad in buff pantaloons and a coat of blue superfine,
and the sort of brooding dark good looks that immediately made her feel completely out of her depth. It
was the same voice that she remembered, mellow and
distinctive. Fortunately he did not appear to have rec-

ognised her, but then, he thought she was her sister…
Lucille jumped visibly. Oh Lord, Seagrave thought she
was Susanna! The scorching heat which had suffused
her body when she had first seen him faded abruptly
to leave her feeling cold and shaken. She had to tell
him at once! For a moment she wavered, within an
inch of revealing her true identity. But he looked so
authoritative, so forbidding, that her courage failed
her. Surely, if she could just get rid of him quickly,
he would not call again…

She sat up straighter with what she hoped was a fair
imitation of her sister's elegance and tried to pull herself together. No doubt he already thought her a lack-
wit, first staring, then silent!

'Lord Seagrave! Excuse me, I was not attending!
How kind of you to call, sir. May I offer you some
refreshment, perhaps? A glass of wine?' Her attempt
at Susanna's husky drawl came out a little strangely.
She sounded as though she had a sore throat.

Seagrave's gaze, coolly assessing, remained focused
on her with disconcerting intentness. 'No, thank you.
This is not a social call, Miss Kellaway.' He strode
over to the fireplace and turned back to face her, awesomely in control.

'When I first heard that you had moved into
Dillingham I thought my informant must be in jest,'
he said conversationally. 'You are hardly renowned
for your interest in country living, are you, Miss
Kellaway? I cannot see what conceivable attraction a
house like this could hold for you. Why, it is not as
though you even own it! Your position is tenuous, to
say the least! You know, of course, that I can terminate the lease at any time?'

Lucille did not know. Susanna's brief instructions

to her sister had not included any information on the lease on Cookes. Marshalling her scattered thoughts in the face of this sudden and unwelcome attack, Lucille tried desperately to work out how Susanna would deal with this situation. She plumped for a certainty.

'Lud, is that so?' She managed to sound quite careless. 'You'll understand, my lord, that I leave such matters to my man of business. But surely you are not about to evict me?' She attempted a melting look at him through her eyelashes. Seagrave seemed totally unmoved. Evidently, Lucille thought, the business of flirtation was more difficult than she had imagined.

'I prefer,' Seagrave said, with scrupulous politeness, 'that you see the error of your ways of your own accord, Miss Kellaway. I feel sure that when you have considered the matter, you will see that the country is not really the place for you. This house can hardly be to your taste, and the village…well, you will find it an uncomfortable place to live.' There was no hint of a threat in his tone, but Lucille felt a shiver go through her. She knew he was trying to intimidate her. There was something powerfully compelling about that tall figure dominating her shabby drawing-room.

She arched her eyebrows in delicate enquiry. 'Whatever can you mean, my lord?' Her tone was provocatively innocent. 'This house is delightful and Dillingham appears to be a charming village!'

Seagrave's dark eyes narrowed momentarily. He had betrayed no temper or even irritation during their exchange, yet Lucille had the unnerving feeling that that was only because he was holding himself on a tight rein. Now he thrust his hands into his jacket pockets as if to restrain himself further, but his voice remained level.

'It is indeed a delightful place, Miss Kellaway, but I doubt that you will find it so. Like many villages it can be insular and intolerant. You will find that the arrival of such a gaudy bird of paradise as yourself amongst the sparrows is not welcomed warmly.' He frowned. 'It puzzles me why you wish to bury yourself in the country in the first place. Are you escaping your creditors, perhaps? Or…' his tone took on a sarcastic edge '…perhaps you have some quarry in your sights and feel that absence will make the heart grow fonder?'

Susanna would almost certainly have used the opportunity to make a push to engage his interest. Lucille, however, momentarily forgot the part she was supposed to be playing and forgot to be afraid of him. How dare he treat her with such contemptuous disdain! 'I'm sure you do not expect me to answer that, sir,' she snapped, and almost immediately realised she had betrayed herself as his gaze sharpened on her with acute interest. He was too quick. She would have to be much more careful. Her gaze suddenly fell on the copy of *Waverley*, lying carelessly on the window-seat. Susanna would never even have had a book in the house, let alone appeared to read one. Would Seagrave know that? Would it be better to attempt to hide it, or just to ignore it? She suddenly realised that the Earl had asked her something else, and was waiting politely for her response. Her colour rose at his steady regard with its edge of scorn. She gave him Susanna's dazzling smile.

'I beg your pardon, sir?'

'I said that you did not strike me as a lady who would enjoy social ostracism, Miss Kellaway,' Seagrave was saying, with weary patience. 'No one will call on you, everyone will cut you dead... Do you really want that? Do not tell me that you do not regard it, for I shall not believe you!'

There was so much repressed violence in his tone that Lucille was suddenly frightened. He was taut with tension. Surely there was more to this than a simple desire to remove her from Cookes? But she was supposed to be Susanna, who would probably be less sensitive to the atmosphere and would no doubt have tried to flirt her way out of trouble. She tried a light, petulant shrug.

'Lud, my lord, you're monstrous serious! What does one small house matter to you? Or perhaps—' she gave him a saucy look over her shoulder '—you have a more personal reason for wishing me off your property?'

It was a shot in the dark but its effect was electric. Seagrave spun round and caught her wrist in a grip that hurt. Lucille looked up at him. His face was expressionless but there was a look in his eyes which chilled her.

'I do, madam, and you know why! Oh, I have no opinion of how you choose to earn a living—I make no judgments. But I do not like you.' He spoke through his teeth. 'You had already brought enough trouble on my family before this latest escapade single-handedly sabotaged my betrothal! You are like a bird of ill omen rather than a bird of paradise!'

Lucille felt her lips twitch at this colourful metaphor. She did not understand his allusion to Susanna's previous entanglement with his family, but could see that he might be justifiably angry that her actions had resulted in a broken engagement. She tried to free her wrist and found herself held fast.

'I am sorry to have unwittingly caused you trouble, sir—'

'Unwittingly!' For a moment his fingers tightened even more cruelly before he dropped her wrist as though he could not bear to touch her. His tone was savage. 'There was nothing *unwitting* about your decision to claim this house, madam! Well, hear this! I shall do everything in my power to drive you out of Dillingham! You will be scorned and reviled at every turn! You will wish you had never come here!'

The slamming of the front door behind him echoed through Lucille's head, causing it to ache again. She rested it in her hands in despair. Oh, why had she not told him the truth when she had had the opportunity? To try to deceive such a man was a piece of complete folly! He was both too acute to be fooled for long, and too forceful to be manipulated with feminine wiles. Feminine wiles! Lucille grimaced. What did she know of such coquetry? Her attempt to impersonate Susanna had been hopeless and she detested the blend of sexual appraisal and contempt with which Seagrave, and no doubt many other men, contemplated her sister. Lucille groaned aloud.

Seagrave... The blood was still singing through her veins from his touch, which was a singularly unhelpful reaction to him, she told herself sternly. It seemed that his slightest glance addled her wits, which was the last thing she needed when she had to have those wits about her! There was no accounting for it. No scientific theory could explain the peculiar mixture of breathlessness and excitement which possessed her in his presence. She had read about romance, of course, but had considered it to be ephemeral and often painful, not something she wished to experience. Then there was physical love, of course—she shuddered, remembering Sir Edwin's licentious gaze and questing hands.

Lucille sighed. She thought of the uncharacteristic excitement with which she had hurried to ask Miss Pym for leave from the school, and her pleased surprise when that good lady had cautiously agreed. Her anticipation at visiting Cookes had reached fever pitch by the time Susanna's summons had arrived. On the day after the meeting at Felixstowe Lucille had rolled into Dillingham village in Susanna's carriage. A bevy of small children had run alongside the coach, chattering and laughing, but their elders had stood silently on the roadside, watching as she passed by. In her ignorance, Lucille had not considered that significant until this day.

But now…she was wearing borrowed plumes and impersonating a notorious woman who, if Seagrave was to be believed, was not at all welcome in the rural tranquillity of Dillingham. She did not doubt that Seagrave had meant every word he had said when he had threatened to drive her out of the village. Lucille sighed again. Why had she given into the cowardly impulse to play along with the masquerade when it would have been so much more sensible to tell him the truth? Now she really was starting to weave a tangled web through her deception!

There was a tap at the door and Mrs Appleton stuck her head around it. Felicity Appleton had accompanied Susanna to Dillingham when she first claimed Cookes, in the hope, Mrs Appleton had said with a wry smile, that the presence of a reputable older woman might reassure the good villagers of Susanna's own respectability. It had been an unsuccessful attempt. The small resident staff at Cookes had walked out in a spirit of righteous indignation as soon as their new employer had arrived, and from then onwards Mrs Appleton had had to run the house single-handedly.

'I do apologise, Miss Kellaway,' Mrs Appleton said now, her plump, motherly face creased with anxiety. 'I tried to tell his lordship that you were not receiving, but he would not be gainsaid!'

Lucille laughed at the thought of Mrs Appleton trying to deter the Earl from his visit. Nicholas Seagrave had hardly struck her as the sort of man to brook any opposition.

'Pray do not concern yourself, Mrs Appleton! His lordship is very forceful, is he not!'

'A man used to command,' Mrs Appleton agreed with a twinkle in her eye. 'I saw him a few times when I was on campaign in the Peninsula with my husband's regiment. He was one of Wellington's brightest officers, you know, and an inspirational leader of men!'

Lucille already knew that Mrs Appleton was the widow of an army sergeant killed at Vittoria, though how this pillar of rectitude had fallen in with Susanna was another matter. Lucille had not pried into their connection, and was only grateful that she had both Mrs Appleton's calm good sense and knowledge of fashion to call upon. The housekeeper had advised her on matters of dress and hairstyle with a patience which Susanna would never have shown, and the result had been surprising. Although Lucille would never achieve the high fashion of her sister, the simple elegance of her new appearance gave her an absurd pleasure that astonished her. She had never been concerned with her dress before, but then, she had not met the Earl of

Seagrave before… She shook her head to drive the thought away.

'Well, would that Seagrave had left his military manners behind in Spain!' she said crossly, still smarting from the Earl's arrogant attitude. 'The man is overbearing to a fault!'

Mrs Appleton laughed. 'But prodigious attractive!' she said shrewdly, and did not miss Lucille's telltale blush. Her smile faded a little. 'I must own myself vastly surprised to see him,' she said thoughtfully. 'Your sister may have told you, Miss Kellaway, that Seagrave never spends time on his estates! I can only assume that the furore caused by Miss Susanna's arrival here has brought him from London! She will be most disappointed to have missed him!'

'A sorry business then, since I had no wish to meet him at all!' Lucille said, with a sigh. It was a half-truth, for whilst Seagrave held a mysteriously strong attraction for her, she certainly had no wish for him to think her Susanna. 'I realise now that I have been very naive about the whole situation!' She continued wryly, 'I truly believed that I would not need to meet anyone during my time here, and that Susanna would only be away a week or two.'

Her worried blue eyes met Mrs Appleton's kind brown ones. 'You must have wondered, ma'am, how I could ever have lent myself to such a deception! I agreed on impulse, you see, wanting a change from a routine that was becoming irksome, and now I am well served for my folly! I do not mind admitting that I almost confessed the whole to Lord Seagrave, and would have done so had he not appeared so terrifying!'

Mrs Appleton sat down, wiping her floury hands carefully on her apron. 'Miss Susanna explained to me her concerns about the lease, and that she had persuaded you to come here to represent her interests whilst she was away.' She shook her head slowly. 'She told me that you were a...' she hesitated, then smiled in a kindly fashion '...forgive me, a bluestocking, was her description of you! She said that you were looking for a rural idyll in which to walk and read! I must confess, Miss Kellaway, that I thought it a foolish scheme from the outset! How Miss Susanna ever thought that you could impersonate a courtesan, I cannot imagine! *You* may have had no notion of having to meet people here in Dillingham, but she has no excuse! She must always have known that there was a chance someone would seek her—you—out!'

Lucille raised a hand in rueful protest. 'Please do not exonerate me of blame entirely, Mrs Appleton! My conscience is happier if I admit to some responsibility! I may not be worldly, but I am not stupid. I should have guessed what might happen! Indeed,' she added thoughtfully, 'deep down I probably knew the risk I was taking, but I wanted to escape the school so much that I was prepared to do it!'

There was a silence whilst both of them contemplated the situation. After a moment, Mrs Appleton spoke a little tentatively. 'I suppose the Earl wants us out of Dillingham? I thought as much, for he has already begun a war of attrition! They will not serve me in the shops, Miss Kellaway, and some most unpleasant things are being said! I would counsel you not to go out into the village. Feeling is running very high!'

Lucille stared at her in growing disbelief. Until that morning it had not occurred to her that the inhabitants of Dillingham would react so badly to her presence among them, but this was all far worse than she could have imagined. She knew that the local gentry would not have condescended to acknowledge Susanna, but that had not worried her as she had had no interest in mixing in rural society. This malicious campaign, though, was another matter again. To be starved out of the village seemed a horrid fate. Mrs Appleton, somewhat shamefacedly, was retrieving something from her apron pocket.

'I had thought not to trouble you with this, Miss Kellaway,' she said a little awkwardly, 'but perhaps you should know… It arrived just like this, with no envelope. Of course, I immediately realised what it was and I will put it in the kitchen fire directly.'

Lucille realised with a sudden shock that it was a letter she was holding out, a letter printed with bold capitals which she could read quite easily, '…nothing but a shameless whore and we do not want your sort here…' She flushed scarlet and looked up at the house-keeper in horrified understanding.

'An anonymous letter! Oh, Mrs Appleton, how dreadful! But when did it arrive? Who could possibly…?' Her voice trailed away as she realised that any one of Dillingham's outraged inhabitants could have composed the missive. Mrs Appleton had not exaggerated when she had spoken of feelings running high.

The housekeeper's mouth was a grim line as she stuck the offending letter back in her pocket. 'I am so sorry that you have been exposed to this, Miss Kellaway! The only advice I can offer is that you return to Oakham at once, before matters become even more unpleasant. Can that be arranged?'

Lucille rested her chin thoughtfully on her hand. 'I cannot return to Oakham for another ten days,' she said dolefully, 'for Miss Pym has closed the school and gone to visit Fanny Burney, the authoress, whilst I am away! Only Mr Kingston, the music master, has been left to keep an eye on matters in her absence. It would not be appropriate for me to stay there alone with him—' She broke off, unable to repress a giggle. 'Gracious, that is tame stuff compared to what our anonymous author thinks of me!'

Mrs Appleton smiled. 'Even so, my dear, do you not have any friends you could go to visit for a little? I do not wish to alarm you, but if you stay here you will not be able to show your face beyond the gates! I imagine Miss Susanna may return in a week or so, but there is no guarantee…' She let the sentence hang but Lucille understood what she meant. Susanna's timekeeping had never been of the most reliable, particularly if it suited her to be doing something else. She would not hesitate to stay with Sir Edwin for as long as it took to get what she wanted out of him.

For a moment, Lucille considered visiting Mrs Markham. Gilbert Markham's widow and daughter were always pleased to see her, but they were living with Mrs Markham's sister and Lucille knew she could not just arrive without warning. And there was no one else. She sighed.

'I am sorry, ma'am! It seems I must stay here another ten days or so. Perhaps it will not be so bad…' She knew she sounded unconvincing. The idea of having to impersonate Susanna for that time seemed suddenly intolerable. From being blissfully happy in her country retreat that morning, she suddenly felt unbearably trapped. After a moment Mrs Appleton sighed as well.

'Very well, Miss Kellaway! Perhaps matters will settle down once the village is over the initial shock of Miss Susanna's arrival.' She sounded as unpersuaded as Lucille herself. She sighed again. 'It is easier in London, where such matters are commonplace. The society in which your sister lives operates in much the same way as the *beau monde*. But here the community is insular and judgmental, and I do not doubt Miss Susanna would detest it!'

'Seagrave said he made no judgments on the way in which Susanna chooses to make a living,' Lucille said slowly, 'yet he would not simply allow her to reside here quietly without interference!'

Mrs Appleton gave a wry smile. 'My dear Miss Kellaway, you will find that most gentlemen have no difficulty in preserving a dual attitude towards ladies such as your sister! They…enjoy their company but they would never marry them, nor even consider them fit company for their sisters! By the same token, I suspect Seagrave believes a Cyprian should stay in London and not cause a stir in his sleepy dovecote!'

Lucille frowned, remembering something else Seagrave had said. 'Does my sister know the Earl?' she asked, carefully. 'He made some reference to her causing trouble for his family before this…'

Mrs Appleton looked disapproving, though whether of Susanna's exploits or Lucille's enquiry was hard to judge. She fidgeted with the edge of her apron before looking up to meet Lucille's gaze. 'I collect he must be referring to Miranda Lethbridge,' she said with constraint. 'I believe she is some connection of the Seagraves. Last winter your sister…' she hesitated, seeing Lucille's innocent blue eyes fixed on her '…well, no point in prevaricating! Miss Susanna took it into her head to seduce Miranda Lethbridge's betrothed, who was also a war comrade of the Earl of Seagrave.

'She did it solely because he was rich, and she was bored! It was a shocking thing, and believe me, Miss Kellaway, I thought myself unshockable! After one night Mr Tatton—Justin Tatton was his name—realised that he had made a mistake and tried to disengage, and Miss Susanna was furious. She spread the rumour that they had been having a lengthy and passionate affair, and she made sure that Miss Lethbridge heard all about it. The poor girl was completely distraught and broke off the engagement immediately.'

Mrs Appleton shook her head. 'I do not condone the behaviour of men such as Mr Tatton, but he had made a mistake and did not deserve to be punished so cruelly. But I fear Miss Susanna detests rejection.'

'I hear very little of Súsanna's exploits, tucked away as I am in Oakham,' Lucille said a little hesitantly, 'but I do remember hearing of a young man, the son of a duke, who was ruined—'

'You mean Adrian Crosby, I collect,' Mrs Appleton said expressionlessly. 'He was just one of many! He was infatuated with Miss Susanna and bought her costly gifts by the barrow load. Worse, she took him to dens—' she saw Lucille's puzzled frown '—gaming dens, Miss Kellaway, where he played deep and lost a fortune to the House who, of course, gave Miss Susanna her share of the pickings! The affair only ended when the boy's father realised the extent of his debt and sent him off to the country to rusticate!'

Mrs Appleton looked unhappy. 'I am in no position to criticise your sister, Miss Kellaway, for she pays my wages! But in my book, men such as Seagrave are fair game for a woman like Miss Susanna, for they know the rules of engagement! But Adrian Crosby was barely more than a boy… And Miranda Lethbridge did not deserve—'

She broke off. 'Forgive me, Miss Kellaway. I am not normally one to gossip, but I thought it only fair that you should know what kind of woman you are impersonating—and why the Earl of Seagrave dislikes your sister so much!'

Lucille's heart felt like lead. Although naive in the ways of the world, she had common sense enough to have realised a long time before that she knew nothing of her sister's way of life, nor did she want to know. She had already learned too much in the inn at Felixstowe. Any lover was good enough, it seemed, as long as he was rich enough to pay Susanna's price. No wonder Seagrave held her in such contempt! Lucille had no time for the double standards of men who kept mistresses and then denounced the very women they would have in keeping, but she had some sympathy with Seagrave's point of view over Miranda Lethbridge. The prospect of being obliged to meet him again, knowing what she did now, made her feel vaguely sick.

Mrs Appleton was watching her sympathetically. 'I thought it best to tell you, Miss Kellaway,' she said apologetically. 'Should you meet Seagrave again—'

'I cannot bear to meet him again!' Lucille said, in anguish. 'Mrs Appleton, forgive my curiosity, but however did you come to work for Susanna? I cannot imagine—' She broke off, aware that her comments could offend. But the housekeeper was smiling, albeit a little sadly.

'You are right in thinking that it was not what I might have chosen, Miss Kellaway, given different cir-

cumstances! After I was widowed I had very little
money, you see, and no means of keeping myself, so
I applied for a post as cook/housekeeper with Miss
Susanna. I knew what sort of an establishment it was,
of course, but without references I could not hope for
a position elsewhere…'

She paused. 'As I said earlier, I am fairly unshockable after ten years on campaign, and am in no way
missish! And indeed I have very little to do with Miss
Susanna's business, for she has a maid to attend to
her.' She smiled suddenly. 'That is not to say that I
haven't had my moments! A gentleman was once
overly amorous to me, but I was able to dissuade him
from his attentions with a saucepan! And believe me,
Miss Kellaway, I could have done a great deal worse
than work for Miss Susanna!'

Lucille was left shaking her head in disbelief. She
knew that *she* was both missish and easily shocked,
and yet she was the one who had so foolishly agreed
to impersonate Susanna. She had not known the half
of it—and now she was trapped by her own folly.
Thinking of this led her thoughts inevitably back to
the Earl of Seagrave.

'Apparently Susanna's arrival at Dillingham has
caused Seagrave's betrothed to cry off,' she told Mrs
Appleton solemnly, 'so he has another reason to dislike her now!' Despite her feelings, she could not suppress a smile. 'He seemed remarkably annoyed by the
fact!'

'I doubt his emotions are involved, only his pride,'
Mrs Appleton said calmly. 'Seagrave is notorious for
having no feelings at all! No more than a month ago
he got engaged to Louise Elliott, a hen-witted girl of
absolutely no distinction other than in her lineage. If

she has thrown him over he may one day come to thank your sister! They say girls become very like their mothers and Lady Elliott is an arrogant, overbearing woman! But enough of this gossiping!' She got to her feet. 'I must make shift to find us some dinner!' She cast a look at Lucille's unhappy face. 'Never fear, Miss Kellaway,' she said bracingly, 'I have found sustenance under far more adverse conditions than this! As for Seagrave, well, we will just have to keep you out of his way in future!'

Chapter Three

Lucille felt that the whole atmosphere of Cookes had changed after that one meeting with the Earl of Seagrave and her illuminating chat with Mrs Appleton. Instead of enjoying the tranquil silence, she began to feel oppressed and lonely. It was the greatest irony that when she had been in ignorance of the villagers' attitude towards her she had not felt the need to leave the house and grounds—now she knew of their hostility, she longed to go out but did not dare. No longer could she lose herself in the pages of a book, or concentrate on her father's esoteric research into eastern civilisations.

Fully awakened, her conscience nagged her and gave her no peace, calling her a stupid little fool for her thoughtless agreement to so damaging a plan as Susanna had suggested. Better by far to have stayed within the safe confines of Miss Pym's school than to perpetrate such a deception.

Then there was the unfortunate effect that the Earl himself appeared to have on her. It seemed that the confusion he had thrown her into that day in Oakham was nothing compared to encountering him at close quarters. Lucille had led a sheltered existence, but none of the fathers or brothers of her pupils had ever made her pulse race in the disconcerting way Seagrave had affected her. His face had a disquieting tendency of imposing itself between her and the written page; the cadences of that mellow voice haunted her thoughts.

None of her reading could help her to understand this peculiar chemistry between them. She even caught herself daydreaming, an indulgence which both puzzled and horrified her. But none of her dreams of him could be in any way encouraging. He thought she was Susanna, after all, and even if he had met her under her own identity she did not flatter herself that he would have any time for a frumpish bluestocking. As for what he would think of her if he discovered her impersonation… She refused to allow herself to even consider that.

Fortunately for Lucille's equilibrium, Seagrave did not appear again at Cookes, although his agent, Mr Josselyn, called with some long and convoluted legal papers for Lucille to sign. She perused these with intense concentration and made a list of points on which she required clarification. She then stopped dead, realising that it was not her place to query the lease, but Susanna's. That inevitably made her recall the masquerade and she found herself out of sorts again. Normally she would have walked off her low spirits, but now she felt she could not even venture outside the gate of Cookes.

On the second day of enforced inactivity, Lucille threw her book aside in despair. It was Sunday evening and the church bells had been calling across the green. The shadows were falling now and all was still in the dusk. It was such a beautiful evening that Lucille was suddenly determined to go out. She put on her bonnet and coat, and slipped out of the front door.

The green was deserted and it was indeed pleasant to be outside now that the heat of the day had gone and the air was full of birdsong. Lucille left the shelter of Cookes's gates and crossed to the duck pond, holding her breath lest anyone see her. But all was quiet. It felt astonishingly liberating to be in the open air. For a while she just stood and enjoyed the neat prettiness of the cottages about the green, their gardens bursting with verdant summer flowers, their white-painted walls reflecting the last rays of the sun. Then she walked slowly across to the ancient stone church, and paused with her hand on the iron gate, suddenly overwhelmed with the need to go inside.

The church, like the village, was deserted now that the evening service was over and the congregation dispersed. Lucille let herself into the green darkness of the interior, and sat in a worn wooden back pew, breathing in the mixture of flower scent and ancient dust. It was so evocative of her childhood with the Markhams that her breath caught in her throat. The familiarity was soothing in an existence that had become so unexpectedly difficult. She said a few heartfelt prayers before letting herself out of the door into the churchyard, which had become full of deep shadows.

The first intimation Lucille had that she was not alone came with the pattering of paws along the path, and then a magnificent chocolate-coloured retriever was before her, sniffing inquisitively at her skirts and pressing its damp nose into the palm of her hand.

Lucille laughed at this shameless bid for attention, bent down, and fondled the creature's silky ears.

'What a beauty you are, aren't you! I wonder what your name is…?'

The dog snuffled softly, rubbing its head against her hand, before turning, suddenly alert, its ears pricking up.

'Her name is Sal, Miss Kellaway, short for Salamanca.'

The Earl of Seagrave had stepped out from the shadows of an ancient yew tree and was viewing Lucille with thoughtful interest. 'She is not usually so friendly to strangers.'

Lucille watched Sal return submissively to her master's heel, and smiled at the look of adoration in those limpid dark eyes. No doubt that was the type of gaze she should be perfecting in the interests of her impersonation. However, there was something about the clear evening, scented with herbs and yew, which made her rebel against the idea of acting a part. She looked up from the dog to see that Seagrave was still watching her.

'Were you at Salamanca, my lord?'

'I was.' He straightened, coming towards her down the path, the dog now close at his heels. 'It was my last battle, Miss Kellaway. I had been in the Peninsula for four years, first serving under General Sir John Moore and then under Wellington—Sir Arthur Wellesley, as he was to begin with. It was July when we came up against the French just south of Salamanca; July, just as it is now. I remember it well.'

Seagrave took a deep breath of cool, scented air. 'It was hot, with the kind of oppressive, airless heat you can get in Spain in the summer. The land around was arid, dry as dust. The dust was everywhere…in our mouths, in our noses, in our clothes… We sat on the flat top of our hill and watched the French lines to the south of us, on the higher ground.'

His voice had taken on a still, reflective quality. 'You may have read that the battle was a great triumph for Wellington. So it was. The French were cut to pieces with at least fourteen thousand casualties. It was carnage. I was wounded advancing across the valley between the two hills. We were in the range of the cannon and I fell with shrapnel in the chest and shoulder. So I was invalided out, and shortly after that I inherited the title and thought to stay at home.'

He stirred slightly and gave a short, bitter laugh. 'My apologies, Miss Kellaway! It is unforgivable to speak of such matters to a lady. You must forgive me.'

Lucille shook her head slightly. She had become caught up in the tale, could almost feel the heat of the Spanish sun and taste the dust. War was an experience so far removed from the lives of most people that it was almost impossible to begin to imagine it. Many did not want to try, finding the contrast with their own easy existence too uncomfortable to contemplate.

'I am sorry,' she began, unsure what she was really apologising for, but aware that the undercurrent of bitterness which had touched his voice briefly was present in that still, shadowed face. 'It must have been very difficult to adapt to civilian life after such experiences.'

Seagrave gave another harsh laugh. 'Indeed it was, Miss Kellaway! After the immediacies of life and death, the delights of the *ton,* whilst entertaining, seem damnably shallow! But it is hardly fashionable to speak so! No doubt you think me most singular!'

'No, sir.' Lucille caught herself just as she was about to express her own preferences for reading and studying over routs and parties. The shock of realising that she had almost betrayed herself caused her to fall silent, her mind suddenly blank. It was impossible to be forever remembering that she was supposed to be Susanna.

'I am glad to see you have overcome your aversion to dogs,' Seagrave observed suddenly, watching as Sal lay down with her head at Lucille's feet. 'I thought you once said that you hated them.'

Lucille froze. Did Susanna hate dogs? She had no idea. Seagrave was looking quite bland, but she suddenly had an unnerving feeling that he was deliberately testing her. She shrugged lightly.

'I do not recall…'

'When you were driving in the Park one day last summer…or was it two summers ago?' Seagrave mused. 'Harriette Wilson's dog bit your arm and I am sure I remember you saying you thought they were hateful creatures and should all be destroyed. You were quite vehement on the subject!'

Lucille mentally added another item to the list of things about Susanna which she found unattractive. The list was getting rather long and she was learning far more about her sister than she had known from the first seventeen years of their lives together. As for Harriette Wilson, Lucille knew her to be a legendary Cyprian in the same mould as Susanna, but her choice in pets was beyond her. 'Oh, well…' she managed to sound quite vague '…that dreadful little, yapping creature—'

'Miss Wilson has a wolfhound, as I recall,'

Seagrave commented, with mild irony. 'Scarcely a small creature, and one which left a scar on your arm.'

Lucille glanced down instinctively, although she was wearing a jacket whose sleeves covered her arms from shoulder to wrist. Which arm would Susanna have injured? How could she tell? This was getting ridiculous. She cast about hastily for a change of topic.

'And what do you call your horse, sir?'

'I beg your pardon?' Seagrave sounded mystified at the sudden change of direction.

'Your horse—that magnificent creature I have heard that you ride about your estate. Surely it must have some equally magnificent name?'

Seagrave laughed. 'I named him after Alexander the Great's steed, Miss Kellaway! A conceit, I suppose, though he is worthy of it!'

'Bucephalus,' Lucille said absently, then recollected herself again as Seagrave shifted slightly, giving her a look that was quizzical to say the least.

'You have an interest in classical history, Miss Kellaway? I would never have suspected it! You must have inherited some of your father's scholarly nature, after all!'

What did he mean, 'after all'? Lucille bit her lip. She was bristling with indignation at the slur on her intelligence but since she knew Seagrave was actually criticising Susanna rather than herself, she realised she should not regard it. She reminded herself that Susanna would shudder to be thought a bluestocking. 'Lud, we were always being fed such tedious facts at school,' she said, as carelessly as she could. 'How tiresome to discover that some of it remains with me! I would rather die than become an intellectual!'

'No danger of that!' Seagrave said laconically. 'I imagine your talents must lie in other directions!'

The comprehensively assessing look he gave her made Lucille tingle suddenly with an awareness which was completely outside her experience. She shivered in the cool air. Strangely she felt no insult, as she had done with Sir Edwin. The shadows were deepening with every moment, creating a dangerously intimate atmosphere about them. The thin, sickle moon rising above the branches of the yew and the scent of honeysuckle on the breeze did nothing to dispel this illusion.

Seagrave took another step towards her. He was now so close that he could have reached out and touched her but as yet he made no move to do so. Lucille's pulse was racing, the blood singing quick and light through her veins. Her mouth was dry and she moistened her lips nervously, watching in fascination as Seagrave's gaze followed the movement of her tongue, the look in his eyes suddenly so sexually explicit that she caught her breath. Then Sal ran forward, barking at shadows and Lucille turned hastily towards the lych-gate.

'I'll bid you good evening, sir.' She hardly recognised her own voice, so shaken it sounded.

Seagrave caught up to her at the gate. 'I saw you coming out of the church, Miss Kellaway,' he said abruptly. 'Can this be some remarkable conversion to moral rectitude?'

The mocking undertone in his voice banished the magical spell his presence had cast on Lucille. She had read about physical attraction, she reminded herself sharply, and knew that it had nothing to do with loving, liking or respecting another person. No doubt she should just be grateful that Seagrave was indeed no Sir Edwin Bolt, with his insultingly lewd comments and disgusting mauling of Susanna's naked flesh. Only she, Lucille, in her inexperience, had for a moment confused that intense physical awareness with feelings of a deeper and more meaningful kind.

'Did you imagine that I was there to steal the candlesticks?' she snapped, angry with herself for her susceptibility and with him for his sarcasm. She gathered up her skirts in one hand to enable her to walk away from him more quickly. 'Do you exercise the right to decree whether your tenants attend church or not, my lord? Take care that you do not assume too many of the Almighty's own privileges!'

Seagrave's eyes narrowed at this before he unexpectedly burst out laughing. 'A well-judged reproof, Miss Kellaway! What a contradictory creature you are! Come, I shall escort you back to Cookes!'

Lucille preferred not to torment herself with his company. 'Thank you, but there is not the least need! Good night, sir!'

Seagrave, who was used to having his companionship actively sought by women rather than abruptly refused, found this rather amusing. He wished he had kissed her when he had had the chance. He watched with a rueful smile as her small, upright figure crossed the green and disappeared in at the gates of Cookes. Susanna Kellaway... He frowned abruptly, recalling what he knew of her. His wits must be a-begging to find her remotely attractive.

He knew she was supposed to exercise a powerful sexual sway over her conquests, but the attraction he had felt had been far more complex than mere lust. God alone knew what had prompted him to tell her

about Salamanca. If he had not forcibly stopped himself, he imagined he would have blurted out all about
his alienation from normal life, the driven madness
which had possessed him when he had returned from
the wars… Damnation! This sojourn in the country
must be making him soft in the head! He called Sal
sharply to heel and set off across the moonlit fields
back to Dillingham Court.

The good weather broke the following day, and
Lucille spent the morning curled up in the drawing-
room with an ancient map of Dillingham that she had
found in her father's study. Each lane and dwelling
was carefully labelled; Cookes was there, though at
that time it was still a row of individual timbered cottages, drawn with skill and precision by the cartogra-
pher's pen. On the other side of Dragon Hill, the only
high land in the area, lay a beautifully stylised house
named on the map as Dillingham Court and surrounded by its pleasure gardens. Lucille's curiosity
was whetted, but she knew it was unlikely that she
would ever see the Court in real life.

There had still been no word from Susanna, and two
weeks had already passed. Lucille no longer really believed that her sister would return in the time she had
promised, and she itched to be away from Cookes.
Wearing Susanna's character, even without an audience, suddenly grated on her. If only Seagrave had not
come to Dillingham! Lucille shifted uncomfortably in
her chair, her conscience pricking her again.

Immediately after luncheon the rain ceased, driven
away by a brisk wind that hurried the ragged clouds
across the sky. Lucille was tired of being cooped up

all day. She put on a pair of stout boots to protect her from the puddles and called for the carriage to be brought round.

'I wish to go to the seaside, John,' she told the startled coachman.

It was six miles to the sea at the nearest point, which was Shingle Street, and the journey was a slow one over rutted tracks. Clearly John thought that she was mad to attempt such an expedition, but Lucille did not care. Once out of the village environs, the lush green fields soon gave way to thick forest and heathland, flat, dark and empty to the horizons. On such a grey day it was both forbidding and desolate, but Lucille found it a fascinating place. When they finally reached the sea, she descended from the carriage to be met by the full force of the wind and was almost blown over. The fresh salty tang of the air was exhilarating.

Feeling much better, Lucille told John that she would walk along the shore for a little way and asked him to meet her at the gates of the only house she had seen in the vicinity. Scratching his head, the coachman watched her walk off along the shingle beach, a slight, lonely figure in her outmoded coat and boots. How could two sisters be so different? he wondered. Miss Susanna Kellaway never walked anywhere if she could ride; more fundamentally, she had never said please or thank you in all the time he had worked for her.

The walking was hard along the shingle, and the power of the waves was awesome at close quarters. The sea was gunmetal grey, a heaving, bad-tempered maelstrom as it hurled itself on the shore. Seabirds screamed and wheeled overhead. Here and there, sea wrack was scattered across the beach; flotsam and jetsam from ships, bent and misshapen after their time in the water. Lucille stooped to consider a few pieces and picked up a piece of wood that had been worn smooth by the force of the waves.

She had reached a point where there was a set of ancient, worn steps cut into the shingle and she turned away from the sea to follow them up the small cliff. On the headland the turf was smooth and springy, the path skirting an ancient fence which marked the boundary of the house Lucille had seen earlier. She paused, wondering who could have chosen to live in so desolate a spot. The house itself was hidden from her view by a well-established shrubbery and cluster of gnarled trees, but it looked a substantial dwelling. And as she considered it, leaning on the fence, a voice from near at hand said:

'Goddess! Excellently bright!'

Lucille jumped and spun around. The voice was of a rich, deep-velvet quality and would have carried from pit to gallery at a Drury Lane theatre. Emerging from the shrubbery was an extraordinary figure, a large woman of indeterminate age, wrapped in what seemed like endless scarves of blue chiffon and purple gauze in complete defiance of the climate. Over her arm was a basket full of roses and at her heels stalked a large fluffy white cat. The most worldly-wise, disillusioned pair of dark eyes that Lucille had ever seen were appraising her thoughtfully.

'That, Miss Kellaway,' the lady said impressively, 'was in tribute to your beauty and was—'

'Ben Jonson,' Lucille said, spontaneously. 'Yes, I know!'

The pessimistic dark eyes focussed on her more intently. 'Would you care to take tea with me, Miss

Kellaway? I have so few visitors here for I am not recognised in the county!'

For a moment, Lucille wondered what on earth she meant. It seemed impossible that such a character would remain unrecognised wherever she went.

'I am Bessie Bellingham,' the lady continued, grandly. 'The Dowager Lady Bellingham! Bessie Bowles, as was!'

She paused, clearly expecting the recognition she deserved, and Lucille did not disappoint her.

'Of course! I have read of you, ma'am—your performance as Viola in *Twelfth Night* was accounted one of the best ever seen at Drury Lane, and the papers were forever arguing over whether comedy or melodrama was your forté!'

'Well, well, before your time, my child!' But Lady Bellingham was smiling, well pleased, and the cat was rubbing around Lucille's ankles and purring. 'My own favourite was Priscilla Tomboy in *The Romp*, but it was a long time ago, before I met dear Bellingham and ended up in this mausoleum!'

She took Lucille's arm and steered her through the shrubbery towards the house. 'You have no idea how delighted I was when I saw you on the beach,' she continued. 'Of course, I had heard that you were staying in Dillingham—my maid, Conchita, knows everything! And I thought that, as we two are the black sheep of the neighbourhood, we could take tea and talk of the London this provincial crowd will never know!'

Lucille remembered, with a sudden uprush of alarm, that Lady Bellingham, in common with the whole of Suffolk, would think that she was Susanna. But it was too late to cry off—the house had come into view and

Lady Bellingham was drawing her forward up the wide, shallow steps and onto the terrace. It was, Lucille thought, a particularly ugly house, foursquare and squat, brick-built and crouching low to the ground as though sheltering from the wind off the sea. And how such a character as Lady Bellingham could choose to immure herself here, Lucille could not imagine.

'I am seldom at home,' Lady Bellingham was saying as though she had read Lucille's thoughts, 'for I travel a great deal on the continent—when the European situation will allow! But for now you find me all alone—' she gave a theatrical shrug '—and happy for some distraction!'

They had gone into the drawing-room, which was stuffed full of furniture mostly in the French style. Lady Bellingham subsided on to the gilt-wood settee, and Lucille somewhat gingerly perched on one of the matching, silk-upholstered chairs, which proved a lot less spindly than it looked. The cat, graciously accepting the bonbon Lady Bellingham held out, curled up in a large *fauteuil* and fell instantly asleep. Lady Bellingham rang a small brass bell and ordered tea, then turned her world-weary gaze back to Lucille.

'So tell me how dear Bertie Penscombe is these days,' she invited, her dark eyes sparkling with malicious enjoyment. 'Is it really true that you have thrown him over for Seagrave? Not that I can fault you there, my dear! Seagrave has to be one of the most charismatic men that I have ever had the pleasure of meeting! Now, if I were thirty years younger…' She helped herself to another bonbon, her eyes never leaving Lucille's face.

Lucille found herself to be completely tongue-tied.

She was unable to comment on the attributes of Susanna's former lover, and was all too aware of the attractions of the Earl of Seagrave. And as she hesitated fatally, Lady Bellingham clapped her hands together in a sudden, energetic gesture that made Lucille jump.

'No, no, no, no, no, no!' she said abruptly and melodramatically. 'I have puzzled over it since we first met, and I cannot account for it! *You* cannot be the Cyprian!'

To be unmasked so emphatically, in tones which would have riveted an entire audience, silenced Lucille completely. Lady Bellingham, seeing her total confusion, smiled in kindly fashion.

'No need to look so shocked, my poor child! It is simply that I have played the Cyprian—oh, many and many times! You do not have the air, the style!' She got to her feet. 'A courtesan minces, so...' it was ludicrous to see that solid figure prancing across the drawing-room in such an accurate and cruel caricature of Susanna's provocatively swaying walk '...and she has the air...' Lady Bellingham stuck her nose in the air and raised a hand to her forehead in an exact parody of Susanna's delicate, die-away affectations. 'I vow,' she said in a languishing drawl, "tis impossible to choose between Lord Rook and Lord Crow, but for their fortune!'

Lucille could not help herself. She gave a peal of laughter.

'And your dress, the hair...' Lady Bellingham was shaking her head sorrowfully. 'My dear Miss Kellaway, if Miss Kellaway you really are, it simply will not do!'

'I know I am very bad at it,' Lucille said regretfully.

'You see, Lady Bellingham, I had no idea…and Susanna had so little time… Oh dear, now I really am in the suds!'

'Tell me All!' Lady Bellingham said impressively, her dark eyes sparkling at Lucille over the rim of her teacup. 'Horace and I—' she eyed the sleeping cat with affection '—have so little excitement! Can you be Susanna Kellaway's sister?'

'I am Lucille Kellaway and I am her twin,' Lucille confirmed sadly, 'and lamentably poor at impersonating her!'

'Well,' Lady Bellingham said astringently, 'that is no bad thing! Why pretend to be a Cyprian when one is not? Lord knows, there's precious little amusement in it, whatever one might think!'

Lucille was beginning to feel better under this unsentimental assessment. Slowly, the whole story came out, of Susanna's request to her and her own foolish agreement. Lady Bellingham nodded and ate biscuits and stroked Horace absentmindedly.

'I only wanted to escape the confines of the school for a little, and visit the place where our father had lived,' Lucille finished ruefully. 'I had no idea that matters would get so complicated! But not only do the villagers detest having Susanna amongst them, but I have been obliged to deceive the Earl of Seagrave— something which I would have wished to avoid at all costs!'

Lady Bellingham put down her cup and brushed the biscuit crumbs absentmindedly from the folds of her scarves. 'Seagrave…yes…' she said thoughtfully. 'He is not the man to try to cozen! His father was another such—an honourable man, but most awe-inspiring! Not like your own dear papa, my dear—' her eyes

twinkled at Lucille '—with whom I once flirted at a
hunt breakfast! A gentleman and a scholar, George
Kellaway, and quite, quite charming! But he had not
an ounce of Seagrave's authority!'

'I plan to leave Dillingham as soon as I may,'
Lucille said in a rush, 'and put an end to this impru-
dent charade! I have been very foolish and do not wish
for matters to go any further!'

'A pity!' Lady Bellingham smiled warmly at her. 'I
am persuaded that I could have taught you sufficient
tricks to pull it off! But if you would rather not...'
She shrugged her ample shoulders. 'Now, I see your
carriage is waiting and I should not delay you, for it
is a slow drive back to Dillingham! But come and see
me again, dear child, for I have enjoyed your visit
immensely!'

'You have been very kind to me, ma'am,' Lucille
said, slowly, 'and I am very glad to have met you! I
was quite blue-devilled today!'

Lady Bellingham enfolded Lucille in a warm embrace and insisted on coming with her to the front
door, where John the coachman was waiting, having
been summoned from his vigil at the gates by the butler. They drove slowly away down the chestnut-lined
drive, and Lucille waved to the bulky, chiffon-draped
figure on the steps until they were out of sight.

The encounter with Lady Bellingham certainly
lifted Lucille's spirits. She now had even less sympathy for a society which could deny itself the pleasure
of the company of such an idiosyncratic character
through pure snobbery. It seemed that former ac-
tresses, like Cyprians, were not to be received or even
acknowledged amongst the bigoted gentry of Suffolk.
The thought bred determination and bravado. There

was not the least need, Lucille told herself, to spend her remaining time in Dillingham moping behind closed doors.

Accordingly she woke the next morning resolved to take a walk, and follow one of the paths she had seen marked on the map the previous day. Her only difficulty lay in negotiating the village green, which she knew was unlikely to be as empty as on the Sunday evening. That was where the bravado came in. Lucille put on her bonnet and raised her chin defiantly. Let the villagers show their disapproval!

Cookes was set back from the road down a short drive, with a carriage sweep at the front and well-tended lawns bordering the gates. Lucille walked slowly down the drive and out on to the green. Despite her defiant thoughts of a few minutes before, she admitted to a large measure of apprehension when she realised that it was market day and the green was packed with stalls and hawkers. There was a wealth of seafood on offer: crab, eels, flounder and oysters tumbled from baskets and across trestles. Nearby were flower girls, and fruit-sellers with panniers of oranges, lemons and cherries. A pieman cheerfully shouted his wares. It was a vivid scene. It was also too late for her to retreat, for she had been noticed. Straightening her spine, she picked her way between the vendors and started to cross the green.

The change in atmosphere was both sudden and tangible. The hostility was all too real. As Lucille passed by a sudden silence fell. Men stared and women pulled their skirts aside as if she might contaminate them. Children were abruptly hushed and summoned to their parents' side. Lucille, who had expected to be able to cope with the animosity, was unprepared for the depth of feeling. It shook her. She actually felt unsafe. Stallholders watched in silence as she walked through the market; trade was suspended. People turned away. One man even spat on the ground at her feet. And behind her she was aware of the crescendo of sound.

'We don't want her sort here…no better than she ought to be…the hussy! She should be driven out! Nothing but a common trollop!'

By the time she had reached the other side of the green and run the gauntlet of so many hostile faces, Lucille found the angry, unshed tears stinging her eyes and blocking her throat. She wanted to shout at them all for their stupid ignorance and intolerance, but equally she wanted to run away and hide, never to have to face them again. Even the curate had emerged from the door of the charming stone church and was watching her progress with hard, condemning eyes. She almost expected him to step forward and denounce her as a harlot before the assembled throng.

Lucille had reached the lane which led out of the village towards the Court, and was starting to feel marginally better, when a stout woman carrying a marketing basket full of vegetables stepped out from a nearby path and blocked her way. Her high colour suggested a choleric nature and her livid gaze made Lucille's heart sink. Behind her lounged a dark young man with a narrow, watchful face, whose bold gaze was appraising Lucille in the presumptuous way that she hated. Her heart started to beat faster.

'Miss Kellaway! I am Serena Mutch, George Kellaway's sister! I had to see with my own eyes if you could really be his daughter!'

Lucille took a deep breath. 'I am delighted to meet

you, Aunt,' she said, carefully. 'It is a pleasure to meet the family I have never known—'

Mrs Mutch snorted with disgust. 'Pleasure! It's a disgrace! You have brought nothing but dishonour on the name of Kellaway, and you should be ashamed to show your face here! You shameless trollop!'

There was a grin on the young man's face now as he leant back against the fence and enjoyed her discomfiture. Lucille itched to slap his arrogance away. If this was Mrs Mutch, the young man could only be her cousin Walter, who had been cut out of his inheritance by Susanna's unexpected claim to Cookes.

'She may be anybody's to ride, but she looks nothing like Farmer Trudgeon's mare!' he said, in a rich country drawl which seemed only to accentuate the insult in the words. Mrs Mutch's face flamed, but whether in anger or embarrassment at her son's coarseness, it was difficult to gauge. She turned to Lucille in a sudden fury.

'Well, what are you waiting for? Get out of this village! Get out, I say!' Her fingers closed around the large cauliflower she had in the basket, and Lucille realised with incredulity that she was about to throw it at her. The insane idea of the villagers pelting her with rotten fruit and vegetables flashed across her mind even as Mrs Mutch raised her arm. It would be messy, Lucille thought hysterically, but not as bad as stoning…

'Good day, Mrs Mutch, Walter…'

The mellow tones, utterly expressionless, cut right across them. Preoccupied in the confrontation, neither Lucille nor her relatives had heard the approaching hoofbeats and Lucille turned in amazement to see the Earl of Seagrave reining in Bucephalus and summing up the entire scene with one swift, assessing glance. He swung down from the saddle and stood next to her. Extraordinarily, there was something so reassuring about his presence that Lucille could feel herself relaxing, despite the fact that her conscious mind was telling her that Seagrave was more likely to join in the denunciation than to defend her.

Mrs Mutch lowered the cauliflower slowly and dropped an embarrassed curtsy. Walter straightened up and threw away the piece of straw he had been chewing.

'Good day, my lord!' Mrs Mutch sounded flustered. 'I was just…greeting my niece!'

Seagrave's gaze rested thoughtfully on the vegetables. 'So I see. A charming family reunion.' He looked at Walter for a moment, and the man's thin face flushed slightly. 'I am loath to interrupt,' Seagrave continued smoothly, 'but I feel Miss Kellaway must be fatigued in this heat. Miss Kellaway, I shall escort you back to Cookes now. Good day, Mrs Mutch.'

His tone brooked no refusal. He looped the horse's reins over his arm and took Lucille's elbow in his other hand, turning back towards the green and walking between her and the avid villagers, effectively shielding her from their view. He steered her down the lane towards Cookes and did not pause or speak until a bend in the road cut them off from sight.

'I did warn you how it would be, Miss Kellaway.' There was no pity in his tone or sympathy in his gaze as he looked down at her. Lucille, shaking with anger and reaction, was so incensed that she looked him straight in the eye.

'You did indeed, Lord Seagrave! I see that you have already been extremely busy putting your threat into practice! A pity you could not have warned me about it the last time we met, instead of making a pretence of civility!'

For some reason her furious comment seemed to touch Seagrave on the raw. The black stallion, a magnificent and highly bred beast, jibbed as he jerked its rein in an involuntary movement.

'It is none of my doing, Miss Kellaway.' The mellow tones were unusually harsh.

Lucille's voice caught on a sob. 'Then it seems you may spare yourself the trouble, my lord! I am already scorned as a scarlet woman and my housekeeper is refused provisions by every stallholder and shopowner in the place! Anyone, it seems, may insult me as they please! Even I am not so brass faced as to stay in a place where I am so clearly despised!'

To her horror, Lucille felt the scalding tears about to overflow. She turned away in anger and distress, covering her face with her hands.

Seagrave's hand tightened on her arm. 'Do not let that old harridan put you out of countenance, Miss Kellaway!' he said, urgently, in her ear. 'Serena Mutch's bad temper springs more from the disappointment and anger of seeing her son disinherited than her disapproval of you!'

Lucille swallowed hard. The insults might have been intended for Susanna, not her, but they were wounding nevertheless. She had never experienced such bitter animosity in her life. 'Whatever her reasons, Mrs Mutch said only what the whole village was thinking!' She took a gulp of air and managed to overcome her tears with an immense effort, even summoning up a wan smile as she remembered the cauliflower.

'At the least, I must thank you for your prompt rescue, sir. I believe I was about to be pilloried with my aunt's vegetables! And on the subject of reputation, I fear that it will scarce do either of us any good for you to be seen in converse with me! You may leave me here, I think. I shall be quite safe!'

'My reputation can stand it,' Seagrave said, with a hint of amusement in his tone, 'and yours, Miss Kellaway—'

'Was lost long since!' Lucille finished for him. She gave a tired shrug. 'As you wish, sir!'

Seagrave, again brought up short by her reluctant toleration of his company, discovered that he wished to prolong the encounter very much. He looked at her, his gaze suddenly intent. She was not beautiful, he thought judiciously, but there was a formidable appeal about her looks which probably in some part explained her success. She was not in the common style, with her oval face set with those magnificent cornflower blue eyes, the small retroussé nose, and the soft pink mouth made for smiling—or to be kissed. Then there was the unconscious challenge of that pert, determined chin and the graceful line of her neck...he could not argue with those who called her looks striking.

Her figure was less voluptuous than he remembered from seeing her in Town, but it showed to advantage in the tight-fitting blue jacket worn over her high-waisted jonquil dress. Less obvious, less easy to explain though, was the clear intelligence in that flashing blue gaze, a very different matter from the cupidity and opportunism that he had seen and despised when he knew her before. Finally, and even more confusingly, she had an air of fragility and innocence which aroused powerful feelings of protectiveness in him.

What else could have sent him to her aid when he could have turned the situation to his own benefit and completed her humiliation? Cursing himself for a susceptible fool, he deliberately tried to distance himself.

'It was foolish of you to venture out in the daylight, all the same,' he drawled. 'I had thought you only dared to flit about the village in the dark!'

'Like a bat, perhaps?' Lucille asked sweetly, and earned herself a quizzical look.

She tried to get a grip on herself, knowing she was in grave danger of giving away the entire masquerade. Susanna would never have spoken thus. But her feelings had swung from misery to a heady relief that she had escaped so unpleasant a scene, and the presence of the Earl of Seagrave added some indefinable element of excitement that was in danger of making her almost too reckless. At that moment she would not even have cared very much had the whole deception come tumbling about her ears, were it not for the thought of Seagrave's inevitable disgust and disapproval. That, on top of her recent humiliation, was more than she could bear.

They continued to walk slowly down the lane that skirted Cookes's orchards, with the mighty Bucephalus trotting along behind in complete disgust. Lucille was finding, disconcertingly, that Seagrave's powerful effect on her had not waned. She was almost unbearably aware of his physical presence, the brush of his sleeve against her arm, the strength of the hand that had held her arm and was now clasping Bucephalus's reins lightly between tanned fingers… For a moment she imagined those same hands sliding over her skin and was transfixed by the image, both dismayed and confused by whatever was happening to her. She did not understand it and could not explain it away. To distract herself, she reminded herself that she was supposed to be Susanna, who would not be thrown into confusion by a staid summer stroll with a charismatic Earl.

'So how do you find Cookes now that you have had time to get to know it a little?' the Earl asked a few moments later.

'Oh, it is a charming little house,' Lucille said, attempting Susanna's condescending drawl, 'though no doubt your lordship would prefer that I thought otherwise!' She looked at him through her eyelashes and saw the slight, cynical smile on his lips. Encouraged, she continued archly, 'Be warned, sir, I may give up Dillingham but I shall not give up the lease so easily!'

She saw that sardonic smile grow. 'I never doubted it for a moment, Miss Kellaway,' Seagrave said smoothly. 'You must be feeling more the thing now, I think, for you have reverted to form! How slow I was in not realising that all I had to do to get you to leave was to offer you enough money!'

Lucille smiled to herself. He certainly had Susanna's measure! 'I would consider any reasonable offer,' she said virtuously. 'After all, a young lady must make shift to take care of herself!' She saw his lip curl in barely concealed distaste and tried not to laugh. She must be a more accomplished actress than she had imagined, to ape Susanna so accurately! She was almost beginning to enjoy herself! Perhaps she should have taken Lady Bellingham up on her offer after all... Half appalled, half exhilarated, Lucille wondered how she had the audacity to further the impersonation.

'I will think about paying you off,' Seagrave said

coolly. 'I am not sure how much the lease of Cookes is really worth to me!'

Lucille cast him a coy look. 'Ah, but it is not merely the lease, is it, my lord! I imagine you would pay a great deal to remove my presence from your estate, but I warn you, my price is high!'

'So I have heard,' Seagrave said, with a searing look sideways at her that made his meaning quite clear. Those dark eyes considered her body with insulting thoroughness, dwelling thoughtfully on the curve of her breasts before moving downwards. Lucille felt as though his gaze stripped every item of clothing from her. She willed herself not to blush. She could hardly complain, after all, if he treated her as the Cyprian she had set herself up to be! And strangely, once again his look evoked none of the squirming disgust she had felt with Sir Edwin, or the outrage provoked by Walter Mutch...

'However,' the Earl continued without interest after a moment, 'it is not a cost I would wish to incur, though I shall offer you a fair price for the lease.'

It was a humiliating setdown, Lucille felt. She remembered Mrs Appleton saying that the one thing Susanna could not bear was rejection. She had never been able to bear the thought that she was not irresistibly attractive, even when a small girl. Accordingly, Lucille set her lips in a mutinous line and pretended to sulk. They walked on a little way in silence. The road was skirting the edge of Cookes's orchards and briar roses tumbled over the ancient wall. Lucille had to stop herself from pausing to breathe in their scent— Susanna had never really appreciated the beauties of nature.

'I am glad that the lease of Cookes prevents you

from evicting me as you threatened that first time,' she said, emulating the spite she had sometimes seen Susanna display when crossed. 'At least matters are not made *that* easy for your lordship!'

Seagrave merely looked amused. 'No,' he agreed affably, 'unfortunately I am not to be rid of you so easily, Miss Kellaway! I am afraid I lied at that first encounter! But you see, it might have worked—and spared me a lot of trouble!'

He was not the only one who lied, Lucille thought, with a sudden and inconvenient return of her guilty conscience. She had done nothing but lie to him since they first met. And here she was parodying her sister to the extent of almost creating a caricature! The enormity of it all rendered her temporarily speechless.

They had reached the wooden gate into Cookes. Bucephalus started to help himself to the hedge. Seagrave turned to Lucille, smiling politely. 'I am glad that your experience in the village has not overset you, Miss Kellaway. You are feeling quite recovered, I hope?'

Lucille managed an artistic shiver. 'Well, I'll own it was most unpleasant, but—simple people…what can one expect but a small-minded, illiterate intolerance!'

'These simple country people often have a very well-developed sense of morality, Miss Kellaway,' Seagrave said dryly, 'which is something I doubt you ever had, or perhaps lost a long time ago! Where did your foster father go wrong, I wonder?'

Lucille tried a delicate yawn, the type of reaction Susanna would most certainly have shown to such moralising. She followed it up with a pert toss of the head.

'Lud, I don't doubt Mr Markham has been spinning in his grave these nine years past! But what a prosy bore you have turned out to be, my lord! I would never have guessed it! You sound just like my foster mother, forever exhorting us to marry well and settle down! I had no taste for respectable, genteel poverty! I declare, if I must give myself to an old man I might as well be paid for it!'

'A most practical attitude, Miss Kellaway,' Seagrave agreed, his face expressionless. 'And your sister, the schoolmistress—I collect she took a different approach to earning a living! How did she feel at being left at the mercy of the world, with Markham dead and Kellaway abroad?'

With a shock, Lucille remembered that *she* was the schoolmistress to whom he was referring. 'La, I do not know! I never asked her!' That, at least was true. 'She spends all her time immured in Miss Pym's school teaching those tiresome little girls! I vow, it's enough to make one run quite mad!' And that, she thought, was quite enough of Susanna for one day. She felt empty and guilt ridden at the things she had said. It was time to make an end.

She turned to Seagrave and held out her hand. 'It seems we may not meet again, so I shall bid you farewell, my lord. I plan to remove from here shortly.'

Seagrave looked down at the small hand in his own, then up again at her face. 'Truly, Miss Kellaway? I did not realise you were in earnest when you said that earlier.'

Lucille tried to free her hand but he was holding on to it. She dropped her gaze from his intent one. 'La, sir, Dillingham is too slow for me!' She gave him one last dazzling smile and tried again to free herself. He had still not let her go and the warm clasp of his fingers was sending small, exquisite sensations trembling along her nerve endings.

'If it is the matter of provisions that is worrying you, I will see that you are sent all that you need,' Seagrave said abruptly, 'and will undertake that you do not have such problems again. And if your housekeeper needs help in running Cookes, I am sure that Josselyn can arrange something. After all, it is in my interests that the upkeep of the house and gardens is maintained.'

Lucille hesitated. This sudden generosity seemed odd and out of character. What new approach was this? Could he be trying to lull her suspicions, pretend to stand her friend, whilst he tried to find a new way to break the lease? No doubt, were she really Susanna, she would be thinking that he had proved susceptible to her charm after all!

'It's monstrous good of you, sir,' she said, giving him a melting look from under her lashes. 'I knew you would relent. I am so grateful…'

'Keep your gratitude within bounds, Miss Kellaway,' Seagrave said coolly. He let go of her at last. 'Make no mistake of it, I want you out of Cookes. But the lease of the property is yours by right of inheritance. I shall not have it said that I have driven you from the house with no recompense. Good day, Miss Kellaway.'

Arrogant man! Lucille let out a huge sigh as she watched him mount a very disgruntled Bucephalus and canter off up the track towards Dillingham Court. She never wanted to have to go through such an encounter again. She felt exhausted, and overcome with remorse. She had behaved in a truly disgraceful way, and if Seagrave had called her bluff and offered her *carte blanche* it would have served her right! Dangling her bonnet from its strings, she made her way slowly through the dappled shade of the orchard towards the house, her mind still full of the charismatic Earl and his quixotic generosity.

Had she but known it, Seagrave's own reaction was just as complicated as her own. Once clear of the village he set the stallion to a gallop across the fields to the Court. The speed was exhilarating, but did nothing to help him clarify his thoughts. He was both puzzled and annoyed by his response to Susanna Kellaway. He was not an inexperienced youth, nor was he willing to delude himself. He was therefore obliged to accept that he was attracted to her, and had been ever since their first encounter. He had lied when he had said that he was not interested in her—he was beginning to want her like a fever in the blood. His feelings prevented him from driving her out of the village with the ruthlessness the situation clearly demanded. It was a completely unexpected reaction and one that was as unwelcome as it was surprising.

Worse, he could not make up his mind about her. She was so contradictory, so unpredictable! One moment she was truly the Susanna he remembered, then a moment later she would reveal unexpected depths before retreating behind that superficial façade once more. It was infuriating, but it was fascinating as well. There was something else, too, that did not fit the case—something at the back of his mind, troubling him…something that his agent had mentioned about the Kellaway sisters when he had first arrived at the Court. He handed over the sweating horse to a stable-hand with a word of thanks and strode into the house, calling for Josselyn as he went. He was so wrapped up in his own thoughts that it escaped his notice that his habitual boredom had vanished like mist in the summer sun.

Chapter Four

There were five days left before Lucille could depart for Oakham, and she felt sometimes as though she were counting the hours. She had not ventured beyond Cookes's boundaries again, contenting herself with strolling through the orchard or sitting beside the pond and watching the brown trout basking in the sun. Lucille had always considered herself to be a solitary soul by choice, with plenty of resources to help her occupy her time, and she was surprised and depressed to find her self-imposed solitude lonely. Since she could not go out, her only companion was Mrs Appleton, and the housekeeper had made it plain in the most pleasant of ways that Lucille's position as her employer's sister precluded a closer friendship between them.

Lucille understood this, but found herself wishing for someone in whom to confide. Over the years Miss Pym had fulfilled this role admirably, and Lucille missed her mentor's advice. She considered going to see Lady Bellingham again, but did not want to impose, and that left only her books for distraction. In an effort to immerse herself once more she turned to

Miss Austen's *Mansfield Park*, hoping that the wittily observed social conventions would divert her from her feeling of isolation.

She had been sitting on the rustic bench beneath the apple tree when she heard the sound of footsteps on the gravel path. For a moment her heart began to race in the absurd hope and conviction that it might be Seagrave, but the man who appeared around the side of the house was a complete stranger to her. Excitement was replaced by apprehension, but she had little time to wonder about his identity as he hurried forward across the grass.

'*Suzanne! Ma belle! Enfin!*' Then, breaking into English: 'You little minx, I have scoured this so-dull countryside just to find you!'

He took her hand and covered it with moist kisses, then held her at arm's length, his berry-black eyes twinkling suggestively. 'But you have lost weight, *mon ange*! Whatever can 'ave 'appened to you?'

'I am very well, I thank you, sir.' Lucille knew she sounded ludicrously formal after his fulsome greeting, but she could not help herself. In the first place she did not have the least idea who he was and she was repelled by his moist breath on her face. She tried surreptitiously to wipe his kisses off her hand.

The gentleman was looking comically crestfallen. 'So cold, *ma belle*? You were not so cruel to your *petit* Charles last spring! Why, we made a fine time of it, you and I, did we not, Suzanne!'

Lucille was fairly certain that she could now place the gentleman as one of Susanna's ex-lovers. And at least she knew his name now. She wished she had been inside when he had called; wished Mrs Appleton had been on hand to help her; wished even that the ground could open up beneath her feet and swallow her up before she had to attempt this difficult conversation. But there was no help on hand. It was a beautiful day, perfect for a romantic tête-à-tête beneath the spreading branches of the apple tree. A turtle dove began to coo above their heads.

She looked at her unexpected visitor thoughtfully. He looked very Gallic, with long black locks, heavily pomaded, and impressive side-whiskers. He was wearing a gaudy purple coat with huge gold buttons, and there was excessive lace at his wrists and throat. There was also a twinkle in his black eyes which Lucille, inexperienced as she was, recognised with misgiving. So far, none of the men who had cast covetous eyes on her in her role as Susanna had actually taken any action, but there was the same lascivious gleam in this man's eyes as she had seen from the occasional father, delivering his daughter back to school, and she had once had to fight off the goaty advances of a repellent geography master. A suspicion that the Frenchman might wish to rekindle his relationship with her sister took shape in her mind.

Lucille gave him a cool smile, moving away to sit down gracefully on the bench. 'My dear Charles, that was then and this is now.' She gave Susanna's light shrug. 'You know how fickle I am, my dear!'

The gentleman seemed to take this in good part, smiling a little cynically as his familiar gaze continued to rove over her. Lucille found this presumptuous but knew by now that Susanna must be used to such attentions. Under his scrutiny the mauve silk and lace dress, another of Susanna's most modest confections, felt as though it was both far too low cut and too transparent. He took a seat at the opposite end of the bench, which was too close to Lucille for comfort, and allowed his arm to lie along the back of the seat, just touching her shoulder. Lucille found she had to steel herself not to flinch away.

'I am *aux anges* to see you again, *mon amour*,' he murmured seductively. 'I have missed you so much!' Lust flared suddenly in his eyes. 'Ah, Suzanne, there is no one quite like you—so warm, so skilful! Do you remember—?'

Lucille broke in rather desperately. 'So how did you find me, Charles?' she asked, certain that Susanna would not have told anyone of her address in Suffolk.

The gentleman rolled his eyes. '*Mon Dieu*, Suzanne, you put me to a lot of trouble! No one at your London house would give your direction—in the end I had to bribe a kitchen maid for the information I wanted! Why are you hiding in this tedious place, *ma belle*?' He raised an interrogative eyebrow.

Lucille shrugged evasively. 'There were reasons, Charles…'

He laughed. 'Reasons? That I understand very well! After all, I have my own reasons for seeking you out, *ma chère*!'

Lucille gave him what she hoped passed for a look of languid enquiry. At least she seemed to have successfully distracted his thoughts from seduction—for the time being. 'Money, my dear?'

Charles looked a little chagrined. '*Alors*, you have no delicacy, you English! I admit to a temporary embarrassment only… If you could see your way clear to advancing me a small loan…'

'My dear…' Lucille hesitated. How difficult it was to achieve the casual intimacy of old lovers! Never having had a lover, old or new, she had no idea.

But the gentleman was on his feet and speaking again. 'A paltry sum, *mon ange*, only my card debts are becoming pressing…'

Lucille felt uncomfortable with him looming over her and stood up. They were of a height and his pleading black eyes, so like a puppy's, gazed melodramatically into hers. She was hard put to it not to laugh.

'My dear Charles,' she began again, 'I would truly love to help you, but I fear I have with me here nowhere near the amount you need. Now, if you were to apply to me in a few weeks' time in London, I might be able to be more forthcoming.'

'You wish to get rid of me,' the gentleman said, hangdog. '*Alors*, Suzanne, be kind to me! I have come all this way—'

Before Lucille had realised it, he had caught her to him and was trying to kiss her. She turned her head just in time and his wet lips landed on her cheek rather than her mouth. She pushed hard but ineffectually against his chest. He was a lot stronger than he appeared and Lucille suddenly wished Mrs Appleton were there with her saucepan.

'Suzanne!' This time there was reproach in his voice. He really was a consummate actor, Lucille thought. Perhaps he could mend his fortunes with a career on the stage. 'To deny a man a little comfort when he has travelled all this way to see you—'

'To borrow money from me, you mean!' Lucille snapped, twisting her head away again to avoid him. 'Let me go at once!' She had no idea how Susanna would have handled this and did not really care. Her only concern was to get away from him. She looked round a little desperately, but there were no suitable objects within reach. If only they had been inside she could have used one of her father's Chinese souvenirs, although it would have been a pity to treat a Ming vase in such a way...

She felt his lips trail wet kisses down her neck and his insinuating hands slipping from her waist to knead her breast. It was disgusting. Freeing one hand at last, she delivered a stinging blow to the side of his face. He let her go with an oath, and at the same time an amused voice from just behind them drawled: 'A very true and proper hit, Miss Kellaway!'

Both Lucille and the gentleman, now nursing his jaw, turned to see the Earl of Seagrave saunter across the path towards them. His muscular height dwarfed the other man and beside Seagrave's severe elegance the gentleman's fussy tailoring suddenly looked completely ridiculous.

Seagrave fixed him with his most quelling look. 'My dear Comte De Vigny, can you not take a hint? I believe the lady expressed a disinclination for your company! You will oblige me by removing yourself at once!'

'*Parbleu!*' De Vigny's gaze moved from Seagrave to Lucille with sudden comprehension. 'So that is how it is, *hein*!'

Lucille opened her mouth to dispel his illusions but Seagrave was before her.

'Precisely so,' he said easily, sliding a proprietorial arm around Lucille's waist, 'so you see how damnably *de trop* you are, do you not, sir?'

There was suddenly an ugly look on De Vigny's face. 'Not your usual style, is it, Seagrave, to deal in such shop-soiled goods? *Merde*, I can tell you all the tricks this one will turn—if you pay her enough—'

'But you will do no such thing!' Seagrave's voice

cut across him like a whiplash. The hostility between the two men was suddenly almost tangible. 'Take yourself off my land, De Vigny, before I call you out!'

De Vigny knew when he was beaten. He muttered a epithet which Lucille, for all her extensive knowledge of French, did not recognise, and sketched a mocking bow. '*Au 'voir* then, Suzanne! I congratulate you on your conquest! *Monsieur*…'

Lucille sat down rather suddenly on the bench, afraid she might faint. Of all her recent insights into Susanna's lifestyle, this had been the most shocking because it had touched her so closely. De Vigny's ugly words had spilled corrosively across the bright beauty of the summer day. Seagrave, who clearly expected her—Susanna—to be inured to such coarseness as De Vigny had shown, was watching the retreating figure with some satisfaction.

'He will not trouble you again,' he said carelessly. He took a closer look at Lucille's white face and gave a quick frown of concern. 'Are you all right, Miss Kellaway? You look a trifle pale. I will fetch you a brandy…'

Lucille closed her eyes, turning her face up to the soothing warmth of the sun and allowing the shock to drain out of her mind. It was absurd to be so affected by an attack which was not really aimed at her, but she had been shaken in the same way as when she was exposed to the malice of the villagers. Yet again the effects of her masquerade had come home to roost in an unexpectedly unpleasant way…

'Your father always kept an excellent brandy. You will find it most restorative.' Seagrave's voice broke into her thoughts and Lucille opened her eyes. He took the seat beside her and handed her the glass.

'The spite of old lovers must be a hazard of your profession,' he said commiseratingly.

Lucille, who had just taken a mouthful of liquid, choked as the fiery spirit caught in her throat.

'That's better,' Seagrave continued approvingly, as the colour returned to her face. 'I had not imagined the encounter would shake you so. I must say, that was a very accurate shot you delivered, Miss Kellaway! One might almost believe that you had learnt cricket, to be so on target!'

'We play rounders at school,' Lucille began thoughtlessly, then caught herself. 'That is, I played when I was at school…'

Seagrave's dark eyes dwelt thoughtfully on her face. 'An unexpected talent, Miss Kellaway.' His voice hardened. 'And no doubt a useful one for a lady in your position. There must be times… But I doubt the Comte was truly dangerous. From what I have heard, I would judge he believes himself more a Lothario than he really is! But, of course—' he inclined his head '—you are the only one who knows the truth of that!'

Lucille was beginning to feel much better. The brandy had restored her natural resilience and added something besides but, unaccustomed to strong liquor, she was in ignorance of its effect on her. She looked at Seagrave pugnaciously. 'You could have intervened to help me, sir! To stand by and do nothing—well, upon my word!'

Seagrave gave her a lopsided grin which seemed to do strange things to Lucille's equilibrium. 'But you might have been wanting to encourage him, ma'am! How was I to judge? Besides, you coped very well on your own, did you not?'

Lucille gave him a fulminating look which met nothing but his unrepentant smile. Another thought occurred to her. 'And now you have led him to believe I'm—' She broke off in confusion.

'My mistress,' Seagrave supplied, with a smile. 'I am not flattered by your aghast expression, Miss Kellaway! Am I then so unattractive that you cannot stomach the idea?'

Lucille blushed. Her fertile imagination, inflamed by the brandy, presented her with the image of herself held close in Seagrave's arms. For a moment she could even feel the hard lines of his body against her own pliancy. Heat suffused her. There was nothing unattractive about the Earl of Seagrave. Those dark, gold-flecked eyes, fringed with thick black lashes, were holding hers with a hint of mockery in their depths that suggested he could read her mind.

Lucille's bemused gaze considered his face thoughtfully. Its delineations were very pleasing, with those high cheekbones, straight nose and firm jaw, and that mouth... Lucille removed her gaze hastily, remembering the fire that had overcome her the last time she had dwelt on its firmly sensuous lines... Yet there was more to Seagrave's face than a mere collection of features. It was the humour and vitality that gave it its character... Lucille suddenly realised that she had not answered his question and blushed even more.

'I...yes...no!' She made a grab for her self-control. 'You are pleased to jest, sir!'

'I assure you, I was never more serious in my life.' Seagrave's gaze was unfaltering. 'We should deal admirably together.' He took the empty glass from her hand and put it gently on one side. Lucille, suddenly gripped by the most terrifying of premonitions, found that the power of movement had temporarily deserted her. She watched, mesmerised, as he leant closer, and closed her eyes when he was too near to be in focus any more. His lips brushed hers in the lightest of kisses, shockingly sweet and piercingly intense. He had already started to withdraw as Lucille gasped with surprise, her eyes opening wide.

'Think about it,' Seagrave said softly, persuasively. He sat back, his tone changing to one of brisk practicality. 'In the meantime, I have another proposal for you to consider. I have a house in Chelsea, which I am willing to offer you on the same terms as this— provided that you give up all claim to the lease of Cookes.'

The kiss completed Lucille's confusion. She struggled to regain some small semblance of control over her wayward reactions. Her whole body was trembling with what she realised was a deep and disturbing sense of anticipation. All that, from one light touch of his lips! There could be no scientific explanation for such a phenomenon. The reassuring thought of the laws of science served to steady her. This could only be a temporary lapse and soon her own innate good sense would be restored.

Then she realised her next dilemma—whilst Susanna might well be thrilled to exchange Cookes for the more appealing prospect of a fashionable London house, Lucille could not make that decision for her.

'Thank you for your offer of the house, sir,' she said, careful to distinguish just which offer she was contemplating. 'I shall let you know my answer as soon as possible.'

She saw his swift frown. 'Can you not give it your consideration now, Miss Kellaway?'

Lucille avoided his eyes. 'I cannot…it is not my—' She broke off, adding carefully, 'It requires much thought, sir.'

Seagrave was still frowning. 'You sound as though you need to consult the wishes of someone else,' he said acutely, and did not miss the sudden rush of colour to her cheeks.

'My lawyer—' Lucille said, constrainedly, and saw his face harden again.

'Of course,' he said politely. 'You will wish to ascertain whether the properties are of equal value. I shall have Josselyn send the details to your man immediately, if you will furnish me with his name and direction.' He raised a questioning eyebrow.

Lucille racked her brains to remember what Susanna had said. She knew Barnes was her sister's man of business, but could not for the life of her remember his address. She said evasively, 'I will send them to Mr Josselyn, sir. Thank you.'

She stood up, suddenly wanting him to leave. Her nerves were distinctly on edge. Worse, she knew that he knew she felt uncomfortable. It was clear in the mocking smile he gave her as he took her hand and bowed over it with grave formality.

'I forgot to thank you,' Lucille added suddenly. 'We were overwhelmed by your generosity, sir! Poultry, game and meat from your own herds; vegetables from your allotments and fruit from your own hothouses!'

Seagrave grinned down at her. 'It was nothing, Miss Kellaway! And I understand that you now have help in the gardens and the house?'

'Yes,' Lucille looked away uncomfortably. 'I am

glad your agent was able to find two villagers whose curiosity outweighed their moral scruples! No doubt they find us a sad disappointment, so quietly do we live!'

'Never mind,' Seagrave said comfortingly. 'Today they will be able to report that you have had a visit from both myself and a dashing French Count! Plenty of scandal to suffice for one day, although plain fare for such as yourself, Miss Kellaway! But perhaps...' he glanced around '...we can do better than that! After all, I have yet to demand payment of the heriot!'

Lucille, who had just started to feel a little calmer, looked up in trepidation to meet the speculative look in Seagrave's eyes. 'My lord?'

'The heriot,' Seagrave repeated, a little satirically, 'is the price, if you like, that I exact for your succession to the lease of Cookes!'

Lucille's heart had begun to beat fast and erratically. 'The price, my lord? I assume you mean a financial transaction?'

The mockery on Seagrave's face deepened. 'Sometimes, Miss Kellaway—but not always.' He moved closer to her. 'In your case, I am tempted to set another payment...this, perhaps...'

This time it was more like Lucille's fevered imaginings. She had no clear idea how she came to be in Seagrave's arms, but as she felt them close around her she started to tremble with the same mixture of apprehension and anticipation that had seized her earlier. The material of his coat was smooth beneath her fingers as her hands came up hard against his chest, as though she were uncertain whether to push him away or draw him closer. And Seagrave seemed in no hurry, determined to prolong the moment of expectation.

'I am inclined to show you how pleasurable you would find it to accept my offer, Miss Kellaway,' he murmured, lowering his head until his mouth barely touched hers and Lucille's lips parted on a gasp of mingled shock and delight. She would not have believed that such a gentle contact could create such an exquisite reaction. That molten heat swept through her again, leaving her weak with longing. This time he did not let her go, but took advantage of her parted lips to deepen the kiss with quite shattering effects.

The seductive warmth of the sun combined with this sensual onslaught went straight to Lucille's head. Her arms slid around Seagrave's neck without any conscious thought on her part. She pulled him closer, a deep shiver running right through her. She was achingly aware of all the points at which his body touched hers and wanted to be closer still. The mingled male scent of his skin and the fresh air filled her senses, intoxicating and heady. The silk dress, made for Susanna's more opulent curves, slid off one shoulder and Lucille felt Seagrave's fingers brush across her bare skin before tracing the edging of the lace that had slipped halfway down her breasts.

Then, to Lucille's immense frustration and disappointment, he had put her gently from him, smiling down into her dazed blue eyes.

'And that is only the start,' he said enigmatically. 'I warn you, I shall exact a heavy price! I'll bid you good day, Miss Kellaway.'

Further up the garden, the boy whom Josselyn had engaged to help keep Cookes's grounds tidy, leant on his hoe, his mouth wide open. So all he had heard about that Miss Kellaway was true after all, and her such a refined and quietly spoken lady as well! Not that anyone could blame the Earl, he thought regretfully. There were plenty who would wish to be in his shoes!

The second poison-pen letter arrived the next morning. Lucille had spent a miserable night. Before she had gone to bed she had stood before her mirror, critically examining her face and figure for any hint as to why the Earl of Seagrave had undergone this strange transformation and suddenly found her so attractive. She could see none. Her soft, fair hair was too straight and too pale, her complexion was positively pallid and her figure was too thin to be at all pleasing. The Earl could only be amusing himself at her expense. Or perhaps he was acting out of a need for revenge, hoping to engage her feelings and, when he had done so, taking great delight in rejecting her? With a heavy sigh, she got into bed, only to be tormented by erotic dreams which caused her to toss and turn all night in a fever of unsatisfied desire.

She felt tired at breakfast time, and the dark smudges beneath her eyes did little to persuade her that her appearance was anything other than old and grey. She was too preoccupied to question the arrival of the neat, white envelope which she found resting on the hall floor, having evidently been pushed under the door. It bore Susanna's name in bold capitals, and after a moment's hesitation Lucille opened it. She was totally unprepared for its contents. In the same bold print as before, the author gave a vindictive and wholly unpleasant opinion of Susanna's character and morals, and ended with the threat that she should remove her vile presence from the neighbourhood or suffer the consequences.

Lucille felt shocked and disgusted in equal measure, horrified once again at the spite and malice represented there. Had the fires been lit, she would have thrust it into the grate with no second thought, but she had to make do with tearing it into little shreds instead. She promised herself that she would not think about it any more, and sat down with her book. Almost immediately she found her mind wandering from the page as she dwelt on the letter's sender instead, and she put her book down in despair, deciding to take a stroll in the garden instead.

It was early, and the garden was shady and cool. Lucille sat down on the little bench in the orchard and reflected once more on the hatred which someone bore towards her sister. Could it be their cousin? she wondered. Walter Mutch had made his contempt very clear that day in the village and since he had the lease of Cookes snatched from beneath his nose he would be bound to bear a grudge. It would be in his interests to drive her out of the village, for the lease might then be settled in his favour. Remembering Seagrave's comments on Serena Mutch's resentment, Lucille supposed that she must also consider her aunt as the anonymous author.

Seagrave… A horrible thought took hold in her mind and refused to be dislodged. Could the Earl have written the letters, or perhaps have instigated their writing as part of his campaign to make her leave Dillingham? The idea made her feel sick. Surely he would not stoop so low? And yet, what did she know of him, after all? For her own peace of mind, Lucille knew she had to avoid seeing Seagrave any more. She had already found herself hoping that he would call, dwelling romantically on their encounters like the veriest schoolgirl! She knew she was close to committing the unutterable folly of falling in love with him.

Lucille plucked a stray leaf from her hair and regarded it rather sadly. She knew she should not be too hard on herself. After all, she had lived almost a nun's life at Miss Pym's, rarely going out into company and never meeting any eligible men. It would have been a rare woman indeed who could have gone from so sequestered an existence into the company of a man as attractive as the Earl of Seagrave, without feeling at least a small pang of the heart. The knowledge did nothing to comfort her, nor could it help her put him from her mind. The thought that she would never see him again once she returned to Oakham made her feel even more unhappy.

Another two days limped past without word from Susanna. Lucille began to pack her small trunk in preparation for the journey back home, no longer prepared to sustain the impersonation just for Susanna's sake. Now that she was close to leaving Cookes she felt relieved and disappointed in almost equal measure, sorry that she had not had more opportunity to explore the countryside and discover more about the county for herself. It had been an educational visit to Suffolk, she thought, a little sadly, but not perhaps in the way that she had intended.

She was just considering whether she dared to take a short walk, and remembering the threats of the anonymous letter-writer, regretfully rejecting the idea, when there was the peal of the front door bell. Hurrying down Cookes's elegantly sweeping stairs, she found Lady Bellingham in the hall, swathed in imperial purple and fur this time, and with a dashing feather-trimmed shako perched on her head. Her ladyship kissed her warmly.

'Dear child! How glad I am to find you still at Cookes!' She scrutinised Lucille closely. 'But you are so wan, my love! How lucky, then, that I am come to take you into Woodbridge!'

Lucille began to say that she did not think this a good idea, but was overruled in the kindest possible way.

'Nonsense!' Lady Bellingham was bracing. 'It is a sadly provincial little place, 'tis true, but it has a certain charm! The outing will do you good!' Her pessimistic, dark gaze took in Lucille's apprehensive face and she smiled a little. 'My poor Miss Kellaway, have they been so cruel to you?' The dark eyes sparkled. 'You must not worry, my love! The gentry may scorn us, but you may be sure that the shopkeepers will welcome us with open arms, for I am so very rich they have no choice!'

And she swept Lucille out of the front door without further ado.

The Bellingham carriage was a remarkable sight: massive, ancient, and unquestionably luxurious. Lucille was not in the least surprised to see Horace curled up asleep inside on a scarlet cushion.

'I cannot abide these modern contraptions,' Lady Bellingham confided, as she settled herself on the thick velvet seat. 'Curricles, phaetons…pah! They may be fast but the workmanship cannot match my barouche! Now, tell me, child, how have you fared since we last met?'

Her tone was so kindly that Lucille almost dissolved into tears. 'It has not been too bad if one has a taste for insults, anonymous letters and *carte blanche*!' she said, aware that in her misery she had probably been losing her sense of proportion. One day, perhaps, she would laugh at this preposterous masquerade and the trouble it had brought her...

Lady Bellingham looked sympathetic. 'Nasty things, poison-pen letters,' she said gruffly. 'You must disregard them, Miss Kellaway! As for the insults, it is no comfort to think that they are directed at your sister rather than you... Small-minded, intolerant people!' She gave a Gallic shrug. 'But the offer of *carte blanche*—now, that sounds far more exciting!'

Lucille found herself smiling, in spite of everything.

'The Comte De Vigny, perhaps?' Lady Bellingham continued. 'Conchita told me that he was in the neighbourhood. He is an old lover of your sister's, is he not? Was he minded to rekindle their *affaire*?'

'I believe he might have been, given the slightest encouragement,' Lucille admitted.

'Not De Vigny, then,' Lady Bellingham said, thoughtfully, watching her face, 'but some more... attractive proposition, perhaps, Miss Kellaway? The Earl of Seagrave, for instance?'

Lucille felt the pink colour stain her cheeks. 'You must be clairvoyant, Lady Bellingham!' she said involuntarily.

'Now, I find that *most* interesting,' Lady Bellingham said, amused. 'Seagrave is always most particular in his choice, and your sister, Miss Kellaway...' she paused delicately '...well, her reputation would normally be too much for such a man to stomach! Which can only mean that either he knows you are not Susanna Kellaway, or he is much drawn to you personally!' she finished triumphantly.

'Neither conclusion gives me much comfort,

ma'am!' Lucille said, shifting uncomfortably on her seat. 'I have to tell you that on one of the occasions we met, I gave Lord Seagrave the impression that I was indeed prepared to be bought off, and so cannot be surprised that he treats me like the Cyprian I set out to play!'

Lady Bellingham was much diverted. 'But you would not accept him, would you, my child,' she said, shrewdly, 'for all that you are as drawn to him as he is to you!'

The hot colour flooded Lucille's face again. 'I…could not do such a thing,' she said, her voice stifled. 'Now, if you please, Lady Bellingham, can we not *please* speak of other matters?'

They were rumbling into the outskirts of the town now, past a working windmill and through narrow streets with their charmingly painted villas set in leafy gardens. The Deben estuary could be seen glinting distantly in the sun. The coach entered the cobbled streets of the centre, where the pavements were crowded with ladies in their summer dresses, their parasols warding off the sun, and the gentlemen were strolling and chatting on the street corners. Lucille and Lady Bellingham descended, her ladyship instructing the coachman to wait for them down by the harbour.

Lucille, made self-conscious by her recent experiences, was sensitive to every curious glance and whispered comment that was being cast their way. Lady Bellingham, on the other hand, ignored the interest of the passers-by with a superb indifference.

'This is a very fine musical instrument makers,' she declared, pausing before a shop where the bow windows displayed a harpsichord and reclining double bass. 'Bellingham bought me a piano from Mr Fenton the second year of our marriage, declaring that it would complement my pretty singing.' She looked most indulgent as she remembered her late spouse. 'Of course,' she continued, 'it is *young* Mr Fenton who keeps the shop now, though he must be all of five and forty! But if you require a guitar to take back to play for those schoolchildren of yours, my dear Lucille, this is the place to buy one!'

Lucille declined the invitation regretfully, explaining that she had neither the money nor the talent for such a purchase. Lady Bellingham was not cast down.

'No instruments, then…' She took Lucille's arm and guided her to the next shopfront. 'Now, how about a gown, my dear?' She wrinkled up her nose. 'I know it says French modes, but the sad truth is that the Misses Browne have not set foot abroad these twenty years or more! No, all their fashions come from London via Ipswich, and it takes several years at that!' She saw the hopeful face of one of the Misses Browne peering from behind the curtains, and hurried on. 'Now, the milliners…'

At last, it seemed, they could make a purchase. A bowing Monsieur Gaston Deneuve was there to greet his noble client almost before Lady Bellingham had reached for the door handle. He tenderly relieved her of the dashing shako, one of his earlier creations, before bringing out a whole range of other hats for them to try.

Lady Bellingham considered them all, gave a blunt opinion on each, and finally settled for a truly outrageous creation with an upstanding poke-front lined with crimson silk, and a high crown adorned with ostrich feathers. Monsieur Gaston, Lucille thought, might well have designed it precisely with Lady

Bellingham in mind. Feeling rather tame in comparison, Lucille chose a rose pink bonnet trimmed with coquelicot ribbons, and was bowed out of the shop by the smiling milliner, hatbox in hand.

The next stop was the drapers for several pairs of embroidered gloves and silk stockings. Lady Bellingham spent copiously, Lucille rather more carefully, for she was aware that she had already parted with a good deal more money than she had intended.

'Now, my love,' Lady Bellingham said, with the satisfaction of one who has already made several desirable purchases, 'I have a small errand to run. I know that you have been surreptitiously eyeing the booksellers this age, so I shall not feel the smallest guilt for deserting you for a little! I will meet you at the carriage within the half hour!'

The time went swiftly for Lucille, browsing amidst the musty interior of the shop, finding old friends on the bookshelves and sighing over the prohibitive cost of new works. By the time she had emerged, with a copy of Fanny Burney's *Evelina* tucked under her arm, the town clock was chiming the half hour and she had almost forgotten that she was supposed to be Susanna Kellaway. She crossed Market Street and turned towards the river.

Remembrance returned swiftly and unpleasantly. The cobbled streets were crowded and Lucille stepped out into the road to avoid a flower seller whose wide panniers threatened to knock her off the pavement. A group of people were moving towards her, and with a slight shock Lucille recognised the Earl of Seagrave, for there was no mistaking his height and breadth of shoulder.

Accompanying him were a young lady and a gentleman whose facial resemblance both to each other and to a horse was striking. The lady, dressed in the first stare of fashion, was hanging on Seagrave's arm in a proprietorial manner as she spoke intimately close in his ear. Her brother, a rather foppish young man who looked as though he were about to impale himself on his shirt points, raised his quizzing glass and gave Lucille the comprehensive stare that she was beginning to recognise as well as resent.

'Gad, if it isn't the Cyprian! How damnably awkward! Who would have thought to meet such a barque of frailty in Woodbridge, of all places! Come away, Thalia, my dear! Were the two of you to meet, Mama would never let me hear the end of it!'

His high-pitched tones carried to Lucille and a number of other curious passers-by. The young lady stared, tittered, and reluctantly allowed herself to be steered in the opposite direction by the Earl, who seemed in a great hurry to depart, and had not acknowledged Lucille by either look or word. Lucille dropped her book. A mixture of fury and anguish rose in her. So he thought nothing of offering her *carte blanche*, but she was not good enough to be introduced to his friends! Although Lucille knew that this was the way of the world, the blatant hypocrisy made her fume. She realised suddenly that she was standing stock-still in the middle of the thoroughfare and that a carter was shouting at her to make way.

'Can I be of assistance, madam?' A gentleman was beside her, handing her parcel back to her and taking her arm to guide her onto the pavement. He removed his curly-brimmed beaver hat and bowed slightly. 'Charles Farrant, at your service, ma'am. Can I escort you anywhere?'

'I…yes, I thank you, sir.' Lucille pulled herself together. 'The carriage is waiting down by the harbour. If you would be so good…'

'Of course.' He put her hand reassuringly through his arm and turned down Quay Street. 'A fine day, is it not, ma'am, although I believe there will be a strong breeze down on the river.'

Lucille realised that he was talking to give her time to recover herself, and felt a rush of gratitude. She looked at him properly for the first time. He was tall and fair, with a pleasant, open face and kind blue eyes that smiled down at hers. His dress was sober rather than elegant—a country gentleman of modest estate, perhaps, or a professional man… She gave him a tremulous smile. The gentleman blinked.

'Indeed, I do thank you, sir, for rescuing me! For a moment I…' Her voice trailed away.

'I saw what happened,' Mr Farrant said, a little abruptly. 'Mr Ditton is unpardonable.'

'Mr Ditton?' Lucille suddenly realised that he must be referring to the fop. 'Oh, I beg your pardon, sir, I did not know the gentleman…'

A slight frown touched Mr Farrant's brow. 'Oh, but I thought—' He broke off, a little self-consciously. 'As you say, madam.'

Clarification burst upon Lucille with a blinding flash. At the time she had been so overcome by the Earl of Seagrave cutting her dead that she had hardly given the other man a thought, but now she understood Mr Farrant's embarrassment. So Mr Ditton was another of them! Well, she had had enough of Susanna and her lovers! Surely there could be no danger in revealing her true identity now that she was on the verge of leaving Suffolk! She stopped dead and turned to her companion.

'Mr Farrant, I believe there must have been some misunderstanding, and largely of my own making. I have not introduced myself.' She stressed the name. 'I am Lucille Kellaway.'

Mr Farrant's open features cleared. He was very easy to read, Lucille thought, amused, for all that he must be at least seven and thirty years old!

'Oh! Miss Kellaway! I thought—' He broke off again, clearly mortified.

'That I was my sister,' Lucille finished for him, without embarrassment. 'An understandable mistake, sir. We are twins and very like in appearance.'

'Yes, although now I come to look at you I can easily see the difference,' Farrant said, loquacious in his attempts to gloss over the difficult moment. 'You are much fairer, Miss Kellaway, and...a most modest style of dress...and the book...I do apologise!' He flushed bright red.

'Not at all,' Lucille said, smiling in spite of herself. 'I collect that you have met my sister, Mr Farrant?' Which gentleman has not? she wondered.

'I've *seen* her, of course,' Farrant said, as though referring to an exotic circus animal, 'and I had heard that she was staying in the neighbourhood, though now I see that it must be you instead!' He frowned. 'But I had heard rumours that your sister was under the protection of the Earl of Seagrave, and I am sure that that cannot be true of you, Miss Kellaway! One has only to look at you to see that you are a woman of unimpeachable virtue! Oh, your pardon, ma'am—' Once again, he broke off in complete confusion.

'Pray do stop apologising, sir,' Lucille said, a little

wearily. 'This is all my fault. I should have known that to appear in public would give rise to this inevitable confusion. I *have* been staying in the neighbourhood, though the rest of your tale is mere gossip!'

Farrant started trying to apologise once again and Lucille could only be grateful that the river was in sight, and beside the harbour wall Lady Bellingham's imposing carriage was waiting. The tide was in on the river and a profusion of craft bobbed at anchor. Seabirds wheeled and soared and the air had a fresh, cutting salty edge. Lucille wished she could have paused to appreciate the scene, but she was anxious to be away. She turned to thank her companion for his escort. Mr Farrant seemed a pleasant enough gentleman, she supposed, though he had nothing of the compulsive attraction of the Earl of Seagrave—

'Your servant, Farrant. Miss Kellaway.'

The last person Lucille wanted to speak to at that moment was Seagrave himself, for her feelings were still very raw. He had evidently parted from the odious Mr Ditton and his sister, and was strolling along the path towards them quite alone.

Farrant bowed awkwardly, clearly at a social disadvantage. Lucille's greeting was cool to the point of frigidity.

'Good day, my lord.' She turned back to Mr Farrant with a warm smile. 'Thank you for your kindness this day, sir. Had you not been so good as to befriend me when others were less amiable, I have no notion how I might have managed!'

Seagrave's eyes narrowed as this point went home and Farrant, acutely uncomfortable, began to stammer that it was a pleasure and that he was always at her disposal. Seagrave watched in sardonic amusement as this flow of words finally dried up and Farrant swallowed convulsively before excusing himself and hurrying off.

'To what do I owe that pretty piece of play-acting?' Seagrave demanded, turning back to Lucille, who was caught between gratitude that Mr Farrant had not inadvertently revealed her identity and annoyance at his inopportune departure. She had no wish for a tête-à-tête with the Earl—or for any conversation with him at all, she told herself fiercely.

'I do not understand you, sir,' Lucille said. There was no need to try to imitate Susanna—she knew she sounded sulky and irritable, and for once it was entirely genuine. She turned towards the carriage, but Seagrave prevented her from moving away by the simple expedient of catching hold of her arm.

'You are being devilishly awkward this afternoon, Susanna!' he said pleasantly. 'All I wanted to know was whether you had considered my offer!'

'The Chelsea house?' Lucille freed herself from his grip and turned to look out over the river so that she did not have to look at him. 'I will let you know as soon as I may, sir.'

'I meant my other offer,' Seagrave said gently.

Lucille turned to stare at him. The sea breeze was ruffling his thick dark hair and she felt a sudden, frighteningly strong urge to reach up and touch it. So he had been serious. He was asking her—Susanna— to become his mistress. For a moment she considered it. Did he really want her, or Susanna? Perhaps the trophy of Susanna hanging on his arm was all that mattered?

If so, how would he react when he discovered it was Lucille he had seduced rather than her sister...

She gave herself an appalled shake. Whatever was she doing, seriously considering this? Fifteen minutes previously, this man had cut her dead, refused to even acknowledge that he knew her. He had no respect for her.

As she hesitated, he took a small blue box out of his pocket. Horrified, Lucille realised that it was a jewellery case. So that was part of the bargain, was it? Some necklace, or bracelet, perhaps, to buy her favours? Perhaps he had just bought it in the town, and now the whole of Woodbridge would know what he intended… She began to feel quite ill with disgust.

'You may keep your bribery, sir!' she snapped, restraining herself from knocking it out of his hand. 'I do not care to be distinguished by your attentions only when it suits you!' Suddenly she did not give a damn about the way Susanna would have treated him. Soon she would be leaving forever, and it made her reckless. Let her sister pick up the threads of the masquerade if she chose! Let Susanna blame her for whistling an Earl down the wind if she dared! Lucille was not about to compromise her own principles just to emulate her sister.

'You are angry that I did not speak to you just now,' Seagrave observed calmly, 'but I thought it best to take the Dittons away as quickly as possible! After all, I understood that your…' he hesitated '…intimate relationship with Mr Ditton ended on less than amicable terms. And as for his sister, even you must surely see that you are not a suitable person to be introduced to Miss Ditton?'

Seagrave sounded so infuriatingly reasonable that Lucille could have slapped him. He had put the box away and was watching her with a degree of cynical humour which suggested that he had assumed she wished to play a scene, but would come around in the end.

'I have no wish to meet that Friday-faced female,' Lucille said scathingly. The cold air and her own anger had brought the pink colour into her face. Her blue eyes were very bright. 'Nor do I wish for a liaison with a man who has no respect for me. Good day, sir!'

She would have walked past him, but he barred her way with one arm on the harbour wall. Lucille was delighted to see that he had stopped smiling.

'Respect? A singular notion, Miss Kellaway! When did you become so fastidious? I dare swear it was not when you allowed Ditton into your bed!' His eyes were almost black with fury but he kept his voice discreetly low. 'Yet you see with what respect he treats you now!'

Lucille knew she was well out of her depth but she was now as angry as he. 'Perhaps I liked Mr Ditton more!' she said, with unforgivable provocation.

Seagrave caught both her arms above the elbow and gave her a shake. 'I see! Perhaps he pandered to your particular tastes? And Farrant?' he added, through his teeth. 'Do you have him lined up as a diversion? A little game to help you pass your time in the country? The poor man is enslaved already! One glance from those limpid blue eyes, one smile, and he is yours! He will be easy meat for you, poor fool!'

At last, too late and with total incredulity, Lucille realised that it was jealousy she could read in his face. Sexual jealousy, certainly, for surely he could have no deep feelings for her. Yet he seemed to resent that Tristan Ditton—and no doubt many others—had apparently taken what she was now refusing him. Lucille suddenly realised how ill-equipped she was to deal with this. She could hardly explain that Charles Farrant knew her to be Lucille Kellaway and not Susanna, and that she had no designs on him of any nature.

'I have the claim to you, Miss Kellaway,' Seagrave said with a soft insistence under which the anger ran hot, 'not Farrant, or any other! Remember that!'

'I think not, sir!' Lucille responded furiously. 'Upon my word, you have a strange concept of possession! What gives you that right?'

'Those who put themselves up for sale, Miss Kellaway—' Seagrave began, only to break off as she interrupted him with no thought for courtesy.

'I am not to be bought, sir, nor have I ever been! You may take your insulting suggestions elsewhere!'

Lucille's bright blue gaze clashed with his own angry one. She found to her amazement that she could not break the contact. The tension between them was almost tangible. The anger drained from Seagrave's eyes as they travelled over her face almost caressingly, as if memorising every detail. His breath stirred a tendril of her hair. Lucille felt as though she were drowning, melting in a sensation completely new to her and dangerously seductive.

She wanted to put her hand up to trace the unyielding line of his jaw, to run her fingers into his hair and bring his head down so that she could touch that firm mouth with her own. Seagrave must have read something of her feelings in her face, for the expression in his eyes changed again to a potent demand, darkening in response to her own need, and he bent his head…

There was a cough, very loud and very deliberate,

just behind them. Seagrave released Lucille and stood aside.

'I beg your pardon, Miss Kellaway, for keeping you waiting,' Lady Bellingham said calmly. She held out a hand to the Earl. 'Good day, Lord Seagrave.'

Seagrave wrenched his gaze and his attention away from Lucille. He took Lady Bellingham's hand and gave her a reluctant smile, appreciative of her tactics. 'How do you do, Lady Bellingham? It is a pleasure to see you forsaking your coastal retreat to be amongst us again!'

Lady Bellingham had her head on one side, considering him with an openly appraising look. She smiled a little regretfully. Then her gaze fell on Lucille, who was so mortified that she had not been able to look at Seagrave for several minutes. Lady Bellingham took her arm gently.

'You look done up, my poor child,' she said gently. 'Come along—we shall go home to Cookes for tea!'

She nodded to Seagrave and steered Lucille like a sleepwalker towards the jetty where the carriage was drawn up. Seagrave, watching their departure, found that he was still breathing hard, as though he had run a mile. He leant on the harbour wall and stared out across the river, where a barge was attempting to navigate the corner called Troublesome Reach.

He knew all that he needed now, had known even before Lady Bellingham had hurried her protégée away with a concern quite misplaced had her charge truly been Susanna Kellaway. And no doubt Josselyn would have the answers to the questions he had posed earlier in the week, but it was unnecessary. He knew that this could not be Susanna. Amidst all the deception and artifice, the one thing that had rung true was her assertion that she was not for sale. He remembered again the blazing honesty of those blue eyes and shifted slightly.

No, Miss Kellaway—if that was her name—had been telling the truth at that moment. And it made sense of all the other matters that had puzzled him: the wit and intelligence that had added spice to their encounters, her shock at De Vigny's behaviour, the way that she had trembled in his arms as he had kissed her, with an innocence that could not have been affectation...

And there was the rub... Seagrave let his breath out on a rueful sigh. He wanted her, whoever she was. He had previously been accustomed to conducting his affairs of the heart as business transactions where emotion never intruded; so, at first, when he had found himself so strongly attracted to the woman he thought was Susanna Kellaway, he had come to the obvious conclusion that his need for her would slake itself if only he could set her up as his mistress.

Now matters were not so simple. His own code of conduct did not permit him to try to seduce an innocent, no matter how much she richly deserved it. Unfortunately that meant that his desire for her was doomed to be unfulfilled and the very idea put him back in a very bad mood indeed.

Seagrave picked up a handful of pebbles and moodily tossed them down into the swirling waters below. Because he was no green youth, he was forced to admit that there was another, more serious aspect to the case. He could no longer dismiss his own feelings as simple physical desire. In a strange way he found he actually *liked* her, enjoyed her company, wanted to be with her, which was far more insidiously dangerous than a mere attraction. Even the fact that she had deceived him, which made a part of him furious with her, could not, it seemed, destroy the feelings he was beginning to have for her.

If he could only sort out this infuriating matter of her masquerade. He groaned aloud, startling a nearby seagull. He could see precisely where his train of thought was leading and it could not be. But one way and another, the arrival of Miss Kellaway in Dillingham was proving far more costly and complicated than he had ever imagined.

Lucille and Lady Bellingham had travelled for a couple of miles in silence before her ladyship ventured a comment.

'Forgive my intrusion, Miss Kellaway,' she said carefully, making a play of adjusting her new embroidered gloves, 'but I thought that you were perhaps in some danger…'

Lucille sighed. 'You were right, ma'am! I was in danger of just about everything! I was in danger of betraying my impersonation of Susanna by stepping completely out of character, I was in danger of either slapping Lord Seagrave's face or kissing him—I am not sure which is worse—and most of all I am in the most serious danger of losing my heart! Now if that is not a sad testament to my folly, I know not what is!'

'Do not reproach yourself, Miss Kellaway,' Lady Bellingham said, so authoritatively that Lucille almost jumped. 'Seagrave is a man of considerable experience, yet judging by your recent encounter, he finds it as difficult as you do to resist the attraction that draws the two of you together. It will do him no harm,' she added, with satisfaction.

Lucille shook her head a little sadly. 'It is of no consequence, Lady Bellingham! I still intend to return to Oakham next week. Mrs Appleton will keep the house open against my sister's return.' She gazed out of the window at the lush Suffolk farmland. 'It will be far better for me to go away,' she finished sadly. 'I can contend with a broken heart only if the cause of it is a long way away from me!'

'Do not be too hard on yourself, Miss Kellaway,' Lady Bellingham said again, with a rueful smile. 'Seagrave is a remarkably attractive man! You are not the first—'

'Nor indeed the last!' Lucille said, bitterly, and Lady Bellingham wisely left it at that as they completed the journey home in silence.

But as her coach pulled out of the drive of Cookes a couple of hours later, she addressed the sleeping cat thoughtfully. 'You know, Horace, unless I miss my guess, Miss Lucille Kellaway will be Countess of Seagrave within six months!'

Horace stretched and yawned widely, showing a very pink mouth and sharp incisors. 'Three months, then!' Lady Bellingham corrected herself, reaching for the bonbon dish.

'I must have been seven sorts of idiot not to have seen it from the first.' The Earl of Seagrave frowned moodily down at his mud-spattered boots. He was sprawled in an armchair on one side of the fireplace, his long legs stretched out in front of him, whilst his brother, who had joined him at the Court a few days previously, had taken the chair opposite. It was almost full dark outside. Inside the room the lamps burned, turning the brandy in the balloon-shaped glasses to a rich amber glow.

Peter Seagrave looked up from the draughtsboard. He had already won two games that evening, a circumstance which only occurred when the Earl was deeply preoccupied. Now, he sat back in his chair and viewed Seagrave with amusement.

'You could scarcely be expected to have to contend with twins!' he said, mildly.

Seagrave looked up, impatiently pushing a hand through his disordered dark hair. 'No, but it only needed a little thought! Josselyn had told me at the outset that there were two daughters—I just didn't realise…' He was shaking his head in patent disbelief. 'And if you had met her, Peter—' His eyes met those of his brother. 'An innocent abroad! Devil take it, how could I have been such a fool! She was like a little girl dressed up in her big sister's clothes—and her sister's personality! She kept forgetting her part: good God, she knew who Bucephalus was; she was even reading *Waverley*!' He finished on a note of total incredulity.

Peter took a mouthful of brandy, savouring the taste. 'The Cyprian and the bluestocking!' he said thoughtfully. 'So whilst Susanna Kellaway has been making a notorious living in London, her twin has been quietly teaching schoolgirls in Oakham! It's an extraordinary idea! But can a woman who lends herself to such a masquerade be the innocent you seem to think her, Nick? Maybe she is really of the same stamp as Susanna Kellaway!'

That went straight to the crux of the matter. Peter

saw a flash of expression in his brother's eyes, too quick to be read, before Seagrave said expressionlessly, 'I think not, Peter. Miss Kellaway may be deceitful, but she is not experienced. I may have been taken in on all other matters, but on that I am convinced.'

Peter raised his eyebrows. He considered Seagrave's judgment to be sound, this latest incident notwithstanding. And he knew his brother well enough to suspect that he was not entirely indifferent to Miss Lucille Kellaway, which was very interesting. Why else this determination to believe her virtuous when all the evidence suggested, at the very least, a rather adaptable attitude towards right and wrong?

'You seem very sure,' he said coolly.

'I am.' Seagrave met his eyes directly. 'I offered her *carte blanche*, Peter!'

His brother almost choked. This was even more interesting! For Seagrave to have been so attracted to the woman he thought was Susanna Kellaway was remarkable! And since she had been proved to be no Cyprian, what now?

'She refused you, I infer?' he said, when he had recovered himself.

'She did,' Seagrave said, a little grimly. 'In no uncertain terms! Miss Lucille Kellaway cannot be bought at any price!'

'Then I wonder why she is playing such a trick,' Peter mused quietly. 'Do you intend to challenge her about it, Nick?'

Seagrave shook his head slowly. There was a wicked glint in his eyes. 'Not just yet! No, I shall play

along with this masquerade and see what I can learn!
Miss Kellaway deserves to be taught a lesson, Peter!'
He reached for his glass and raised it in silent toast.
'It should provide some sport!'

Chapter Five

'You cannot really refuse to see him,' Mrs Appleton said, in an agitated whisper. Her arms were full of hothouse flowers as she hovered in the bedroom doorway. Lucille stared at her, completely at a loss, her headache all but forgotten.

'But Mrs Appleton, he cannot possibly expect to come up to my bedroom—'

'When I told him that you had a sick headache and were resting, he assured me that he knew just the cure, and I do not imagine that he was referring to Dr James' Antimonial Powders!' the housekeeper said, grimly. 'Now we are undone, Miss Kellaway! If the Earl of Seagrave is intent on setting you up as his mistress—'

'I must get up at once,' Lucille said, throwing back the covers only to dive back under them again in horror, as she heard the sound of footsteps on the stair. Her horrified gaze met Mrs Appleton's. 'Oh no, he would not—' she began, breaking off as the Earl of Seagrave himself strolled casually into the bedroom as though he was accustomed to being there every day. He perched on the end of the bed, one booted foot swinging, and viewed Mrs Appleton's outraged consternation with amusement.

'Go and put those flowers in water, ma'am, and leave me to cure Miss Kellaway! I know you are reputed to be a dragon of respectability, but Miss Kellaway is, after all, accustomed to receiving gentlemen in her bedchamber and does not need your chaperonage!' The wicked dark gaze swung back to Lucille, who was shrinking as far beneath the bedclothes as she was able. 'Come, my dear! Such modesty! I am persuaded that you will soon be much more comfortable with me when we are intimate together!'

'My lord!' Mrs Appleton was doing her best. 'Miss Kellaway really is very unwell today! Perhaps it would be better—'

'Nonsense,' Seagrave said bracingly, his assessing gaze resting warmly on Lucille's flushed face. 'A fit of the blue devils, that is all! Perhaps I could take you for a drive later, Miss Kellaway—the fresh air will do you good! But first, we have a small matter to discuss, do we not?'

'I do not understand your lordship.' Lucille's voice, very small, came muffled from even further beneath the blankets. 'It was my belief that we had no more to say to each other and I would be obliged if you would leave immediately!'

'A lovers' tiff, perhaps!' Seagrave shrugged casually. He gave Mrs Appleton a conspiratorial smile. 'The necklace was a little paltry, I'll own, but it was the best that a provincial jeweller could muster! Miss Kellaway was quite right to draw my attention to its deficiencies!' He turned back to Lucille. 'I will make up for it, I swear!'

There was an outraged squeak from beneath the

covers. Seagrave's smile grew. He got up and strolled towards the window, admiring the view across the orchards to the open country beyond. 'This is a charming house, and most conveniently placed for our liaison,' he observed thoughtfully. He turned to consider the room. 'The bed is perhaps a trifle small, but we shall see!' He raised his eyebrows questioningly as Lucille's red, outraged face appeared.

'I wish that you would go and leave me alone! At once!' Lucille had abandoned finesse in her anxiety to be rid of him. She was thoroughly confused by this ludicrously out-of-character behaviour on Seagrave's part, this burlesque, but she was so much at a disadvantage that all she wanted to do was make him go away. Now was not the moment to challenge him on his behaviour, when she was half-naked and he had that particularly mischievous look in his eye.

Surely, she thought in horrified disbelief, he could not have misread their encounter of the previous day so profoundly as to believe that it was an attempt on her part to exact a higher price from him? He was far too astute to believe that! But Seagrave was sitting back down on the bed, far too close for comfort, and Lucille abandoned her attempt to puzzle out his motives given the overwhelming need to preserve her own modesty.

'I feel sick,' she said plaintively. 'No!' It came out as a small shriek as she realised that Mrs Appleton was about to hurry off to fetch a bowl. 'Do not leave me, dear ma'am! I shall be quite better directly!'

'That's the spirit!' Seagrave said approvingly, patting her thigh through the blankets. 'I have been thinking,' he added reflectively, 'that it might be a good idea for you to invite your sister to spend some time with you here! It might improve your humour and also give her the opportunity of a change of scene. What do you think, Susanna?'

Lucille did not know what to think. She had never seen him in so carefree a mood. And for him to suggest that she should invite herself to visit Cookes… She gave a faint moan. Seagrave took her hand comfortingly.

'Well, perhaps not. If we are to be spending a great deal of time together it would not be convenient…and no doubt she is one of those tiresomely puritanical and dry spinsters who thinks of nothing but her books!' He stood up, stretching with a lithe movement that drew Lucille's attention to his rippling muscles. She looked hastily away, the colour flooding her face again.

'I will leave you to recover,' Seagrave was saying, the devils dancing in his eyes. 'But do not keep me waiting long to taste your delights, Susanna!' He leant forward and placed a lingering kiss on Lucille's round, outraged mouth. 'That cambric nightgown will have to go,' he added thoughtfully. 'It is far too concealing!'

'He knows the truth!' Lucille averred, her face no longer red with affront but ashen pale. As soon as her unwanted visitor had left she had thrown back the covers and leapt out of bed, her headache quite forgotten. She paced the room in her reviled nightdress, thankful only that it was as all-concealing as Seagrave had said.

Mrs Appleton put down the flowers she was still clutching and sat down on the end of the bed.

'I agree it was most singular behaviour,' she said

worriedly. 'Are you sure that there was nothing in your conversation yesterday, Miss Kellaway, that might have led him to believe—?'

Lucille shook her head stubbornly, wrapping her arms about her for comfort. 'At first I wondered, but as an explanation it will not serve. No, he has somehow divined the truth and is intent on making me suffer! I know it!' she finished fiercely. 'Seagrave would never normally behave thus! It was a parody, a caricature! Oh, that I had never started this! I must go away at once!'

She stared blindly out of the window. As soon as the idea that Seagrave might know the truth had taken hold, Lucille was convinced that it was the right one. Not only did it explain his ridiculous behaviour, but some deeper instinct told her that he knew; that he was making a game of her as small recompense for what she had done.

The idea threw her into a panic. What would his next step be? To attempt wholesale seduction, perhaps, still pretending that he thought she was Susanna? And she had only two alternatives—to play along with the charade, or to tell him the truth. Three alternatives, she corrected herself. She had been intending to leave on the morrow—why not now instead? She started to pull her half-filled trunk from under the bed, only to be stayed by Mrs Appleton's calm voice.

'Forgive me, Miss Kellaway, but is this hasty departure really the best thing to do? In the first place, Seagrave is quite capable of stopping you if he really wanted to, and John has the wheel off the carriage, as he did not think you would be going until tomorrow!'

Seeing Lucille's look of despair, she came across and laid a comforting hand on her arm. 'Do nothing precipitate,' she counselled in kindly fashion. 'Think about whether you wish to tell him the truth, and if you decide that you cannot, go tomorrow, as you had intended.'

Lucille nodded slowly. Her emotions were so jumbled that all she could think of was her overwhelming need to escape. 'But it must be tomorrow,' she said miserably. 'I have to go! Nothing must stop me!'

A sudden and violent summer storm kept Lucille indoors that afternoon, and she tried to while away the hours with a copy of Samuel Richardson's *Clarissa Harlowe*, which she had found on one of her father's bookshelves. It had proved quite impossible to concentrate, for her mind was occupied solely by the thought of the Earl, and fruitless speculation on how he could have realised her impersonation, and what he intended to do about it. She felt as though her customary good sense had completely deserted her, leaving her feeling hopelessly vulnerable.

The late morning had brought another huge bunch of flowers, this time from Charles Farrant, and a note expressing the hope that he might call upon her the following day. As Lucille planned to start her journey back to Oakham at first light, she knew this was not possible and felt a vague regret. She would have liked to have had the opportunity to thank him properly for his assistance. Charles Farrant had none of Seagrave's dash and brilliance, but he also lacked the Earl's arrogance and was, Lucille told herself severely, a very pleasant gentleman. Unfortunately, that seemed to weigh little with her. Lucille gave a little despairing sigh.

The thunder was retreating by the time four o'clock

struck, and Mrs Appleton had just brought in some afternoon tea and cakes, when there was the sound of carriage wheels on the gravel outside, and a sudden and imperative knock on the front door. Lucille put her book down quickly, wondering if Susanna could have chosen this moment to return at last, but a moment later she heard a man's voice, followed swiftly by an exclamation from Mrs Appleton. Lucille hurried across to the drawing-room door and out into the hall.

The scene that met her gaze was a startling one. The gentleman in the hall was sufficiently like the Earl of Seagrave to make identification immediate, and to make Lucille's heart turn over, but he was more slender than his brother and had an open, youthful, boyish look that was very appealing. He carried in his arms a very slight young lady who appeared to have fainted. Her face was very pale and her soaking wet curls just brushed his chin as he held her with her head resting against his shoulder. Her clothing, the demure sprigged muslin gown of a schoolroom miss under her cloak, was also drenched and dripping onto the floor. She did not stir at all. In complete astonishment, Lucille recognised her to be Henrietta Markham, her adoptive sister.

'Hetty! Good God!' Lucille forgot her own preoccupations and hurried forward. 'Whatever can have happened?'

Mrs Appleton turned to her. 'This gentleman—the Honourable Peter Seagrave—says that he found the young lady on the road from Woodbridge, madam. She must have been caught in the thunderstorm. Shall I prepare a bedroom, ma'am? She looks as though she may have taken a chill!'

'We will put her in my room, I think, Mrs

Appleton.' Lucille touched Hetty's cold cheek tentatively. 'Could you prepare a hot posset whilst I show this gentleman the way? Oh, and please bring some smelling salts if you can find any!' Lucille turned to Peter Seagrave. 'If you would be so good as to carry her upstairs, sir? I will show you to the room.'

Peter carried Hetty up Cookes's sweeping stairway and put her down very gently on Lucille's bed. He stood back, looking down at her with an anxiety that drew Lucille's attention even though her main concern was to try to rouse her sister. She sat down on the side of the bed and took Hetty's cold hands in hers.

'Hetty? Wake up, my love! You are quite safe!' She looked up at Peter. 'She was not injured when you found her, was she, sir?'

He heard the fear in her voice and was quick to reassure her.

'No, ma'am. Miss Markham was wet and tired, and I believe she had not eaten for some time, but she was not injured.'

At the sound of his voice, Hetty stirred. Her eyelids fluttered, then lifted.

'Lucille! Oh, thank goodness!' Her voice was a thread of a whisper and it caught on a sob. 'I was so afraid that I was wrong and I would not find you here…' Her gaze went past Lucille to Peter Seagrave and a little colour came into her cheeks. She struggled to sit up. Lucille pressed her back firmly against the pillows.

'You had better rest now, my love. Mrs Appleton will come up to help you. Can you manage a little food?' Then, seeing that Hetty's gaze was still riveted on Peter, she said: 'I will say all that is proper to Mr Seagrave. Perhaps, sir—'

Peter Seagrave took the hint. 'I will wait for you downstairs, Miss Kellaway.' The smile he gave Hetty had so much tenderness in it that Lucille blinked in shock. 'I shall hope to see you again soon and in better health, Miss Markham,' he said, and reluctantly made for the door.

Thirty minutes later, Hetty had been washed, fed and put to bed wearing one of Lucille's nightdresses. Lucille went slowly back downstairs to find Peter Seagrave standing by the drawing- room window, his hands deep in his pockets as he gazed out across the wilderness garden. He turned swiftly at her entrance.

'Miss Kellaway! Will Miss Markham be all right?'

Lucille smiled reassuringly. 'With a little rest and some care I am sure she will be perfectly all right, sir! And I have not yet had a chance to thank you for bringing her to us—I cannot bear to think what might have happened had you not rescued her!'

She took a seat, and gestured to him to do the same. 'Did Hetty explain how she came to be wandering so far from home? I did not like to press her just now, but I am rather concerned…'

Peter Seagrave's warm brown eyes rested on her thoughtfully. 'I cannot throw much light on the circumstances, I fear, ma'am! I found Miss Markham on the Dillingham road just outside Woodbridge. At first she would not consent to speak to me…' a reminiscent smile touched his lips '…for she claimed she had no need of help from strange gentlemen, although a more bedraggled and woebegone sight would have been difficult to find! Eventually I persuaded her to let me take her up, and she unbent sufficiently to confide that she had run away from home and was seeking out a relative with whom she hoped to find shelter.'

Peter got to his feet again restlessly, moving back to the window. 'Miss Kellaway, there is no easy way for me to say this. When Miss Markham told me that she was seeking Miss Kellaway of Cookes, I was horrified. I was convinced she must be mistaken, but she was adamant. Good God, an innocent like Miss Markham asking to be escorted to the house of a notorious Cyprian! At first I thought I had mistaken Miss Markham's quality, but it only takes one look to ascertain that she is a schoolroom miss!' He turned back to look at her, a deep frown on his brow. 'I knew Miss Markham's reputation was compromised the moment she was over this threshold, but I had no choice! I could not take her to Dillingham Court with only myself and my brother there and I did not know of anyone else nearby who could give her shelter. But devil take it, I cannot stand by and see her ruined by association with—' He broke off. 'I beg your pardon,' he said with constraint.

Lucille looked down at her clasped hands. The same thoughts had been preoccupying her ever since Hetty had arrived so unexpectedly. Given her state of health, it was clearly impossible to send her adoptive sister straight home, and it sounded as though there had been serious reasons that had driven Hetty to run away in the first place. Until she had had the chance to find out what had happened, Lucille did not want to upset Hetty by trying to explain why she could not stay at Cookes.

But Peter was right—news of Hetty's arrival at the house would inevitably leak out and her reputation would be ruined. Suddenly Lucille felt close to tears. It was bad enough that by her foolish masquerade she had landed herself in so much trouble, but that Hetty should now be compromised was utterly unfair!

Lucille, whose thoughts on her own circumstances had gone quite out of her mind, suddenly realised that she could not possibly remove from Cookes the following day as she had planned. Now all her problems were compounding themselves with a vengeance!

'Forgive me, Miss Kellaway, but there is more,' Peter Seagrave said suddenly. His fair, open face flushed. 'As I am being so frank, I may as well go further. I think that you should know that Nick—my brother, Lord Seagrave—knows that you are not Susanna Kellaway, although I understand that you have been using her identity...'

Lucille, who had been pondering how on earth Hetty had managed to trace her to Cookes, was all at sea for a moment. In her concern for Hetty she had given no thought to the fact that her adoptive sister had called her by her name—or that Hetty might well have referred to her as Lucille when talking to Peter on the journey. Yet now it seemed that it did not matter anyway! Peter knew that she was not Susanna! Seagrave knew, just as she had suspected...

The mortification overcame her in a huge wave. She felt ready to sink with embarrassment now that she had received this confirmation. How did he know? How long had he known for? Why had he not spoken? The thoughts tumbled over themselves inside her head.

'You have been using her identity...' It sounded so cheap, so deceitful! And so it was, Lucille told herself fiercely, blinking back the hot tears which threatened to overwhelm her. She had known all along that if unmasked she would appear both dishonest and immoral.

'Forgive me, ma'am,' Peter said again, a note of real concern in his voice. 'I had no wish to upset you. It was anxiety for Miss Markham that prompted me to speak.' He moved swiftly across to the desk, where the bottle of brandy reposed. 'Drink this…' He pressed the glass into her hand. 'It will make you feel better.'

'More brandy!' Lucille thought ruefully, taking a mouthful. The Seagrave family seemed intent on turning her into a toper! She felt the strong spirit burn her throat and realised that she had needed it.

'Mr Seagrave—I should explain…'

Peter ran a hand through his dishevelled dark hair. 'I have no wish to pry, ma'am,' he said, with constraint. 'I understand that there must be reasons…' His gaze swept over her comprehensively and he could not contain himself. 'But devil take it, Nick must be a slow-top not to have seen it from the start! I have never met your sister, Miss Kellaway, but it doesn't take much to see that *you* are no bird of paradise!'

Lucille could not help laughing, in spite of everything. 'Do not be too hard on your brother, sir! Susanna and I are identical twins, and as you have correctly stated, I deliberately deceived him as to my identity!' Her laughter died as she reflected on this. 'Indeed,' she added softly, 'unlike Hetty, I deserve the opprobrium of the world! I came to Cookes in the full knowledge that it belonged to my sister who is considered—let us not boggle at it—to be a fallen woman. Worse, I pretended to be that very woman! Hetty is an innocent who has been compromised through no fault of her own. I do not have her excuse.'

'You are too harsh on yourself, ma'am,' Peter Seagrave said, slowly. 'I do not pretend to understand why you should choose to perpetrate such a fraud on my brother, but no one who has spent any time in your company would think you other than a gentlewoman and,' he added in a rush of gallantry, 'I can understand why Miss Markham sought you out when she needed help!'

Lucille smiled a little sadly. 'Thank you, sir! I do not deserve your good opinion. But none of this helps Hetty,' she added quietly. 'Since the world believes me to be Susanna and this is indubitably her house…'

'Yes,' Peter agreed thoughtfully. 'Miss Markham's reputation is damaged just the same.' He squared his shoulders. 'Miss Kellaway, I really feel we should ask Nick's help in this. But that will inevitably entail bringing your…masquerade…into the open. Can you—are you prepared to talk to him about this?'

Lucille bit her lip. 'For Hetty's sake I am prepared to face your brother and explain,' she agreed quietly. She saw his swift nod of approval and said quickly, 'Mr Seagrave, I would account for my actions to you if I could, but I must talk to your brother first. All I ask is that you believe that my main concern is to spare Miss Markham distress, and in that, I believe, we are one.'

'Very well, Miss Kellaway.' Peter stood up. 'I must go now, for Nick will be wondering if I've had an accident on the road!' He took her hand. 'Thank you for your frankness. I am sure we can resolve this predicament one way or another.' He flashed a grin, so like his brother's sudden smile that Lucille's heart missed a beat. 'Please give Miss Markham my best wishes for her recovery,' he added. 'I shall call in a day or two to see how she progresses.'

Lucille was sure that he would. As Peter Seagrave went out to his cold and patient horses, Lucille wondered how such a youthful innocent as Hetty Markham could possibly have caught him in her toils. There was no doubt of it though. Peter Seagrave was already fathoms deep in love with her.

When the Earl of Seagrave called the following morning, Lucille was in such a state of pent-up nervousness that she almost refused to see him. She had lain awake for what had seemed like many long, dark hours, reflecting in equal measure on the coil in which Hetty was caught and on the frightening prospect of confessing to Seagrave. Neither situation provided a single comforting thought, and in the end she had fallen into a light doze from which she had awakened unrefreshed as soon as the sky began to lighten.

Hetty was still sleeping soundly by mid-morning and Lucille did not have the heart to wake her. She spent a lonely breakfast staring blankly into space over her coffee cup, then trailed off to the drawing-room to continue her reading of *Clarissa*, only to find that her thoughts distracted her so much that she did not take in a single word. Far from spending time at Cookes pursuing her favourite hobby of reading, she seemed to have done little but cast her books to one side! In a fit of annoyance she went out into the garden, but it was a grey day with a chill breeze. It seemed to suit her mood. She went back inside and tried to compose a letter to Mrs Markham.

Twenty minutes later, Lucille finished her carefully worded letter, acquainting Mrs Markham of her daughter's whereabouts, and blotted it thoughtfully. She had left out all reference to Cookes being Susanna's house now, simply informing that good matron that she was taking a short break in the house that had been her father's and that Hetty, having presumably gained her direction from the school, had sought her out there. That at least, she thought, should allay Mrs Markham's maternal fears and prevent her from descending on the neighbourhood in a fit of moralistic fury.

How to keep Hetty's presence a secret from the village was another matter, and one which Lucille considered a hopeless task. She was still frowning over this problem when Mrs Appleton announced the Earl of Seagrave. It was almost a relief to know that he had come. Lucille drew herself up a little straighter, stilled her shaking hands by putting them behind her back, and faced the door.

Seagrave came into the room with all the careless assurance which Lucille had come to expect of him. He accepted her offer of refreshments and sat down, allowing his dark gaze to travel over her very deliberately. Lucille found this distinctly disconcerting. She had chosen a gown of Susanna's in palest blue, from which she had ruthlessly removed all the yards of tulle and lace, and the result had been simple and pleasing. The appreciation in Seagrave's eyes suggested he considered it very flattering.

'Good morning, Miss Kellaway,' he murmured. 'You look entirely delightful. Now…' the observant gaze appeared to be fixed on her face '…how may I help you?'

'I beg your pardon, sir?' Lucille tried to get a grip on herself.

'My brother told me that you had something most particular to say to me.' Seagrave raised his eyebrows. 'I came as soon as I was able. So…what is it all about, Miss Kellaway?'

To her horror, Lucille found that she could not speak. She had keyed herself up to such a state of pent-up tension that the words simply would not come out.

After a moment, Seagrave said patiently, 'You appear to be in some difficulty, Miss Kellaway. Am I to understand that the problem involves Miss Markham? Peter told me a little of his meeting with her yesterday.' He studied the high gloss of his boots with sudden intensity. 'Certainly her situation appears most irregular. She is, I collect, a vicar's daughter fresh out of school—your adoptive parents' child, as I understand it! What desperate set of circumstances could have forced her to seek refuge with you?'

Lucille winced. Reflecting ruefully on the difference between Peter Seagrave's diffident courtesy and his brother's high-handed arrogance, she realised that every word he spoke made it more difficult for her to summon up the courage to explain her pretence. She had to do it. Sitting there, knowing that he knew her to be Lucille not Susanna, but with the fact unspoken between them, was extraordinary. And there was no possible way to help Hetty without touching on her own situation, but her courage almost failed her. She cleared her throat.

'My lord—'

'Miss Kellaway?' He was waiting for her to speak, a look of ironic patience on his face. Lucille took a deep breath.

The door opened and Hetty Markham skipped into the room, demure in her freshly laundered sprigged muslin gown.

'Good morning, Lucille! I feel so much better! I was never so glad as when I found you here—' She stopped dead on seeing Seagrave, then dropped a neat curtsy. 'I beg your pardon, sir, I had not realised that my sister was not alone!'

Lucille felt the ground give way beneath her feet. She pinned on the best semblance of a smile that she could muster. Why could Hetty not have recovered half an hour later? However, all was not lost if she could only manoeuvre her from the room.

'Good morning, Hetty,' she said rapidly. 'I am glad to see you so much improved this morning. Mrs Appleton will help you to breakfast in the parlour—'

'Oh, I have had my breakfast in bed!' Miss Markham announced insouciantly. She caught Lucille's eye. 'Oh! But I will wait for you in the parlour, of course!' She turned impulsively to Seagrave. 'Excuse me, sir—'

'Do not leave on my account, ma'am,' Seagrave said, getting to his feet and giving Hetty a smile so full of charm that she looked quite dazzled. 'I imagine that you must be Miss Markham. I am Nicholas Seagrave—I believe that you met my brother Peter yesterday?'

'Oh…yes, sir…how do you do!' Hetty blushed adorably. 'I am so grateful to Mr Seagrave for rescuing me!' She opened her huge blue eyes even wider. 'I am so very sorry that I was not able to thank him properly! Please could you convey my gratitude to your brother, sir, for the service he rendered me yesterday?'

Lucille saw Seagrave's lips twitch slightly. 'Certainly, Miss Markham! But I believe my brother is hoping to call on you himself. He was only waiting until you were well enough to receive him. He will be delighted when I tell him that you are so much recovered!'

'Oh!' Hetty turned to Lucille, her eyes shining. 'Please say that I may see him, dearest Lucille!'

Two pairs of eyes, one blue, one dark, were fixed on Lucille, although the expression in Seagrave's was somewhat more sardonic than Hetty's. Lucille could feel matters slipping beyond her control.

'I am sure it would be perfectly proper for you to see Mr Seagrave later and thank him for his help,' she said weakly. 'But for the time being, would you not prefer to rest? We must be sure that you did not take a chill yesterday.'

Hetty's glowing peaches and cream complexion could not have looked less feverish, and she gave a little laugh. 'Oh, no, I feel wonderful!' She sat down beside Seagrave with a confiding smile. 'I cannot tell you, sir, how glad I was to have Lucille here to turn to when I needed help! She has always been the best of sisters to me—why, she always used to write to me every month when I was at school, and even came to visit me sometimes when she was not needed at Miss Pym's!'

Across her glossy chestnut curls, Seagrave's eyes met Lucille's. His expression was quite unreadable. 'The best of sisters indeed,' he murmured smoothly. 'Tell me, Miss Markham, how did you find Miss Kellaway's direction, now that she is no longer at the school?'

'Oh, it was the easiest thing!' Hetty said, artlessly. 'I wrote to the school, of course, expecting Lucille to be there, but a gentleman—the music master or some such—returned my letter immediately, with a note explaining that Lucille had been here at Cookes for the past month! So I took the stage to Woodbridge and it was only by the worst chance that I got caught in the rain and could not find anyone to bring me to Dillingham! But, of course, it was not so bad at all, for then your brother came along and saved me! He seemed most surprised when I asked to be taken to Miss Kellaway's house, and I feared that there had been some misunderstanding, but all was resolved when I saw Lucille—' She broke off. 'I do beg your pardon, sir! I am always running on, and Mama says it is very bad of me!'

Seagrave smiled. 'Do not apologise, Miss Markham, you interest me vastly!' Again, his eyes met Lucille's. She put a hand to her head in despair and saw his smile deepen. Seagrave got to his feet. 'But you must have a hundred and one things to discuss with Miss Kellaway, so I shall leave you for now. It was a pleasure to meet you, Miss Markham! Miss Kellaway—' There was wicked amusement deep in his eyes, but to Lucille it was no laughing matter. She could have cried.

'I am sorry that you have not had the chance to discuss whatever you wished with me, Miss Kellaway,' Seagrave said pleasantly. He took her hand and drew her to one side. 'Tell me, did you learn your amateur dramatics at Miss Pym's school?' He pressed a kiss on her hand. 'I will call again tomorrow, when perhaps we may talk. Until then…' The amusement was still in his eyes, but beneath it Lucille thought she could sense anger—and the promise of retribution.

'Well!' Hetty said, when Seagrave had been shown out. 'He is a vastly handsome man, but somehow rather frightening! Do you like him, dearest Lucille?'

Lucille hesitated. At that precise moment, her feelings for Nick Seagrave defied description. 'He is charming enough,' she said as casually as she was able. 'But he is vastly above me, my dear! Why, Lord Seagrave is an Earl and his family owns most of the land hereabouts! Cookes is merely one of his tenant properties!'

Hetty drooped. 'I see,' she said despondently. 'Then I suppose Mr Seagrave is far too important to think of me!'

Lucille patted her hand bracingly. It was far too late to counsel Hetty not to fall in love with Peter Seagrave, for the damage was already done. 'The Earl said that his brother would call and I am sure that you may believe him. But Hetty, there are other more important things I need to discuss with you.'

Hetty looked as though she thought nothing could be more important than Peter Seagrave, but obligingly sat down to listen. Lucille looked her over carefully. It was no wonder that Peter was smitten. Henrietta Markham had blossomed into a remarkably pretty girl. She had a sweet, round face, dominated by the huge blue eyes, and complemented by her mass of soft, curly brown hair.

'Now, Hetty,' Lucille said severely, 'what is all this about? I understand from Mr Seagrave that you told him you had run away from home!'

Miss Markham blushed. 'Oh, Lucy, please don't send me back! It's all Aunt Dorinda's fault!' She looked at Lucille with desperation. 'She plans to marry me off to that dreadful curate, Mr Gillies! Did you ever meet him, Lucy? He is the most dreadful bore! His clothes smell of mothballs and his breath smells even worse! I'd rather die than marry him!'

Lucille was beginning to feel rather more than nine years older than her youthful relative. She sighed. 'I'm sure it will not come to that, my dear! Mrs Pledgeley will surely not force you into marriage against your will! And what does your mother have to say to this?'

Hetty looked up at Lucille's severe face, her own expression tragic. 'Oh, Mother would be glad to see me safely settled! She thinks I'm too wild—she says it's the Kellaway connection! And you've no idea how ruthless Aunt Dorinda can be! I know she looks fat and fluffy and indolent, but she has a heart of steel underneath and Mother is no match for her! And Mr Gillies is always calling and paying me unctuous compliments—I knew what they were at! I couldn't think what else to do except come to you!' She was determined to make a clean breast of it and hurried on. 'You know how I found out your direction! Then I waited until Aunt had gone into Ipswich with Mrs Berry, then I took out my valise—I had already packed it in preparation—and walked to the King's Arms. It's at least a mile, you know! I knew the stage passed through there at ten, for John, the gardener's boy, had mentioned it once to me. So I waited, and they took me up as far as Woodbridge, and the rest you know!'

She finished, and looked as though she were about to burst into tears. 'I'm s-s-sorry, Lucy! I didn't know what else to do! And now if you send me back they will make me marry Mr Gillies and I'll never see Peter again!' She stifled a sob and reached up her sleeve for a cambric handkerchief.

Lucille sighed again. 'Well, my love, you have been most resourceful in finding me, and I suppose you will have to stay at least until you are fit to travel!' She saw Hetty's blue eyes peeking at her hopefully above the handkerchief. 'I have written to your mother already to let her know that you are safe. There is, however, one other thing that you should know.' She drew a deep breath. 'This is in fact Susanna's house, not mine.'

Hetty, for all her youthful innocence, was not slow to grasp the significance of this. Although Mrs Markham disapproved of Susanna to the point of never mentioning her name, it had not been possible to keep the truth of Susanna's occupation from Hetty, particularly when it was deplored so loudly and avidly by all and sundry. She quite forgot her tears, her eyes growing huge as saucers.

'But I thought this was your house! Oh glory, Mama will be furious! You did not tell her in your letter?'

'I left that bit out,' Lucille said austerely, and frowned as Hetty stifled a giggle.

'Hetty, it's more serious than just your mama's disapproval! The very fact of your coming to Susanna's house—well, it's bound to reflect on your own reputation in a most unfortunate way. It is not your fault, for you did not know, but you know how unpleasant people can be—'

Lucille broke off, for Hetty had paled visibly as she realised what Lucille meant. 'Mr Seagrave!' she whispered through white lips. 'He seemed shocked when I asked for Cookes and now I see why! Oh, what must he think of me!' Her huge blue eyes filled with tears and overflowed. 'Oh, I cannot bear it! He must think me a loose woman!'

Lucille thought that this was most unlikely. She moved swiftly to Hetty's side and took both her hands. 'I can assure you that he thinks no such thing!' she said briskly. 'He and I spoke last night, and he is perfectly aware that you are a young lady of impeccable reputation! He is as concerned as I to prevent any scandal touching your name, and has pledged himself to help us! Now, dry your eyes, my love! It will not do for you to look woebegone when he arrives!'

Hetty brightened immediately, with the adaptability of the young. 'Oh, Lucy! Do you think he really does like me?'

'I'm sure he does! Now, I shall get Mrs Appleton to bring you in some tea and pastries whilst I arrange to send the letter to your mama.'

Lucille went out feeling exhausted. She supposed that it was not so strange for Hetty to fall head over heels in love with Peter Seagrave on the strength of one meeting. He was, after all, a personable man and he had come to her rescue like a knight from the romances. When contrasted with the odious Mr Gillies, his charm would have bowled her over.

Lucille sighed. She had little doubt that Henrietta was right in thinking that her aunt planned to marry her off, although whether she would have forced the match was another matter. With two daughters of her own approaching marriageable age, Dorinda Pledgeley would have wanted to get so pretty a rival off her hands as soon as possible. Mrs Pledgeley was an overbearing woman, Lucille reflected, and had made the Markhams feel like poor relations ever since she had provided them with a home after the death of the Reverend Gilbert Markham. Just for a moment, Lucille permitted herself to imagine the flutter in the Pledgeley dovecote were Hetty to catch herself an Earl's younger brother. Then she told herself severely not to count her—or in this case Hetty's—chickens before they were hatched.

The thought of an Earl brought her thoughts inevitably on to Seagrave. Hetty's artless confidences had wrecked all possible chance of her explaining the situation to him before he heard of it from anyone else. Lucille shivered as she remembered the look in his eyes as he had left her. The tension of waiting until the following day to see him was almost intolerable. Oh lord, how had she ever got herself into this knot? With hindsight she could see that Seagrave was the last possible person to try to hoodwink. She knew she was a fool to have got herself so entangled. Worse, she knew she would not emerge unscathed.

Peter Seagrave called that afternoon, bringing a huge bunch of flowers for Hetty which made her eyes open to their fullest extent. Lucille, reflecting that the house would soon look like a horticultural show, took them away to put in water whilst Peter took Hetty off for a sedate tour of the garden. Mrs Appleton, looking more indulgent than Lucille had ever seen her, strolled along with them as Hetty's chaperon.

Lucille stood in the scullery, half-heartedly trying to arrange the flowers in one of George Kellaway's more outlandish china vases, and watching as Peter settled both Hetty and Mrs Appleton on the seat beneath the apple tree and proceeded to charm them both. Lucille knew that she was in danger of envying Hetty Markham. Hetty had fallen madly in love in the most unexpected way and it seemed her feelings were returned.

Lucille pushed one unfortunate rosebud forcibly into the vase and stabbed herself painfully on the thorns. Her own situation, she reflected miserably, could hardly have been more different. She too, had

fallen hopelessly in love, for in her own way she was
as inexperienced in the ways of the world as Hetty.
Her nine years' seniority counted for nothing. She had
gone from the confines of Miss Pym's school and met
the Earl of Seagrave, who had somehow been the per-
sonification of all her ideals. And now she had been
exposed to him as a liar and a cheat. He had never
had any respect for her when he thought she was
Susanna, but this was worse, for now he knew her true
identity and could have nothing but contempt for her.

Chapter Six

Lucille slept surprisingly well that night. She had been convinced that the combination of dread and a guilty conscience would keep her awake, but in the event she was too tired to be troubled by either. She awoke to a bright, sunny day, and decided to take a walk before the house was astir. No doubt the fresh air would make her feel more cheerful. She slipped through the garden and orchard, where the dew was fresh on the grass, and took a path that set off across the fields.

The sky was already bright blue, and the air had that fresh, keen edge that came straight from the sea. Skylarks were already singing high above. Lucille's spirits began to lift. She came to a stile and crossed another field. A hay wain rumbled down the gentle hill towards the village, but nothing else moved in the still landscape. Reaching the next lane, Lucille rested on a gate and considered the view.

'Good morning, Miss Kellaway. A beautiful day, is it not?'

How quietly he moved! Lucille had already recognised those distinctive tones when she turned her head to confront the Earl of Seagrave, who was clearly on a morning constitutional about his estate. It was now too late to deplore the fact that Susanna had no clothes remotely suited for a walk in the country, and that she had chosen to wear her own drab brown jacket and skirt, and sturdy boots. Very likely it would make no difference to Seagrave's opinion of her anyway, but he had obviously noticed, for he was looking at her with unconcealed interest.

'I had no idea your wardrobe contained anything so unflattering,' he observed with amusement.

Lucille, her heart beating suddenly in her throat as a result of his unexpected appearance, could think of no suitable rejoinder. Surely now that he knew she was not Susanna he would not expect her to be forever appearing in her borrowed plumes?

'It seemed sensible for a walk across fields,' she said after a moment, noting that his riding boots were liberally spattered with mud and that he was wearing what were obviously old trousers and a casual jacket. The neckerchief carelessly knotted at his throat completed an ensemble which had an informal elegance that did nothing to detract from his air of authority.

'Indeed it is,' Seagrave said, with a glimmer of an approving smile. 'But what a surprise to find you out walking at this hour, Miss Kellaway! Evidently a dislike of early hours is not something which you have in common with your sister! Unless, of course,' he gave her a speculative look, 'it is simply a bad conscience which has kept you awake!'

There it was, out in the open between them! Seeing Lucille blush, Seagrave continued kindly, 'Shall we continue walking whilst you tell me about it? I often find that it is easier to talk on delicate matters if one has some other occupation on which to concentrate as well!'

He fell into step beside her, shortening his stride to match her steps. 'My route back to the Court takes me past Clockhouse Woods—will you accompany me? Let me help you over this stile.'

Lucille knew she really had no choice. She put her hand reluctantly into his as she stepped up on to the stile. His touch was quite impersonal but Lucille felt a deep shiver go through her which she tried to pretend was the effect of the summer breeze. As though she did not have enough to contend with, without the added distraction of this disturbing physical attraction!

The path climbed slightly up a small hill, and Lucille preserved her breath to cope with the incline. She knew it was only a small stay of execution. At the top she paused for a rest and considered the view across to the River Deben and the silver sea beyond.

'This is one of the highest points in the county,' Seagrave commented, as Lucille gradually turned to look across the patchwork fields inland, momentarily diverted from the matter at hand. 'I had forgotten, in fact, what a beautiful county Suffolk is. It is a landscape made for artists, I think. Do you draw, Miss Kellaway?'

'Indifferently, my lord.'

'Ah, a pity. But perhaps you will try your skill? Such a view can only encourage you.'

Lucille had to agree. 'I can understand why John Constable finds it so inspirational,' she said, spontaneously. 'The light and the colour…the limitless space—why the sky seems to go on forever…' She turned a glowing face to Seagrave and almost immediately recollected the barrier between them. She fell silent and the silence seemed to last several hours.

At last he said, a little drily, 'It does not surprise me that you evidently know Constable's work well, Miss Kellaway. You must come to Dillingham Court some time and see the work I have commissioned from him, if that would please you.'

'I…yes, that would be delightful.' All animation had gone out of Lucille's manner.

'My lord, I must tell you…explain…'

Seagrave drove his hands into his jacket pockets. 'Indeed you must, Miss Kellaway. Why not start with the most important point, which is why it was necessary for you to impersonate your sister in the first place? For it was an impersonation, was it not? You had plenty of opportunities to tell me the truth, yet you deliberately chose not to avail yourself of them!'

His tone was quite gentle but with an underlying thread of steel which made refusal quite impossible. Lucille was aware of nothing except her misery. She had always prided herself on her integrity and could not bear him to think her deceitful. The regard she had for him just made matters worse. Plain, prim Miss Kellaway, playing a role in a masquerade and meeting her handsome Earl…

She shrugged away the fanciful idea. Practical Miss Kellaway did not believe in fairy stories. Soon, after all, she would have to return to her dull existence—very soon, now that the truth had come out. There could be no point in remaining in Dillingham and carrying on the charade. While she hesitated, he spoke again.

'Of course, I may be doing your sister an injustice, for I assumed her to be involved in this deception! But perhaps you claimed Cookes in her name and she is unaware of the impersonation?'

That got through to Lucille, as it had been intended to do. Her chin jerked up and she eyed him furiously.

'There is no need to represent matters in a worse light than they are, sir!' she said, hotly. 'Susanna claimed Cookes, as was her right by inheritance. But she found she had to go away for a short time and was anxious that her absence should not give your lawyers a lever to break the lease. And judging by your words to me when first we met, my lord, her fears were justified!'

Seagrave inclined his head with a slight smile. 'Touché, Miss Kellaway! That at least explains her motive in asking you to impersonate her. But what of your own motives?' He stopped walking and turned towards her. 'What did she offer you to make it worth your while, Miss Kellaway? You told me that you could not be bought, but it seems that is not true! So what is your price?'

Lucille bit her lip. Her throat was as dry and stiff as paper, and tears of strain and unhappiness were not far away. Suddenly all she wanted to do was go home and indulge in a hearty cry. The one man in all her twenty-seven years with whom she had fallen disastrously in love regarded her as nothing more than a mercenary adventuress!

'My price, as you put it, my lord, was the peace I believed I could find at Cookes, more fool I!' she said bitterly, pushing back the tendrils of silver hair which the breeze was tugging free from her bonnet. She faced him out stormily. 'I would not expect your lordship to understand—or pity—the restrictions of a proscribed existence, day in, day out, with no thought of change! When Susanna came to me I agreed to her proposal in a moment of weakness, wanting nothing but to escape! I never thought that I would have to meet anyone, or sustain the masquerade! Well, I am well served for my folly now, am I not!' She swallowed the lump in her throat. 'I had better go, I think. Your lordship must be wanting me from Cookes immediately!'

She turned aside, but Seagrave put a hand on her arm, restraining her. 'A moment, Miss Kellaway.' His face wore its customary inscrutable expression and there was no way of telling what he had thought of her words. He ran his hand through his dishevelled dark hair. 'There is no immediate necessity for you to leave Cookes.'

Lucille could not meet his eyes. 'Indeed, I think I must, sir.'

'And I say you shall not.' There was steel in his tone now. 'Be so good as to walk with me a little further, Miss Kellaway. There is something which you should know, I think.'

Lucille fell into step beside him, wondering what else he could possibly have to say to her. Seagrave did not look at her as they continued the downward path, which was now skirting the wall of the field and the woods beyond.

'This morning,' he said conversationally, 'I received word that a lady reliably identified as Miss Susanna Kellaway was in Paris and would shortly be leaving for Vienna in the company of Sir Edwin Bolt.' He swung round to look at Lucille. 'I do not believe your sister will be returning to Cookes for a while, Miss Kellaway.'

Lucille's heart sank at the news but a moment's

reflection told her that it made no difference. She would have to leave Cookes, and if that meant that Susanna lost the lease then so be it. At least her hopes of Sir Edwin had not as yet been dashed if Seagrave's intelligence of them was correct.

They had reached the point where the path to Dillingham Court struck off at right angles beneath the spreading canopy of oak trees. Lucille paused in the shadows.

'I cannot allow that to weigh with me, I think, sir,' she said carefully. 'I promised Susanna that I would stay at Cookes until she returned, but now my circumstances have changed, have they not? Nothing remains but for me to apologise to you for the pretence, and take myself back to Oakham.'

Seagrave was watching her with a slightly mocking smile. 'You are very certain that I will let you go, Miss Kellaway! What if I should choose to press charges to punish you for your duplicity? Obtaining property by deception…false representation…I am sure that I could make the crime fit the charge!'

Lucille felt the earth rock beneath her feet. She had not even thought of that. 'Surely you would not—' she gasped.

'Wouldn't I?' Seagrave looked thoughtful. 'I have a great dislike of being duped, Miss Kellaway! Am I to let you get away so easily?' He leant against the trunk of one vast oak and viewed her with amusement. 'You look horrified, Miss Kellaway! Did you never think of this when you and your sister hatched your plot? Were you so sure of remaining undetected?' He straightened up and Lucille took an instinctive step backwards and he followed. She could sense some force at work in him which she did not understand. It was comparatively dark beneath the trees and his face was in shadow.

'Just how far would you have gone to emulate your sister, I wonder?' Seagrave said slowly. 'I remember you now, of course, Miss Kellaway. We met in the inn at Felixstowe. No wonder you were so discomposed to overhear that I was intending to travel to Dillingham! And now that I know you are from Oakham I remember that I once caught sight of you during a brief stop there.' His inexorable gaze lingered on the strands of silver hair escaping from her bonnet, the sudden wild rose colour which had flooded her face. 'It was a revelatory moment, one might say,' he observed, in a caressing tone that made Lucille shiver, 'and I imagine you remember it too, do you not, Miss Kellaway? How charming you looked at that window—' His hand came up to touch her cheek with feather-light fingers and she felt herself tremble. She knew he could feel it too.

'How charming and how virginal,' Seagrave repeated, with sudden predatory intensity. 'As you do now. But is it possible for a woman who can play the Cyprian to be virtuous herself? I doubt it!'

Lucille tried to speak, but found she could not. She moistened her lips with the tip of her tongue. 'I do not—' She broke off, realising how husky her voice was. His proximity was having a disastrous effect on her, turning her knees to water and her mind to a morass of fevered thought, none of it intelligible. 'I do not understand you, sir,' she managed, and saw his eyes narrow with a mixture of exasperation and a less easily defined emotion. She took another step back, only to find that her back was against another of the broad oaks. Seagrave followed her without apparent hurry, placing one hand on each side of her head against the trunk of the tree so that she could not escape.

'I think you do, Lucille,' he said harshly. 'How far were you prepared to go to further your charade? Would you have eventually accepted my offer of *carte blanche*? Do I really have to take you here and now, against this tree, to discover the truth? Because, believe me, I will do so if I must!' He held her wide, horrified eyes with his very deliberately as he straightened and stepped even closer to her. Lucille instinctively closed her eyes and a moment later she felt his mouth on hers.

A small corner of Lucille's mind acknowledged that she had wanted this ever since he had first kissed her in the garden, then all conscious thought was lost in the sensations that he aroused in her. His anger apparently forgotten, Seagrave's mouth explored hers with a searching but gentle expertise which created such acute excitement that Lucille was lost in a maze of tactile pleasure. She became almost unbearably aware of the hard strength of Seagrave's body pressing her backwards against the unyielding tree trunk, the softness of her own curves as they moulded themselves to the taut lines of his.

The kiss deepened, intoxicatingly sweet. She wanted it to go on forever. Nothing in her experience could explain this delicious torment. And then she felt his fingers at the neck of her jacket, slowly undoing the tiny pearl buttons. The rush of cool air against her heated flesh was utterly delightful. Lucille moaned softly with pleasure. Half of her mind was telling her that she should make him stop, that he would think her as free with her favours as her sister was; the other

half was shamelessly telling her that it did not care
what he thought as long as he carried on arousing
these pleasurable sensations within her...

All buttons unfastened, Seagrave parted the lapels
of her jacket to reveal the fine lawn of her petticoat
beneath. He traced the delicate line of her neck, her
jaw, then her collarbone, with the lightest, most tantalising touch of his lips. Lucille's head fell back, the
silver-gilt hair spilling from its pins to tumble down
her back in a pale waterfall.

She no longer had any inclination to break off their
encounter. Equally, she was so innocent, she had no
real idea of what was happening to her, other than that
it was wonderful. Above them, the breeze stirred the
thick green canopy of leaves and the shifting shadows
played over them. Though her eyes were still closed,
Lucille, all senses fully alert, could feel Seagrave slide
the soft material of her chemise away from her skin
so smoothly, so seductively, every touch only serving
to inflame her further. And when his lips continued
their path downwards from her collarbone over the
exposed curves of her upper breasts, she gasped aloud,
arching against him, digging her fingers into his shoulders.

'Is that far enough, Miss Kellaway, or will you take
more?' That mocking voice was so slurred that she
scarcely recognised it. Lucille thought she would melt
from sheer devastating pleasure. Here was a side of
her nature which she had never even suspected, a side
which even now was demanding that she take this
much further and grant it the ultimate satisfaction.

'Well, Miss Lucille Kellaway? What a surprising
girl you have turned out to be!' Seagrave's mouth was
now an inch from her own, though his fingers had

moved inside her jacket to torment the over-sensitised tips of her breasts. His tongue teased the corners of her mouth before returning fully to cover it again, drinking deeply. When at last he paused for breath, Lucille opened her eyes for the first time and saw the intensity of desire in those narrowed dark eyes so close to her own. She reached out to pull him closer.

His hands circled her waist, holding her against him. The linen of his shirt was rough against her skin as she slid her hands beneath his coat and over the firm muscles of his back, making him gasp in turn. He bit gently at the side of her neck until Lucille arched her head back once more, allowing his questing mouth to return to its teasing assault upon her heated skin. She felt his hands move to unfasten her chemise and she wanted nothing more in the whole world. But—

'No, oh no!' Lucille did not want sanity to return, but it was already there at the edges of her mind, persistent, telling her what unbelievable liberties she had permitted him, what was the next logical step... She had not cared that he had kissed her out of anger; that he thought her a cheap deceiver. She knew that she loved him, and that had been enough for her. But now! This time the touch of the cool breath of summer breeze on her skin brought reality back and Lucille struggled to free herself. She was instantly released.

'Thus far and no farther?' Seagrave said. His voice was rougher than usual and he was breathing hard. 'You would need to take matters much further, I fear, to imitate your sister!'

Lucille was desperately trying to regain control of her disordered senses. She knew he had only intended to punish her and in a strange way this helped to steady her. It could not be expected that an experience which had had such a cataclysmic effect on her would leave him similarly moved. She straightened her bodice, fastening the buttons of her jacket with fingers that shook and slipped. She could not look at Seagrave.

As her mind slowly assimilated what had happened to her she felt more and more horrified, desperately shocked at her own behaviour. Prudish, priggish Miss Lucille Kellaway, who lived life vicariously through her books, had turned out to be a flesh-and-blood creature whose passionate nature, whose needs and desires, could have been her own undoing. So before, Seagrave had thought her a cheat. Now he would think her of easy virtue as well!

The scalding tears which had threatened before welled up in her eyes.

'I have no ambition to emulate Susanna, sir.' Her voice wavered and she pressed her hand to her mouth in a desperate attempt to regain her self-control. She heard Seagrave swear softly under his breath, but whether his anger was directed at her or at himself, she could not tell. Nor did she care. Her sole attention now was focussed on getting herself back to Cookes in one piece. She turned aside from him, but he caught her arm to restrain her.

'Miss Kellaway—'

It was too much. Lucille burst into tears.

Her eyes felt gritty and swollen with crying, her cheeks were burning hot and her nose felt as though it were twice its normal size. However, the greatest shock to Lucille was that the Earl of Seagrave was suddenly behaving as though she were his sister, and had enfolded her in arms that were tenderly protective but not remotely loverlike. Gentle fingers were brushing the damp hair away from her face whilst he pressed his own laundered handkerchief into her hand. His lips brushed her cheek and she heard him murmur gentle words of comfort in her ear. She was astounded.

Seagrave let her go. She felt bereft. 'Forgive me, Miss Kellaway,' he said, with less assurance than she had ever heard from him before. 'I have behaved appallingly and I must apologise.'

'No, sir,' Lucille said unsteadily, scrupulously fair, even through her misery, 'it was all entirely my fault! I am the one who should be apologising—'

'Oh, to hell with apologies!' Seagrave said, with uncharacteristic irritation. 'Miss Kellaway, this is no time for polite prevarication. You are in no state to go back to Cookes on your own—you must allow me to escort you to Dillingham Court. My housekeeper will look after you until you are well enough to return home.'

Lucille almost argued with him, but she had no energy left to do so. Instead, she allowed him to place her unresisting hand on his arm and lead her back on to the path to the Court. She was amazed to see that the sun still shone and to feel the gentle breeze on her hot face. She could not begin to understand all that had just passed between them.

'You need not worry that you will meet anyone at the Court,' Seagrave said abruptly. 'Peter will not be rising before lunch, for he spent the night at the gaming tables, no doubt trying to win enough money to enable him to support a wife!' He slanted a look down at her and sighed as he took in the look of blank incomprehension on her face. Lucille Kellaway had had a tremendous shock and he was entirely responsible for it. He took a deep breath.

'Miss Kellaway...' his voice was very gentle '...forgive the necessity of referring to what has happened, which I know no gentleman should do. You are a lady of considerable intellect. What happened between us just now is what is termed, I believe, a chemical reaction. I imagine that you have studied the physical sciences and understand the concept. It was unpardonable of me to act in such a manner and it will not happen again. Do not regard it.'

Do not regard it! So that was how he considered an encounter which had left her shaken to the core! A part of Lucille was more miserable than she had ever been in her life, but for her own sake she could not allow it ascendancy. It was far better to be angry than to be humiliated. She turned on him furiously.

'I certainly understand your intention to punish and shame me, sir! It is a lesson I shall never forget!'

'Such was not my intention, Miss Kellaway,' Seagrave said quietly. 'Oh, it may have started that way, but I was as much a victim of my desires as you were! The only difference was that I knew what I was about, which you did not!'

Lucille knew that she could not allow herself to feel this insidious sense of empathy which was threatening to draw them together. There was no future for her with him, and to believe so only to be disappointed would destroy her completely. She tried to whip up her fury further. 'And to offer me *carte blanche* when you must already have guessed that I was not Susanna! That was not the action of a gentleman!'

'No.' Seagrave had followed her lead and sounded his inscrutable self once more. The brief flash of tenderness she had seen in him might never have been. 'It was not. But *that* you brought on yourself, Miss

Kellaway! If you choose to play the Cyprian, you cannot complain when people treat you thus!'

Lucille knew that he was right and it made her even more furious. Anger with herself mingled with the hurt he had inflicted. Her feelings for him were mocking her and goaded her even further.

'I have explained my reasons, I have apologised for my actions and I can do no more,' she said in a voice which shook. 'And now I am going home! I would rather walk across coals of fire than spend another moment in your company, my lord!'

'You forget Miss Markham's situation.' Seagrave's voice halted her when she had taken only three steps away from him. There was no expression in his face to indicate his reaction to her impulsive words.

Lucille hesitated. She had indeed forgotten Hetty's predicament in the tumult of emotions that surrounded her own relationship with Seagrave. And now, reminded, she closed her eyes briefly for a moment in complete despair.

'Miss Kellaway.' There was a real determination in Seagrave's voice now, and for once the habitual mockery was absent. 'If we are to help Miss Markham, we must, I think, bury our own differences.' He rested one booted foot on a fallen log and looked at her thoughtfully. 'You should know that once I realised your true identity, I never for one moment suspected you to be a courtesan. There is a transparent innocence about you that makes such an idea nonsense! In fact, our recent passage of arms would never have happened had you truly been such a woman. It is only your inexperience which—' He broke off, seeing the colour flood her cheeks. 'But we will never speak of it again! As for the rest, I've heard and understood what you have said about coming to Cookes and—' he shrugged '—am willing to forget about it. Now are you also willing to put the past behind us?'

Lucille was filled with desolation. She understood that this was all she could expect of him; understood that he was being more generous than she might have expected. It was her own feelings that made it so difficult for her to accept this. Loving him as she did, she would always want more than this, more than he was prepared to give. At all costs she must keep him from discovering her true feelings. That would be the ultimate humiliation.

'Very well,' she said hesitantly, 'for Hetty's sake, I suppose…'

'Thank you. I believe I may have a solution to the problem. Now…' his dark eyes scrutinised her face carefully '…do you feel strong enough at present to cope with this, or are you quite overset?'

His words had the desired effect. Lucille's chin came up and a little colour crept back into her face. 'Of course I am! I am not an invalid! I have not had an accident!'

Seagrave's lips twitched at this. 'Just so,' he said, noncommittally. They began to walk once more, out of the edge of the shady woods and into the parkland that was the start of the Court's grounds. Dillingham Court itself could be seen in the hollow of the hill, its golden stone glowing in the summer sun. Normally Lucille would have paused to admire such a charming aspect, but now she did not feel like stopping to appreciate the view. At least it made it easier to forget what had happened between them when she had another more pressing problem on which to concentrate.

'If you have thought of a way of saving Hetty I

shall be forever in your debt, sir!' she admitted honestly. 'I could never have foreseen that she would seek me out here and unwittingly embroil herself in this! I could not bear for her reputation to be ruined as a result!'

'A tangled web indeed, Miss Kellaway,' Seagrave said, gently. 'Society's rules are very harsh sometimes, and I agree that Miss Markham should not suffer as a result of the sins of others!'

For Hetty's sake Lucille swallowed her anger and mortification. It seemed that, despite his previous words, Seagrave would be forever reminding her of her folly and deceit, but who could blame him? And if she had to bear that for Hetty it seemed the least she could do.

They were descending to the house now, through groves of late rhododendron and glades of wild flowers. It was an enchanting place, but Lucille's spirits were lower than they had ever been. As they reached the gravel of the forecourt, Seagrave gave an exclamation.

'Good God, my mother is here!' Lucille followed his gaze to where a smart travelling coach with the family crest was disgorging what seemed like vast quantities of luggage onto the front steps. Seagrave swung round on her and caught both her hands. She met his imperative dark gaze.

'Listen to me, Miss Kellaway. You can save Miss Markham's reputation, but only if you are prepared to save your own in the process. You must stay at Cookes, and you *must* assume your own identity. Now, are you prepared to do so?'

He was so close. Lucille's bemused blue gaze was trapped by the intensity of those dark eyes. Once again, that peculiar empathy seemed to draw them together. She found that she could not look away.

'Yes, but I do not understand—'

To Lucille's astonishment he gave her hands a reassuring squeeze before letting her go. 'Trust me! Everything will be all right!'

Lucille gave up the attempt to think straight. In the course of one brief hour they appeared to have gone from opposition through a dangerous, if transient, physical intimacy, and were now united for the sake of Hetty's cause. She shook her head in disbelief.

Seagrave hurried her across the gravel sweep and into the entrance hall, which was an impressive room with its waxed flagstone floor and porphyry scagliola pillars. It seemed to be full of portmanteaux and harassed servants. A pregnant silence fell as they entered. One unfortunate footman was so startled to see Lucille that he dropped the bags he was carrying. Seagrave ignored him.

'Medlyn,' he addressed the butler, 'I see my mother has arrived! Where is she, please?'

'Lady Seagrave and Mr Peter are in the blue drawing-room, sir,' the butler said, expressionless. 'Her ladyship is partaking of refreshment. Lady Polly is currently in her room.' His thoughtful gaze swept over Lucille. 'Would the young lady wish to have a moment to compose herself before going through, my lord?'

Seagrave's gaze contemplated Lucille, taking in the twigs in her tumbled hair and the creased clothes. He smiled slightly. 'A good idea, Medlyn! Do ask Mrs Hazeldine to look after Miss Kellaway, whilst I have a word with my mother!' He turned to Lucille. 'Join us when you are ready, Miss Kellaway!' He bent closer. 'And don't run away!'

For some reason, his words and the warmth of his smile made Lucille feel marginally better. She went docilely with the housekeeper to a nearby cloakroom, and allowed herself to be led back to the drawing-room when once she had tidied her appearance and washed her hands and face. Her courage did not fail her until the door of the room swung open.

The drawing-room looked out across the park to the lake and Peter Seagrave and the Dowager Countess were sitting by the long windows, drinking tea. It was, Lucille thought, a particularly elegantly furnished room, with a pair of rosewood card tables and matching rosewood sofa and chairs. Seagrave, who had been speaking as she came in, broke off in the middle of his sentence and came swiftly across to her, ushering her into the room as Peter jumped to his feet.

'How do you do, ma'am? May we make you known to our mother?'

There was a pause. The diminutive, dark-haired lady put down her teacup and rose to her feet. Her lack of inches did not detract from her air of authority. She was impeccably elegant, her hair immaculately coiffed and her dress the epitome of understated good taste. Lucille immediately felt that her hasty preparations had been insufficient and was hideously aware of her own shabby state. She would not have been surprised to discover that she had done up all her buttons in the wrong holes.

Lady Seagrave raised one eyebrow. Her eyes were as dark as those of her sons, and just as inscrutable. They swept over Lucille appraisingly. Then the

Countess gave an exclamation and hurried forward, enfolding Lucille in a warm and scented embrace.

'Miss Kellaway! When Nicholas said that he had brought you here I was hoping—! Thank goodness I've found you at last!'

Chapter Seven

The Earl of Seagrave was seldom put out of countenance, but even he could feel his composure slipping
in the face of this unexpected and totally inexplicable
welcome. He shot Peter a quizzical glance, but his
brother's jaw had dropped so far that it was obvious
he could not throw any light on the situation.

'Mama,' Seagrave began, 'I did not have time to
explain fully—' He stopped and started again. 'This
is Miss Kellaway—'

The Countess let Lucille go. 'Of course it is! I told
you, I've been looking for her for several months!'

'Miss *Lucille* Kellaway,' Seagrave stressed, 'not
Susanna Kellaway—'

The Dowager Countess looked scandalised. 'Why
should I be looking for Susanna Kellaway? What an
extraordinary idea!'

Seagrave, realising that the servants were providing
them with a large and fascinated audience, closed the
drawing-room door. 'You must tell us all about it,
Mama!' he said smoothly. 'I am amazed you had not
mentioned your…ah…mission to find Miss Kellaway
to either of us before!'

The Countess had the grace to look a little embarrassed. 'Lord, Nicholas, I never see you or Peter at Everden from one year to the next!' She viewed her recalcitrant sons with exasperation. 'Both your sister and I would have been happy to tell you of our quest for Lucille had you put in an appearance!'

'So Polly is involved in this as well, is she?' Seagrave marvelled. 'You perceive me positively agog, Mama...'

'Your sister will join us later, I am sure,' Lady Seagrave said. 'She has gone upstairs to rest for a little. She has the headache.' She turned a glowing face to Lucille. 'Oh, she will be so pleased when I tell her! We had quite given up hope of ever finding you!'

Peter was shaking his head in disbelief. Seagrave looked as though he was trying not to laugh. He opened the door briefly to order some more refreshments, then closed it again very firmly.

Lady Seagrave subsided on to the couch in a sussuration of silks and laces, and patted the seat beside her to encourage Lucille to sit down. Seagrave took an armchair opposite, crossing his long legs at the ankle, and Peter moved across to the window and propped himself against the sill. The Countess gave Lucille her enchanting smile.

'You look completely bowled over, my poor child, and no wonder! What a splendid coincidence that Nicholas should have brought you here this morning! But...' she turned her enquiring gaze on her elder son '...I understood you to be saying that there was a particular purpose to Miss Kellaway's visit?'

'That can wait, Mama,' Seagrave interposed swiftly, with a warning glance at Lucille. 'As it turns out, we need your help, but for now we are all on tenterhooks to hear your story!'

Lucille, sitting where the Countess directed, was completely confused by the turn of events. She had steeled herself to expect hostility from Lady Seagrave, if not direct rudeness. This dazzling warmth was so completely unexpected that she was almost afraid she was dreaming. The events of the entire morning now seemed strangely unreal. Any moment she would awaken in her bed at Cookes—or perhaps in her bed at Miss Pym's school, to find that it had all been an impossible dream…

'You are all kindness, ma'am,' she stammered. 'I had not expected such a welcome.'

Lady Seagrave touched her hand lightly. 'I have long been hoping to meet you, my dear. I have been shockingly remiss towards you in the past, I know, but I hope you will forgive me!' She saw that Lucille's look of perplexity had deepened and added, 'You see, Miss Kellaway—may I call you Lucille?—I am your godmother!'

'Godmother!' Both Seagrave brothers spoke simultaneously. Lady Seagrave frowned at them. 'Now, how am I to explain matters when you keep interrupting me? I do wish you would both be quiet!'

There was silence in the room. Lady Seagrave settled herself more comfortably, and addressed Lucille.

'Just as background, my dear, I wonder how well you know your parents' family situation?'

'Not at all well, ma'am,' Lucille said, even more confused than she had been before. Surely the Countess could not be her godmother? She had thought that the Markhams were godparents to both herself and Susanna, as well as being their guardians.

'Well,' Lady Seagrave said with a sigh, 'I suppose I should tell you a little, for it is pertinent to the situation. The Kellaways were once a respected county family—very wild, of course, and when that odious girl Serena ran off and married beneath her there were plenty to say it was no more than they expected...' She heard Seagrave give an exaggerated sigh at this digression and gave him a quelling look. 'Anyway, your father, my dear, inherited a tidy estate over at Westwell, and promptly sold it to finance his travels! He had been a contemporary of my dear husband's at Oxford, and Gerald offered him the lease of Cookes so that he at least had a roof over his head! Not that he was often in Dillingham, for he travelled nearly all the time.' She paused for breath and smiled to see that she had the rapt attention of her audience.

'It was on one of his tours of Italy that he met your mother, Lucille. Oh, Grace Kellaway was a lovely girl! So fair, so delicate! You have a great look of her, you know! She was distantly related to the Hampshire Fordhams, I believe, but her branch of the family never had any money and so she was acting as companion to a rich old woman. The Fordhams are so high in the instep as to be ridiculous, given that—' She broke off, having caught Seagrave's eye. 'Well, that's nothing to the purpose! But George swept Grace off her feet, married her and brought her back to Dillingham.'

Her gaze, misty eyed for a moment, rested on Lucille, who had propped her chin on her hand as she listened, absorbed, to the tale of her parents' romance. 'A year later Grace gave birth to you and your sister,' the Countess said, a little gruffly. 'You were beautiful babies! And at first all was well with her. George asked his cousins, the Markhams, to stand as godparents for your sister, but he asked Gerald and myself to sponsor you. "The elder always has all the advantages," he said to me, "so it seems only fair for the younger to have you." Of course, we agreed.' Lady Seagrave paused to wipe away a surreptitious tear. 'After that, it all went wrong! Grace was taken ill with childbed fever and George was devastated.'

She sniffed away the tears and this time it was Lucille who put a hand out to comfort her.

'Oh, dear ma'am, please do not distress yourself!'

'No, no, my child, it's all right.' The Countess took out her lacy handkerchief. 'It was just a terrible tragedy, for George Kellaway was so deep in love with his bride! I think the only way he could cope with his loss was to go travelling again, and after that he was seldom at home. And then there were the Markhams, so anxious to have a family that they offered to take you and your sister and give you a home! It seemed for the best.'

There was a tentative knock at the door and a bashful footman appeared with a tray of refreshments. He looked so startled to see Lady Seagrave and Lucille sitting next to each other that he would have dropped the tray had Peter not moved swiftly to intercept it.

'Of course, we lost touch with what happened to you and your sister,' Lady Seagrave resumed. 'I was not even aware until quite recently that Gilbert Markham had died. An old friend, unaware of my connection with the Kellaway family, was recounting the scandalous tale of how your sister came to become—' She caught Seagrave's eye again, and cleared her throat. 'Anyway, she told me that it was entirely because you had been left destitute on the death of your adoptive father that Susanna had turned to…her profession. I took this with a pinch of salt, for I knew George Kellaway was still alive and thought that he must have provided for you. It was only when I received the letter that I realised!'

Seagrave stirred in his armchair. Lucille jumped. She had almost forgotten he was there—almost, but not quite, since it was impossible to ignore his physical presence.

'The letter, Mama?' he said patiently.

'From Churchward and Churchward, of course!' The Countess turned back to Lucille. 'They wrote to me, enclosing a letter from your father. They are our family lawyers, you know, and quite by chance they also looked after George Kellaway's estate. They also held his will.'

Lucille frowned. 'I was not aware that he had any estate, ma'am! And as for his will—did he not die intestate?'

The Countess snorted. 'Certainly not! Kellaway may have been a ramshackle fellow, but he knew better than that!'

'But Susanna said that there was no will! Her man of business had checked! She was entitled to nothing but the lease of Cookes!' Lucille blushed as she caught Seagrave watching her. 'I beg your pardon, sir, I understand that the lease of Cookes is within your gift! But the fact remains that there was nothing else for her to inherit except the contents of the house!'

'There was nothing for *her* to inherit because she was not in the will!' Lady Seagrave said, with asperity. 'George explained it all to me. At the last, he was remorseful that he had been abroad when Markham died, and that he had never done anything to help you both. He had heard that you had become a teacher, Lucille, and I think he admired you for that. He hoped that you had inherited some of his interest in scholarship. Perhaps he even regretted that he had never had the opportunity to discuss it with you.' She saw the cloud that touched Lucille's face and sighed. 'Anyway, he left it too late. And the only recompense he could think of was to leave you his fortune.'

'That is nothing in comparison, ma'am—' Lucille said, in a choked voice.

'True.' Lady Seagrave looked approving. 'I imagine that you must sometimes have wondered about him, longed to meet him… He asked me, as your godmother, to try to find you and acquaint you with the news of your inheritance. Unfortunately, he did not say where you were teaching, and I was not at first able to find your direction. I had lost touch with the Markhams long ago, so first I had to trace them to ask after you. I finally found Mrs Markham about four weeks ago, and was directed by her to Miss Pym's school. Of course, by the time I had discovered the school, you had left for Cookes… So here I am, my dear, mightily glad to have found you at last!'

Lucille spared a thought for Mr Kingston, who had been left to hold the fort at Miss Pym's and must have been quite taken aback by the sudden and inexplicable popularity of their junior mistress. First Hetty, and then Lady Seagrave seeking her out!

'Dare we ask about George Kellaway's estate, Mama?' Peter enquired with a grin. He turned to Lucille. 'I apologise for my curiosity, Miss Kellaway, but I now view you quite as one of the family, and I hope that excuses me!'

Lucille met Seagrave's sardonic gaze again and

blushed. It was impossible to believe that he could hold the same sentiments. How he could feel at discovering this unwanted link between them, she dared not even imagine.

'George Kellaway asked me to be utterly discreet about his fortune,' Lady Seagrave said, virtuously. 'He had no wish to publicise his daughter's prospects! He knew it would give rise to an ill-bred curiosity! However,' she added to Lucille, her dark eyes sparkling, 'your father was an unconventional man, my dear, so it is no surprise that he made his fortune working for a Chinese warlord! Make no enquiry into the service he rendered him—suffice it to say that the gentleman in question paid him in precious stones and solid gold bars!'

As Lucille gasped in shock, Seagrave and his brother exchanged a look.

'Now that,' Seagrave said with feeling, 'is a story well worth putting about, Mama!'

'Extraordinary business,' Peter Seagrave said, chalking the end of his billiard cue. 'And Miss Kellaway an heiress! I don't mind admitting, Nick, when you ushered her through the door this morning I thought Mama would cut up rough! When she fell on Miss Kellaway's neck like a long-lost relative, you could have knocked me down with a feather! Thought she was touched in the upper works, though I dare say I shouldn't say such a thing.'

Seagrave laughed. The brothers had been imperiously banished from the drawing-room by their mother, who had declared that she wanted to spend some time getting to know her goddaughter. They were now playing a desultory game of billiards whilst they waited for their idiosyncratic parent to summon them again, though both of their thoughts were pre-occupied, if for different reasons.

'Mustn't forget about Miss Markham in all of this,' Peter said suddenly. 'It's all very well Miss Kellaway suddenly being rich and respectable, but where does that leave her adoptive sister?'

'Don't worry, Peter.' Seagrave measured his shot and sank the ball with expert precision. 'If I know Miss Kellaway, she'll be confessing all to Mama at this very moment! By the time we see them again,' he added sardonically, 'they will have hatched some plot to explain Miss Kellaway's masquerade and have saved Miss Markham's reputation into the bargain!'

There was a note in his voice which made Peter glance up at him curiously. 'Miss Kellaway told you, then? What did you make of it all?'

'An extraordinary business,' Seagrave echoed his brother's words dryly. 'Miss Kellaway must have more of her father's wildness than one might have previously imagined! And now she is so rich, you see, she will be tolerated as an Original! No doubt she will buy a cottage, keep cats and hold bluestocking soirées!' This time there was no mistaking the undertone of bitterness in his voice.

Peter hesitated a moment. 'Did she tell you why she did it?' he asked tentatively, uncertain how far he could trespass. Despite their seven-year age gap he had always been close to Seagrave, but there were times when Peter knew better than to pry.

'Yes.' Seagrave turned to look beyond the formal gardens to the meadows, shimmering in a heat haze. His expression was distant. 'I understand from what she said that she wanted to escape; the school stifled

her and the society in which she found herself was not
stimulating... She is fortunate that she now has the
means to indulge herself without having to resort to
subterfuge!'

Peter almost said that he would expect his brother
to sympathise with Miss Kellaway, since one of the
features of his own existence had been the overriding
boredom that had beset him in civilian life. However,
one glance at Seagrave's face suggested that this
would not be wise. The Earl was looking angry, an
observation which was borne out by his next shot,
which was wildly off target and played with more
force than accuracy.

Peter sank his shot and won the game.

'Damnation,' Seagrave said emotionlessly. 'Something else for which to blame Miss Kellaway!'

'Devil take it, Nick!' Peter was moved to protest,
against his better judgement. 'She's a nice girl, not up
to snuff in the ways of the world, perhaps, but scarcely
the hardened deceiver you make her out to be! Why,
I'll wager the trick was a schoolgirl game, one sister
pretending to be the other! I'm sure Miss Kellaway
never imagined it would get her into trouble—'

He broke off at the look of cynical amusement on
Seagrave's face. 'Now there,' he said, 'I must agree
with you, little brother! Miss Kellaway had no notion
of the difficulties in which she would find herself!'
His amusement died. 'An innocent abroad,' he said
softly, as he had done the night he had discovered the
masquerade, 'and with no more idea of how to go on!'

Peter stared. He had never heard that tone from his
brother before. And as their eyes met there was an
expression there he had never seen before either.

'I think you should know that I would have done a

great deal to save Miss Kellaway from the consequences of her own folly.' For once Seagrave's voice
was devoid of mockery. 'Now that circumstances have
changed, though, I imagine it will not be necessary,
and I find that…disappointing…'

Peter paused, resting on his cue, and viewed his
brother with a mixture of amazement and disbelief.
'Nick! Are you saying—?'

Seagrave turned away. 'I find Miss Kellaway…
interesting, Peter. She is not at all in the common style!
And she is hardly an antidote, is she?'

'Hardly,' Peter agreed with feeling. He found himself standing with his mouth open. He had never, ever
heard his brother admit to an *interest* in a woman,
other than in the purely physical sense.

'Do you know whether she intends to stay in
Dillingham for long?' he asked, obliquely trying to
discover the precise nature of his brother's feelings.
Seagrave was not deceived. He grinned.

'I believe that Miss Kellaway would flee Cookes
immediately were I to let her! However, I have managed to persuade her that it is in Miss Markham's best
interests for her to stay a little while, and by the time
you and Miss Markham are formally betrothed—' he
gave his brother a look of sardonic amusement '—I
shall have persuaded Miss Kellaway to marry me!'

Peter swallowed hard, running a finger around the
inside of his collar, unsure how many shocks his con-
stitution could take in a single morning. 'You're very
sure of my intentions towards Miss Markham,' he
said, with a grin. 'And what of yourself, Nick? Are
you suggesting another marriage of convenience?'

'Like my proposal to Miss Elliott?' Seagrave smiled
slightly. 'At that time I thought that if I had to marry

someone then she would be as good as any! An insufferably arrogant attitude, although I console myself by thinking it would have been as much of a business arrangement on her part as mine! But Miss Kellaway…' His voice softened with a betraying tenderness. 'She is a very different matter. Not least because I wonder if she would accept me!' His smile faded. 'I *do* care for her, but I find I can love her no more than I could anyone else. I would not wish to delude myself or deceive her. I wonder, is it truly fair to offer marriage to such a woman on those terms?'

Peter expelled his breath on a long sigh. He had been afraid of this, afraid that Seagrave's coldness, although showing all the signs of thawing, would not melt into love for his future bride. Perhaps a strong mutual regard was the best that could be hoped for, but it seemed very sad, and a pale reflection of what could be…

'No,' he said quietly, 'it is not fair to offer Miss Kellaway marriage on those terms. But—you will do it anyway, will you not, Nick?'

Their eyes met. 'Yes,' the Earl of Seagrave said slowly. 'I do not intend to let her go.'

With his own perceptions heightened by his feelings for Hetty Markham, Peter was ready to dispute his brother's claim that he could not love Lucille Kellaway. He suspected that Seagrave's feelings ran far deeper than he might know himself, and hoped that he would not discover this too late.

'You seem very certain that your heart will remain untouched, Nick,' he said with gentle satire. 'I think you mistake! You have so much reprehensible experience, and yet you still do not realise that your feelings are truly engaged this time!'

Upon which challenging statement he sauntered out of the room, whistling under his breath, and leaving his brother staring at the door panels with a suddenly arrested expression on his face.

Lucille had indeed confessed to Lady Seagrave, for she felt that she could do no other. The story of her impersonation of Susanna came out haltingly and shamefacedly, whilst her godmother sat quietly listening and asking the odd question here and there for clarity. Lucille said nothing of her feelings for Seagrave, or of his offer of *carte blanche*, for her feelings on the subject were too raw, but Lady Seagrave was no fool and could discern a great deal about the state of Lucille's emotions simply from her narrative.

'Well, my dear,' she said, at the end of this recital of woes, 'it is a sad tangle, is it not, but do not despair! Mrs Appleton had the right of it when she said it was a foolish idea from the start! But enough of that—you have castigated yourself far too much as it is! I think it best if we call Nicholas and Peter back in now, for it seems they both have a stake in the matter!' She did not miss the betraying blush which came into Lucille's cheeks and patted her hand encouragingly. 'I know Nicholas seems formidable at times,' she said comfortingly, 'but if he has said he has forgiven you, you must believe it, Lucille. He does not bear grudges.'

Lucille felt less confident of this, but had no time to dispute the Countess's words, as she was ringing the bell briskly and sending a footman to summon the brothers. Once again, the sight of Seagrave strolling carelessly into the room made Lucille's heart do a somersault. It was not fair, she thought resentfully, that her feelings should be in such a turmoil when he appeared utterly impassive, not a flicker of emotion visible on his face.

The Countess went straight to the point. 'Lucille has told me everything,' she said, with a very straight look at her elder son, 'and it seems our first concern must be for Miss Markham. May I count on help from both of you in this?'

Peter nodded immediately. Seagrave was slower, and Lucille's heart sank. She was not to know that he had been momentarily transported back to childhood and was suffering from the guilt both he and Peter had always felt when confronted with some misdemeanour. Surely Lucille could not have told his mother *everything*? Once again, he remembered with perfect clarity the warmth and sweetness of her mouth beneath his own, the softness—

'Nicholas?' His mother's voice was sharp. 'You will, I hope, support my efforts to restore Miss Markham's reputation?'

'Certainly, Mama,' Seagrave said, obligingly, dragging his thoughts away from certain aspects of Lucille which he had an urgent need to explore further. His gaze was very dark and unreadable as it rested on her. 'And what do we do about Miss Kellaway's situation?'

Lady Seagrave waved a dismissive hand. ''Tis a simple matter! The only two facts which people know for certain are that Susanna Kellaway claimed Cookes, and that Miss Markham went to stay there. The rest is complete speculation!' She sounded most pugnacious. 'So we put it about that I invited Lucille, my *goddaughter*,' she stressed the word, 'to visit me at the Court, but my journey was delayed and so she was obliged to stay at Cookes in the meantime. Being a girl from a sheltered background, Lucille was not aware that people would take her for Susanna and did not realise this for some considerable time. When she discovered the fact, she sought you out for advice, Nicholas!' She saw the look of sardonic enjoyment on Seagrave's face, and hurried on.

'To compound Miss Kellaway's problems, she had invited Miss Markham to join our party, and now discovered that her adoptive sister was also tarred with the brush of Susanna Kellaway's reputation.' She caught Peter's eye. 'It will not help the tale if it becomes known that Miss Markham ran away from home, Peter, but I know I may rely on your discretion there!'

Peter nodded. 'And then, I imagine, you arrive, Mama, and decide that the best course of action is for us to make the true facts known, explaining that it was Miss Lucille Kellaway in residence all the time and not her sister. Miss Markham is vindicated and no one will care to dispute us, I think!'

'With Miss Kellaway's fortune to sweeten the pill,' Seagrave said sarcastically, 'I do not doubt that you are right, Peter!'

Lucille flushed and Lady Seagrave turned on her son. 'You are become monstrous disagreeable all of a sudden, Nicholas! Perhaps it is the heat! So, do I have your agreement to the plan?'

Three heads nodded solemnly. 'Excuse me, ma'am,' Lucille said suddenly, 'but must the solution depend on my remaining at Cookes? I have told Miss Pym that I shall be returning to Oakham shortly and the school holiday will soon be at an end! Would it not be better for you to take Miss Markham up, out of your kindness, and for me to return to my teaching?'

Lady Seagrave looked up and caught the expression in Seagrave's eyes as they rested on Lucille's down-bent head. So that was how the land lay! It seemed that, despite her feelings, Lucille wanted only to escape from both Dillingham and the Earl, and that for his part, Seagrave was not inclined to allow her to do so. Her heart lifted. She did not yet know her god-daughter well, but already liked what she knew. And, if Seagrave had formed a *tendre* for Lucille, she was fairly certain that he would manage the situation to his advantage. And she would do her best to help him.

She framed her words carefully. 'I think, my love, that you must resign yourself to staying at least a little while.' Lucille's unhappy blue eyes met hers and she smiled encouragingly. 'The story of Miss Markham's predicament will ring true only if you are present to give the lie to the fact that Susanna was at Cookes. Once Miss Markham is creditably established, you may, of course, do as you please. And indeed, you have your own future to think of now that you have your own fortune!'

She saw Lucille's shoulders slump. Never had a newly discovered heiress looked so unhappy! 'You look worn out, poor child! So much to consider in one morning!'

Lady Seagrave knew only half the story, Lucille reflected tiredly. She could not believe that it was not yet luncheon. Half a century seemed to have passed in the brief time since she had stepped out from Cookes that morning. In a daze, she heard Seagrave ordering his carriage to be brought round to take Lucille back to Cookes, and Lady Seagrave murmuring that she would write to both Miss Pym and Mrs Markham, to acquaint them of the latest situation.

Lucille nodded wearily. Mrs Markham would be beside herself to hear that Hetty was being taken up by the Countess of Seagrave.

Lady Seagrave pressed her hand in concern. 'Why, you are done up, are you not, my love! Well, we shall leave our plans until tomorrow! I shall call on you in the morning! Oh, we shall all have such fun! And Miss Markham will be just the companion for Polly—it is all working out so perfectly!'

Lucille wished she could summon up just an ounce of Lady Seagrave's delight. To be obliged to prolong her time in Seagrave's company was well-nigh intolerable. Amidst the pleasure of Lady Seagrave and Peter, his own silence stood out markedly. His tone was cool as he handed her into the carriage and bid her farewell, and as the coach rumbled over the rutted tracks taking her back to the village, Lucille allowed two solitary tears to run down her cheeks. The discovery of an anonymous letter waiting for her at Cookes felt like the last straw and she tore it up with a viciousness that went a long way towards relieving her feelings.

Chapter Eight

'I cannot match the colour of the sea,' Lady Polly Seagrave was saying, laying down her paintbrush and shading her eyes against the dazzling sunshine. 'It is so bright, today! Only look, Lucille, I have made it appear the same colour as Mrs Ditton's turban!' She sighed. 'I fear I shall never be an accomplished artist!'

Lucille put her book down on the rug and went to look over Polly's shoulder at the water-colour on the easel. 'You have made The House of Tides look very pretty,' she pointed out consolingly. 'Lady Bellingham will be so surprised that she will want to buy your painting!'

Polly giggled. 'It is an ugly house, isn't it! I cannot understand why such a character as Lady Bellingham should choose to live there!' She smiled shyly at Lucille. 'I was so very glad to meet her—and surprised that Mama permitted it!'

Lucille had been surprised too. When she had expressed her intention of calling on Lady Bellingham that afternoon, a silence had fallen in the Dillingham Court drawing-room, broken only by Thalia Ditton saying in her fluting voice that her mama would never allow her to call on a former actress. Miss Ditton had then fixed Lucille with her limpid blue eyes and said that she supposed that Miss Kellaway must, through her family connections, have met some utterly *fascinating* people, but not those of whom the respectable members of the *ton* could possibly approve.

It was left to the Earl of Seagrave to break the uncomfortable silence, saying that for his part he had always found Lady Bellingham to be absolutely charming, and that he would be glad to escort Lucille to The House of Tides. Miss Ditton had pouted, but brightened when Peter had hurried to the rescue by suggesting a picnic outing to Shingle Street, given that the weather was so fine.

The Earl had caught up with Lucille in the drawing-room doorway. 'I see that you are loyal to your friends, Miss Kellaway,' he observed, with a lazy lift of one eyebrow. 'A number of people come so newly into fortune and fashion might be tempted to drop their previous acquaintances…'

Lucille's clear blue gaze met his. 'I collect that you mean Lady Bellingham? But she was very kind to me when…' her gaze fell '…before…' she finished lamely. 'I find it tiresome that society judges on outward appearance and not character. You will not find me snubbing Lady Bellingham, I assure you!'

'Bravo, Miss Kellaway!' Seagrave said warmly. 'It is what I would have expected of you and I admire you for it! Now, Polly has told me she would like to come with us, but what a pity Miss Ditton cannot be one of our party!'

Lucille gave him a sharp glance, but Seagrave's face was as bland as ever.

'I find I cannot regret Miss Ditton's absence,'

Lucille said sweetly. 'She is not at all the sort of person that Lady Bellingham would wish to meet with!'

Seagrave's laughter followed her out of the room.

And now here they all were, seated on the springy turf, out of the cooling east breeze and having partaken of a delicious picnic. Peter and Hetty were sitting a little way off, the two dark heads close together, under the watchful eye of Lady Seagrave. Nearer at hand, Miss Ditton was chatting engagingly to Seagrave, her parasol at a flirtatious angle as she gazed up teasingly into his face. Mrs Ditton was looking on with the calculating expression of an ambitious mama who has her quarry within her sights. Lucille found that the scene put her out of humour. She put her book down and looked out to sea.

How dramatically life had changed at Cookes since Lady Seagrave had taken them up, Lucille reflected. As Lady Seagrave's goddaughter and an heiress to boot, Miss Kellaway was no longer to be scorned and ignored. Several prominent members of Dillingham society had soon been overheard to say that they had always known that so sweet and prettily mannered a girl could not have been the Cyprian, despite the fact that they had never actually met her. Thalia Ditton had actually had the temerity to claim a friendship, based on the unpleasant encounter in Woodbridge, and had brought her brother to call. It became apparent that Mr Tristan Ditton did not regard his previous relationship with Susanna as a bar to courting Lucille for her fortune.

Lucille's failure to disclose her true identity had been neatly glossed over and put down to a becoming modesty—or possibly the allowable eccentricity of a bluestocking of independent means. Many expected the schoolmistress-turned-heiress to be both original and quaint, and applauded her for it. Local society wished to take her to its bosom and so she became fashionable. Hetty considered it to be a great joke, and Lucille, who privately found it both shallow and hypocritical that she should be fêted wherever she went, tried to tell herself not to be so pompous.

Lucille had swiftly discovered that Lady Seagrave's plans for presenting Hetty into society meant that she would have to make some concessions. She had tried to resist, but the Dowager Countess was adamant.

'I understand your reluctance to appear in society, my love,' Lady Seagrave had said sympathetically, 'for I know that you are interested only in more bookish occupations. And clearly a lady of your independent means and...' she paused delicately '...and your age will not be concerned to be settled creditably. But it is essential that we establish Miss Markham's good reputation, and you did offer your help in that. I am afraid that it will involve a degree of self-sacrifice.'

Lucille had reluctantly acquiesced, knowing that to refuse would appear ungracious when Lady Seagrave had done so much for them. As for her own plans, she had seldom considered marriage in her scheme of things, for she had known from an early age that her prospects were not bright. She had had no family, fortune or opportunity to help her, and now that she had suddenly acquired all these things, she was obviously considered too old to be making a brilliant match. Lady Seagrave had hinted that there might now be many dubious fortune hunters dangling after her for her money, but had suggested that her best course of action might lie elsewhere.

'I realise that you do not have any ambitions towards the married state, Lucille,' she said carefully, 'being of scholarly inclination and possibly a follower of the ideas expressed by Mary Wollstonecraft in her *Vindication of the Rights of Women*.' She wrinkled up her nose. 'A very good sort of woman, I am sure, but some of her suggestions are most impractical. Now, where was I? Oh, yes, I think that under the circumstances you might consider buying yourself a cottage, hiring a companion and spending your time reading and so forth. I am persuaded that you would find such an existence most agreeable.'

Lucille, who six months previously would have said that such a life would be her idea of bliss, found that this suggestion made her want to cry. The Dowager Countess's next words made her feel even worse, and forced her to confront the truth rather painfully.

'Of course,' her godmother had said in a kindly tone, 'should you discover that you are not averse to the married state, you would do best to settle for a solid country squire, the type of man like Charles Farrant, who is so *reliable*.' She gave Lucille an affectionate smile and continued, 'Such men may not be very exciting, of course, but you are past the age of wanting romance! A sensible match to a worthy man—what could be better?'

Lucille had missed the look of wicked amusement on Lady Seagrave's face as she contemplated her goddaughter's pale, unhappy expression. The Dowager Countess had already observed that the mere mention of her elder son's name could put Miss Kellaway to the blush and she was determined to keep him at the forefront of Lucille's mind. Lucille was not naturally unsociable, but her attempts to avoid the Earl of

Seagrave were making her appear so. If there was the slightest chance that he would be present at a breakfast or *fête champêtre*, Lucille would cry off, employing a range of half-truths and creative excuses. It was therefore both disconcerting and annoying to find that somehow her avoidance tactics did not appear to be working.

On one occasion she had pleaded a sick headache, only for him to call on her in the afternoon to ask after her health. Worse, she had refused an invitation to the Dittons at Westwardene, an outing on which she was certain he would be present, only to stumble across him as she took a walk. He had fallen into step beside her and had invited himself back to Cookes for afternoon tea. His manner towards her was faultless but she seemed unable to escape his company, which, given that it gave her pain just to see him, was very difficult for her. Her feelings gave her no rest—Nicholas Seagrave haunted her thoughts when she was awake and walked through her dreams at night.

Meanwhile, Peter Seagrave was paying serious court to Hetty, whose schoolgirl prettiness was blooming into luminous beauty in the warmth of his attentions. He would call at Cookes each day to take her driving through the country lanes, or to visit with friends, or simply to walk together in the gardens. The blossoming romance clearly had the blessing of Lady Seagrave, who would sigh extravagantly over young love, thereby making Lucille feel even more as though she were at her last prayers.

It was in Polly Seagrave's company that Lucille found some solace. For some reason she had expected Lady Polly to be a female version of Peter, extrovert and vivacious, and had been surprised to discover her to be both shy and studious. Polly had the Seagrave features, the rich chestnut hair and gold-flecked eyes, but there was a gravity in her manner that resembled the Earl more than his younger brother.

Early on, Polly had confided in Lucille that she was in disgrace with her mother for being too particular over her suitors; she had rejected eight potential husbands in her first season and had thereafter been labelled as 'the fastidious Lady Polly.' She was now three and twenty, and considered herself to be firmly on the shelf. Once again, Lucille felt the weight of her own twenty-seven years crush her. It could not be wondered that Seagrave would not look twice at such a faded spinster!

Charles Farrant was a regular caller at Cookes these days and was happy to escort Lucille into Woodbridge or on any expedition she chose. Together they were making a study of the history of the windmills in the area, and would spend hours poring over old maps and documents. Hetty was thrilled, convinced that her sister and the bashful Mr Farrant would make a match of it, and she had done all she could to encourage him. She was so in love that she wanted everyone else to be happy too. And it was not Mr Farrant's fault, Lucille thought fairly, that he had kind blue eyes rather than dark, gold-flecked ones, and that his gentle, slightly stammering tones had none of the mellow timbre of the Earl's voice.

'Do you come with us on a walk along the beach, Miss Kellaway?' Thalia Ditton's piping voice cut across Lucille's thoughts. 'Lord Seagrave—' she cast a coy, sideways glance at him under her eyelashes '—suggested it. He has offered to show us a stone sculpture wrought entirely by the sea over the centuries! Too thrilling!'

Lucille knew that the last thing Miss Ditton wanted was for her to be an unwanted third to her tête-à-tête with Seagrave, and since Lucille had no wish to feel like an unwelcome chaperon, she graciously declined the invitation. Peter was pulling a reluctant Hetty to her feet in order to join them on the trip to the beach and Polly was packing up her paints and going across the grass to join her mother and Mrs Ditton in the sun. Lucille tilted the brim of her straw hat against the sunlight and settled down again with her book. Gradually the piping voice and girlish giggles of Miss Ditton faded away, as did the low tones of Peter and Hetty, engrossed in their conversation. A bee buzzed near at hand amid the sea thrift. Lucille's eyelids grew heavy, the dazzling bright light and the heat all combining to make her feel very sleepy.

It was a blade of grass tickling her nose which brought her back to the present. She opened her eyes to find that she was looking directly into those of the Earl of Seagrave, in much the same way as she had done the time he had found her asleep in Cookes's drawing-room. The difference this time was that he was smiling at her and the effect on her was consequently greater than before, both mesmeric and compelling. She felt light-headed at his proximity. Lucille blinked and cleared her throat, determined not to lose her common sense in the face of this unexpected attack on her emotions. The blade of grass was not now in evidence, but she was certain that he had been teasing her with it all the same.

'Surely you cannot have abandoned Miss Ditton on the beach, my lord? She may be swept away by the tide!' Lucille struggled to sit up straighter, aware that Seagrave's lazy gaze was appraising her in a way far too reminiscent of the looks he used to give her before she had been transformed into a respectable young lady. Since she had resumed her own identity, his behaviour had been impeccably proper, underlining to Lucille just what the differences were in the way society treated a lady and a Cyprian.

Only occasionally did she catch him looking at her with a watchful, almost calculating look which puzzled her, and once she was surprised to see in his eyes the same heat she remembered from their encounter in the woods, before his customary, cool detachment had closed his expression down again.

'I am sure Peter is capable of taking care of Miss Ditton, even given his preference for Miss Markham's company!' Seagrave said indolently.

'But it is not Mr Seagrave's society Miss Ditton sought!' Lucille said tartly, then realised that her waspishness could be easily attributed to jealousy. She changed the subject hastily. 'Are the rock formations very fine, my lord? I have read of some in Derbyshire which are accounted well worth seeing!'

'Well, ours certainly cannot compare with the Derbyshire peaks,' Seagrave acknowledged wryly. 'I think it must have been some drunken fisherman who first espied an outcrop of rock here and likened it to Queen Elizabeth's face! I cannot see the likeness myself! And any caves around here are used for more serious purposes than pleasure visiting!' He sounded quite grim for a moment.

'Smuggling, my lord?'

'That and other things.' The gold-flecked eyes were

very serious as they met hers. 'Will you walk with me a little, Miss Kellaway?'

Lucille looked round. Polly had gone to join the others on the beach and Mrs Ditton was asleep, overcome by the warmth of the sun, her mouth slightly open as she snored quietly. Lady Seagrave also looked as though she were dozing, although Lucille could have sworn that she had seen the Countess's eyes open and close again very quickly a moment previously. In the meantime, Seagrave had, with his usual authority, decided that she would agree to his proposal, and had pulled her to her feet. He took her arm and steered her towards a path that was cut through the springy turf.

'Have you heard of the Fen Tigers, Miss Kellaway?' Seagrave asked as they fell into step together.

'I understood them to be the men who had originally drained the fenland in the seventeenth century, sir,' Lucille said, wondering what he meant.

'That's true,' Seagrave smiled down at her. 'How very knowledgeable you are, Miss Kellaway! However, there is a band of men calling themselves the Fen Tigers who are currently roaming the land around Ely and Cambridge. They are mainly disaffected farm workers and even tenant farmers who claim that rents are too high and wages too low.' Seagrave sighed, looking out across the dazzling waves. 'I have always tried to preserve good relations with my tenants here at Dillingham, but I have heard that such unrest is spreading eastward. They burn barns down and attack farms and their owners. They have many hiding places, both for men and their weapons.'

Lucille shivered as the sun went behind a solitary cloud. For some reason the talk of unrest and discontent had made her think of the anonymous letter-writer and his threats to drive her from Dillingham. She had thought to receive no more letters after her true identity was announced, assuming that the author would realise his mistake. But the letter that had been awaiting her on her return from Dillingham Court that day had been followed by two more, always delivered after dark, and each more lurid than the last.

'That was what you meant about the caves being used for other purposes,' she said, shivering again.

Seagrave nodded sombrely. 'I have frightened you,' he said, watching her. 'I do apologise, Miss Kellaway. I have not, I hope, inadvertently touched on matters which are distressing to you?'

Lucille's startled blue gaze met his dark, unreadable one. The sun had emerged from behind its cloud and she suddenly felt far too hot. The words of the most recent anonymous letter seemed to burn into her mind, with their implication that she and Seagrave were lovers. Looking up, she realised that he was still watching her with that stilled, concentrated look that was far too perceptive. She gave herself a little shake.

'Gracious, my lord, how could that be so?' She knew that she sounded both shaken and unconvincing. 'I know nothing of secret hiding places or rural unrest! It all sounds most disagreeable!'

'As you say, Miss Kellaway.' Seagrave was still watching her intently. 'But there might be something else, something closer to home—'

'No, indeed!' Lucille bit her lip, realising immediately that she had betrayed herself with that hasty denial.

They had stopped walking, and were standing facing each other across the grass, almost in the manner of antagonists.

'You always were a bad actress,' Seagrave said softly, almost consideringly. 'I do not believe you, Miss Kellaway! Can it be that Cookes has some secrets too? Perhaps as a hiding place… But no—' it was frightening how quickly he could read her '—it is something else, isn't it, something more personal—?'

'Lucille! Nicholas!' Polly was coming across the turf towards them, dangling her straw hat from its ribbons. 'The others are ready to go now. Are you—?' She broke off, looking from her brother's tense face to Lucille's studiously blank one. 'I beg your pardon! I did not realise that I was intruding.'

'You were not, Polly!' Lucille was quick to reassure her friend. 'I shall be ready directly!' She slipped her hand through Polly's arm and turned gratefully away from Seagrave. She did not look back, but she knew that he was watching them as they made their way to where the carriages were waiting.

Seagrave chose to travel back with Mrs and Miss Ditton, a fact which made Lucille glad for once. She felt sure that the constant scrutiny of those dark eyes would have broken down her resistance. But as she was once again surrounded by the lively chatter of Polly and Hetty on the way home, she reflected that there were some undercurrents beneath the bright and happy surface of life in Dillingham, and some had already touched her too closely.

Lucille was not by nature given to melancholy, however, and by the time the night of Lady Seagrave's impromptu ball had come round, two weeks later, she had managed to throw off her low spirits and was looking forward to the event with almost as much excitement as Hetty. Lady Seagrave had helped her to choose a dress, a simple confection of sapphire silk and silver gauze which perfectly matched the blue of her eyes. That was one benefit conferred by age, Lucille thought wryly—she was not obliged to wear the whites and pastels of the younger girls! With her silver hair drawn into an artistic chignon rather than a severe bun, she felt agreeably chic in an understated way, which was perfectly appropriate for a lady of her mature years who would be seen rather in the light of a chaperon to Hetty than her older sister.

Hetty, heartbreakingly pretty in a plain white figured gown, was waiting in the drawing-room for Lucille to give her the seal of approval. When she saw her adopted sister she rushed forward to give her an impulsive hug.

'Oh, Lucy, you do look fine! You will not want for partners tonight!' She gave her a sly, sideways look. 'I'll wager Mr Farrant will be quite tongue-tied when he sees you!'

Lucille sighed, thinking Hetty was probably right. It was unlikely that the Earl of Seagrave would be affected in the same way.

She held Hetty at arm's length and smiled. 'Well, my love, you are no dowd yourself! I take it that Mr Seagrave cannot have arrived yet, or no doubt I would have found him paying you the most extravagant compliments!'

Hetty blushed. 'Oh, Lucille! He isn't…he cannot be trifling with me, can he? I try not to hope too much, but—' She broke off, her pleading blue eyes fixed on her sister.

Lucille gave her hands a comforting squeeze. 'Mr Seagrave has been most particular in his attentions,' she said thoughtfully, 'and I am sure that he would not be so careless of your reputation as to draw such attention to you only to dash your hopes. But you have not known him long, Hetty...' she hesitated '...are you certain of your own feelings?'

Hetty's eyes lit with a shine that was almost incandescent. 'Oh, yes! I knew from the moment I first saw him! Even when I was refusing his help, I knew my protests were in vain for—' she gave a delicious little shiver '—what happened between us was inevitable!'

Lucille did not have the heart to utter any warnings in the face of such transparent happiness. She heard the sound of the Seagrave carriage draw up outside and found herself hoping fiercely that matters would work out for Hetty. That way the Seagrave brothers would only have broken one heart between them rather than two.

The ballroom at Dillingham Court was brilliantly lit and already full when Hetty and Lucille arrived. This was Lucille's first ball, and she suddenly found herself daunted by the prospect. Clearly Lady Seagrave's idea of 'a small party for close friends' involved a hundred people and a monstrous amount of organisation. The Earl, looking immaculate in the severe black and white of evening dress, was waiting with his mother to greet their guests. Lucille, suddenly overcome by shyness, had to be almost pushed into the ballroom by Hetty, and found herself confronting Seagrave with all thoughts flown completely from her head. He gave a charming but entirely impersonal smile.

'Good evening, Miss Kellaway. I hope that you enjoy the ball.'

His indifference piqued Lucille. 'You are all goodness, my lord. I shall endeavour to do so.'

At that, his gaze focused properly on her face in the most disconcerting manner and Lucille's heart gave a little jump of apprehension. Why could she not have held her tongue! Then Seagrave smiled with genuine amusement.

'I had forgotten that you would probably have preferred to be at home with your books this evening, Miss Kellaway,' he said. 'No doubt our frivolous pursuits will not interest you!'

Lucille gave him a dazzling smile, reminiscent of Susanna at her best. 'On the contrary, my lord, I am growing a little tired of the assumption that I am only interested in scholarship! It should be possible to dance every dance, I imagine!'

'Entirely possible,' the Earl murmured, with a cynical look at the ranks of men barely holding back from besieging her. 'But only if you spare one for me, Miss Kellaway! Astringent conversation is the antidote I shall need this evening!' He gave her his rare, heart-shaking smile and continued, 'But here is a gentleman who, I am persuaded, will do his best to entertain you in the meantime!'

He stood back to allow Charles Farrant to approach Lucille, and watched in amusement as Lucille's pack of admirers closed in.

Mr Farrant was delighted to see her and he was more tenacious than he appeared. Before anyone else could cut him out, he grasped her hand firmly and pulled her onto the dance floor. 'Miss Kellaway! How charming you look, ma'am! May I beg the honour of the first dance?'

One of Lucille's responsibilities at Miss Pym's was to teach the young girls dancing, so she was not entirely unfamiliar with the dances that were taking place. However, there was a great deal of difference between a schoolroom and a fashionable ballroom, and she was glad that it was Charles Farrant guiding her through the set of country dances. Had she been dancing with Seagrave, she reflected ruefully, she would have been so distracted that she would no doubt have stepped all over his feet.

Charles Farrant escorted her off the floor and stuck by her side like a limpet, his face becoming gradually more flushed as one man after another attempted to prise Lucille loose. She secretly found it a charming novelty to be so much in demand, although a natural cynicism, confirmed by the sardonic amusement she saw on Seagrave's face as he contemplated her, made her realise that it was mostly her fortune that was the attraction. She emerged from the mêlée with her dance card full for most of the evening and her new circle of admirers vying with each other to entertain her. The experience was not an unpleasant one, particularly in view of Seagrave's obvious indifference.

Lucille's exertions on the dance floor gave her little time to worry about Hetty, whom Lady Seagrave had promised to chaperon anyway, and it was not until the first break in the dancing that she had the chance to look around and espy her sister in the middle of a group of debutantes and their beaux. Hetty was tilting her head to listen to the words of a lovelorn potential poet, but her eyes were drawn repeatedly to Peter

Seagrave, who was lounging just beside her chair in a distinctly possessive manner.

'Peter is *épris,* is he not, Lucille,' a soft voice said in her ear, and Lucille turned to find Polly Seagrave beside her, her warm brown eyes smiling. She was looking slender and fragile in silver gauze, but it seemed only to accentuate the pallor of her complexion and her faintly sad expression as it lingered on Peter and Hetty.

'I am glad,' Polly added consideringly, 'for Hetty is a lovely girl and she cares for him too.' She drooped a little. 'I wish—' she began, and broke off as her gaze alighted on a gentleman across the other side of the ballroom. She caught her breath on a slight gasp and dropped her fan, bending hastily to retrieve it.

Lucille, much diverted by this, wondered who the gentleman could be who had so disturbed Lady Polly's composure. She had made no secret of the fact that she found most of her admirers tiresome boys or men without anything to commend them. Lucille had wondered whether this dissatisfaction related to some disappointment in the past, or perhaps to some ideal with whom she compared everyone.

'Lady Polly, who is that gentleman—' she began, only to be interrupted by a flustered Polly, whose manners were usually immaculate.

'Gracious, it is so hot in here!' She plied her fan rapidly and nervously, and spoke with more animation than usual. 'Oh, look Lucille! That spiteful cat Thalia Ditton is here, and she has brought Louise Elliott with her, of all people! I had heard that the Elliotts were staying with the Dittons, but how Louise dares to show her face after throwing Nicholas over, I cannot imagine!' Polly wrinkled up her pert little nose. 'Did you hear that she tried to pass off the broken engagement as a misunderstanding? Perhaps she thinks to engage his interest again, but she'll catch cold at that! Nicholas had a lucky escape there!'

Lucille, distracted as Polly had intended her to be, turned to consider Miss Elliott with curiosity and jealousy in equal measure. She had never suffered from jealousy before, and found it too painful to view as an educational experience. Miss Elliott, plump and fair, was smiling up at her recently betrothed with a winning charm and Seagrave did not look in any way averse to her company. As Lucille watched, he murmured something in Miss Elliott's ear and swept her into the dance. Polly gave a snort of disgust.

'Lord, this ball is hardly better than the London crushes! Silly girls, tiresome men—'

Lucille laughed. 'Are your admirers not to your taste then, Polly?'

Lady Polly grimaced. 'They are such boys! Oh, I know some of them are older than I am, but they are so immature!' She saw Lucille's sympathetic smile and said hastily, 'No doubt you think me too particular, for I know that I am generally held to be so! But—'

'But what you need is a real man, Lady Polly!'

Polly jumped and blushed vividly, spinning around. 'Oh, Lord Henry, I did not see you there!' She got a grip on herself although her colour was still high. 'Have you met Miss Kellaway before? Lucille, may I introduce Lord Henry Marchnight?'

Lucille found herself being appraised by the gentleman she had seen across the room. He certainly was a man who knew how to invest a look with all sorts of meaning. His warm grey gaze started at the top of her head and travelled languorously down her in open appreciation, before returning to her face as he gave her a broad smile.

'Miss Kellaway...' his voice lingered caressingly over her name '...it is a pleasure to meet the new sensation!'

Lord Henry was, Lucille thought, possibly the most handsome man she had ever met. He was tall, well built and fair, with a lithe physique which must be the envy of every aspiring sprig of fashion. And there was absolutely nothing about him which made her heart beat any faster. Polly, on the other hand, had a becoming blush in her pale cheeks and was plying her fan rather fast to cool it. Reflecting ruefully on the unpredictable nature of attraction, Lucille held out her hand to him. Her smile was serene but it was belied by the twinkle in her eye. She could not help but like Lord Henry.

'How do you do, sir!'

The grey eyes widened as Lord Henry took in the self-possessed nature of her greeting, and his smile grew. It was not the response to which he was accustomed.

'So do I find you ladies bereft of suitable masculine company?' he enquired, raising a lazy eyebrow at Polly. 'Or should I perhaps say unsuitable company?'

Despite the lightness of his tone, Lucille picked up a barely detectable hint of bitterness, an impression confirmed when the colour rushed back into Polly's face and she answered with constraint, 'We were reflecting on the sad lack of serious conversation at such a gathering as this, sir!'

'Ah, conversation!' Lord Henry smiled satirically. 'But surely such is not the purpose of these events, for the more opportunity a lady and gentleman have to converse, the less likelihood that they will discover any ground of mutual interest! Surely, Lady Polly—'

'Your servant, Marchnight.' The shadow of the Earl of Seagrave had fallen across the three of them and his dark eyes moved thoughtfully from Lord Henry's amused face to Polly's flushed one, then lingered for a moment on Lucille, who was looking studiously blank. He turned to his sister.

'I believe you promised me the boulanger, Polly!'

Lord Henry watched them walk away, a slight, cynical smile on his lips. 'Seagrave doesn't approve of me making up to his little sister,' he said ruefully.

He sounded unconcerned, but once again Lucille picked up the nuance of bitterness and frustration and thought she briefly caught an expression of real unhappiness in those grey eyes.

'Why is that, sir?' Lucille was wondering whether Seagrave's willingness to leave *her* in Lord Henry's company sprang from indifference or the belief that she was too old or unattractive to warrant his attentions. 'Are you, then, considered very dangerous?'

Lord Henry almost choked at this. 'I believe the relatives of youthful females consider me excessively so,' he said drily. 'I wonder that you dare be seen in my company, ma'am!'

Lucille felt her lips twitch. 'Ah, but then I am not precisely an impressionable girl, am I, Lord Henry? No doubt Lord Seagrave believes me to be quite safe!'

Now it was Lord Henry's turn to grin broadly. 'Do not depend upon it,' he said seriously, allowing his admiring glance to linger on her animated face. 'However, if you are feeling really brave, you might consent to walk a little with me, ma'am? The Seagraves have a charming conservatory which would be most suitable for…furthering our acquaintance!'

Lucille held his eyes for several seconds, but could read there nothing but a limpid innocence. She did not believe herself to be in any danger from him. She had already divined that his real interest lay with Polly and that anything else was merely distraction. And she was curious to find out what barriers were preventing Lord Henry's courtship of Lady Polly Seagrave. Polly, for all her studious ways and proclaimed lack of interest in her suitors was not, Lucille thought, at all indifferent to his lordship.

All the same, strolling with him in the conservatory might not be the wisest course of action. She was about to suggest a convenient alcove as a more suitable place for their conversation, when the dancers turned and she saw Seagrave glaring at them from across the set. That decided her. She gave Lord Henry a dazzling smile.

'Thank you, sir. I should be delighted!'

She saw the quick flash of surprise in Lord Henry's eyes before he offered her his arm and escorted her around the edge of the dance floor. One set of double doors were open and led directly into the conservatory, which was humid and dimly lit with paper lanterns. It was an intimate atmosphere, but the number of couples strolling amidst the ferny darkness made it an unlikely place for dalliance.

Which was just as well, Lucille thought, for that was the last thing she wanted. They admired the pond, with its series of waterfalls tumbling over rocks into the central pool and Lucille stopped to identify a number of exotic lilies. When they reached the stone seat at the end of the glasshouse, she sank down onto it with an encouraging smile at Lord Henry to join her. He took the seat, saying, 'Now we may get to know each other a little better, ma'am!'

Lucille sat up straight. 'Yes, indeed. I am so glad, for I wished to talk to you of Lady Polly. She is a charming girl, is she not?' She added thoughtfully, 'In fact, I noticed that you find her more than charming, Lord Henry!'

There was a long, chagrined silence.

'Miss Kellaway,' Lord Henry said at length, in tones of rueful amusement, 'you are possibly the only lady I have ever been in such a situation with, who did not wish to talk about herself! Or at least—' he sounded very slightly piqued '—about herself in conjunction with me!'

Lucille smiled at him apologetically. 'I am sorry, sir! I have been told my ways are somewhat unconventional! I had formed the opinion that you might wish to talk about Lady Polly, but if I was mistaken—'

'You were not, ma'am.' Lord Henry sighed. 'In the absence of being able to talk *to* Lady Polly, I suppose that talking about her is the best alternative! You must be most perceptive, ma'am, to have guessed my feelings for Lady Polly on so short an acquaintance. But the simple fact is that I shall never be considered suitable to pay my addresses to her!'

There was such a wealth of bitterness in his voice that Lucille felt her heart go out to him. 'But surely there can be no objection—' she said, knowing that he was a younger son of the Duke of Marchnight. 'Your family—'

'Oh, my family credentials are impeccable, Miss Kellaway!' Lord Henry could not stop himself once he had started. 'There could be no objection to the

Marchnight name, only to me personally!' He sighed heavily. 'I met Lady Polly five years ago when she was first Out. Amongst all those silly debutantes she was like a breath of fresh air. I was attracted to her at once.' He paused. 'She had a friend—a lady I shall not name for reasons which will become obvious. She was forever in Lady Polly's company. I did not...' he hesitated, looking endearingly self-conscious '...I was not aware that she cherished any hopes for the two of us, for Lady Polly was the only one who occupied my thoughts! But one day the young lady contrived that her coach broke down in the neighbourhood of my house in Hertfordshire.' He sighed. 'She knew that I was out of Town and claimed to be passing quite by chance. Whatever the case, she was obliged to stay at Ruthford overnight. We were not alone, of course, for Miss—the lady—had a cousin travelling with her as chaperon and my housekeeper was, of course, in residence. Nevertheless, the gossip, much of it on the part of the chaperon, was harmful and it was made very clear to me that the honourable course of action could entail nothing other than a proposal of marriage.'

His unhappy grey eyes sought Lucille's. 'If only you could know, ma'am, the sleepless nights I spent trying to work out what I should do. I had been on the point of making Lady Polly Seagrave a declaration, you see, and I could not bear to consider deliberately cutting myself off from a future with her. It seemed hopeless. And in the end I made it clear that I would *not* be offering for Miss—for the lady who had stayed at Ruthford.'

He shook his head, staring into the dark pools of shadow between the lanterns. 'I then went to old Lord Seagrave, the current Earl's father, and asked his permission to pay my addresses to Lady Polly. I was fool-ish—I should have waited for all the gossip to die down, but I could not! Anyway, he turned me down flat, calling me a man without honour who trifled with young women! Everyone was shunning me for my be-haviour—I was in despair! I could not see why I should be called upon to pay such a heavy price for a situation that had not even been of my contriving.' He shrugged uncomfortably. 'Oh, I know that as a gentle-man I was supposed to take the responsibility, and under other circumstances I might possibly—' He broke off. 'But I was furious at being manipulated and even more angry at being condemned in such a fash-ion. I managed to see Polly alone and tried to persuade her to elope with me. She refused to go against her father's wishes.'

There was a silence but for the faint splash of the waterfall into the pool below. Lord Henry stirred. 'Since then I am afraid that I have achieved a well-deserved reputation for wildness. My amorous exploits are always loudly decried by the *ton* and seen as con-firmation of my bad character!' He met Lucille's intent gaze and broke off self-consciously. 'I beg your par-don, ma'am, I cannot believe that I am broaching such a subject with you—'

Lucille raised a hand in a slight gesture of appease-ment. 'Have no concern on my account, sir, for I have always been told I have no sensibility! You do not shock me!'

'I shock myself,' Lord Henry said feelingly. 'It is unpardonable of me to burden you with this story—I cannot think why—' He broke off again and finished, puzzled, 'Upon my word, Miss Kellaway, there is something remarkably sympathetic about your character! I do not usually confide in complete strangers!'

Lucille smiled slightly. 'I can believe it, sir! But I count Lady Polly my friend and I know that she is not happy. Is there anything I can do?'

'You are all goodness, ma'am, but I am persuaded that it is too late for Lady Polly and myself to settle our differences. And I am sure the current Lord Seagrave sees me in no kinder light than his late father did!'

'Well,' Lucille said, and this time the note of bitterness was in her own voice, 'I cannot offer to help you there, that is true! It would do your cause no good for me to approach Lord Seagrave!' She stopped before she betrayed herself completely, but Lord Henry had clearly sensed her distress and put a hand comfortingly on one of hers.

'Then it seems you are in no better case than I—' he had begun, when Seagrave himself interrupted them. Neither of them had noticed his approach.

'Miss Kellaway! I am come to escort you to supper!' Lucille looked up to see him at his most inscrutable, but there was a wealth of meaning in his voice if not his face, and it made her bristle instinctively. She had no idea whether he had been close enough to hear her last comment, but she certainly resented the way his gaze lingered suggestively on Lord Henry, and in particular on their clasped hands. She began to withdraw her own, and Lord Henry let her go with what appeared to be deliberate and regretful slowness. She knew that he was only doing it to annoy Seagrave.

'Are you constituted as my Nemesis for this evening, Seagrave?' Lord Henry was saying, with lazy disdain. 'To be torn away from the company of not one charming lady but two seems more than mere co-incidence!'

'If you wish to consider it deliberate, Marchnight,' Seagrave said pleasantly, 'then please do so!' There was an ugly expression in his eyes. He turned back to Lucille. 'If you please, Miss Kellaway—'

'I believe that Mr Farrant is my escort for supper,' Lucille said, feeling a secret pleasure at being able to thwart Seagrave's high-handed tactics, but rather ashamed of herself at the same time. 'Oh, look, here he is come to claim me! If you two gentlemen will excuse me…' She bestowed a particularly warm smile on Lord Henry, and got to her feet.

'Good God, I am falling over your admirers to-night!' Seagrave said, with a rare show of ill temper. He turned on his heel and strode out of the conservatory.

Chapter Nine

Lucille enjoyed her supper with Charles Farrant, Polly Seagrave and Polly's partner, George Templeton, who was evidently considered to be far more suitable than the luckless Henry Marchnight. As she watched Polly picking at her food and attempting to appear animated, Lucille reflected on the story which Lord Henry had told her. Polly could only have been eighteen at the time of the proposed elopement, and it was quite understandable that she would not have dared to flout her father's wishes. What seemed so sad now, however, was that Polly had clearly had a regard for Henry Marchnight—feelings which had not faded or been replaced with the passage of time. To be obliged to see him socially, to be drawn to him and yet to be forever separated from him must, Lucille thought, be a torment to her.

Across the room, Henry Marchnight was ostentatiously feeding grapes to a fast-looking lady in vivid red. There was much banter and flirtatious laughter, and Lucille saw the shadow that touched Polly's face. Nearer at hand, Hetty was laughing with shy coquetry at some comment of Peter Seagrave as he sat beside her. Peter's attentions were becoming so marked that it could not be long before he made Hetty a declaration. Lucille had no doubts that he was in earnest. His feelings were clear from the way his gaze lingered on Hetty's piquant little face, the proud possessiveness with which he watched her.

Lucille felt as though a hand had squeezed her heart, both sad and happy in one complicated rush of feeling. Hetty was very lucky, she thought fiercely, and perhaps did not know how fortunate she really was. She prayed hard that Hetty would never know the pain of being disillusioned in love.

As if in an echo of her thoughts, the Earl of Seagrave crossed her line of vision, leading Thalia Ditton into the first set after dinner. A romance in that quarter would certainly strain the friendship between Miss Ditton and Miss Elliott, Lucille thought, digging her spoon viciously into her ice. Miss Elliott was looking very sulky.

Lucille danced the next with Charles Farrant and was expecting to sit out the following dance, which was a waltz. She was rather diverted to find Henry Marchnight approaching her. He swept her onto the floor with aplomb.

'The next time you wish to make Seagrave jealous, you may rely on me, Miss Kellaway,' Lord Henry said, with one of his dizzying smiles. 'I have not had so much entertainment in an age!'

Lucille tried to looked severe and could not repress a smile. 'I do not know what you mean, sir!'

'Oh, come! Since we are already such good friends, Miss Kellaway, I should tell you that I have never seen Seagrave behave so! He is notorious for having no feelings, and yet he betrayed plenty tonight!' Lord

Henry's smile deepened. 'Do not mistake me,' he added hastily. 'I actually like Seagrave, and in common with many of his acquaintances I was distressed to see the change wrought in him by his time in the Peninsula. He used to be far more…approachable. But I truly believe that if anyone can reach him, it must be you, Miss Kellaway.'

Lucille looked up into his face to see if he was teasing her, but Lord Henry looked completely sincere. For one glorious moment she allowed herself to believe him, to think that perhaps she might be able to make Seagrave return her regard. But only for a moment. Lord Henry did not know about the masquerade, after all. Had he done so, he could never for one minute have thought that Seagrave would hold her in anything other than contempt. At that moment the movement of the dance brought them round in a circle, and Lucille saw that Seagrave was waltzing with Louise Elliott. Miss Elliott was pressing herself against him with far more abandon than the dance required, and was smiling archly up into Seagrave's face as she did so.

The light went out of Lucille's eyes. Lord Henry, following her gaze, gave an exaggerated sigh.

'What a tiresome little piece Miss Elliott is! Do not regard it, Miss Kellaway. Unless I miss my guess, Seagrave is only doing his duty dances!' He cast a sly look down at Lucille. 'And if it has the added benefit of making you jealous, Seagrave will consider it well worthwhile!'

Lucille shook her head. 'I wish you would not persist in this mistaken belief that Lord Seagrave could in any way care about my reaction,' she said tiredly. 'You could not be further from the truth, sir!'

Lord Henry seemed unconvinced. 'There is a simple way to put it to the test, ma'am,' he drawled. 'You have only to show a modicum of interest in flirting with me to bring Lord Seagrave to heel! I would stake on it!'

For a moment, Lucille was tempted. But she knew that, whatever the effect on Seagrave, it would twist a knife in Polly's heart. She shook her head reluctantly, giving him a slight smile to temper her rejection.

'I am vastly flattered by your offer, sir, but it would not serve.'

Lord Henry was not despondent. As the music stopped he let her go, raising her hand to his lips. 'Should you change your mind, ma'am, just let me know! It would be no hardship!' He gave her one last, wicked smile and took himself off into the cardroom.

It was unfortunate that the movements of the dance had left Lucille standing just to the left of an alcove, and one which contained the Misses Ditton and Elliott. They had found a way to be united, Lucille discovered, and that was by denouncing her as the common enemy.

'...thirty years old, if she's a day,' Miss Ditton was saying, 'no style, no air, no address...she would have done better to stay in the schoolroom! Flirting in that ill-bred way with Harry Marchnight, whom everyone knows will take up with any woman if she throws herself at his head!'

'It will take more than a fortune in gold to improve her chances of marriage,' Miss Elliott agreed, with a spiteful laugh. 'The Cyprian's sister! What man would wish for that connection in the family!'

Lucille turned aside a little blindly, and went out into the hall, taking the first door that she found. Her

gaze was blurred with tears and she was suddenly
afraid that she might disgrace herself by fainting. She
found that she was in the library, a room which was
fortunately deserted and lit only dimly with a lamp at
either end. She sank gratefully into an armchair.

How strange that Miss Ditton's cruel jibes could
hardly touch her, when Miss Elliott, who was only
stating the truth after all, had made her feel so exposed, so vulnerable. It *is* true, Lucille thought hopelessly. No one, not even Lady Seagrave, had been
blunt enough to point it out to her before, but how
many men would want to marry a woman whose sister
was a notorious courtesan? Certainly not the sons of
noble families, with a proud name and title to uphold.
Not even the country gentlemen such as Charles
Farrant, whose upright moral ideas would be outraged
at the thought. Lucille had never wanted to marry before and so her sister's situation had never affected her
in that way—now she suddenly saw it as the biggest
stumbling block of all.

She looked up, dry eyed. So she must put any secret
dreams of marriage to Seagrave behind her, and just
be grateful that she now had her fortune to sweeten
the pill of her inevitable loneliness. And perhaps,
given time, she might no longer be haunted by those
dark, perceptive eyes, the mellow cadences of that
voice…

'Are you unwell, Miss Kellaway?'

The Earl of Seagrave was coming down the library
towards her. Lucille felt hot and then cold. How curious, a part of her observed, that the brilliant charm
of Harry Marchnight had left her unmoved when the
slightest word from Seagrave could throw her into
complete confusion. She cleared her throat.

'No, my lord, I thank you. I am quite well.'

'Then why are you hiding away in here? Your hordes of admirers are quite desolate, I assure you!'

Seagrave took a chair opposite Lucille and scrutinised her carefully. His tone softened.

'What is the matter, Miss Kellaway? And do not try to fob me off with the answer that nothing is wrong, for I shall not believe you!'

Lucille hesitated. The temptation to tell him about Miss Elliott's carelessly spiteful words was very strong, but she knew she had to resist. Such a confidence could only lead on to dangerous ground.

'I am tired, I think, my lord,' she said, avoiding his too-observant gaze. She tried to smile. 'This is my first ball, after all, and I am accustomed to living quietly. I came in here for a little solitude.'

Seagrave's steadfast gaze had not faltered and she knew that he did not believe her, but after a moment he said lightly, 'This is a fine room, is it not, Miss Kellaway? Perhaps you include an appreciation of architecture amongst your interests?'

Lucille looked at her surroundings properly for the first time. The library was indeed beautifully proportioned, with arches at either end and long windows opening onto the terrace outside. As well as the shelves of books behind their glass cases, there was a fine collection of sculpture and some paintings which she could not see clearly in the dim light.

'A part of the sculpture collection was accumulated by my father on his Grand Tour,' Seagrave was saying, 'but your father also brought back pieces for him over the years. You may have realised from what my mother has said that your father and mine were great friends. He was both a prodigious scholar and also a traveller who had remarkable stories to tell of his time abroad. I used to come to Cookes when I was down from Cambridge, to hear tell of his adventures.'

'I have read some of his manuscripts,' Lucille admitted. 'He must have been a fascinating man to talk with.'

'Indeed he was.' Seagrave was looking at her with that same watchful consideration that Lucille found so disconcerting. Then he smiled at her suddenly, which was even more disturbing. 'He would have liked you, I think, Miss Kellaway! In some ways you have much of the same unconventionality. Tell me, what were you discussing with Henry Marchnight?'

How clever of him, Lucille thought, with reluctant admiration, to lull her into a false sense of security before springing on her the question that really mattered. No doubt his concern for Polly was prompting the enquiry—he must be concerned that Henry could not make an approach to his sister through Lucille. Suddenly she felt reckless. She might have to let go of her own hopes, but she would do her utmost to help Henry.

'Lord Henry was telling me of his regard for your sister,' she stated boldly. 'He has not, I believe, recovered from the disappointment he suffered in that direction several years ago.'

There was a short, sharp silence.

'He hides his disappointment remarkably well,' Seagrave said drily. 'And how does Polly feel?'

'I have not asked her, sir,' Lucille said calmly. 'I had intended to speak to Lady Polly, for I saw that Lord Henry's presence discommoded her. However, if you prefer, I shall not broach the topic. I imagine that you would not wish to encourage a friendship between your sister and myself!'

Seagrave's eyes narrowed slightly. 'A curious assumption, Miss Kellaway! I assure you that I have been pleased to see the growing friendship between the two of you! Polly has lacked friends within her own circle—whilst she enjoys all the usual society diversions, there is a seriousness about her that relishes sensible conversation. I understand that, for in some ways she and I are very alike. So please do not imagine that I would wish to discourage you from spending time together. But Lord Henry is another matter, perhaps.' His voice took on a reflective quality. 'I have always liked him, but there has been an undeniable rake's progress in his behaviour in recent years.'

'Perhaps it is the aimless seeking after distraction of one who has lost the only woman he truly cared about,' Lucille said boldly. She could not believe that she was speaking thus. Perhaps the lemonade had contained a secretly alcoholic component which had loosened her tongue.

'Lord Henry seems to have gained a champion in you very swiftly,' Seagrave said, and there was an element in his tone which Lucille could not interpret. Nor could she read his face, which was in shadow. 'I should perhaps warn you that Lord Henry is accounted very dangerous!'

'So I understand!' Lucille said tartly. 'That is, however, rather like Satan rebuking sin, is it not, my lord!'

Again there was a sharp silence, then Seagrave laughed. 'Once again you have surprised me, Miss Kellaway. I would have you know that Harry Marchnight has far worse a reputation than I have!'

'In general terms that may be so, sir,' Lucille allowed fairly, 'but I can only speak as I have found and Lord Henry has always treated me with perfect chivalry. However,' she added kindly, 'I daresay that you have had more provocation than he did, sir!'

Seagrave was shaking his head in amused disbelief. 'I cannot dispute your words, Miss Kellaway! I have indeed behaved towards you like the veriest rake, but yes, the provocation has been excessive!'

He stood up, and a sudden ripple of anticipation went through Lucille.

'There is something about you, Miss Kellaway,' Seagrave continued reflectively, 'that makes me wish to live up to my reputation!'

He put a hand down and pulled her to her feet, and Lucille wondered whether he was about to kiss her. The orchestra had stuck up for a waltz in the ballroom next door, and the faint strains of the music floated into the library.

'You promised me a dance,' Seagrave said, softly. 'Dance with me now.' He pulled her into his arms before she had time to reply. Lucille's eyes widened as she felt the response of her body to his proximity. Waltzing with Henry Marchnight had not been like this. Just the brush of his thigh against her was suffi-cient to send a shiver of sensation right through her. His arm was hard around her and she seemed acutely aware of every line of bone and muscle in his body.

The dimly lit room, with the sculptures watching them with unseeing eyes, the soft lilt of the music, the darkness outside, all seemed to combine to create that secret, magical atmosphere which spun its web around them. Once again, as in the churchyard in Dillingham, Lucille scarcely dared to breathe for fear of breaking the spell.

Her dress brushed against a sheaf of lilies arranged in a large basalt pot, and their scent suddenly filled the room, heady and sweet. Seagrave's face was in shadow, defeating her attempts to read his expression once more, although she thought that he was smiling slightly. The music swept on, the distant notes all part of the dream. Lucille could feel the warmth of his body and had to fight against the surprisingly strong urge to slide her hands beneath his coat and press closer to him.

This time it was the sound of voices from immediately outside the door that interrupted them. Their dancing feet faltered and Seagrave's arms fell away from her as he stepped back.

'I believe that I hear Miss Markham's voice.' He glanced at the clock. 'No doubt she is ready to leave for home, as I understand that you did not wish to stay the night at the Court.' His voice had regained its habitual coolness. 'Good evening, Miss Kellaway!'

That had dropped her down to earth with a bump, Lucille thought resentfully. When would she learn? As she slipped out of the door, she saw Seagrave reach for a book and settle himself in an armchair. He seemed to have forgotten about her already.

In the hallway she was pounced on by Hetty who, together with Lady Seagrave and Polly, had been hunting for her.

'Lucille! Are you all right? We looked for you everywhere but could not find you!'

Lady Seagrave's observant brown eyes were scanning her face and Lucille could feel a betraying warmth rising in her cheeks. She tried not to look towards the library door, and found it almost impossible not to do so.

'I am sorry to keep you waiting, Hetty,' she said hastily. 'I had a headache and went to sit down quietly for a while.'

Hetty chattered about the ball all the way back to Cookes, and only fell silent when she saw the lines of genuine strain and tiredness in Lucille's face. She parted from Lucille in the hall at Cookes and wafted up the staircase on a wave of euphoria after a barely coherent good-night. Lucille, in comparison, felt bone tired. Mrs Appleton had left a tray of food out for her in case she had wanted anything, but all she felt ready for was her bed. She picked up the candle and as she turned to go upstairs, her gaze was caught by something white lying on the tiles of the hall floor.

Lucille bent closer, then recoiled as she recognised the bold black writing on the white envelope. Another anonymous letter! But surely, now that her identity was so well known in the neighbourhood there could be no reason— Very gingerly, she bent down and picked the letter up. It must have been left there after Mrs Appleton had retired to bed, which could only mean that her mysterious accuser was out wandering the village that very night. The thought made her uneasy and she glanced towards the door to make sure that it was securely locked. Taking the letter in one hand and the candle in the other, Lucille made her way slowly upstairs. Suddenly she had never felt less like sleeping. In her room, she put the candle down on the washstand, and ripped open the envelope.

'You are still pretending to be a respectable lady, you slut, but we all know the truth. You are Seagrave's whore and if you are not out of this house within a sen'night it will go badly for you.'

Lucille held out the letter to the candle flame with

a hand that shook. Not just insults, but threats as well now! Either the writer did not believe the story of her identity, or he thought her of easy virtue anyway. Lucille remembered the kiss in the garden, this time with a shudder of horror rather than pleasure. Had someone been spying on her then? Perhaps, even now, an unseen watcher was outside, his gaze trained on her window where the faint light still burned, knowing that she must have read his letter… The flimsy ashes of that letter stirred in a slight breeze from the casement. Lucille shivered. Now she was getting fanciful, and at all costs she could not let her imagination run away with her. Perhaps, if she told Seagrave… She paused for a moment, all too aware of the difficulties of explaining to the Earl that an anonymous member of the village thought that she was his mistress. And yet, the matter was becoming too dangerous to be simply ignored.

There was a scream, sudden and shocking in the quiet house. Lucille grabbed the candle, leapt to her feet and rushed to the door. On the landing she collided with Mrs Appleton, resplendent in a voluminous nightdress and lacy bedcap, and grasping her bedroom poker very firmly in her right hand.

'Miss Kellaway, what on earth is going on? Was it you who screamed just now?'

'Hetty!' Lucille grasped Mrs Appleton's sleeve with an urgent hand. 'Go and waken John the coachman, Mrs Appleton! I will—'

She got no further as the door of Hetty's room burst open and her sister ran along the landing and flung herself into Lucille's arms, sobbing wildly. Lucille nearly dropped the candle.

'Lucille, there was someone in my room just now!'

Hetty cast a terrified look over her shoulder towards the half-open door. 'I opened my eyes and saw a face looking at me through the bedcurtains! I thought I would die of fright!'

As Lucille wrapped an arm around the terrified girl, Mrs Appleton took the candle and advanced purposefully towards the door.

'Oh, no!' Hetty gasped fearfully. 'Mrs Appleton, do not! He may be dangerous!'

Lucille, who would have wagered any day on Mrs Appleton against any unknown intruder, drew her sister into her own bedroom and encouraged her to curl up under the eiderdown. Hetty was still pale and shaking, her hair a mass of tumbled curls, her thin nightgown providing no warmth against the shivers that assailed her. She clung to Lucille's hands.

Lucille tried gently to free herself, but Hetty clung harder. 'Do not leave me, Lucille!'

At that moment, Mrs Appleton appeared in the doorway, shaking her head. 'There is nobody there, ma'am. I have checked thoroughly, behind the furniture and under the bed, but there is no one.'

Hetty gave another sob. 'I know he was there! I saw him!' She looked at Lucille defiantly. 'I know you think I was dreaming, but I swear I was not! I had not even gone to sleep, and I turned over and opened my eyes and there was a pale face staring at me through the curtains!' She gave another shudder and looked as though she was about to burst into tears again.

Lucille hugged her. 'Of course we do not think you imagined it! It is just difficult to see where the man can have gone!'

Hetty looked mutinous. 'I don't know, but I know he was there!'

'What manner of man was he?' Lucille asked. 'Tall or short, dark or fair, young or old?'

'I don't know!' Hetty burrowed under the covers, drawing her knees up to her chin. 'He was dark, I think, and not old…I only saw his face for a moment!' Her voice wavered and she shuddered.

'I shall make us a nice pot of tea,' Mrs Appleton interposed comfortably, 'and no doubt we shall all feel better for it. Miss Kellaway, if you have a moment…'

Lucille tucked Hetty up and went out on to the landing. Mrs Appleton was holding something in the palm of her hand. It looked like grey dust.

'I did not say anything in front of the young lady, ma'am,' she began, 'but I thought that you should see this. I found it in the room, by the side of the fireplace.'

Lucille touched the powder and held it up to her nose. She almost sneezed as the pungent smell filled her nostrils. 'Snuff! But—'

Her puzzled gaze met Mrs Appleton's. 'I cleaned that room only this morning, ma'am,' the housekeeper said quietly, 'and there was no trace of this then. But someone has been in the room tonight—there can be no doubt!'

They looked at one another in silence for a moment, then Mrs Appleton patted her arm reassuringly. 'Let us leave it until the morning, Miss Kellaway! I'll go and make us that tea!'

None of them slept very well that night, and the morning saw Hetty keep to her bed pleading tiredness. Lucille took breakfast alone, knowing she looked pale and drawn, her mind full of anonymous letters and unknown intruders in equal measure. She scoured the room, with Mrs Appleton in attendance, but they could find no further trace of the mysterious trespasser. Yet there was no denying the small pile of snuff which Mrs Appleton had carefully collected and put in a little glass bottle.

Lady Seagrave and Polly called in the afternoon, and were distressed to find Hetty indisposed and Lucille looking so wan. Lucille told them of Hetty's experience, but did not mention the snuff. For the time being she thought it better that the episode be explained away as a bad dream. She had still not decided whether or not to tell Seagrave. Polly too, was looking a little jaded, and Lady Seagrave seemed rather annoyed that such a splendid social occasion had left all her protégées looking rather the worse for wear.

'Here's a to-do!' she said, crossly. 'I thought you young people would have had more stamina! Peter is nursing a sore head, and Seagrave is in some kind of bad mood! I despair of the lot of you!'

Lucille laughed, but as they were leaving she took the chance to draw Polly aside for a quick word and promised to visit her the next day. Polly smiled at her, but still looked sad.

That night, both Lucille and Hetty had retired to bed early, Hetty having been moved to the second guest bedroom and the door of her original room locked. The house was very quiet. Lucille was attempting to read and was experiencing the most enormous difficulties in keeping her mind on the written page. Why was somebody apparently waging this campaign against them? Surely it could not be Seagrave, still intent on ridding the village of them? It would take the greatest hypocrisy to fall in with his mother's plans whilst simultaneously working secretly against them. She could not believe it of him. And were the letter-writer and the intruder one and the same? Lucille sighed, blew out her candle and lay down with no real hope of going to sleep.

Surprisingly, she fell asleep almost immediately, and did not dream. It was an unquantifiable time later that she woke suddenly, unsure what had disturbed her. The wind had got up during the night and was sighing in the trees outside. The house creaked a little. Lucille's nerves prickled. She opened her eyes and stared into the dark. Then she heard it again, the noise which must have woken her. It was a soft, scraping sound, and it came from immediately outside her window.

Lucille slipped silently out of bed and crossed the bare boards to the window, hesitating only slightly before she slipped behind the heavy curtains. The night was dark, for the wind had brought up some cloud which was harrying the full moon. Its silver light was fitful, one moment lighting the whole garden, the next plunging everything into darkness as it disappeared. A branch tapped against the glass and made Lucille jump. Nothing moved in the silent garden.

Then, as she was about to return to her bed, Lucille saw a shadow detach itself from the side of the house just below her. There was the quietest of clicks as the window was closed behind him. The moon disappeared behind a cloud. When it came out again, there was nothing to be seen.

Lucille returned to bed and sat shivering beneath the covers in much the same way as Hetty had the previous night. There was no doubt that there had been someone there—someone who had broken into the house for some secret purpose, and had left like the thief in the night that he was. Lucille had absolutely no inclination to go downstairs and investigate. She lay awake until the first hint of dawn light crept into the sky outside.

'This is a very serious business, Miss Kellaway.' The Earl of Seagrave had been with his agent in the estate office when Lucille had hesitantly asked to see him, but he had sent Josselyn away immediately and gestured to her to take a chair. He leant on the desk, viewing her unsmilingly.

'Since the end of the wars there have been many masterless men roaming the countryside trying to find a living. I suppose it is hardly surprising if some of them have turned to crime, though it is puzzling that you could find nothing missing this morning.'

'No, sir.' Lucille had also seen the men in tattered uniforms who had been dismissed immediately after Waterloo. Some swept the streets or cleared the gutters, but it was humiliating for them to have sunk so low when they might justifiably have expected their country to treat them as heroes. 'I checked the house thoroughly, but none of the contents appeared to have been stolen.'

'There has been unrest on the land, as well.' Seagrave straightened up and drove his hands into the pockets of his casual shooting jacket. 'We talked about it that day at the beach, did we not? I have heard that the rick burning and rioting have moved closer. I wonder…?'

He seemed lost in thought for a moment.

'Wool prices were higher during the war, were they

not?' Lucille observed thoughtfully. 'That cannot have helped. And I have read that the enclosure of common land has deprived those who used to use the land for grazing. It must be very difficult for them to earn enough to feed their families.'

'Yes, indeed. Unless one can farm enough land, there is little money in it,' Seagrave agreed, 'and with many clergymen and landowners putting up rents, it is no wonder that there has been arson and damage to farm buildings. But your problem, Miss Kellaway, appears to be more specific than this.' He held the small bottle of snuff up to the light and took a careful sniff. 'Is there anything else which might throw some light on the activities of your mysterious intruder?'

This was what Lucille had dreaded. It had almost been sufficient to prevent her from seeking his help at all. Since the day at the beach she had been afraid that he would try once again to prise from her the secret of whatever was troubling her. She had hoped that he had forgotten, but now he was watching her once more with that unsettling perspicacity. Nothing would have induced her to mention the letters and their malicious accusations. Even so, she felt a blush rising to her cheeks and met his eyes defiantly.

'No, my lord, that is all.'

'I see.' His gaze, searching and too penetrating, lingered thoughtfully on her face, noting her high colour. 'Well, if you remember anything else, be sure to tell me. I cannot imagine that you will have any more trouble, but perhaps it would be a good idea for the three of you to remove to the Court? The whole village must be aware that three women are living alone at Cookes, even though your coachman is close at hand in the coach-house. I would feel better were I to know that you were all under my roof.'

He spoke with only the most impersonal concern, and once again Lucille was reminded of the burden that they already constituted to him. She shook her head slowly. To be in such close proximity to Seagrave and be obliged to treat him with the same indifferent courtesy that he was showing her could not be borne.

'You are very good, sir, but I am sure we will do very well where we are. As you say, we are unlikely to encounter any further trouble.' She got to her feet.

'As you wish.' To her faint disappointment, Seagrave made no attempt to press her to change her mind. Once again, Lucille castigated herself for wishing that he would do so. How contrary of her to wish to avoid him and yet be annoyed when he showed her nothing but impersonal concern! It put her out of all patience with herself.

Seagrave held the door open for her with scrupulous politeness. Lucille found that even this was beginning to irritate her. 'We shall see you tonight at Mama's card party, I hope,' he was saying, still with that irritatingly casual lack of interest. 'The Dittons and Miss Elliott shall be here, amongst others! Good day, Miss Kellaway!' And Lucille was left standing in the passageway reflecting that even for Hetty's sake she was unprepared to make such a sacrifice as that evening would entail.

When she got back to Cookes, to complete her illhumour, the latest anonymous letter was waiting for her.

Chapter Ten

In the event, neither Hetty nor Lucille were able to go to Dillingham Court that night for the card party. When John went to put the horses to, he discovered that someone had sawed very neatly through the front axle of the coach, making it completely unusable. There was no doubt that the damage was deliberate and malicious. Lucille sent him over to Dillingham Court with a message for Lady Seagrave, and settled down to play a hand of whist with a disappointed Hetty. Before long, however, there was the sound of wheels on the gravel outside and then Peter Seagrave's accents were heard in the hall, greeting Mrs Appleton. Hetty threw down her cards with a glad cry and rushed out to greet him.

'Oh, Peter, how glad I am to see you! The most extraordinary things are going on here—it makes me quite frightened!'

Over her tangled curls, Peter's eyes met Lucille's. She had tried to make light of the incident to Hetty, but could not deny that the atmosphere of tension in the house was strong and she felt as uncomfortable as anyone. Peter put Hetty gently away from him, but retained a grip on her hand.

'Miss Kellaway, my mother has sent me to convey you all at once to Dillingham Court. When she heard of this latest accident that had befallen you, she felt that the best thing would be for you to come to stay with us until the matter is resolved. If you could all pack a few necessities, I can take you straight back to the Court and we may return for the rest of your belongings in the morning.'

Lucille looked at his guileless face suspiciously. For some reason she was certain that Seagrave's high-handedness was behind this, presented in its most acceptable form by Peter and Lady Seagrave. Hetty, however, was looking so relieved that Lucille did not have the heart to refuse and it was with very little real reluctance that she went to pack a case for their remove to Dillingham Court.

Life at the Court gave Lucille a real insight into how a family like the Seagraves would live when they chose to take up their appointed place in the neighbourhood. There was no doubt that they were considered to be the first family in the locality. Invitations to the Court, or to join the Seagrave party on some outing or assembly, were highly prized. The family breakfasted late, usually at ten or eleven, for the previous evening's entertainment would only end in the small hours.

After breakfast Seagrave would often go off to the estate room to attend to business, or go out riding or shooting with Peter and a number of their male acquaintances. Lady Seagrave, Polly, Hetty and Lucille would embark on a round of visiting in the neighbourhood, often staying out for luncheon with friends, or returning to the Court to read, wander in the gardens or play croquet on the lawns.

Dinner was a vastly formal occasion. The family rarely dined alone and seemed to have guests almost every night, sometimes staying, sometimes not. The meal was served in splendour, with footmen behind every chair and much plate on display. Later, the ladies withdrew to the drawing-room and the men smoked, drank and chatted before joining them for cards or impromptu dancing. It was a relentlessly sociable if superficial existence, and Lucille, who had been daunted by it to start with, soon found it bored her.

She was considered odd because she often wished to stay in her room to read, or wandered off alone in the gardens. The indulgence with which her eccentricity had been treated at first was now declining and a vociferous minority, led by Thalia Ditton, were both open in criticising her obliquely for her unconventional ways and decrying her connection with so disreputable a person as Susanna. Lucille knew Miss Ditton's sniping sprang mostly from resentment, but it hurt nevertheless. She rarely thought of Susanna these days, except to wonder how long it would be before her sister reappeared to throw Dillingham into turmoil. She longed to return to Oakham, but Lady Seagrave was still adamant that Hetty needed her.

Under the circumstances, Charles Farrant's uncomplicated admiration was balm to her soul, particularly as Seagrave was an attentive but wholly indifferent host. It shook Lucille to realise that this aloofness on his part made no difference to her feelings for him. She had learned more about love in the space of three months than she would ever have wanted to know, she told herself sadly. That led her thoughts on to Polly Seagrave, for Henry Marchnight had apparently left Suffolk for London. Lucille saw that Polly was pining, and her heart ached for her, but it seemed that in Polly's case as in her own, nothing could be done.

At the end of the second week of their stay at the Court, Lucille let herself out of the house just as the sun was starting to set. She made her way cautiously through the gardens, heavy with the scent of honey-suckle and night-scented stock, and set off up the path that led up to Dragon Hill. She paused to look at Dillingham Court, illuminated by the rosy rays of the setting sun. How tranquil it looked! But this world was not for her. Lucille made a secret promise to herself that as soon as Hetty was officially betrothed to Peter, she would make her excuses and return to Miss Pym's school. That would give her a little time to decide what she wanted to do with the fortune she had so unexpectedly inherited—and start to recover from the effect that the Earl of Seagrave had had on her life.

She had reached the place where the path left the Dillingham park and climbed up beside the wood, had even placed her foot upon the stile, when her name was called from close at hand.

'Miss Kellaway! A moment, if you please!' The Earl of Seagrave himself was striding down the bridleway towards her in the dusk, a deep frown on his brow. Lucille bit her lip. Damnation! Was the man omniscient? She had laid her plans so carefully, crying off from an evening party at Westwardene, the home of the Dittons. As far as she knew, the entire Seagrave family had been intending to go—but it seemed she had been mistaken. And now Seagrave was bound to cut up rough and spoil her outing. She took her foot from the step and placed her basket upon it. It was starting to feel heavy.

Seagrave reached her side in five strides. 'What the devil can you be doing out alone at this time of night, Miss Kellaway?' he said, without preamble. 'Have you taken leave of your senses?'

Lucille looked mutinous. 'I felt in need of an evening constitutional, my lord,' she said, knowing she sounded sulky. 'It is such a delightful night, is it not? I see that you too are enjoying the evening air!'

Seagrave's lips twitched. 'Cut line, Miss Kellaway! You do not go for an evening walk with a heavy basket! Now, what's afoot?'

Lucille gave up. He would insist on escorting her back to the Court, so it mattered little if he knew the truth.

'I was going up the hill to look for the comet, my lord,' she said baldly.

There was perfect silence. A pheasant scuttered away from beneath their feet, uttering its harsh cry. Far away in the wood, a tawny owl called. Then Seagrave stirred.

'You never cease to surprise me, Miss Kellaway,' he said affably. 'I did not realise that your scientific leanings had recently taken an astronomical turn. I take it that you refer to the comet discovered recently by Sir Edmund Grantly, who put a paper on it to the Royal Society? I recollect reading about it in the *Morning Post*.'

'Yes, sir.' Lucille looked up at the sky, which was already darkening to a deep blue. 'I discovered an old treatise in my father's library which predicted that a certain comet would return seventy-one years hence, a date which brought it close to the present. I then remembered reading a report of the same scientific paper you mentioned, sir. So I concluded that it could be the same comet and decided to look for it myself.'

'You fascinate me, Miss Kellaway,' Seagrave said, with perfect truth. 'A most enterprising adventure! And in the basket?'

Lucille pulled the rug aside and produced a telescope in a battered leather case. Seagrave took it and considered it thoughtfully. 'I remember this, for your father used to allow me to look at the stars through it when I was a boy! Good lord, I had quite forgot…' He handed it back to her and looked curiously into the depths of the basket. 'And a picnic as well! How well prepared you are, Miss Kellaway! Do I detect some of Mrs Appleton's famous pastries? And a Cornish pasty? You will be telling me next that you have a bottle of wine tucked away in there as well!'

'I have port wine, sir,' Lucille said primly, and could not resist smiling at his laughter. 'I thought it would be useful against the cold!'

'Capital! Then we have all we need, though I suppose—' he slanted a look down at her '—we shall have to share the glass—unless you intended to drink it from the bottle!'

'We?' Lucille was all at sea. Bemused, she watched him pick up the basket and climb over the stile in one lithe movement.

'Yes, indeed!' He was holding out an imperative hand to help her over. 'I cannot permit you to go star—or comet—gazing alone, so I shall accompany you. That way, you shall be quite safe!'

Lucille doubted that severely. Whilst his recent behaviour towards her had been irreproachable, he was a threat to her peace of mind at the very least, and could be far more dangerous than that, as experience had taught her. Her recent forays into society had confirmed that Seagrave was much sought after as a matrimonial prize, but the same calculating mamas who threw their daughters in his path considered him to be both cold and unfeeling. Privately, Louise Elliott was thought to be the veriest fool for throwing Seagrave over, but there were those who thought she had had a lucky escape.

Cold, unemotional, heartless, were all words which Lucille had heard used to describe the Earl of Seagrave and they were impossible to equate with her experience of the complex, charismatic man who was now proposing that she take a midnight picnic alone with him. As she stepped over the top bar of the stile, his strong hands caught her about the waist and swung her to the ground. Breathless and dizzy, she felt her spirits soaring. No matter that he was a dangerous threat to her hard-won composure—for one moonlit evening he was hers alone, and though it would be cold comfort when she was back in the narrow world of Miss Pym's school, memories would be all she had.

He kept a hold on her hand as they climbed Dragon Hill together. The sun was setting in the west in a flurry of blues and gold, and a sliver of moon was rising above the hill. There were only wisps of cloud and a breath of wind. It was indeed a perfect night. Seagrave spread the rug for them in the shelter of the wall and watched with amusement as Lucille unpacked the picnic. 'Not just pastries, but tomatoes, strawberries... You are a remarkable woman, Miss Kellaway!'

The light was draining from the sky, leaving Seagrave's face in shadow. Deep within her woollen coat, Lucille shivered. It was only a slight movement, but he saw it.

'I hope you are well wrapped up, Miss Kellaway. Sitting still at night is a cold business! I used to go out looking for badgers with the gamekeeper's son when I was a lad, and a long cold night we had of it sometimes!'

'Did you see any?' Lucille enquired, pouring some port into the glass and passing it to him. Their fingers touched. She repressed another shiver.

'Yes, and charming creatures they were too! We found one ancient sett in the woods behind us—doubtless it is still there, for I imagine it has been inhabited for centuries! Have you ever seen a badger, Miss Kellaway, or do you not rate natural history as highly as astronomy?'

Lucille laughed. 'Being a girl, I led a more circumscribed existence than you, my lord! I fear I was not allowed out at night to look for badgers, owls, or any other creatures—much to my regret!'

'I am surprised that you did not escape from under your adoptive parents' vigilant eye and go anyway,' Seagrave observed.

'I expect Susanna would have told tales,' Lucille said thoughtlessly, then stopped. Seagrave appeared not to have noticed.

'Were you close to your sister?' he enquired, draining the glass and passing it back to her.

'As a child, I suppose…' Lucille paused '…we were quite close, but always very different. I always had my nose in a book, whilst Susanna hated bookish things. She could not wait to escape from the constraints of school!'

'And of everything else,' Seagrave said dryly. He was stretched out beside Lucille, propped on one elbow, and his nearness was having its usual disturbing effect on her senses. But tonight was so extraordinary, so unexpected, that she had at last given in to the impulse which was telling her to forget the future and simply relish the pleasure of his company whilst she could. 'Despite her wildness, though, it must have been a severe shock to you all when she decided to go on the Town!'

Lucille giggled. She could feel the port wine warming her inside—and prompting her to further confidences. 'Oh, it was terrible! Mrs Markham went into a spasm and had a fit of the vapours that lasted a week. We had to call the doctor! I tried to persuade Susanna against it, but she was adamant! She said it was the only career for which she had a talent!' Lucille sobered. 'We practically lost touch with each other after that, which was a pity. I would have given a lot...' Her voice trailed away.

'It was a shame for you to lose what family you had,' Seagrave agreed, sinking his strong white teeth into one of Mrs Appleton's excellent pasties. 'But mine have taken you to their bosom! I am glad that Polly has found such a friend in you, Miss Kellaway, and with the connection between Peter and Miss Markham about to be formalised... I am breaking no confidences when I tell you that he plans to travel to Kingsmarton tomorrow to ask Mrs Markham's permission to address her daughter.'

Lucille was silent, thinking of the bleak future she had mapped out for herself by comparison. It seemed that her release would come sooner than she had realised. 'I am so very glad for Hetty,' she said sincerely, deploring the self-pity she could not help feeling.

'And what about you, Miss Kellaway?' Seagrave asked softly. 'What plans do you have?'

He was too quick, Lucille thought resentfully. Perhaps having the Earl of Seagrave's undivided attention was not such a good thing after all.

'Now that I know Hetty is settled suitably I shall go back to Oakham,' Lucille said, expressionlessly. 'Once I am back at the school I shall have time to decide what to do in the future.'

'The school, yes...' Seagrave sounded thoughtful. 'How different can two sisters be, I wonder? You are evidently both well-read and enthusiastic about learning, and whilst I can claim only the barest acquaintance with Susanna, I do remember hearing her say she would rather die than read a book, an over-exaggeration which no doubt accounts for why I remember it!' He turned sideways to look at Lucille, whose clear profile was etched against the darker sky. 'Miss Kellaway, when you were pretending to be your sister, how much of what you said was true?'

Lucille hesitated. Though he had spoken casually, she sensed somehow that this was a very important question. Her impersonation of Susanna had never been mentioned between them since the day the Dowager Countess had come to Dillingham. On Lucille's part this was because she had no wish to expose herself to Seagrave's scorn and denunciation once again, and she had assumed that he had not spoken to her of it because he deplored the whole episode. It was an uncomfortable issue which lay between them, only partially resolved, and added to the barriers which kept him remote and her unhappy. But now he was actually asking her…

She fidgeted with the edge of the rug, unable to meet his eyes. 'Oh, most of it was nonsense, my lord! I do not know Susanna well enough to know what her opinions would be on most things, so I made them up! I imagine that I was in danger of creating a most ridiculous caricature! And…' her voice took on a desperate edge '…the deeper I got, the more guilty I felt. I was on the point of abandoning the whole sorry charade and going back to Oakham on the very day that Hetty arrived and put a spoke in my wheel!'

'Your assumptions about Susanna's opinions were quite accurate, I believe,' Seagrave said. It was too dark to see his expression, or tell what he had made of her words. 'But it must have been difficult, when your own thoughts and tastes are so well established.' His voice took on a reflective quality. 'I cannot believe that it took me so long to realise! I knew Susanna hated reading, yet you left your novels lying about the place, and a fine variety of them there were too! I knew she hated walking and travelled everywhere in her carriage, yet I found you out walking on more than one occasion! And when we talked you would step out of your part every so often when you forgot yourself! You do not even really look like Susanna, since you evidently refused to lard yourself with cosmetics, or drench yourself in chypre!'

'No,' Lucille said slowly. 'I would have expected that anyone who knew Susanna really well would quickly see through the masquerade for the sham it was! That was why I was so grateful that you got rid of the Comte De Vigny so quickly, my lord! That, and—' She stopped, colouring up.

'That, and his distressing inclination to refer to your sister's undoubted talents between the sheets!' Seagrave finished drily. 'Yes, you were most shaken by that, were you not, Miss Kellaway! The penalty for deception?'

'If that were the only penalty, then I would consider myself to have been let off lightly, sir,' Lucille said, subdued. 'To lose—or never gain—the good opinion of those one respects—that is of more serious consequence!'

'If you value such things, that must be true,' Seagrave agreed, pensively. 'Not everyone would believe that it mattered. But how important is that to you, Miss Kellaway?'

Lucille felt as though she were suffocating. There seemed to be a great lump wedged in her throat. She had said nothing of any stronger feelings—she knew she could never have his love. But just to know that he liked her a little, respected her even...would that not be enough?

'It means a very great deal to me, my lord.' In her desperation she dared more than she would have thought possible. 'Through my own folly I have forfeited the right to your respect, and when this whole sorry episode is just a memory that knowledge will stay with me forever!'

There was a silence.

'It must have been difficult for you to remain at Dillingham for Miss Markham's sake, when all you must have wanted to do was escape,' Seagrave observed. Lucille cursed the darkness and his own inscrutability, which made it impossible for her to judge his response to her words.

'It was.' Lucille knew there was still a raw edge to

her voice and suddenly wished she had never started this painful soul-baring. It was too humiliating. If he were to say something cutting after all she had revealed, she would probably run away down the hill in tears.

'You explained to me at the time what had prompted your actions,' Seagrave said, still in that same contemplative tone. 'Let me tell you something, Miss Kellaway. I was never proud of some of the things I had to do whilst on campaign with Wellington. I saw some hideous atrocities, and was obliged to take some actions which would haunt any man. Such experiences change people, and when I was invalided out I was profoundly glad.

'Imagine, then, my horror on discovering that I could not simply adapt back to civilian life! I missed the uncertainty, the challenge, the excitement of the army. I was deeply bored.'

He shifted slightly. 'I ran through every pleasure that life in Town had to offer! Women, gambling, any dangerous sport, and the more hazardous the better! I was a fool, and I was able to indulge that folly because I had the means to do it.'

His voice took on the same bitterness that Lucille had heard that evening in the churchyard. 'Poor Harry Marchnight is pilloried for one youthful indiscretion, and yet I revelled in every kind of reckless behaviour and it was all forgiven me because I was a supposed hero! The more I tried to tarnish the image, the more people indulged me. And after a year of foolishness, during which I lost more money and trifled with more women than I care to remember, I was challenged to a duel by one outraged husband, and let him shoot me because I could not be bothered to defend myself and knew in my heart that I deserved it! Such madness eclipses anything that your boredom could ever have driven you to, Miss Kellaway, so let us hear no more of that!

'And the worst of it is,' Seagrave finished savagely, 'that when this temporary madness had gone, I found I still cared little, felt nothing! Oh, I care for my family, perhaps, for I owe them a great deal, but my estates, my responsibilities, the lady to whom I was betrothed…they meant nothing to me! I am still uncertain whether anything ever will!'

Lucille was silent. All words seemed inadequate, platitudes he must have heard from well-meaning friends a hundred times. She remembered Polly confiding in her how much the War had changed Seagrave, and how Henry Marchnight had said how sorry his friends were to see this remoteness in him.

Instinctively, impulsively, prompted only by the love and concern she felt, she reached out a hand and touched the back of his in a gesture of comfort. She was about to draw back, appalled at her own effrontery, when his fingers closed over hers, warm and reassuringly alive after all that he had said.

'The stars are coming out, Miss Kellaway,' Seagrave said a little huskily, pulling her closer.

It was true. Engrossed in their conversation, Lucille had not realised that the sky had turned a deep velvet blue and that the first stars were shining far above them. The sky was clear but for a few scattered clouds, and the new sickle moon swooped low over the wood. The owls were calling again. It was a beautiful night.

She got to her feet a little stiffly, helped by Seagrave's hand under her elbow. He was standing very close to her.

'Where is this comet to be found, Miss Kellaway?'

'In the constellation of Cassiopeia, sir,' Lucille said, as briskly as she could. 'There…above the point of the central star. Why, I can see it even without the aid of the telescope! How beautiful!' She raised the telescope to study that smudgy pinpoint of light. 'Why, it has a tail rather like one of your tropical fish, my lord! Only look—'

Excitedly she passed him the telescope and waited whilst Seagrave focused on the heavens. After a while he sighed. 'It is…quite awesome, is it not, Miss Kellaway? And all those stars—how very humbling!'

The breeze rustled in the woods behind them. Some small creature of the night scattered away through the undergrowth. Lucille shivered. There was a strange timeless quality about the night as though it were not really happening.

'Are you cold, Miss Kellaway?' Seagrave turned to her. 'Would you like to go back?'

'No!' Lucille saw him smile in the moonlight and added hastily, 'That is, it is such a beautiful night, my lord, that I did not wish to go back inside immediately, but—'

'But you must not get cold,' Seagrave observed. 'Here, take my coat!'

He draped it around her shoulders. It smelled of the fresh air and a faint cologne, and whatever that indefinable smell was that was the essence of Nicholas Seagrave himself. Lucille breathed it in and felt herself go weak at the knees.

'Oh, no!' She realised how husky her voice sounded. 'You will be cold yourself, my lord! Please—I have my coat—'

'And I have my jacket, Miss Kellaway, and will do

very well with that.' Seagrave stooped to pick up the rug and the basket. 'Come, I will show you the lake in the moonlight. It should look very pretty.'

They went slowly down the hill to the stile. As Lucille stepped over the top bar, Seagrave picked her up as he had before, but this time he did not swing her down to the ground, but let her slide slowly down against him. When her feet touched the ground he did not let her go. Lucille's heart started to hammer. A most delicious, terrifying anticipation was causing butterflies in her stomach.

'I have tried,' Seagrave said, with a note of exasperation in his voice, 'God knows, I really have tried to behave with circumspection, Miss Kellaway! But it is impossible—' He put a hand under her chin and turned her face up to his. 'Lucille,' he said softly, consideringly. His fingers traced the line of her jaw with the gentlest of touches before he bent his head to kiss her.

The flash flood of desire swept through Lucille immediately, as though it had only been waiting for this moment and all her attempts to deny it had been in vain. She could feel the heat of Seagrave's body, feel the racing of his heart against her hand, where her palm rested against his shirt. She slid her arms around him, and heard him groan against her mouth.

'Lucille…' he said again, gently, caressingly, his breath stirring her hair. 'Who would have thought…?'

Lucille's senses were full of the scent of his skin. She ran her fingers into the thick dark hair at the nape of his neck, and drew his mouth back down to hers. His arms tightened about her. Then she remembered their encounter in the wood, her heated response to him, the danger she was in from her own wayward senses, and she drew back slightly.

'Don't be afraid…' Seagrave murmured, his lips touching the hollow at the base of her throat.

'Last time…' Lucille said, uncertainly.

'I know.' He sounded as though he really did understand. 'But this is different, Lucille. It will never be like that again, I promise.'

'Oh…' It was more a sigh than a word, and Lucille heard the betraying note of disappointment in her own voice. So did Seagrave. He laughed softly.

'Unless, perhaps, that is what you want. But that wasn't what you meant, was it, Lucille?'

It was so difficult to concentrate, Lucille found, when the brush of his lips against the tender skin of her neck was making her shiver from head to toe. Shiver, but with a consuming heat that burned into her soul.

'I know you meant only to punish me.'

'To start with there was something of that in it,' Seagrave agreed softly, thoughtfully, 'but I wanted you, Lucille. From the very first moment I saw you, I wanted you…' His lips returned to hers again with a searching insistence that robbed her of all thought.

Neither of them heard the approaching footsteps until the stranger was almost upon them in the darkness, and then the effect on Seagrave was electric. He pulled Lucille further back into the shadows, held hard against him, but this time it was his hand across her mouth that silenced her.

'My lord! Are you there?' The quiet whisper barely reached them. Swearing under his breath, Seagrave let Lucille go.

'The devil! Jem, you scared me half to death!'

'Sorry, sir.' The man came out into the moonlight, and Lucille recognised him as one of the grooms at the Court. 'But it's past the time we said we'd meet, and there's trouble over at Cookes, sir. Evening, ma'am,' he added to Lucille, showing not the least surprise that she was there.

The change in Seagrave was remarkable. Lucille was still in a dazed and dreamlike trance, but he had snapped back to reality without appearing to draw breath in between. 'Right, Jem.' His voice was hard and incisive. 'You get back to Cookes and stay with Will—I'll join you as soon as I've escorted Miss Kellaway back to the Court—'

'Too late, sir!' Jem turned to point to the hill behind them. 'They're coming this way. About twenty men, my lord, armed with pitchforks and scythes in the main, but in an ugly mood! Walter Mutch kept the weapons at Cookes—'

Lucille woke up. 'Cookes! But how—?'

'There's no time!' Seagrave took her arm tightly. 'Jem, get over to Martock Farm and warn them. I'd heard word that they would be heading that way sometime soon. Take the fastest horse—and don't let them see you. I'll send someone to call out the yeomanry and follow you over there. Now, Miss Kellaway—'

'Sir!' Jem's urgent whisper cut across his words. 'Look, there!'

There were torches flaring at the top of the hill. The mob were making no secret of their approach. The tramp of feet echoed through the still night, a ragged rhythm with an undertone of violence. Voices were raised in angry clamour. Lucille saw with a shock that their faces were blackened, emphasising the bright, at-avistic excitement in their eyes. She shrank back into the enveloping thickness of the bushes, pulled close against Seagrave's body. The warmth and strength of his arms was reassuring, but she was still trembling with fear.

The mob passed over the hill and the torchlight flickered and died behind them, the roar of voices fading away. The bushes rustled beside them and Jem was gone. Lucille and Seagrave stepped out onto the path. The moonlight was as bright but the night had lost all its magic. Lucille shivered convulsively in the cold breeze and folded her arms tight against her.

'The Fen Tigers!' she said in a choked whisper. 'And you knew that they were connected with Cookes—'

'I will tell you everything later, Lucille,' Seagrave said in a tone which brooked no opposition. He had set off for the house at a fast pace, obliging her to run to keep up. 'For now, you will oblige me by going back to the Court and not stirring a foot outside until I return!'

Lucille clutched his arm. 'You will not go to Martock Farm alone? The danger—'

She saw Seagrave grin in the darkness. 'Never fear for me! I have faced far worse than this!' He gave her a brief, hard kiss and was gone.

Chapter Eleven

Lucille did not even try to read, but sat by the window in her room, looking out over the darkened gardens. Her mind was split; half of it was marvelling over the magical evening that she had spent with Seagrave and the precious, fragile rapport that seemed to be building between them, and the other was wrenched with fear for him. Every moment she spent with him only served to make her fall deeper in love, but Lucille had long given up trying to explain her feelings to herself or to dismiss them. She knew now that the life she led at Miss Pym's school, which had already begin to pall when she had come to Dillingham, could never be fulfilling again. She did not know if there was an alternative.

A diversion to her thoughts was caused by the return of the rest of the family from Westwardene. Hetty knocked on the door on her way to bed, and regaled Lucille with a highly amusing account of the card party. Both Miss Ditton and Miss Elliott had been as mad as wet hens, she said, to discover that Seagrave was not of the party, and the odious Mr Ditton had declared himself desolated at Lucille's absence.

Yawning, Hetty had kissed her sister and gone off to bed, having extracted a promise from Lucille that she would join them on their visit to the ruins at Allingham Castle the following day.

The minutes ticked past and Lucille dozed in her chair. She was just wondering whether Seagrave would wait until the morning to acquaint her with the events at Martock Farm, when there was a knock at the door. She opened it to find an impassive footman on the landing.

'His lordship's compliments, ma'am, and would you join him in the drawing-room.'

There were no concessions to politeness: if she would be so good, if she were not too tired… A prickle of apprehension ran down Lucille's spine. She looked at the man's face, but he appeared quite blank. It seemed that none of Seagrave's staff were going to question their master's right to peremptorily summon one of his guests in the middle of the night.

Her first view of Seagrave did nothing to allay her fears. He was standing before the fireplace, his arm stretched along the mantelpiece and one booted foot resting on the fender. There was a moody scowl on his face which even the dim, shadowed room could not disguise. It was almost impossible to equate this man with the one who had held her so tenderly in his arms only a few hours earlier. Lucille's heart sank.

'Sit down, Miss Kellaway.' His tone was curt. 'There are a couple of matters I wish to discuss with you. I regret that they cannot wait until the morning!'

Lucille was starting to feel very nervous. She sat on the edge of her chair, looking up at him. He turned away.

'You should know that I have had Cookes under

surveillance ever since you told me of the curious occurrences there,' he began, without preamble. 'That was why I wanted you all out of the house and installed here at the Court, but as usual, your damnable independence—' He broke off, glaring at her, and ran a hand through his ruffled dark hair. 'I had already received intelligence that the Fen Tigers intended a strike in this neighbourhood, the fenland becoming too hot for them. Walter Mutch's name was mentioned. Your cousin, I am sorry to say, is a young man who has been involved in various dubious enterprises over the years.'

Seagrave's dark eyes searched Lucille's pale face thoughtfully. 'The Kellaway wildness runs deep in him, they say. Walter had anticipated that Cookes would be his before Susanna's unexpected claim overset his plans. He had already begun to use the house as a base for his activities.' Seagrave shrugged. 'A little smuggling, perhaps; storage of stolen goods, certainly... In addition, he had been accustomed to helping himself to the contents of the house during your father's prolonged absences abroad. He is always fathoms deep in debt, for he is an extravagant gambler, and he found it useful to take the odd item here and there to settle his bills. I believe the house to be so cluttered with artefacts that no one would have noticed.'

Lucille nodded tiredly. 'No, I am sure no one would have realised... Oh, dear! And then Susanna upset his plans by moving in! I suppose that it was Walter that Hetty saw that night?'

Seagrave nodded. 'Yes. I imagine he was hoping to scare you all away, since he seems to have deliberately set out to frighten Miss Markham. I had heard that

Walter is partial to snuff—it is one of his extravagances—which was one of the reasons I suspected him when Mrs Appleton found the snuff dropped by the fireplace. I imagine he must have slipped out in the confusion after Miss Markham screamed and before you all came running. As he knew the house, it would not be difficult for him to slip away unnoticed. Certainly your presence at Cookes was very unwelcome, especially with Walter's connection with the Fen Tigers. He had a quantity of arms hidden in one of the outhouses—I have been over there tonight after the insurrection at the farm was put down—and I imagine that he was on tenterhooks lest you discovered his secret.'

Lucille was momentarily distracted. 'The farm! I almost forgot! Whatever happened?'

Seagrave smiled for the first time. 'Very little, Miss Kellaway! These mob outings are usually characterised by a lot of shouting and swearing but very little real violence! When I reached Martock, Jem had already warned the farmer and the place was barricaded. The rabble were milling about threatening to burn the place down. Then the farmer doused them all with buckets of water which he had thoughtfully filled in advance in case of fire, the yeomanry arrived, and the whole thing degenerated into an ignominious retreat!'

His smile faded. 'Walter Mutch was taken by the yeomanry. I understand that he has…acknowledged the error of his ways, and decided that a future in America might possibly be for the best!'

Lucille considered him with misgiving. 'You mean that you have persuaded him! Oh, poor Mrs Mutch! How dreadful for her!'

'Better to have a son emigrate than have a son de-

nounced as a rabble-rouser and a thief!' Seagrave said
strongly. 'I imagine that you would not have wished
to press charges and cause trouble in the family, Miss
Kellaway, but the contents of Cookes actually belong
to your sister, who may not be so forgiving!'

Lucille hesitated, certain that he was right. Were
Susanna to return and consider herself defrauded, no
consideration of family feeling would be likely to
sway her. An idea occurred to her. 'Perhaps I could
settle his debts,' she said eagerly. 'After all, now that
I have a fortune at my disposal—'

She stopped as Seagrave held up a hand, a look of
amused resignation on his face. 'You are most generous, ma'am, but I have to tell you that I have already
instructed Mutch to seek settlement of his debts
through Mr Josselyn, and have included, in addition,
a sum to speed him on his way abroad!'

Lucille's heart sank. Was there no end to the responsibilities that her family would lay at his door?
She got to her feet. 'Then you must let me repay—'

'Certainly not.' Seagrave was standing over her,
awesomely authoritative. 'You will not argue with me,
Miss Kellaway.' The gold-flecked eyes scrutinised
Lucille's pale face with a hard look. 'The matter is
closed. But I infinitely regret that there is a more important issue which I need to discuss with you.'
Lucille sensed something in his manner—tension?
Anger? She was not sure, but her nerves tightened in
response.

'That day at the beach, I asked you if you were
hiding something from me,' Seagrave was saying. 'I
wondered if you had, in fact, discovered Walter's
cache of arms, and were too afraid to say anything,
but I thought it unlikely.' He was taking from his

jacket pocket what looked like an envelope, a white envelope with black writing. 'And now,' Seagrave said grimly, holding the letter out to her, 'I realise just what it was you were omitting to tell me, Miss Kellaway.'

'Oh!' Lucille recoiled in horrified remembrance. She had left the last anonymous letter carelessly discarded on a table in Cookes drawing-room and had forgotten about it completely. And Seagrave had said that he had been to Cookes that evening, and must have gone inside, into the drawing-room, where he would have seen the letter... She remembered what was written there, and the colour flooded into her face.

'Well might you look so!' Seagrave said, with soft vehemence. He was very close, his physical presence, trapping her, intimidating her completely. 'Why did you not tell me, Miss Kellaway?'

Lucille tried to speak calmly though her heart was hammering. Those furious gold-flecked eyes were only inches from her own.

'Oh, because such letters are best ignored, my lord! They were spiteful and malicious, and I did not care to take them seriously! And I was embarrassed—I admit it!' She met his eyes defiantly. 'I did not wish you to see what was written there!'

Seagrave moved slightly away from her, although his angry gaze never left her for a moment. 'How many letters have there been, Miss Kellaway?'

'I don't know...five...six, maybe. I threw them away!' Lucille was horrified to find that she was nearly in tears, more upset by his anger than she had ever been by the hurtful accusations of the anonymous writer. The lamplight blurred into puddles of gold as she felt her tears spill over and she dashed them away.

'Forgive me for pressing you on this, but I must

know—' There was constraint in Seagrave's voice now. 'Were they all like this? Did they all suggest that there was an…illicit relationship between the two of us?'

Lucille looked miserably down at the carpet. 'No. The first two were purely personal attacks on me—on Susanna. It was only after I…resumed my real identity that the letters suggested that I—that we…' Her voice trailed away.

'I see.' Seagrave sounded quite expressionless. He came across to her once again. She sensed that he was standing close to her, but she could not look up into his face. 'Miss Kellaway—' his voice was very gentle '—I understand that aversion to such poisonous malice as this might make you wish to destroy the letters; pretend, perhaps, that they never existed. Unfortunately, in a small place such as Dillingham it is not so easy to escape such spite. Although country society appears to have taken you to its heart, below the surface, not everyone is so generous! A word here or there, and a reputation dies. Your reputation, Miss Kellaway.' He tapped the letter. 'There are plenty of people who would be willing to believe this libel.'

Lucille looked up at him then, her eyes very bright. 'But I am going away soon—it does not matter!'

Seagrave was shaking his head. 'Such malevolence travels, Miss Kellaway. By devious means it will work its way back to the school, back to the parents of the children in your care… They will hear that Miss Lucille Kellaway is not a fit person to take charge of their offspring, that she is a woman of shady morality, perhaps.' He sighed regretfully. 'Or suppose that you decide to use some of your fortune to settle in some comfortable town, a seaside resort, perhaps. How long would it be before someone hears a rumour, a tantalising tale of a lady and a nobleman...scandalous details...Miss Lucille Kellaway is, after all, the sister of a notorious Cyprian. How piquant, that the respectable sister should, after all, be proved as licentious as the courtesan... You will never be free of it, Miss Kellaway!'

He looked down into her face and gave a short laugh. 'You look horrified, Miss Kellaway! Had it never occurred to you that *this* might be the natural outcome of your masquerade? I see it had not!'

'No, sir.' Lucille's voice came out as a shaken thread of sound. 'I had never thought that my good name would be compromised...not my own name... I know I pretended to be Susanna, but I always intended to resume my life as before, and no one had ever questioned my own integrity...'

Seagrave took her hand and pulled her round to face him. 'Nor mine, Miss Kellaway. This touches my honour. But fortunately the solution is easy to hand. You will marry me.'

Lucille withdrew her hand hastily. 'Oh, no, sir! I could not possibly allow—'

'I was not asking you, Miss Kellaway,' Seagrave said, with a hint of humour, 'I was telling you. The only way I can protect your reputation—and restore my own—is for us to wed. So perhaps we can dispose of your objections relatively quickly?'

He took the chair opposite hers and raised a quizzical eyebrow. Lucille sat down a little abruptly. Her mind was spinning. To be Countess of Seagrave—it was all that she had wanted; all that she had dreamed of. But not like this! This quixotic proposal, borne out of necessity...

'I am very sensible of the honour that you do me, my lord…'

'But? Do, please, be frank, Miss Kellaway. If you have any objections to me personally—'

'Oh, no!' Lucille was struggling already. 'But I am a schoolteacher, sir—'

'Yes?'

'And as such must be a most unsuitable person to become a Countess.'

Seagrave waved a hand. 'A trifling objection, Miss Kellaway! I cannot regard it! Your family is an old and respected one in this County. What could be more suitable?'

'But I do not fit into County society—it bores me.'

'It bores me too,' Seagrave agreed affably. 'We shall not mix with our neighbours if we do not wish!'

Lucille was thinking of Louise Elliott's cruel words. 'And my sister is a Cyprian, sir! A barque of frailty, a—'

'Say no more, Miss Kellaway!' Seagrave was actually grinning. 'I understand you perfectly! But I think you misjudge your sister!' He lips twitched again. 'The next time you see her, I confidently predict that she will be Lady Bolt, and as such above reproach!'

'And I deceived you, sir!' Lucille finished tragically. 'I pretended to be the Cyprian!'

To her amazement, Seagrave still had that wicked grin on his face. 'Yes, I own that I shall be very interested to see how you intend to further your impersonation in the marriage bed!'

The hot colour flooded Lucille's face. 'But—'

'Lucille,' the Earl said, suddenly losing patience, 'if

you have no more substantive points to make, I suggest that you accept!'

'Yes, my lord,' Lucille said, slowly. 'It does seem to be for the best…'

'A little more enthusiasm might not go amiss,' Seagrave said humorously. He got up and pulled her to her feet. 'Before I let you go, perhaps we should seal our bargain…'

It was impossible, Lucille thought, to resist that dizzying, demanding spiral of desire that overcame her at his lightest touch. But she was remembering the words he had spoken only that night when he had told her that he could never care deeply for anyone ever again… He had told her he wanted her and the urgent claim of his hands and his mouth was now making that very clear. But love? When she loved him so much, was it not the ultimate folly to accept this compromise and marry him? For she would always be striving to make him love her, making herself unhappy when it was obvious that he did not feel as she did. The subtle, sensuous touch of his tongue parting her lips distracted her thoughts for a moment and she struggled to free herself.

'My lord—'

'Yes, Lucille? I really think that you should call me Nicholas now.' Seagrave's lips were just grazing the soft skin beneath her ear, sending ripples of feeling along all her nerve endings. His mouth moved, brushing her neck, to pause at the base of her throat and slip even further to the hollow between her breasts. Lucille gasped.

'My lord…Nicholas…an intense physical awareness is not a good basis for a marriage…'

'True, my clever little Lucille—' Seagrave's words

were barely above a whisper '—but it is intensely pleasurable, is it not?' He raised his head and looked down at her, his eyes brilliant with desire. 'I like to tease my cool, practical Miss Kellaway...' His mouth was doing precisely that, following the marauding hands that were sliding the lace edging of her bodice aside.

'Nicholas...' Lucille tried again, although she was finding it almost impossible to remember what she was trying to say. His thumb was skimming the tip of one breast whilst his tongue savoured the delicate curves he had uncovered.

'If I am not to take you here and now, I must let you go,' Seagrave was saying huskily, regretfully, his glance lingering on her flushed face and feverishly sparkling eyes. He gave her one last, deliciously leisurely kiss. 'But we shall be married very soon! On that you may depend!'

'Oh, Lady B., what am I to do!' Lucille put down her cup of chocolate and fixed her visitor with anxious blue eyes.

Lady Bellingham, awesome in puce velvet with matching turban, raised her eyebrows. 'Do? I do not immediately perceive your problem, my dear!' A humorous light entered her dark eyes. 'You are an heiress who is to be married to one of the County's most eligible bachelors in less than a sen'night! What could be more suitable? Why do you have to do anything?'

'I am wondering,' Lucille said slowly, 'whether I should cry off from the marriage!'

When Lady Bellingham's huge coach had lumbered through the gates of Dillingham Court that morning, Lucille had been both surprised and very glad. She had been intending to call at The House of Tides, but had never seemed to have a moment to herself from the time the engagement had been announced.

Good news had travelled fast. The morning after her passage of arms with Seagrave had taken place, the maid who brought Lucille's hot chocolate dropped a respectful curtsy and told her how pleased all the staff were that she was to be Lady Seagrave. Five minutes later, the Dowager Countess, in a dashing negligee of lace and gauze, had swept into the room and enfolded Lucille in her warm embrace.

'My love! I am so happy!' She had paused to look indulgently at her future daughter-in-law. 'I knew you were just right for Nicholas the moment I met you! Oh, this has all worked out so much better than I dared to hope!'

Hetty had been no less ecstatic. 'Now we shall be sisters twice over!' she had declared, hugging Lucille tightly.

Peter and Hetty were to be married the following spring in St George's Church, Hanover Square. Seagrave, however, had decreed that he had no intention of making a fashionable spectacle out of his wedding, and had declared that the service would take place in two weeks' time in the Dillingham village church. This announcement had thrown his mother into a frenzy of preparation. She had sent to London for her own dressmaker, and Lucille had then undergone what seemed to be endless fittings for her wedding dress and talk of nothing but trousseaux. And in less than a week…

Recalled to where she was, Lucille looked up to see Lady Bellingham watching her with the same humour still lurking in her gaze.

'A change of heart?' she mused. 'But what are the alternatives? A country cottage and a country companion? Or perhaps a home by the sea, with your books? And yet I could swear that you were in love with him!'

The words, delivered in the best tradition of melodrama, caused Lucille to start and look round nervously, but they were alone in the library.

'That is the problem,' she acknowledged baldly. 'I am in love with him—but he does not love me, Lady Bellingham!'

Lady Bellingham helped herself to another cup of chocolate from the silver pot, and took two of the bonbons which Lady Seagrave's housekeeper had thoughtfully provided.

'You are in the habit of thinking too much, Lucille,' she observed equably after she had munched her way through the sweets. 'You should, in common parlance, let nature take its course. Seagrave is much attracted to you—furthermore, he finds you interesting.' She wrinkled up her nose thoughtfully. 'On the day he escorted you to The House of Tides, I noticed that he scarcely took his eyes from you the whole time! Men can be notoriously foolish when it comes to discovering their feelings—I fear you will just have to give him time.'

'Will you come to the wedding?' Lucille asked eagerly.

Lady Bellingham's eyes twinkled. 'My child, I would not miss it for the world! To be Received and Recognised—' she rolled her 'Rs' impressively '—in the County! It is beyond my wildest dreams!'

Lucille viewed her with misgiving. 'Now, Lady B.,

you are not going to be naughty, are you? I doubt Mrs Ditton would be able to cope with it!'

Lady Bellingham opened her eyes to their widest extent. 'You may rely on me, my dear! But what a pity your sister cannot be present! Lord, I would give a monkey to see Mrs Ditton's face were the Cyprian to make an entrance!' She stood up and pulled on her gloves. 'I have it in mind to go travelling again,' she added. 'I leave next week. Mayhap I shall see your sister whilst I am abroad!' She presented her cheek to Lucille to kiss. 'I shall give her the new Countess of Seagrave's greetings!'

Lucille felt bereft as she watched the carriage roll away down the drive. Suddenly she could not bear the thought of dress fittings and interminable talk of weddings. She let herself out of the French windows and set off down the Green Walk towards the lake.

The thick tree canopy shaded her from the heat of the sun and the dappled grassy glades were filled with the scent of summer flowers.

A slight figure was sitting on the stone bench beside the lake. With surprise, Lucille recognised Polly Seagrave, her shoulders slumped beneath the gay parasol, one hand shading her eyes against the bright reflected light from the water. She turned at the sound of Lucille's approach and her melancholy expression lightened slightly into a smile.

'Have you escaped Mama's clutches, Lucille? It is too fine a day to be indoors, bridal fittings or no!'

She turned away slightly, but Lucille's observant gaze had already noticed the betraying tears drying on Polly's cheeks, the hastily concealed handkerchief that seemed suspiciously damp. Polly had seemed genuinely happy when told the news of Seagrave's betrothal to Lucille, but Lucille had wondered on more than one occasion whether all the talk of weddings was not putting a strain on her friend. Polly was even quieter and more withdrawn these days.

Lucille sat down beside her on the bench. 'If you would rather I went away, just tell me,' she offered. 'I know that sometimes, when one is miserable, it is far better to be left alone!'

Her words had the desired effect. Polly looked as though she was about to deny that she was in any way unhappy, then she took a deep breath.

'No, Lucille, please stay! The truth is…the truth is…' she hesitated, then went on in a rush, 'You will have heard that Lord Henry had returned to London? I keep telling myself that it must be for the best, but in my heart…' She burst into tears.

Lucille passed her a dry handkerchief and waited until Polly's sobs had subsided a little before giving her a hug.

'I thought that all this talk of weddings would be upsetting to you,' she said regretfully. 'Oh, Polly, I am so very sorry! Is there no chance—?'

But Polly was shaking her head. 'I think not. Yet now, after five years, I can no longer deny that I love him! If he asked me to run away with him now, I would not hesitate a moment! Yet of course, I know he will not!' She sighed despondently. 'Enough of this! I do not wish to dwell on it!'

She stood up and took Lucille's arm, saying with studied brightness, 'You must come and see the new greenhouses! Mama swears we shall soon be able to feed an army on our own produce! It was Nicholas's idea, you know—he has become a model landowner! I believe Mr Josselyn is quite overcome!' The brittle cheerfulness of her tone softened a little. 'Oh, Lucille, this is all your influence, you know!'

Then, as Lucille tried to demur, she insisted, 'No, indeed! It is on your account that Nicholas has stayed in Dillingham and found an interest in the estate. He has become much more the brother I remember!' She frowned. 'Oh, no! There is Mrs Hazeldine come to fetch us.' She gave an involuntary giggle. 'She looks very hot and bothered, rushing around in the full sun!'

In the light of Polly's genuine praise, Lucille thought a little wryly, her half-formed plan to run away from the wedding seemed rather ungracious. She allowed the housekeeper to catch them up and submitted obediently to dress fittings for the rest of the afternoon.

Chapter Twelve

The wedding was a great success and Dillingham Church was packed to the rafters. A proud Mrs Markham sat in the front row with Hetty on one side and her sister Mrs Pledgeley on the other, that matron puffed up out of all proportion at her tenuous connection with the nobility. Miss Pym was there, celebrating the occasion by forsaking her customary dress of black bombazine for one of grey instead, adorned with a string of pearls. Best of all was Lady Bellingham, magnificent in jet black taffeta and the most outrageous diamonds that the County had ever seen.

Mrs Ditton, already furious at the failure of her daughter to catch the Earl, seethed with envy and outraged respectability across the aisle. She had been silenced totally by the cordial way in which Lady Seagrave had greeted Lady Bellingham, and had only managed to murmur *sotto voce* to Mrs Elliott that she could not imagine what the County was coming to when an *actress* was thought fit to grace such an event.

The only absentee was Mrs Mutch, who had been so distraught at Walter's downfall that she had taken to her bed and not re-emerged. However, her second son, Ben, was there with his young family, and Lucille had made a point of speaking to him, to Mrs Ditton's further disapproval. Ben Mutch was a pleasant young man, with none of Walter's unsteadiness, and Lucille was sure that, given time, she might heal the breach with her father's family.

Lucille had been horribly nervous at the start of the day, but felt nothing but happiness all through the service and the long wedding breakfast which followed at the Court. Just the presence of Seagrave beside her, his attentiveness, the warm approval in his eyes, made her feel wonderfully cherished. At the back of her mind was the thought of the night that was to come, and a shiver of anticipation and awareness went through her as Seagrave's hand brushed against hers.

It was very late when all the guests left. Lady Seagrave escorted Lucille upstairs and helped her out of the beautiful embroidered dress of white satin and into one of the delicious filmy concoctions from her trousseau which passed as a nightdress. Lucille sat dreamily before the dressing-table whilst the maid brushed her hair, the nervous expectation just starting to stir within her. Lady Seagrave fussed about, picking items off the table and putting them down again, and finally dismissing the maid a little abruptly. She sat down on the end of the bed and fixed Lucille with her bright gaze.

'With no mother of your own to speak of such matters, Lucille, I feel that I should be the one to broach the subject of the intimate side of marriage—' Lady Seagrave broke off in annoyance as the maid slipped back into the room and whispered something in her ear. She frowned.

'Well, tell him that I shall be but a moment! Really—!'

The maid whispered something even more urgently, and Lady Seagrave sighed and stood up. She swooped on a bewildered Lucille and wrapped her in her scented embrace, kissing her soundly. 'You look beautiful, my love! I wish you very happy!'

It was only as her new mother-in-law's exit was followed immediately by her husband's entrance into the bedroom that Lucille realised why Lady Seagrave had left so rapidly. Clearly the Earl had been in a hurry to claim his new bride. Lucille was suddenly gripped by shyness as Seagrave's intent gaze swept over her, lingering on the diaphanous lines of the nightdress as they softly skimmed her body.

In the candlelight he looked more magnificent than ever. He had discarded his coat and his white linen shirt was open, revealing the strong, brown column of his neck. He strolled across the room with his customary easy grace, and leant one hand against the bedpost, still studying her. Lucille's tension grew, particularly as Seagrave had neither smiled nor spoken since he had entered the room, had done nothing but contemplate her with that inscrutable, lingering regard.

And then, at last, he spoke.

'You look…' The Earl hesitated and Lucille held her breath. Perhaps radiant, or lovely, was the word that he was looking for? But no…

'You look tired, my dear,' the Earl of Seagrave said to his new wife, with a chill courtesy that struck Lucille in the heart. 'I shall bid you goodnight.'

He kissed her forehead gently, passionlessly, and went out of the room.

* * *

At the end of the third week, Lucille acknowledged to herself that her new husband appeared to have no interest in consummating their marriage. She had no idea why his feelings for her appeared to have undergone so sudden a change. He had said that he needed her, wanted her, and yet it seemed that that was no longer so. At first Lucille had been perplexed; now she was beginning to feel hurt and angry.

During the day, they appeared to live their lives in charming harmony. They took breakfast together, then Seagrave would attend to estate business and Lucille would continue her instruction with Lady Seagrave on the art of running a great house. There were endless visits to be made about the estate and equally endless calls from their neighbours; they dined out or entertained at home; they were seldom alone.

Gradually the warm respect of the servants had given way to commiserating looks; conversations were broken off hastily as she entered the room. The visitors, with an ear for scandal, probed gently but implacably. And through it all, Seagrave was attentive but distant, as impossible to read as he had ever been.

At the start of the fourth week, when it became apparent to Lucille that she was to spend another night alone, she put her book to one side, and slipped out of the huge bed, pulling her lacy negligee on over the entrancing confection of lace and gauze that was her nightdress. Its transparent, silky lines mocked her. Evidently it took more than this to tempt the Earl of Seagrave. To tempt an Earl... For a moment she hesitated, her nerves almost persuading her back to bed— alone. Then she steeled herself and turned to the door.

The landing was deserted. At the bottom of the

stairs, the grandfather clock struck eleven-thirty with its melodious chime. It felt like a very long way across to the door of the Earl's bedroom. Lucille raised her hand and knocked softly on the panels. There was no sound. She knocked again, a little louder. A sound from downstairs made her start, and without conscious thought she turned the handle. The door was unlocked. And the bedroom was empty.

'I beg your pardon, madam.' It was Medlyn who was standing behind her, his face its usual impassive mask.

Lucille jumped and spun round. Under other circumstances she might have been embarrassed to be found thus, particularly considering the filmy nature of the nightgown, which Medlyn was studiously avoiding looking at too closely. Now, however, her anxiety over Seagrave's disappearance overrode all other concerns.

'The Earl, Medlyn—do you know where he is?'

She waited in an agony of doubt for the shadow to fall across his face, the shadow which would suggest that her husband had left her and gone up to London, or was gambling away his substance to avoid having to face his responsibilities, or, worse still, was in the arms of another woman…

Medlyn looked thoughtful, grave. 'His lordship went out about an hour ago, my lady,' he said, carefully expressionless. 'He did not say where he was going. However…' he hesitated '…I believe he may have gone to Cookes, ma'am. He has been there twice before in the last couple of weeks.'

'To Cookes?' Lucille was dumbstruck. 'But why? The house is closed.'

Medlyn was shaking his head. 'I do not know, ma'am. However…' again he hesitated, before putting considerable weight on his words '…if you were seeking him, ma'am, I believe that you would find him there.'

Their eyes met. 'Thank you, Medlyn,' Lucille said, slowly. 'I am persuaded that you are right.'

The butler nodded. The faintest suspicion of a smile seemed to touch his lips for so brief a moment that Lucille was sure she had imagined it. 'Good luck, my lady,' he said.

Lucille dressed swiftly and donned a warm cloak, before slipping down the stairs and out of the house. A light was still burning in the hall, but she saw no one, not even the man whom Medlyn had instructed to follow her and keep her safe. It was a clear night and she had no difficulty in following the track to Cookes, a journey which took her a mere twenty minutes. She was not afraid. The necessity of confronting Seagrave was the sole thought in her mind. She reached the village green with its slumbering cottages and paused, a little out of breath.

The front of Cookes was all in darkness. Holding her breath, Lucille tip-toed up the drive and around the side of the house. The drawing-room curtains were drawn, but a thread of light showed beneath them. She knew that the French door must be unlocked, for Walter Mutch had tampered with the latch when he had broken in and unless Seagrave had had it mended it would still be damaged.

Her heart was suddenly beating in her throat. She pushed the door open, and stepped into the room.

The Earl of Seagrave was sprawled in one of the faded velvet and brocade chairs before the fireplace. He had discarded his coat and loosened his cravat, and was staring into the fire, an empty brandy glass held carelessly in one hand. As Lucille closed the door behind her with a soft click, his gaze came up and fixed on her with unnerving intensity. With a slight shock she realised that he was not as drunk as she had at first imagined, although the half-empty brandy bottle at his elbow was testament to the fact that he was also nowhere near sober.

'What the devil are you doing here?' he demanded unceremoniously, the mellow voice much harsher than usual.

Lucille took off her cloak and folded it over the back of a chair, trying to ignore the shaking of her hands as she did so. This was going to be even more difficult than she had imagined. Sheer determination had brought her this far. She raised her chin. She was not going to let her courage desert her now.

'I came to find you, my lord,' she said, with far more calmness than she was feeling. 'I was somewhat…concerned to discover you from home.'

'Very wifely,' the Earl said coldly. 'Well, since you are here, my dear, you may as well join me in a drink to toast this hollow marriage of ours!'

Lucille began to feel angry. It was the only way to keep out the hurt that she knew would destroy her if she let her defences slip for one moment. She moved over to the table and poured Seagrave another glass of brandy—and a generous one for herself.

'A pity that you did not discover this aversion to my company before we were married rather than after, my lord,' she observed sweetly, as she sat down opposite him. 'Your timing is rather unfortunate.'

Her anger was growing now, warming her. She saw his eyes narrow on her and continued recklessly, 'Do you wish to be released from this marriage which you contracted so hurriedly? If so, you need only say the word!'

'Are you suggesting a divorce?' Seagrave asked, his tone so soft that Lucille could barely detect the thread of anger than ran through it. Her own rage was like a fire in her blood now, its effect as strong as a rush of adrenalin.

'I thought more in the way of an annulment,' Lucille waved her hand airily. 'It would be easy to prove, after all! And think of the speculation, my lord! Why, no one would know which were the greater piece of gossip—to suggest that the Countess of Seagrave was so unattractive that her husband found her repellent, or that the Earl was incapable of consummating his marriage!'

She swallowed half her brandy in one go. It was making her feel quite marvellously uninhibited. Seagrave's gaze was now a dark glitter focused on her unwaveringly. There was a tension in him that Lucille recognised, the tautness of a man who is barely holding himself under control. He said slowly, 'I understand that you are trying to provoke me, Lucille. Appearances may be to the contrary, but I am not a patient man. Take care that you do not push me too far!'

Lucille shrugged carelessly, although her frustration and the need to hurt him were consuming her. 'My words can have no power to move you, my lord, since you do not care for me. At least in *that* you have been honest! You never pretended to love me! But I would have settled for much less, for what you offered on the night you proposed to me! Now it seems you intend to deny me even that!' She downed the rest of her brandy with a gulp.

Seagrave's very stillness was terrifying. His face was inscrutable. 'It is not as you imagine, Lucille. You do not understand—'

'Oh, I understand very well!' Lucille's bitterness spilled over. 'It is simply that you regret what you have done!' She leant across for the brandy bottle. Seagrave moved it out of her grasp. Suddenly infuriated, she got up and reached across him, determined that in this small matter at least, she would have her way.

Seagrave's hand closed around her wrist. 'The only thing I regret,' he said very softly, 'is not doing this sooner.' He gave her arm a sharp tug. Lucille was caught off balance and the brandy, which had gone straight to her head, did the rest. She tumbled on to his knee.

'And now, my Lady Seagrave,' the Earl said, through his teeth, 'you will be able to judge for yourself whether your husband is incapable of consummating his marriage!'

Despite his anger, it soon became apparent that the Earl of Seagrave was in no hurry. The kiss was long, insistent and utterly inescapable. Lucille was immediately assailed by the same treacherous weakness that always invaded her senses when he touched her. She gave a little sigh deep in her throat, the telltale sign of her pleasure. Instantly, the fierce sweetness of the kiss intensified. Seagrave entwined one hand in the cloud of silver hair, holding her face upturned to his so that he could plunder her mouth at will. Still kissing her, he stood up, holding her in his arms. Lucille tore her mouth away from his with an effort.

'What—'

'Hush.' He silenced her again. The searing passion washed through Lucille in a tide that left her trembling. This time when he raised his head she did not speak, simply resting her cheek against his broad shoulder as he carried her out of the drawing-room and up the stairs into her own bedroom. Her eyes were closed, waiting for the onslaught on her senses to begin again, wanting nothing but to touch him, taste him, explore the sensations which she still only half-understood. Seagrave kicked the bedroom door shut behind them.

The curtains were not drawn, but neither of them paid any attention. Seagrave tossed her down into the middle of the big bed and was beside her before Lucille had time to draw breath. His mouth reclaimed hers immediately, but Lucille was aware that his fingers were busy with the buttons at the back of her dress, skilfully unfastening it to slide it off her shoulders and down to her waist. When he realised that she was wearing no chemise beneath, wearing nothing beneath, Seagrave paused, a slow smile curving his lips.

'Well, Lucille, whatever were you about to forget to dress properly?'

'I was in a hurry,' Lucille whispered, and saw his smile deepen as he lowered his head to her exposed breasts.

Lucille arched upwards against the demand of his lips and fingers. She tugged hard at his shirt and felt it come loose, sliding her hands beneath the linen and gasping as she touched his naked skin for the first time. Her quick, indrawn breath was smothered against his lips.

Seagrave drew away a little to pull off his boots and

toss them with an impatient hand into a corner of the room. He discarded the rest of his clothes in a couple of quick movements before rejoining her on the bed. Lucille watched the silver moonlight slide over his muscular physique and reached out to pull him down beside her. She ran her hands over his chest, spellbound by the texture of his skin, wanting to feel it against her own. Her fingers drifted lower, over his stomach and across his ribs, and he groaned, pulling her against him.

Lucille had never seen a naked man before and the classical statues she had seen in pictures, whilst beautiful, were in no way as compelling as the real thing. Her exploring hands stilled as coherent thought returned for the first time in a long while. Her reading and observation of real life had given her an understanding of how animals mated, but as to how that would apply to her—

'Nicholas…' There was a thread of anxiety now in her whispered words.

Seagrave heard it and was quick to reassure her. 'Trust me.' His voice was soft. 'It will be all right. You will see…'

He was still stroking her skin and the gentle touch was both relaxing and at the same time oddly exciting. Lucille felt her worries slip to the edge of her mind as pleasure began to cloud her thoughts again. Her skirt was tiresomely in the way, she thought crossly, and she was grateful as she felt Seagrave easing it over her hips to fall, an empty shell, on the floor. She felt his hand run the whole length of her near-naked body and opened her eyes. Seagrave was looking at her, her silver hair spread across the pillows, her slender body illuminated in the sharp moonlight. His narrowed, concentrated gaze only served to excite Lucille further.

'Silk stockings?' he said musingly, a hint of amusement detectable in his voice. 'That was the only piece of underwear you stopped long enough to put on?' His hand was stroking her silken thigh, slowly, tantalisingly, and its touch was deliciously stimulating. Lucille remembered vaguely that the stockings, part of her trousseau, had been nearest to hand as she had dressed and before her haste to find him had overcome her. She tried to form the words to explain to Seagrave, but he was already kissing her again. Anyway, he did not seem to mind, Lucille thought hazily, for he had not taken them off. As his hands lingered on her thighs a feeling of unbearable anticipation was growing in her, warming the pit of her stomach, demanding satisfaction. She felt his fingers part her legs, still stroking persuasively, urgently. Lucille dug her fingernails into his shoulders.

'Nicholas, please…'

She did not know exactly what she was asking, but he did. He slid into her, hard and deep, and Lucille's instinctive gasp of pain was lost as he moved inside her, replacing pain with pleasure, such unimaginable pleasure that she cried out as the inexorable tide of sensation tumbled over and through her. She was dimly aware of Seagrave gasping her name as the same hot, sweet tide took hold of him almost immediately.

It was a long time before the ripples of that pleasure died away, and Seagrave rolled over, pulled Lucille into the crook of his arm and wrapped the blankets firmly around them. She felt wonderfully warm and secure there, her head resting against his shoulder, watching the taut lines of his face relax into sleep. Her own eyelids grew heavy. Soon she too was asleep.

When Lucille awoke again the moon had moved round and the room was in near darkness. It was still night outside and she could hear the wind in the trees. She propped herself on one elbow to look down at her husband. He looked boyish in sleep, the thick dark lashes resting against the hard line of his cheek and the tousled dark hair falling across his brow. Lucille was swept by an intensely strong, protective love. She also felt rather pleased with herself and was half-ashamed to be so brazen.

Seagrave might not love her, but she had made him consummate the marriage in an entirely satisfactory manner. Her body ached pleasantly with the aftermath of an unfamiliar pleasure and a little smile curved her lips. It was then that she realised that Seagrave was awake and watching her. In one swift movement he had pulled her beneath him.

'That was a very self-satisfied smile I saw just now,' he said huskily. 'No doubt you are pleased with yourself, madam?'

Lucille's eyes widened. She was unable to gauge his mood and her heart began to race with a mixture of genuine nerves and anticipation. What if he was angry with her for provoking him and pushing him too far? He might have genuinely intended an annulment. She stared up at him. If he repudiated her now, she did not think she could bear it...

Seagrave's gaze shifted from her face to her bare shoulders, and Lucille suddenly became acutely aware of her nakedness. Worse, she became aware of his nakedness, of his body poised above hers. That strange but delightful ache was invading her body again, making her want to offer herself shamelessly to him again. She frowned. How very odd to discover such wayward impulses that she had never before suspected… She was just debating with herself whether a study of genetics would be instructive, when Seagrave's mouth took hers roughly at the same time as his hand came up to her breast. Lucille gasped with shock.

'This is no time to be thinking scientifically, my demanding little wife.' Seagrave had read her thoughts. His voice was soft, but with a mocking undertone. 'I understood you to have found me lacking in my husbandly duty. Allow me to make up for lost time!'

Lucille's eyes widened still further. 'Nicholas, again? But…' Once again she lost her train of thought as his mouth plundered the softness of hers.

'Yes, again,' Seagrave confirmed with a grin. 'You will find that I can also be a demanding husband!'

It was quite different from the first time, less gentle but no less exciting. The relentless rhythm of their bodies was building now, pushing them both over the edge once more and leaving them exhausted with pure pleasure, to doze, wake in the dawn, love again and finally fall into a fulfilled and dreamless sleep.

It was very late when Lucille finally awoke. The room was filled with daylight and she was alone. She lay still for a moment, wondering whether she had dreamed the whole of the previous night, but the tumbled bedclothes and the indentation in the pillow where Seagrave's head had lain suggested that it had been real. So did the faint marks on her body, the unaccustomed but wholly pleasing differences she felt in herself. The colour rose to her cheeks as she remembered all that had happened.

How innocent she had been, and how he had delighted in instructing her, promising that this was only the start... Lucille frowned. But where was Seagrave now? Surely he could not just have left her... Even as the first doubts began to infiltrate her mind, she heard a sound downstairs and, wrapping the sheet tightly around her, hurried down to see if he was there.

The scene which met Lucille's startled gaze was a chaotic one. The entrance hall was full of empty packing cases, and from the dining-room came the rustle of paper and the chink of china and glass. Lucille pushed the door wider and walked in.

Susanna was standing at the table, a frown marring her brow as she tried to wrap a pair of outlandish china figures, whose outstretched arms were defying the tissue paper. She looked up crossly as Lucille came in.

'So there you are!' she said, peevishly. 'Where is Mrs Appleton? I need her to help me wrap these pieces. How am I to take it all away with me if I have to do it all myself?'

Her petulant blue gaze took in the hastily wrapped sheet and Lucille's sleep-filled eyes and tumbled fair hair. 'Well, upon my word! Country living must have wrought some strange changes in you! It is high noon! Whatever can you have been doing?'

As if in answer to that precise question, there was the sound of the front door closing and the Earl of Seagrave strolled into the room. He was dressed casually in breeches and a linen shirt. In one hand was a can of milk and in the other a loaf of bread and a pat of butter. His dark brows rose as he saw the two sisters, Lucille in her sheet and Susanna in plunging emerald silk.

Susanna's face was a picture. 'Lucille! Seagrave! What—! Surely—!'

Seagrave, a wicked grin on his face, put the food down carefully and crossed to Lucille's side, sliding his arm around her waist and pulling her intimately close.

'You look entirely delightful, my darling,' he said softly, his breath stirring her hair. 'I hoped to be back before you awoke.' He dropped a kiss on her bare shoulder. 'How I look forward to exploring again what is hidden beneath that sheet...' He straightened up.

'Your servant, Lady Bolt,' he said easily. 'Congratulations on your recent marriage. Is Sir Edwin with you, or in London?' His gaze took in the packing boxes and the serried ranks of glass and china. 'I take it you are removing from Cookes? Do not trouble to pack for yourself—my agent will arrange to have all the items you wish transported to your new home, or pay you for those you wish to leave behind. I have a new tenant for Cookes, but no doubt Josselyn and your man of business can sort matters to your satisfaction.'

Susanna's avid gaze was travelling from one to the other. There was only one matter that interested her at the moment, and for once it was not money. 'Seagrave, surely you have not seduced my sister!'

'On the contrary,' Seagrave said smoothly, 'she seduced me! You must have more in common than might immediately be apparent!'

Lucille was scarlet. 'Nicholas...' she said, beseechingly.

Seagrave relented. He took her hand. 'You may

wish us happy, Lady Bolt,' he said softly. 'Your sister became my wife a month ago.'

'Your wife! A Countess!' Susanna's face was working like milk coming to the boil. 'Lucille, you sly minx! To think that I leave you here to impersonate me and return to find you married to Seagrave! Of all the conniving starts! Why, it could have been me—' She broke off at Seagrave's look of amused disbelief. 'Well,' she said grudgingly, getting a grip on herself, 'I suppose I must wish you happy! And—' she was recovering herself fast and gave Seagrave a flirtatious look '—I must beg your lordship's indulgence for the masquerade! I hope you will forgive me!'

There was a silence. Seagrave looked thoughtful. 'I believe I owe you my thanks, Lady Bolt,' he said coolly, at length. 'Had it not been for your idea to change places with Lucille, I should never have met her. And now…' his warm gaze dwelled on his wife and he smiled gently '…I discover that I love her with all my heart.'

Lucille caught her breath as their eyes met. There was such a deep tenderness in those brown eyes that she felt quite dizzy. 'I am so very fortunate,' he said, softly, 'to have found out how much I love you, Lucille, and I think you love me too, do you not?'

'Lud, how affecting,' Susanna drawled. They had both temporarily forgotten that she was there. She picked up her gloves. 'There is nothing so tiresomely unfashionable as a husband and wife in love with each other,' she continued. 'I will leave the two of you to bill and coo! You may find me at the Hope and Anchor in Woodbridge when your agent wishes to talk terms!'

She swept out and slammed the door behind her.

There was a silence, then Seagrave sat down, pulling Lucille onto his lap. 'When we first married, I had truly not realised the depth of my feelings for you, Lucille,' he said quietly. 'On our wedding night, the truth hit me with such a blinding flash that I think I was in shock with it. I did not know what to do or what to think. Suddenly all the feelings and emotions that had deserted me years ago returned with such intensity that I could not believe it. You had the most terrifying power over me, for I knew that to lose you would be my undoing. And whilst I tried to come to terms with that fact, I almost did lose you in the process!'

Lucille snuggled closer, turning her face into his neck. 'I am so very glad,' she said, muffled, 'for I love you so much I do not think I could bear it if you did not care for me!'

There was a contented silence whilst they just held each other, then Lucille said, 'What did you mean when you told Susanna that you had a new tenant for Cookes?'

Seagrave smiled. 'Ben Mutch, Walter's younger brother, has petitioned to take over the house. I think he will make an admirable tenant and I hope it will go some way to healing the breach with Mrs Mutch caused by Walter's misdeeds.'

Lucille kissed him. 'And now Susanna will exact a high price for removing herself from Cookes—she will fleece you!'

Seagrave pulled her closer. 'This time,' he said, with a smile, 'it is a price I am willing to pay!' He had found the end of the sheet now and was starting to unwrap it with single-minded concentration, raining little kisses over her bare shoulders. Lucille pushed him away.

'Really, Nicholas! When you had gone to all that trouble to fetch some food! Can we not have something to eat first?'

Seagrave paused, appearing to give the matter his consideration. 'In a little while, perhaps. First…'

Susanna Kellaway, returning a minute later to collect the reticule she had accidentally left behind, and to surreptitiously pick up a rather attractive silver watch chain she had earmarked to pay the landlord of the Hope and Anchor, found them equally entwined in the sheet and in each other's arms, oblivious to interruption.

'Disgusting!' she said, to her waiting coachman, as she closed the door of Cookes and hurried out to her carriage. 'There is nothing so odious to a Cyprian as a husband who prefers his own wife!'

*   *   *   *   *

THE UNCONVENTIONAL
MISS DANE
by
Francesca Shaw

Francesca Shaw is not one, but two authors, working together under the same name. Both are librarians by profession, working in Hertfordshire, and living within easy distance of each other in Bedfordshire. They first began writing under a tree in a Burgundian vineyard, but although they have published other romances, they have only come to writing historical novels in the last ten years. Their shared interests include travel, good food, reading and, of course, writing.

Also by Francesca Shaw
in Mills & Boon Historical Romance™

A SCANDALOUS LADY

Look for

THE REBELLIOUS BRIDE

Coming January 2003

Chapter One

The stagecoach lurched, then with infinite slowness toppled on to its right-hand side, precipitating Miss Antonia Dane into the lap of the portly bank clerk next to her. Wildly clutching at his lapels only served to take both of them on to the floor of the coach, where they were shortly joined by a curate, a basket of apples and a small child who promptly set up a piercing wail.

"Donna!" Antonia looked round anxiously for her companion as she attempted to lever herself upright from the mass of tumbled humanity. "Oh, I do beg your pardon, sir," she apologised, removing her elbow from the clerk's midriff. "Donna, there you are! Are you unhurt?"

"A little shaken, my dear, but otherwise unhurt, I believe." Miss Maria Donaldson came into Antonia's view over the heap of bodies, patting her neatly coiled hair into place, her pince-nez already firmly back in position on the tip of her nose. "But I think we should alight as soon as may be." She turned to the red-faced farmer wedged next to her. "If you could force open the door, sir, I believe I could climb through."

After considerable upheavals, the farmer managed to

assist Donna's slight frame through the door and on to
the sloping side of the coach. Sensing escape, the small
child set up a fresh wail and to Antonia's relief was
handed up to his mother who followed Miss Donaldson
into the spring sunshine.

It was a shaken but unhurt group of passengers who
eventually assembled on the rutted road to view the
wreck of their conveyance. The driver and guard un-
hitched and calmed the horses, but further useful activity
then seemed beyond them. The driver removed a filthy
hat the better to scratch his equally dirty hair, the guard
helpfully kicked the nearest wheel and the men amongst
the passengers stood around sucking their teeth in contemplation of the depth of the ditch into which the coach
had fallen.

"Really, my dear Antonia," Miss Donaldson murmured gently. "I have never been able to understand
why men feel that giving something a sharp kick will
restore it to working order."

Antonia's lips quirked in amusement. "It never
works, but I think it must make them feel better. Come,
let us see if our luggage is still safely strapped on behind."

"Your elbow has come through the sleeve of your
gown," Miss Donaldson observed as they turned from
their scrutiny of the large luggage basket at the rear of
the stagecoach. "Is your pelisse still in the coach?"

"It must be," Antonia responded indifferently, her
fingers twitching together the hole in the threadbare linen
sleeve. "It proves I was right to wear this old gown for
the journey—I have too few good dresses to damage like
this."

She set her straw bonnet straight on her head, tucking
in a straggling brown curl and retying the ribbons under

her chin. "I think we will achieve little by waiting here until the coachman finally realises he must send for help. The last fingerpost said Rybury was only three miles; if we take our pelisses and handbags from the coach, we can walk and at least wait for our luggage in comfort at the inn."

The curate, who was more than happy to assist the ladies, was just handing out their things from inside the coach when, with a thud of hooves on the wet chalk, two horsemen rounded the bend and reined in at the sight of the shambles in their path.

"My lord!" exclaimed the curate with delighted recognition of the man who sat astride the tall chestnut gelding. "This is Providence indeed, if you would be so kind as to instruct your groom to get help to right the coach."

The nobleman thus addressed dismounted, tossing his reins to his groom before striding over to regard the wreck. "Has anyone been hurt, Mr Todd?" he enquired of the curate, his glance keenly surveying the ill-assorted group of passengers.

Antonia encountered the brief scrutiny of a pair of dark brown eyes before they moved on to as swiftly peruse and dismiss the small birdlike figure of her companion. She found herself colouring, with what had to be indignation, at such a cursory survey. For although shabbily dressed, and undoubtedly not at her best after a long coach journey, Miss Antonia Dane with her tall figure and striking dark looks was accustomed to attracting more attention than this man had afforded her!

Her eyes followed the tall, carelessly elegant figure as he stood, hands on hips, regarding the stage coach and the ditch. Bareheaded, the light breeze ruffled his dark blond hair which was, Miss Dane decided, in sore need of his barber's attention. He might appear careless of his dress, but cut and cloth were of the finest and the burnished leather of his long boots spoke of a man who need not, unlike Miss Dane, watch every penny.

Mr Todd the curate trailed after him, explaining to his lordship the circumstances of the accident and the fortunate fact that no one had been injured. The groom nudged his own hack forward. "Shall I ride to the village for help, my lord?"

"No need, Saye. We passed Shoebridge and Otterly hedging the Long Meadow back around the bend; fetch them and we will have enough men to right the thing."

As the groom cantered off, his lordship turned to the coachman and guard who shuffled to attention, recognising authority when they saw it. "You—hitch the horses up on long traces, and you two, fetch cut poles from that pile there…"

Antonia watched him take command, organising and ordering until the male passengers were marshalled into an obedient team, some levering up the wheel, others with their shoulders to the rear of the vehicle. With the addition of two sturdy hedgers and with Saye at the horses' heads, the stranded coach began to teeter upright, then stuck again in the soft soil of the bank top.

"I fear we cannot do it, Lord Allington," Mr Todd gasped, his clerical black besmirched by mud. "We must summon more help from the village."

Without reply, his lordship stripped off his buff coat, rolled up his sleeves, and applied his shoulder to the coach. Thus encouraged, the men exerted themselves to the utmost and heaved. Seconds later, with a shuddering crash, the vehicle once more stood on four wheels.

The coachman and groom rehitched the team, the grateful passengers picked up their luggage and began to climb aboard and Lord Allington, fending off the flustered attempts of the curate to brush down his coat, remounted and rode off.

"How very gratifying," Miss Dane remarked waspishly, pausing on the step of the coach to regard Lord Allington's retreating back, "to have the leisure to ride round the countryside setting we lesser mortals to rights."

Miss Donaldson cast a sideways glance at her former pupil, noting the pinkness of her cheeks and the brightness of her dark hazel eyes. Antonia always exhibited an independence of spirit, more to be expected of a fashionable matron than an unmarried lady of four-and-twenty, but even so, Lord Allington seemed to have ruffled her out of her habitual well-bred composure.

"He is a local gentleman, by all accounts," Miss Donaldson observed calmly. "And even you must concede, Miss Dane, that it was fortunate that he had the leisure to rescue us today."

Mr Todd, catching the reference to their rescuer as he handed her into the coach, added, "That was Marcus, Lord Allington, from Brightshill. He is of an old Hertfordshire family and owns all the land on this side of Berkhamsted to the crest of the Downs."

Antonia settled in her place before remarking, with a deceptively gentle smile, "Not quite all, Mr Todd. You forget, do you not, the Rye End Hall lands?"

"One hardly regards those any longer," the curate responded dismissively. "The lands and Hall are sadly neglected, as one might expect after the scandalous behaviour of the last owner—but I shall say no more of that in front of ladies. It will be a good thing if the rumours are correct and Lord Allington does intend to add them all to his own extensive estate. They will then be subject to the good husbandry which characterises the Brightshill lands—and the tenants will be employed. There is too much want in Rybury.''

Antonia opened her mouth as if to speak, then closed it, staring out of the window with furrowed brow. Miss Donaldson, seeing the look of worry, said low-voiced, ''Did you never meet Marcus Allington when you still lived at Rye End Hall?''

''You forget, Donna, in the ten years since I left home to live with Great Aunt in London, I have never been back to Rye End Hall. It must have been this man's father who was at Brightshill when I was a child, and he would have been away at school and university, I suppose. I would not know if my father or brother knew them well.''

Miss Donaldson reflected that, from what she had heard of the late and unlamented Sir Humphrey Dane, normal social intercourse with his neighbours would not have figured large either for himself, or for Antonia's late brother Howard.

The coach was finally rumbling into Rybury and pulling up before the only inn the village boasted. The host of the Bell walked out to greet the passengers, all of whom were only too pleased at the chance to sit in comfort and drink his ale while exclaiming loudly over their recent misadventure.

The coachman and guard lifted down the ladies' luggage and Antonia and Donna stood looking round. Rybury, neat rather than picturesque, looked at its best in the spring sunshine with primroses on the green and children fishing for tiddlers in the Rye Brook. The pike road cut across the green and a by-road led over a bridge to a straggle of cottages, on the edge of a fine stand of woodland already touched with new green.

"Would you ladies be requiring the use of a cart?" the landlord enquired, wiping his hands on his apron as he approached.

"Yes, thank you, landlord. We will need these trunks taking to Rye End Hall; is there a carter who can help?"

"Our Jem can do that for you, ma'am, just as soon as he's finished serving the coach passengers. It's a nice clean cart for you ladies, better than that old thing." He nodded towards the stagecoach. "Would you care to step into the private parlour and take some refreshment while you wait, ma'am?"

As he ushered them into a rather dingy front room, he chatted on. "Going to be staying at the Hall, then? That's been empty this last six months since Sir Humphrey and Master Howard were both carried off within a fortnight of each other." He shook his head. "Sometimes I wonder if it weren't a judgement on them both and the wicked life they led…"

Miss Donaldson cleared her throat reprovingly and he darted a quick glance at her frosty profile. "Begging your pardon, ladies, you did know what had occurred…?"

"Sir Humphrey was my father, Mr Howard Dane was my only brother," Antonia supplied quietly.

"Oh…ah! Sorry, ma'am, if I've spoken out of turn. The coach is just leaving now, I'll get young Jem out directly." He hurried away, clearly realising he had overstepped the mark.

"I can see the local people held my father and brother in as high regard as we, Donna," Antonia remarked bitterly, pacing up and down the rather lurid Turkey rug before the fire. "The lord knows what we will find when we finally get to Rye End Hall!"

Young Jem, a skinny version of his father the landlord, soon appeared with the cart, drawn by a neat cob, and set to loading the baggage and trunks before fetching his passengers.

Miss Donaldson, regarding the narrow seat, began to climb into the back, saying, "I can sit here on the trunk, my dear."

"I shall not hear of it Donna!" Antonia protested. "You sit up here in the front with Jem—I will walk through the woods. I have a headache coming on, and it is less than a mile by the footpath," she added as Donna still looked unsure.

She followed the cart across the green and past the cottages, pleased to find, after a few yards, the beginning of the footpath she remembered. As she picked up the hem of her skirts and hopped over the frequent muddy patches in her stout boots, Antonia reflected that it must be a full ten years since she had last trodden this path.

Then her mother had just died and her father had not yet embarked on the course of drinking, gambling and philandering which had ruined the family fortunes and corrupted her brother. As soon as rumours of his conduct began to reach polite Society, her great aunt, Lady Honoria Granger, had descended and borne her off to Town. Honoria had expected some opposition from her niece's husband, but Sir Humphrey had been only too pleased to be spared the trouble of bringing up a daughter.

It had been fortunate that Lady Honoria had been left well provided for by her late husband and had been able to afford to educate and then bring out Antonia, for Sir Humphrey, with the girl off his hands, had shown every sign of forgetting he had ever had a daughter.

Antonia stopped every now and again to pick primroses, feeling more at ease now she was out of that wretched public conveyance. How right she had been to wear her old gown, she thought, seeing the chalky mud spatters around the hem.

Whilst she had lived with her great aunt, she had wanted for nothing, but when the old lady had finally succumbed to increasing old age and had gone to live under her grandson's roof, her cousin, mindful of his own inheritance, had wasted no time in pointing out to Antonia that she could expect no more support from that quarter.

Antonia had been under the misapprehension that she had been living on income from her mother's legacy to her, but Cousin Hewitt had soon, and with smug satisfaction, put her right. Not only would she now have to manage without great aunt Honoria's beneficence, but Hewitt Granger had also made it pretty plain that she and her companion, Miss Donaldson, must find alternative accommodation.

Slowly following the winding path, Antonia found herself in a clearing full of sunlight. Shedding her bonnet and pelisse, she perched on a fallen tree and held her face up to the warmth, grateful to be in the clear air and out of London.

In the midst of the upheavals of her aunt's infirmity and removal, the death in a driving accident of a brother who had been almost unknown to her and the sudden demise of her father from an apoplexy a mere two weeks afterwards had passed as though they had been no concern of hers. The family solicitor had dealt with everything. After a precarious half-year in lodgings whilst the lawyer sold all he could find to settle Sir Humphrey's debts, Antonia had finally received word that only the house and land remained.

She was just reflecting, and not for the first time, on how fortunate she was that Donna, her old governess, had offered to accompany her to Rye End Hall, when she heard a boy's voice raised in a yelp of pain. Heedless of her discarded bonnet and cloak, Antonia ran across the clearing, pushed through a straggle of branches and found herself in the company of two urchins, neither of them a day over ten years of age.

One, a wiry redhead, was disentangling himself from the bramble bush into which he had tripped. His companion, an even grubbier child, was holding by the feet four limp-necked, and very dead, cock pheasants.

There was a long moment while the children stared at her, round-eyed with terror, then, as she took a step towards them, they dropped the birds and took to their heels.

Well! The local poachers certainly started young hereabouts, Antonia thought, stooping to pick up the still-warm pheasants. No doubt they were encouraged by a lack of keepering, for in the depths of debt Sir Humphrey had discharged all his servants but for a slatternly housekeeper. Still, the birds were hers, snared on her own land, and they would at least serve as supper tonight!

"Caught red-handed!" a triumphant, rough voice said behind her. Antonia spun round to find two burly individuals in decent homespuns, shotguns under their arms and a couple of terriers at their heels, confronting her. "Did you ever see the like, Nat? A female poacher, as I live and breathe. You give us those birds, my pretty, and come along of us quiet-like."

Antonia opened her mouth to protest that she had just

picked up the birds; then the thought of those two skinny, frightened children, and what would happen to them if these men caught them, kept her silent.

The two keepers advanced towards her, one taking the birds from her limp grasp, the other seizing her roughly by the arm, tearing the old gown even more. Shocked by the contact, Antonia gasped and pulled away.

"Let me go!" she demanded breathlessly.

"Let you go? Oh dear, no! After we've caught you on his lordship's land, with his lordship's pheasants?" He grinned, exposing stained teeth. "It's your lucky day, my pretty, you won't have to cool your heels in the village lock-up. Oh, no, his lordship's at home, and him being a Justice of the Peace, he likes to see a poacher whenever we catch one. And he'll like to see this one, won't he, Nat?"

Both men eyed Antonia slyly. She was suddenly very aware that she was without bonnet or pelisse, that her old linen gown clung around her limbs and she was quite unchaperoned.

Who could they mean by "his lordship"? This was Rye End Hall land—her land—but the humiliation of arguing about her identity with these two was more than she could countenance. No, better to go along with it and get out of this wood as quickly as possible. Whoever this magistrate was, at least he would be a gentleman and she could make her explanations to him in decent privacy.

The keeper's fingers were moving suggestively on her bare skin through the tear in her gown. Antonia turned such a look of glacial fury on him that he let go of her elbow, then, recalling himself, seized her painfully by the wrist instead.

The walk back through the woods was mercifully

short, but by the time they reached the stable block of a big house she did not recognise Antonia was flushed and breathless, her hair tumbling about her face and her skirts torn and bedraggled.

Her captors marched her through the servants' quarters, up the backstairs, through a green baize door and into a hallway that seemed vaguely familiar to Antonia. The butler, alerted by the commotion, emerged from the dining room to hear the gamekeeper's explanations. He looked her up and down with utter disdain, before departing to inform his master of the arrival of a felon for his attention.

Antonia stood, inwardly shuddering with mortification, forcing herself not to struggle and thus appear even more undignified and unladylike than she already must. After all, when in the presence of this gentleman, she could explain the circumstances of this unfortunate incident. And what was more, she fumed, she expected an apology for the behaviour of his keepers for their overzealousness in straying onto her land and their insulting familiarity with her person!

When the butler finally reappeared to usher them in, she straightened her back, raised her chin and stalked with as much hauteur as she could manage in the circumstances, into the study.

The magistrate into whose presence she had been hauled was sitting behind a wide mahogany desk, his fingers drumming impatiently on the leather surface beside a pile of papers which had been pushed to one side.

Antonia stared in horrified recognition at the man she had seen only hours before. Lord Allington, for it was indeed he, returned her stare without the slightest sign he had ever set eyes on her before.

Raising one tawny brow, he remarked, "Well done,

Sparrow: you have enlivened what was proving to. be a thoroughly dull day. I was hoping for a diversion from this tedious correspondence—'' his long fingers flicked the pile of papers dismissively ''—but a female poacher is more than I could have looked for. Thank you, Sparrow, you and Carling may go.''

''What, and just leave her, my lord?'' The senior gamekeeper was surprised.

''Well, I hardly feel she is likely to prove more than I can handle; or do you think she has a dangerous weapon concealed somewhere?'' The dark brown eyes were warm as he surveyed the clinging, bedraggled gown that did nothing to hide the form beneath. Antonia flushed angrily, but gritted her teeth, determined not to bandy words with him in front of the keepers.

With barely concealed reluctance the two men shuffled out, closing the door behind them. Antonia put up a hand to push the hair off her face and realised she had succeeded in spreading dirt, and what felt horribly like pheasant's blood, all over her forehead.

Marcus Allington got up and came round the desk to look at her more closely. ''You are certainly a novelty, my dear, and a considerable improvement on the usual crew who plunder my birds. At least, if you were cleaned up, you might be...'' He continued to stroll round her.

Antonia felt the blood burning up her throat and cheeks at the insolence of the scrutiny.

''Now, what shall we do with you, I wonder?'' He came back round to face her. ''I suppose you realise I could sentence you to hard labour for this—your fingers would not be so ready for setting snares after that.''

He lifted Antonia's right hand, turning it over caressingly between strong fingers whilst holding her furious gaze with his eyes. Even in the midst of her anger, she saw the sudden surprise as his touch registered the soft skin where he had expected work-hardened roughness.

Seizing her advantage, Antonia snatched her hand away and, in a swirl of muddy skirts, put a heavy chair between herself and Lord Allington.

"You are no village wench, not with hands like that! So…who the devil are you? And what are you doing with my birds?" he demanded, voice suddenly hard.

Antonia found her tongue at last, and spoke with all the hauteur at her command. "A lady, sir, and one who does not relish being manhandled by either you or your men."

"Damn it, woman, do you expect me to believe that? Look at yourself!" His scornful stare swept from the top of her disordered hair to her boots emerging from beneath her muddy hem.

"Kindly mind your language, my lord," Antonia said frostily, sinking on to the chair with as much grace as if she were at Almack's, and not in danger of having her knees give way beneath her.

Marcus Allington sketched her an ironic bow before leaning indolently against the edge of the desk. "My humble apologies, madam. I should have realised, from the moment I set eyes upon you, that I was dealing with a member of the Quality."

Flushing, Antonia looked down at herself. Mud-caked walking boots were all too obvious below a torn and besmirched hemline. Her old and faded gown was ripped, there were bloodstains where the birds had touched the skirts and her elbow protruded through the hopelessly threadbare sleeve. Without her bonnet, her dark brown curls, always hard to manage, now cascaded about her shoulders and she could feel her face was filthy.

She glared at him, resenting his easy elegance, even in the riding apparel he still wore. Marcus Allington's broad shoulders and long, muscular legs were set off to perfection by the country clothes... Antonia recollected herself, annoyed at the spark of attraction she had felt for an instant.

"If I present a disordered appearance, it is no wonder," she retorted sharply. "Having been set upon, dragged through the mire and brambles—is it any wonder? And," she pursued, before he had a chance to reply, "all I was doing was walking in the woods."

"Trespassing on my land, in possession of my game." His voice was flat, his face hard. "I expect my keepers to earn their wages. Madam," he added sarcastically.

"Your land? I hardly think so, my lord. Those woods are Rye End Hall land."

"Not for these past five years." He regarded her with sudden interest. "What do you know of Rye End Hall?"

"I own it," Antonia informed him coldly. With an effort she tried to hide her dismay at the discovery that her father had sold off land. How much more had gone without her knowing? It had never occurred to her to scrutinise the estate maps when the solicitor had handed them back to her: she knew the extent of Rye End Hall lands too well. If Sir Humphrey had sold off woods so close to the house, what else might have gone?

"You appear surprised, madam?" It was a question, but his voice held more sympathy than previously. "Surely you have not been sold short in your purchase of Rye End Hall?"

"I have not purchased it, my lord; it came to me on the death of my father."

"Your father?" Now it was Marcus Allington's turn

to be taken aback. "You cannot be Sir Humphrey Dane's daughter!"

"And why not?" Antonia's chin came up defiantly. Whatever her father and her brother had become, the Danes were an old and proud family, and all her instincts and her great aunt's training were evident in her bearing now.

Despite her ludicrous appearance, Marcus could not now doubt she was telling the truth. The more he looked at her, the more he saw a family resemblance. He remembered her grandfather, white-haired and patrician, visiting his own grandparents; how as a young boy he had been overawed by the bearing he now saw traces of in this woman.

"You have to admit, Miss Dane, that your appearance, and the circumstances in which we meet, are much against you." He straightened, crossing to the bellpull beside the fireplace. "Let me order you some refreshment, and then you must tell me how I may help you."

Antonia realised just how hungry she was: they had set forth from the Golden Fleece in Holborn before dawn and a hastily snatched meal of bacon and bread at Abbots Langley was hours in the past.

The footman was hard put to disguise his amazement at being sent for sherry and biscuits for the female who had just been dragged through the servants' quarters as a common criminal.

She fell to hungrily when the refreshment arrived, then recollected herself and nibbled delicately at the almond wafer. "You are very kind, my lord, but I am in no need of assistance."

Marcus Allington possessed the irritating ability to raise one eyebrow. He said nothing, but the quirked brow and the ironic twist to his lips, spoke volumes.

Antonia flushed, goaded into an explanation she did not want to make. "I can see you wonder at my gown, sir, but if one travels on the public stage, naturally one does not don one's best attire for the journey." His eyes were resting thoughtfully on the torn sleeve and Antonia hurried on, "Your men tore my garment when they apprehended me!"

"No..." Amused recollection lit the brown eyes. "It was already torn after the accident to the stagecoach."

Antonia, scarcely acknowledging to herself that she had been piqued by his lack of recognition, blurted out, "When I was dragged into your presence, you made no sign you had seen me before."

"You must forgive me," he said smoothly, sipping his sherry. "I remembered the tear, but not, I regret, you. Although, now I come to think of it, you were, were you not, wearing a bonnet and pelisse?"

"I had laid them aside in the woods, just before your men came upon me."

"All the better to catch my pheasants, no doubt," he said drily.

"I have already told you, I did not know they were yours. And of course I did not catch them—I...I found them upon the footpath." She had no intention of betraying the two urchins.

"Tsk, tsk, Miss Dane," Lord Allington admonished. "You really are a very poor liar." His voice hardened. "Let us stop playing games. I believe neither that you caught those birds nor that you found them. Describe the culprit you had them of, madam, for you do yourself no favours in my eyes in protecting him."

"Liar? How dare you, sir! Being in or out of your favour counts as nothing to me. If I prevaricated, it was simply because I have no intention of delivering up to your tender mercies one of your unfortunate tenants, forced into poaching merely to stay alive!'' She was upright and quivering with fury in the chair.

"It is not my tenants who are starving, Miss Dane.'' Marcus strode over to where she sat. When he put one hand on each arm of her chair, she had to will herself not to shrink back from his cold regard. "When you reach your inheritance, madam, look around you and see the state in which your departed father left his people, before you come preaching to me of mine.''

Antonia stared back into his hard face, appalled at what he had told her. She did not know how to respond: he was too close, too overpoweringly male…

With a swift movement he bent his tawny head and kissed her full on the lips with a hard, possessive, sensuality. Momentarily she was too stunned to resist, then she broke away from the heat of his mouth, bringing up her right hand to slap his cheek.

Marcus straightened, ruefully rubbing his face. "I suppose I deserved that, but I must confess, Miss Dane, that your…eccentricity quite robbed me of my good sense.''

Antonia sprang from the chair in a swirl of skirts. "I think not, sir! I believe that your overweening arrogance leads you to believe you can take whatever you want! Do not trouble to ring for the butler, my lord—I can see myself out!''

Her hand was on the doorknob when he said softly, "Miss Dane.''

Hating herself for responding, Antonia turned to look at him. "Well?''

"Feed your tenants, Miss Dane, then at least they will not have to steal my property to survive.''

Chapter Two

Antonia swept past a startled footman, who leapt to open the front door for her, down the shallow flight of stone steps and halfway down the gravelled drive before her anger calmed enough for her to slow to a stop. As consumed by anger as she was, there was no point in storming off into the Hertfordshire countryside without getting her bearings first.

Now she could see the front of the house, she realised that she could recall it from rare visits as a small child with her grandfather. But her memories were of a far less elegant effect: it was obvious that Marcus Allington had applied both an admirable taste and considerable amounts of money to Brightshill.

The pleasure grounds were beautifully kept, with close-scythed lawns sweeping to stands of specimen trees. Through the trees she could see the glimmer of water where she could have sworn none had been before and the drive was bordered by classical statuary, each pedestal nestling in a group of flowering shrubs.

"Insufferable man!" Antonia fumed aloud. She felt even more down at heel and grimy in this setting, the only discordant note in a perfect landscape. "Well, I am

glad of it!'' she exclaimed. ''Serve him right if I lower
the tone!'' She realised she was scuffing the perfectly
raked gravel with her boot, to the betterment of neither.
She was in danger of forgetting who she was, although
after being mauled like a loose woman by that…
that…man, it was little wonder.

She shot a fulminating glance in the direction of the
study window and was startled to see Marcus Allington
standing at the casement, regarding her. Antonia
straightened her shoulders, gathered up her frightful
skirts in one hand and swept an elaborate curtsy to the
semi-clad deity on the nearest pedestal. Looking closer,
she saw he bore a quite remarkable resemblance to the
Prince Regent—although without the corsets—a thought
that brought back her natural sense of the ridiculous.

Giggling faintly, and without a second backward
glance, Antonia walked down the drive as though she
owned it. Once through the gates she began to hurry,
half-running, conscious that it must be a good two hours
since she had parted from her companion and that Donna
would be becoming anxious.

The wind through the bare hedges was turning sharp
as the afternoon drew in and she was reminded that,
however pleasant the day had been, it was still only
March and she was without her pelisse and bonnet.

Suddenly the neatly cut and laid hedges and sharply
defined ditches gave way to a raggle-taggle of overgrown bushes and choked muddy puddles. Through one
of many gaps in the boundary, Antonia could see an ill-
drained field with clumps of dead thistles here and there.
There was no doubt she was now on Rye End Hall land.
The fruits of her father's and brother's neglect were only
too evident: Antonia remembered uneasily Lord Allington's comment about her tenants.

She turned into the entrance of the Hall, between rusted gates hanging crazily from the tall posts. The lodge houses were empty; their neat little gardens, which she remembered from her childhood, were now lost under brambles and nettles.

Hurrying up the drive, Antonia formulated a light-hearted version of her adventures to tell Donna, carefully omitting all references to that insolent, exciting kiss. Miss Donaldson might be small in stature and a gentle-woman to her backbone, but she would have no compunction in marching round to Brightshill and telling his lordship precisely what she thought of his outrageously forward behaviour!

The front door opened as she approached and there was Donna, her anxious expression lifting in relief. "There you are, my dear! I was just trying to decide whether I should go in search of you." She broke off as her eyes took in the full awfulness of Antonia's appearance.

"What have you been doing? There is blood on your face—are you hurt? Have you fallen in the woods?" She ushered Antonia in as she spoke, hurrying her through the hall and into the kitchens at the rear of the house.

"No, no," Antonia hastened to reassure her. "It is pheasant blood, not my own. I have had quite an adventure, Donna—and another encounter with Lord Allington, our infuriating neighbour."

"Infuriating, dear? Oh, bother this fire, it will never get the water warm if I cannot induce it to draw better." She raked at the smouldering logs in the grate but to little effect.

Antonia sank wearily on to a settle and stared round at the dereliction that was the kitchens. The walls she had always remembered as lime-washed twice a year were begrimed with smoke and hung with cobwebs. The chimney crane and jacks were rusted and the wide shelves and dressers were either empty or heaped with filthy piles of chipped crockery. Miss Donaldson had obviously found a broom, for the flags in front of the hearth and settle had been swept, only to reveal the ingrained grime of the floor beneath.

"It cannot have become so squalid in a mere six months," Antonia said despairingly. "No wonder the lawyer advised against our returning here! Well, perhaps this is the worst room. If Father hired some slattern of a cook…" Her voice trailed away as she saw Donna's face. "Are they all as bad as this?" she asked despairingly.

Donna came and sat next to her on the settle, taking her hand in hers as if to give the younger woman strength. "I have not looked into all of the rooms—perhaps the kitchen seems worse because you remember it as a place of bustling activity, bright and clean in your dear mama's day—but all seem filthy and there is hardly any furniture remaining."

Antonia took a deep breath, ruthlessly quashing the strong desire to burst into tears and run pell-mell down the drive to take refuge in the inn. This was their home now, and they were going to have to make the best of it. "Well, it is getting dark and we must find some candles, heat some water and have something to eat before we go to bed. It is too late now to try and improve matters."

Faint steam was at last rising off the kettle. Antonia poured a little into a bowl and washed her face and hands while Donna fastidiously brushed off the surface of the table, spread a cloth she had brought in the food hamper upon it and began to unpack their provisions.

Their simple supper was soon spread out: some potted ham, cheese, apples, bread and butter and a fruit cake. Donna made tea, after scouring a cracked teapot she found on a shelf, and they drank it, grateful for its warmth. As they ate, Donna prompted Antonia to recount the tale of her afternoon's adventure. Even the heavily censored version she received was enough to make her shudder, and exclaim at intervals.

Replete, Antonia sat back and pushed out her feet towards the faint heat from the range. "Let us simply leave everything as it is until the morning. We cannot see to do anything, and we have had a long and wearisome day." Even as she spoke, there was a rustling and a scuttling from behind the dresser. "Oh, no! Mice!"

"If we are fortunate," Donna replied grimly, packing the food back into the wicker hamper as she spoke. "I did not like to tell you, my dear, but when I first entered the kitchen I fear I saw a rat."

"Urgh! Well, that is tomorrow's first task—to find a ratcatcher and a large cat. Let us see if we can find a bedroom fit to sleep in."

A dispiriting survey by candlelight revealed a series of filthy chambers, only three of which contained beds. They finally decided on the room that evidently had been occupied by the housekeeper, before she had finally been driven out by Sir Humphrey's outrageous behaviour and total unwillingness to pay wages.

Made up with their own linen, the bed was at least clean, if not particularly comfortable. But even the pervading smell of damp was not enough to keep the ladies awake; both were asleep almost as soon as their heads touched the pillows.

By seven o'clock the next morning, they were already breakfasted and holding a council of war in the kitchen.

Antonia was attempting to make a list on a piece of paper retrieved from Sir Humphrey's study, along with a blunt quill pen and a pot of thick brown ink. "I will put down some ink on the list first of all!"

Miss Donaldson watched her young companion's bent head with a worried frown in her eyes. The candlelight struck burnished lights from her hair and her pleasant voice was light and amused. Really, Miss Donaldson mused, any other young lady of her acquaintance would be having a fit of the vapours by now.

In the years Donna had known Antonia, she had come to respect her spirit, the courage that allowed her to rise above all the misfortunes that had come her way. She would cope with this disaster of a house, that was certain: but she did not deserve the burden.

"Donna... Donna?" Antonia tapped her hand with the quill. "You have not been listening to a word I have said! We need to make a list of provisions and one of us must walk into Rybury and see what we may purchase there. No doubt young Jem from the inn would be willing to fetch the rest from Berkhamsted for a small consideration. He seems a reliable lad, do you not agree?"

A furtive scratching in the wainscot reminded them of another pressing need. "And send up the ratcatcher," said Donna with a shudder. "There must be a woman in the village who will come up to scrub..."

"Let us hire two if we can," Antonia interrupted. "It will take more than one woman and our own efforts to set this place to rights!"

The light from a fresh, sunny morning was struggling through the begrimed windows. Donna blew out the candles and crossed the kitchen floor to throw open the back door, letting in a flood of spring sunshine and the smell of damp earth. It also admitted young Jem, cap in hand and pink with the importance of his message.

"Good morning, and begging your pardon, ladies, but my ma says, do you need some things fetching, or any help, like?"

"Jem, you are a godsend," Antonia beamed at him, deepening his confusion. "Come in and sit down while we finish this list of provisions. And tell me, Jem, are there any women in the village who would come and clean for us?"

"Oh yes, ma'am." Then a look of doubt came over his face. "Well, that is…er…"

"For a regular weekly wage, of course," Miss Donaldson supplied firmly. She knew enough of Sir Humphrey to realise why Jem was doubtful. "And a ratcatcher."

"That'll be Walter Armitage, so long as he's over his rheum," Jem said helpfully. "And what about a cat, ma'am?"

"That would be perfect, Jem, if you can find one. Now, here is the list. Do you remember everything we need?"

"Provisions, ratcatcher, cat, charwomen," Jem recited confidently. "And would you be needing a boy, ma'am—for odd jobs, like?" He stood twisting his cap in his hands and looking hopeful.

"We will," said Antonia, regarding his cheerful open face, which was as clean as one could reasonably expect of a fourteen-year-old. "But will your father not be requiring you to help around the inn?"

"I can do all my chores by ten, ma'am, and then be up here directly."

"Very well, Jem." Antonia settled on a daily wage

which, although very modest, made the boy's eyes gleam, then he shot off through the back door, clutching the list tightly.

"That was fortuitous," Donna announced. "And the first thing I am going to do when that boy gets back is to send him up the kitchen chimney to get rid of the birds' nests." She unfurled a vast white apron, wrapped a cloth around her neat coiffure and, hands on hips, regarded the kitchen.

"If you begin here," Antonia suggested, "I will attack the bedroom, then at least we can eat and sleep in comparative comfort."

Pausing only to drop yesterday's wrecked dress into a tub of cold water in the hope that, once clean, some of the cloth could be saved, Antonia too swathed herself in an apron and marched upstairs.

She scrubbed at the misted glass hanging on the bedroom wall until she could see her own reflection in it and twisted up her hair under a turban like Donna's. Really, her coiffure was a disgrace, she thought. The unruly curls needed the attention of a hairdresser regularly if she were not to look a complete romp, but just now she had neither time nor resources for such fripperies.

She was wearing a sprig muslin dress that, although faded, at least had no rips or tears. Antonia rolled up the sleeves, flung open the casement and set to with a duster on a stick to knock down the cobwebs that swathed the walls. As one large spider after another was dislodged from its eyrie and scuttled for the open door, Antonia reflected how glad she was that the light the night before had been so poor. She chased a particularly hairy specimen out with a broom and began to take down the curtains.

* * *

By midmorning the room was swept, dusted and aired. The hangings were in a heap on the floor for the washerwoman; only the bed remained to be attacked. Pulling off the sheets they had put on the previous night, Antonia was relieved to find the mattress not as fusty as she had feared. Even so, it, and the pillows, needed a thorough shake and air. She dragged it to the window and hung it out to refresh the flattened goosefeathers. It was too heavy to shake, so Antonia hung over the sill and pummelled it vigorously with her hands.

There was an indignant shout from the side path beneath as a shower of dust and stray feathers rained down. Startled, red-faced and still folded in two across the sill, Antonia raised her head to find Marcus Allington beating the dust from his jacket with his gloves.

"Lord Allington! I am so sorry…" Antonia looked down into his upturned face, noticing he seemed amused rather than annoyed. She bit her lip, regretting the instinctive apology to a man who had treated her in such a cavalier fashion only the day before. It was bad enough to be manhandled by his keepers, but to have him force his attentions upon her and then arrive at her house unannounced was the outside of enough! "Were we expecting you, my lord?" she enquired coldly. "Perhaps you are missing a pheasant or two?"

"I would not know, Miss Dane: I leave counting my birds to my keepers. And after your very convincing explanation of the circumstances yesterday, I would not dream of looking for them here in any case." He seemed very cheerful this morning, and quite unperturbed both by her coldness and the unconventional circumstances. Antonia was visited by the sudden insight that, beneath his conventional exterior, Marcus Allington was a man who enjoyed the unexpected.

A strangely comfortable silence ensued. Then she realised his gaze was resting appreciatively on the quite indecorous amount of cleavage she was displaying in her upside-down position.

Hastily she scrambled back over the sill, pulled the gown up at the neck then, with as much dignity as she could muster, looked out again. "If you follow the path round to the back of the house you will find my companion, Miss Donaldson, in the kitchen, my lord."

Marcus Allington bowed rather ironically before sauntering off round the corner. Antonia watched him, the blond hair on which he had not replaced his hat ruffled by the breeze, the breadth of his shoulders even more impressive seen from above. Recalling herself sharply, Antonia put up her hands to remove her turban; then stilled the action. No! Why should she titivate herself for him when he had coolly arrived without a word of warning or a by-your-leave?

She shook out her skirts and apron and sailed down the stairs, only to discover as she reached the hall that her heart was beating uncomfortably fast. Well, he had caught her at a disadvantage, hanging out of the window in an unseemly manner, entirely inappropriate to her status as a gentlewoman. Anyone would be flustered in such circumstances. Why, she would have felt just the same if it had been the vicar's wife…

Thus reassured, Antonia entered the kitchen with a calm smile and the firm intention of treating Marcus Allington as if yesterday—that kiss—had never occurred.

She found Miss Donaldson uncharacteristically discommoded by being discovered, duster in hand, standing on a chair. "Do allow me to hand you down, ma'am," Marcus was saying in a tone that suggested he was used to assisting middle-aged gentlewomen down off kitchen chairs every day of his life.

"Thank you, Lord Allington, I am most grateful." Donna's cheeks were pink as she hastily tossed the duster behind the settle. "Will you not take a cup of tea…oh, dear, I do wish I could suggest you took it in the drawing-room, but really, it is not…"

"…fit for habitation," supplied Antonia, entering behind them. "Good morning, Lord Allington. How kind of you to call, I do trust you have had a pleasant ride over from Brightshill. I regret to say there is at least one dead pigeon—ours, I hasten to add—in the drawing-room, so I feel you would be more comfortable here on the settle."

"Good morning, Miss Dane," he returned easily. "I felt I should look in on you and assure myself you had recovered from yesterday's excitements." His eyes met hers with a mischievous gleam in their dark brown depths. "You will, I know, forgive me for the informality of not leaving my card first."

"Allow me to introduce my companion, Miss Donaldson. Please sit down, my lord," Antonia said repressively as she went to help Donna with the tea things.

His lordship, unwilling to sit whilst the ladies stood, glanced round the kitchen. "Have your servants not yet arrived, Miss Dane? Allow me." He took the cups from Donna and set them on the now clean table.

"We have…" The word "none" was on the tip of her tongue, but then she broke off, remembering his great house and the quantity of servants therein. To admit that she and Donna were of such limited means that employing a maid and one or two charwomen was the only prudent course open to them was suddenly insupportable.

''The London house is still being closed down,'' she said airily, implying that a multitude of menservants and maids were busy with dustcovers and the packing of trunks. ''And with this house being in such a state, I thought it best to leave it a while before deciding how many to engage.'' Beyond him, she caught a glimpse of the look of pained shock on Miss Donaldson's face at this barefaced deceit.

''Meanwhile, young Jem from the inn has gone to hire us some charwomen in the village. London servants would take one look at Rye End Hall at present and turn tail immediately.'' Antonia managed a light social laugh. ''You know what servants are—or perhaps not? Perhaps Lady Allington deals with all such matters?''

Marcus's lips quirked in acknowledgement of such a blatant piece of fishing and Miss Donaldson cast up her eyes to the cobwebbed beams. ''I very much regret to inform you, Miss Dane, that I find myself without a wife at present.'' He crossed his booted legs, quite at ease on the hard settle, his eyes twinkling with amusement, his tone totally lacking in the regret he professed to feel.

Antonia had the grace to colour at her own boldness. ''That is a pity, Lord Allington, for I had hoped to find a congenial neighbour. More tea?''

''I hope you will find me a congenial neighbour, Miss Dane—I am generally reckoned so to be.''

''But women are different,'' Antonia remarked without thinking.

''How very true, ma'am. I have often observed that to be the case. As to more tea, I must decline. I am on my way to see Mr Todd; I believe you are acquainted with our curate?''

''Yes, indeed, we were travelling together yesterday.''

Antonia was blushing in earnest now. "Good morning, my lord."

As soon as the door had closed behind his lordship, Miss Donaldson protested. "Antonia! I had never dreamed you capable of such gaucheness! And such dissembling about our supposed servants...I do not wonder you blush so! What will his lordship think when he discovers the true state of our affairs?"

"I suspect he already knows," Antonia replied ruefully. "There is not much escapes Lord Allington's sharp eye. I know I behaved badly, Donna, but he aggravates me so! And he wants Rye End Hall to add to the land he bought from my father: he will be asking to buy more land soon and, if he realises just how badly things stand with us, the offer will be very small."

"You just say no," Miss Donaldson replied robustly.

"But I suspect I may have to sell some land to raise the money to repair the fabric of the house—and we have not even seen it properly in daylight. If he realises how desperate I am I will have lost all my bargaining advantage."

"How dreadful to think of a young lady having to understand such matters," her companion murmured, her eyes glittering behind her pince-nez. "But I do take your meaning. However, it is not the only reason you have behaved so—shall we say—out of character, is it, my dear?"

Antonia returned the shrewd glance with a guilty smile. "I know, Donna; it is pride, I am afraid, the pride of the Danes. I cannot bear to have people know to what straits we have been reduced. And after that humiliating encounter yesterday..."

Miss Donaldson was too wise a woman to pursue the topic, but as she gathered up the teacups, she thought that there must have been more to yesterday's events than had been recounted to her. There was a tension that was almost palpable between that man and her young friend.

"At least we now have two rooms that are habitable and we can eat and sleep in cleanliness and relative comfort." Antonia replaced the tea cups on the freshly scrubbed oak dresser. "Let us undertake a complete survey of the house and see what we have in the way of furniture and linen."

It took them until three in the afternoon to complete their tour. Antonia was sitting at the kitchen table, sorting the disappointingly short lists of furniture remaining, while Donna sliced bread and butter for their belated luncheon.

"Father must have either sold a great deal or it has had to go to satisfy the creditors," she sighed sadly. "All the lovely French pieces from my mother's chamber and the blue drawing-room have gone. By the time we have thrown away the pieces that are too full of worm to keep, we will be rattling around like two peas in a drum."

Miss Donaldson laid down a platter and paused on her way to fetch the butter to con the lists. "You know, my dear, this list would be quite adequate if only we were in a modest house. I do not say that everything is of the first height of elegance, but it will be passable with polishing and some repairs. The linen needs darning, but it is of good quality."

"If wishes were horses, Donna… We are in a mansion with twenty-two rooms, to say nothing of the servants' quarters. Unless we move into the stables, there is no smaller accommodation.'' Antonia cut a piece of bread and butter, her brow furrowing in thought.

''The one saving grace is that, with the exception of those few slates off on the west wing, the fabric of the house appears remarkably sound. It needs cleaning and many minor repairs, but nothing beyond the skill of the village craftsmen. We must fashion ourselves a small suite of rooms and close up the rest of the house.''

Further conversation was interrupted by the arrival of young Jem looking mightily pleased with himself. He was laden with two wicker baskets, one of which was brimful of provisions, the other spilling over with kittens.

''Good heavens, Jem! I asked for one cat, not every stray in the village!''

The boy extracted a fine tabby from the centre of the basket. ''But she's just had kittens, miss, and she's a good mouser. With all the kittens she'll work even harder, miss, and when they grow up, they'll be catching, too.''

''Well done, Jem, that is a sensible thought,'' Antonia praised him. ''There are certainly enough mice in this house to feed such a hopeful family. Put the basket in the scullery and find her a saucer of water.''

Donna inspected the shopping while the cat was settled into her new home. ''This is excellent, Jem.'' As she sorted through she asked, ''Did you manage to engage the charwomen for us? And the ratcatcher?''

''Widow Brown and her daughter will be coming up first light tomorrow. The ratcatcher can't come until Wednesday, but he's bringing his dogs and a boy, so they'll do the house and the stables and all. And my dad says, I ought to do the chimneys for you.''

The lad gratefully accepted a platter of bread and

cheese from Donna and set to with a will, talking with his mouth full. "I got the provisions from Berkhamsted, my mum saying I should, you being Quality, like. Everyone is pleased to hear the Hall is occupied again, I 'spec you'll have lots of tradesmen calling…"

Antonia left Donna pinning old sacking over the fireplaces while Jem readied a motley collection of brushes and sticks to attack the chimneys. The sunshine was warm on her shoulders as she found the gate into the kitchen garden. The warm brick walls still retained their trained fruit trees, and the shape of the beds could be descried despite the rank growth of weeds and dead vegetables.

She walked up and down the brick paths, looking hopefully for anything edible, but could recognise nothing except some mint and thyme. The fruit trees needed pruning, but the new growth on the fans was vigorous and were promising for later in the year. That exhausted her sum of horticultural knowledge, which was worrying, for a flourishing kitchen garden would make all the difference to the degree of comfort they could expect.

Jem had just emerged sootily from the kitchen chimney when Antonia returned to the house. "Is there anyone in the village who would tend the kitchen garden for us, Jem?"

He stood fidgeting on the piece of sackcloth to which Donna had banished him whilst she swept up his sooty footprints. "Old Walter Johnson, who used to do the gardens here, is still alive, miss. He's got the rheumatics something awful, but he knows what he's doing right enough, and he could bring a lad with him for the heavy digging."

"That sounds excellent, if you think the old man can manage."

"He'll do right enough, and be glad of the money. You could have had his eldest son, but he's in Hertford gaol."

"Goodness!" Miss Donaldson exclaimed. "I do not think we would want to employ someone of that kind."

"Was only poaching, miss. Caught red-handed, he was, and his lordship at Brightshill sent him down. He's devilish hard on poachers, is his lordship."

"Lord Allington, you mean?" Antonia enquired, flushing at the recollection of her own experience of his lordship's treatment of poachers. When Jem nodded, she asked, "Is poaching much of a problem around here, then, for him to be so strict?"

"It has been—folks have got to eat, when all's said and done, but it'll be all right now you are here, miss," said Jem confidently. "There'll be work again on the land and the grounds and in the house, I'll be bound. But all your tenants have had it hard the last few years. A lot of families would have starved if it hadn't been for the odd pheasant or rabbit off your land or his lordship's."

Antonia was suddenly consumed by a great blaze of anger against her father and brother for their negligence and profligate behaviour. She had been aware of the effect their ruinous ways had had on the family fortune and name and on her own prospects. Now she was reminded how they had betrayed their responsibility to their tenants, who seemed to be starving at the very gates of the Hall.

And as for Lord Allington, how could one defend a man who was willing to imprison breadwinners for putting food into the mouths of their children? It was iniquitous! The man was inhumane, there was no other word for him, she fumed inwardly. She knew that all landowners took a hard line over poaching, as they did over any offence against property, but surely a rational man could show some leniency where people were starving?

Looking uncharacteristically grim, she found Jem some coppers from her reticule for his day's labours and sent him off home with an apple to munch and an injunction to approach the old gardener in the morning.

After supper, Donna sat placidly cutting up hopelessly worn sheets to make pillowcases while Antonia remained at the table with a pile of papers and a quill pen.

After an hour Donna, tired of hearing her heavy sighs, enquired, "What are you doing, my dear? It cannot be good for your eyes and it certainly seems to be giving you no satisfaction."

"I am reviewing our financial position. You recall we agreed that we should be able to afford to engage a maid, a footman and a cook?"

"Indeed. Were we mistaken? Do we have less money than we thought?"

"No, we were accurate in our calculations. But, Donna, how can we in all conscience bring in smart town servants to look after our comfort and consequence when the people on the estate are in such straits? We must spend the money on charwomen and gardeners and men to do the repairs; then, at least, the money will be going to as many families as possible. You and I must look after our own clothes and do the light cleaning and the cooking."

There was a short silence after this outburst while Miss Donaldson removed and polished her pince-nez. "I applaud the sentiment, my dear, but I do at least think you should have a maid to lend you some consequence and to answer the door. It is going to make receiving guests most difficult and what any prospective suitor would think…''

''It will give any prospective suitors a very clear idea of my true position!'' Antonia responded briskly. ''I hardly feel, in view of my father's reputation locally, that the local gentry will be beating a path to my door.'' She left unsaid the thought that, at her age and in her financial position, the sooner she resigned herself to spinsterhood, the better.

''How true,'' agreed Donna. ''It is such a pity that Lord Allington is unmarried. His wife would be just the person to introduce you to local society.''

''I agree; and if his lordship were married, I am certain his disposition would be considerably more conciliatory.''

It was on the tip of Miss Donaldson's tongue to reply that she found Lord Allington quite agreeable as he was, but a glance at Antonia's stubborn face persuaded her that this was best left unsaid. She folded her sewing away and rose from her seat by the fire. ''I think we should retire, my dear; we have yet another long day before us.''

Chapter Three

"Antonia, what are those chimneys over there through the trees?" Donna's voice floated faintly down the stairs from the servants' attics.

"Which chimneys? And what are you doing up there?" Antonia responded, puzzled. She pushed back a wayward strand of hair behind her ear, put down the polishing cloth with which she had been attempting to restore some lustre to the newel posts of the main stair, and climbed towards the sound of her companion's voice.

Miss Donaldson was leaning on the sill of one of the dormer windows that looked out across the leads to the woods lying to the west of the house. "How verdant the countryside has become in the three weeks we have been here! I feel spring has come at last—it quite fills one with hope for the future."

Antonia looked at Donna's thin cheeks, usually so sallow, now touched with colour, and realised her friend was flourishing in the face of this new challenge. The daughter of an impoverished India army officer, she had had no choice after his death, when she was in her early twenties, but to become a governess.

Although she had spoken little of her previous employers, Antonia knew she had not found the role a congenial one. Becoming companion-governess to the fourteen-year-old Antonia had better suited her temperament and the two had soon become fast friends.

"Yes, it is lovely." Antonia came to lean on the ledge next to Donna, and for a moment neither spoke as they breathed in the fresh smell of the breeze wafting softly across the beechwoods from the Downs. "What brought you up here?"

"It occurred to me that we gave these rooms only the most scant scrutiny that first day; I wanted to see if we had missed anything, but there is only a chair with a broken leg—and another damp spot we had failed to notice. But then I noticed those chimney stacks—see?"

Antonia followed the pointing finger to where ancient twisting brick stacks just broke the tree-line. "Good heavens! The Dower House! I had quite forgot it. The last time I was there, I must almost have been a babe in arms: my father's elderly cousin Anne lived there for years but, since they had quarrelled violently long ago, we never visited. She is long dead now."

"Will the house be yours, then?" Donna enquired, the germ of an idea growing in her mind.

"Well…yes, it must be, for it is part of the estate." She met Donna's eye and they thought and spoke as one. "Furniture!"

"Of course, it may have been cleared out by your father and sold when his cousin died," Donna said with the practical air of someone who was determined not to be disappointed.

"Perhaps not." Antonia thought out loud. "They were on such bad terms and he had other things to occupy him…"

"Such as his wine cellar," Miss Donaldson supplied waspishly. "Well, we must go and have a look, and the sooner the better. Just let me look in at the kitchen first, I left Widow Brown preparing the vegetables for dinner."

A scene of chaos greeted them as they stood on the threshold. The charwoman was chasing the tabby cat round the kitchen with a broom, a badly mauled, skinned rabbit was bleeding damply on the hearthrug and a pot of giblet stock boiled over on the range.

"Mrs Brown, whatever is the matter?" Donna demanded.

The charwoman grounded the broom and stood panting, red in the face. "Dratted cat, miss! It's the rats it's meant to be eating, not what's in the pantry!" The cat, seizing its opportunity, dragged the rabbit off into the scullery and Antonia darted across to save the stock pot before it boiled dry.

"Oh, dear," lamented Donna. "I fear that rabbit was all that is left of our dinner. Did the boys leave any other game this morning, Mrs Brown?"

Shortly after they had arrived, Antonia had had the notion of encouraging her tenants to "poach" the plentiful game that infested her neglected lands. She had struck a bargain: she would take a cut of the animals they snared or shot; in return, they could keep the rest to feed their families. She had laid down the strict condition that they did not stray by so much as a toe into Brightshill or any other estate in the neighbourhood.

The scheme was already starting to work well. Her tenants would be better fed and she felt confident that they were now safely removed from all temptation to run foul of the law—or Lord Allington's gamekeepers. In return, she and Donna dined well on rabbit, pheasant, pigeons, and on one occasion, venison. They had become adept at plucking, skinning and stewing to the great benefit of the housekeeping account and, perhaps more importantly, had begun to heal the rift between landlord and tenant that her father's dissolute and neglectful behaviour had opened. Whenever she met any of her tenants, Antonia had been warmed by their obvious gratitude.

And there was still the river and the lake to consider; Antonia had looked at her late brother's fishing rods, but after becoming entangled in hook and line when removing them from the cupboard, had regretfully decided she needed lessons before threatening the local pike and perch.

"I believe there is still a brace of wood pigeons." Donna peered into the larder. "But I had better stay here and see what I can retrieve; will you go on to the Dower House without me, Antonia? Now, Mrs Brown, let us see what we can do here…"

Antonia, glad to escape from the smell of burnt stock, slipped out of the back door with relief. Rain earlier that day had given way to sunshine, although she had to watch her step with the mud as she picked her way across the freshly gravelled paths through the walled vegetable gardens.

Old Johnson was hoeing between lines of seedling vegetables, grumbling without bothering to straighten up at the skinny lad who was putting in pea sticks along newly dug trenches. Knowing full well that the gardener could—and would—hold forth at length with incomprehensible gardening questions if she gave him the opportunity, Antonia gave them a cheery wave and went out through a wicket gate into the ruins of the pleasure grounds beyond.

She negotiated clumps of brambles and nettles, remembering with sadness the smooth sweep of lawn and
well-tended shrubberies that had once occupied the area.
Her mother had loved to stroll in the cool of the evening
in the formal rose garden she had created: now Antonia
could not even recognise where they had walked together arm in arm.

She swallowed hard against the almost physical pain
of remembering and resolutely walked on to the belt of
trees that fringed the pleasure grounds, separating them
from the gardens of the Dower House and the pastures
beyond.

A small group of fallow deer started away, almost
under her feet, reminding her that the fences must be in
disrepair. The animals were lovely to watch, but would
swiftly lay to waste any efforts to civilise the gardens.
Gloomily Antonia walked on, attempting to calculate
how much fencing would cost, not only for the grounds
but, more importantly, the fields and pasture land.

The Dower House was hidden behind a rampant
hedge of briar and thorn, taller than her head. Approaching as she was the rear of the house, Antonia came first
to the garden gate, which hung crazily from one hinge,
the wood quite rotten and covered in lichens. Antonia
lifted it aside gingerly and walked through, finding herself in a paved yard with a well in the middle.

The house had been the original farm on the estate.
Built in the reign of the first James, it was a two-storey
building of two wings constructed of local red brick,
under a tiled roof capped by the twisting chimney stacks
Donna had espied from the attic that morning.

The yard in which she now stood had once been the
farmyard, but when the house had become the Dower
House and the new Home Farm was built, the outbuild-

ings were demolished and the yard became part of the gardens.

The small mullioned windows reflected only dully, despite the bright sunshine; as Antonia approached, she saw the leaded panes were thick with grime and festooned with cobwebs. There was a low back door under a heavy porch; she tried it and found it, not surprisingly, locked. She hesitated, realising she would probably have to ask young Jem to break in, for they had found no keys that could belong to this house up at the Hall.

Disappointed, for by now she was quite excited at the prospect of exploring, she was turning away when she saw a key hanging on a hook on a beam in the porch. It was red with rust and obviously not, judging by its size, the key to this door. Antonia turned it in her hand, staining her fingers with the rust. It could be the front-door key: it was worth trying. Gathering up her skirts, she took the drive that led round the side to the front of the house, facing across overgrown lawns to the main gates beyond.

Antonia could still remember the only occasion she had visited the house. She had been with her mother and they had driven in the carriage the short distance down the lanes from the Hall; the strange old house and the crabby old lady in her old-fashioned clothes were a vivid memory, even twenty years on.

Not expecting it to work, Antonia tried the key in the front-door lock. It grated and resisted, then suddenly turned with a loud click and the panelled oak swung open. The hall beyond was dark and gloomy with shadowed recesses and the black gaping holes of opened doors. Antonia hesitated, unwelcome memories of every Gothick tale she had ever read welling up in her mind. She stood, one hand on the door frame, her toes safely on the outside of the threshold, poised to run at the first ominous creak.

Then the ridiculousness of her position struck her: a grown woman frightened to enter her own property in broad daylight! What would she say to Donna—that she was too afraid to look for the furniture they so badly needed? Boldly Antonia stepped into the hall—but left the door wide open behind her.

As she moved from room to room, her skirts raised puffs of dust. But, to her amazement, everything was completely dry: there were no damp stains or musty smells, only dry dust and airlessness shrouding the contents of the house, left just as they had been when Cousin Anne had died nine years before. Relations between Sir Humphrey and his querulous relative had been so poor her father must have ordered the place shut up and had never troubled himself to investigate further.

The ancient brick and oak had stood the test of time and the elements in a way more recent buildings had not. Quite at her ease now, for the old house had a homely, safe feeling to it, Antonia roamed from room to room, lifting dust sheets, peering at hangings in the gloom, running her fingers along the dark wood of the sturdy old furniture. The stairs were wide and shallow and led her up to a gallery and a suite of bedrooms.

Antonia was just inside the door of what must have been Cousin Anne's chamber when she heard the floorboards creaking in the hall below. Her hand flew to her throat and she froze, all the tales of ghosts alive again in her mind. Panic gripped her and with it a blind urge to get out into the sunlight. Whoever—or whatever it was—had reached the foot of the stairs; she could hear the boards groaning.

There must be back stairs… Antonia picked up her

skirts and flew down the landing on tip-toe; down a passageway, through a doorway and found herself at the head of a flight of narrow, winding stairs. She stumbled down, the very act of running feeding her panic, round a dark bend and crashed into something large, solid and alive.

"Got you!" Strong hands seized her roughly by the shoulders and shook her. Muffled against woollen cloth, Antonia turned her head frantically and screamed. She could see nothing in the gloom. The man holding her was clenching her upper arms in a vice-like grip that brought tears to her eyes and her heart was leaping in her chest till she felt quite sick.

There was no one within earshot to come to her aid: Antonia held back her screams and saved her breath for struggling. She began to kick with a vengeance, stubbing her toes against unyielding leather boots. Suddenly released, Antonia stumbled back against the wall, but before she could open her mouth the man seized her by the wrist and dragged her down the last few stairs into the kitchen.

"Come on, wench, let me have a look at you in the light...out to see what you could steal, were you?" The light from the casements fell on Antonia's dust-stained face and her captor released her with an oath. "Hell's teeth! You again!"

Shaking and furious, Antonia glared into the hard face of Marcus Allington. She found her voice. "How dare you assault me in my own house!" But although she was angry, she was also shaking with relief that it was he.

"I thought you were a housebreaker—the front door was wide open, I could hear somebody moving about upstairs.'' He glared back. ''What do you expect me to do? Pass by and let the place be ransacked?''

Antonia's knees sagged and she let the kitchen table take her weight as she rubbed her stinging wrists. ''I thought you...I thought you...''

''You thought I was the vagrant, someone who was going to attack you?'' He took a step forward, seeing how white her face was under the dust, noticing a cobweb caught up in her dark curls, seeing with a pang of guilt a bruise forming on her wrist where his unyielding grip had held her fast.

''No...'' Her voice quavered, then broke. ''I thought you were a headless ghoul!''

''A ghoul! Really, Miss Dane!'' Marcus began to smile then, seeing her tears, softened. ''Antonia...I am sorry, come here.'' Antonia found herself pulled gently against his broad chest and held. The ridiculous tears of fright kept welling up and she gave in to them, sobbing in earnest as he stroked her hair and quietly murmured reassurance. It had been so long since anyone had held her, offered her the comfort of their arms. Miss Donaldson's brisk sympathy and sensible friendship were not the same.

The tears dried in a few minutes, but Antonia stayed in the shelter of Marcus's arms, her cheek nestled against his waistcoat, his heart beating steadily under her ear. Indeed, he seemed quite content to hold her and stroke her hair as though gentling a startled foal.

Antonia stirred against him as a realisation of the situation overcame her instinctive need to be held. As though her movement had triggered something in him, his hand stopped stroking and moved to caress her nape and the hand holding her against him came up to tip up her face.

"Lord Allington…"

"You look adorable with cobwebs in your hair, like a kitten that has been exploring." His voice was husky and amused.

"I d-do not t-think this is…" Antonia knew she was stammering, knew this was neither wise nor proper, but she had no will to break free from his encircling arms.

"Then do not think at all," he murmured softly, his mouth coming down on hers with infinite gentleness. She clung to him as his mouth moved insinuatingly on hers, drawing her deeper into the kiss. Dizzily Antonia clung to him, drowning in unfamiliar sensation, overwhelmed by the feeling of security his strong arms gave her. From deep within her came a little moan of longing as she clung to him more fiercely.

Marcus lifted his mouth from hers and looked down into her innocent eyes. "I think I had better take you home."

"Home?" she quavered, suddenly overcome by a desire to be carried in his arms to Brightshill.

"Yes, your companion will be wondering what has become of you," he said almost briskly, holding open the door for her to pass through. "Where is your horse?"

His abrupt return to conventional manners underscored just how improper her behaviour had been. Antonia's face flamed. "I walked over. My lord…you must disregard, I beg you, my behaviour just now. I was frightened, driven by relief after such a scare. Normally I would never…"

"I quite understand," he responded coolly. "You are not normally in fear of headless ghouls."

They were now on the other side of the front door. Marcus twisted the key in the lock, then handed it to her, his fingers brushing hers momentarily as he did so.

His horse was cropping the grass, its reins thrown over the branch of a tree.

"I will walk back with you to Rye End Hall," he announced, taking the reins in his hand.

She flushed again at the coolness in his voice, confused by the welter of emotions she was feeling. Yes, she supposed she had offended him by implying that the only reason she had returned his kiss was relief that he was not some vagabond, but he should never have kissed her in the first place! She had no intention of trying to make amends—after all, it was the second occasion on which he had taken liberties with her.

"It will not be necessary for you to accompany me, Lord Allington," she said with equal coolness.

"I think it is." He fell into step beside her. "Even if there are no ghouls, there may well be undesirables in the woods. With no keepering on your lands, anyone could be roaming."

Stung, Antonia snapped back, "Do not keep harping on my foolishness, my lord! Have you never read a Gothick tale and then wondered at a creak in the night?"

"No, I have no time for such nonsense."

In the face of such a comprehensive snub, Antonia fell silent and they walked without speaking along the rutted lane until they reached the gates of the Hall.

"Goodbye, Lord Allington, thank you for your concern for my property," she said politely but dismissively, holding out her hand to him.

He accepted neither her hand, nor his dismissal. "If you have recovered your composure, Miss Dane, there is something I wished to speak of to you."

"Any loss of composure I may have suffered, my lord, is entirely attributable to you," Antonia said frostily, then realised what a double-edged remark that was.

Marcus smiled thinly. "None the less, if you could spare me a moment of your time?"

"Very well, Lord Allington, we are still some minutes from the house."

"I do wish you would call me Marcus. After all, we are near neighbours: if, that is, you are intending to stay here."

Antonia raised her brows, "There is no question of my leaving, my lord... Marcus. This is my family home and I intend to stay here."

Marcus allowed his eyes to stray over the ruins of the pleasure grounds where one deer could be seen nibbling delicately at the remains of a rose bush. "It must be a powerful attachment you feel that overcomes the many disadvantages of the situation," he remarked.

"What disadvantages?" Antonia demanded hotly.

"To find yourself without friends, in a property that is tumbling around your ears, set amid derelict lands which can be bringing you no income—forgive me for speaking frankly, but that appears to constitute not one but several disadvantages."

"The house is not tumbling about my ears: there is merely a little damp; that can soon be rectified."

Marcus nodded sagely, "Then no doubt it is the damp that prevents you from furnishing Rye End Hall?"

"And how would you know in what condition my furnishings are, sir?" Antonia demanded, her colour rising.

"It is difficult to keep secrets in the country. Let us be frank, Miss Dane: financially, you are at a standstill. If you have any concern for your tenants, or indeed yourself, you must look to raise income."

"This is being frank, indeed!" Antonia stopped abruptly and faced him. "I believe, sir, you cross beyond frankness! What concern can you have with my private affairs?''

Marcus's dark brown eyes looked at her measuringly. ''I am, after all, a neighbour, but more than that, I am in a position to alleviate your situation.''

Antonia stared at him in wild surmise. Marcus Allington, offering her marriage? Surely there was no other interpretation to put on his words, especially after that kiss just now...?

''M-Marcus,'' she stammered, ''this is so sudden! I scarcely k-know you...'' She broke off at the look of astonishment dawning on his face. He had it under control in a second, but not before she realised the apalling error she had fallen into. Burning with a humiliation she struggled to conceal, she blundered on, ''That is to say, it is very kind of you to offer help to someone you scarcely know...''

''Our families have been neighbours for centuries.'' He spoke smoothly, but she could see a trace of colour on his cheekbones. His attempts at tact were as humiliating to her as her original error had been. ''Your father sold me some land several years ago: I would give you a fair price for the farmlands and the woods. It would leave you the pleasure grounds; with the house restored you would be able to sell it easily, perhaps to a London merchant seeking a country retreat. There are many such these days.''

Humiliation turned to anger as his words sank in. So, Marcus Allington had only kissed her, been so sympathetic, in order to gain her confidence as a prelude to snapping up her lands. His impression of her as an empty-headed female must have been compounded by her falling into his arms not once, but twice! To be arrested as a poacher, to be found in a twitter over ghosts and then to so misinterpret his intentions on the flimsiest of evidence—he must think her so foolish she would accept his offer without hesitation or calculation.

"The day will never come when I am prepared to sell so much as one yard of my land, my lord—to you or anyone else!" She gathered up her skirts and swept off, turning as a further thought struck her. "And your protestations of neighbourly concern would ring more true, sir, if you conducted yourself as a gentleman and did not manhandle me at every opportunity!"

He had swung up into the saddle. Her words obviously stung, for the horse tossed its head in protest as his hand tightened on the reins. "I am not in the habit of manhandling unwilling ladies, ma'am; I would suggest you look to your own behaviour before you criticise mine. I would hardly characterise you as unwilling just now."

Before Antonia could do more than gasp at this attack, he had dug his heels into the horse's flank and cantered off down the track. She was still angry when she re-entered the kitchen, now mercifully restored to its habitual order. Miss Donaldson was placidly brewing a pot of tea, the stock was simmering fragrantly on the range, mixing with the delicious odour of roasting pigeon, Mrs Brown had gone and the cats were sleeping off an excess of rabbit in the scullery.

"My dear, whatever is the matter?" Donna put down the teapot at the sight of Antonia's flushed cheeks and furious expression.

"That insufferable man!"

"Which man?" Donna asked, not unreasonably.

"Well, there is only one in the neighbourhood determined to interfere in my life at every turn—Marcus Allington, of course!" She plumped down in a chair and began to fiddle irritably with a folded paper which lay on the table.

"Lord Allington? Why, what has he done to discommode you so, Antonia? Drink this tea and calm yourself." Donna pushed the cup of tea across and waited anxiously, her eyes fixed on her young friend's stormy countenance.

Antonia took a deep breath. "I was in the Dower House, exploring; it was very dark and gloomy in there, and in truth, rather frightening. He saw the front door standing open and followed me in; I have never been so scared in my life! And then he…then he…I was agitated and naturally…er…clung to him. He…" She found herself unable to say the words to finish the sentence.

"Are you trying to tell me he kissed you?" Miss Donaldson seemed inclined to be amused rather than shocked, which only fuelled Antonia's annoyance.

"Really, Donna, I am surprised at you! I would not have thought you would regard such unseemly behaviour so lightly."

"Well, if you had cast yourself into his arms…he is but a man, after all, my dear. And," she added, musingly, "a most eligible one at that."

This was too palpable a hit. Antonia sank her head into her hands, much to Miss Donaldson's alarm. "Antonia, my dear! Are you telling me he offered you some insult?"

"No! Oh, Donna, I made such an abject fool of myself. I thought he was making a declaration of marriage, but he was only offering to buy the land!"

"If he misled you in any way," her companion began hotly, "he must do the honourable thing and…"

Antonia cut across her. "No, no, it was entirely my own stupidity, and I said nothing which could not be explained away. But I know he knew what assumption I had made—it is so humiliating.''

''But when you came in just now you seemed angry, not embarrassed. Did you quarrel?''

''I told him I would never sell Rye End Hall lands to him.''

There was a short silence, then Miss Donaldson said gently, ''I fear you may have to sell some of them to someone; that paper under your hand is the bill of estimate from Mr Watts the builder from Berkhamsted, who came last week. It seems there are more roof timbers to replace than we had realised and, of course, we had not allowed for the cost of lead…'' Her voice trailed off as Antonia spread open the paper.

''It seems a reasonable and honest estimate,'' she said blankly when she had read it carefully, ''but quite beyond our means.'' The two women stared at each other across the table, the tea cooling between them.

The gloomy silence was broken by the arrival of young Jem, whistling cheerily. ''Good day! Is there anything you'd like me to do, miss? Ma's sent the eggs you wanted, and Pa thought you might like a look at the Lunnon paper, it got left behind yesterday at the inn.''

Donna pulled herself together with a little shake, thanked Jem for the eggs and paper and hustled him outside to sweep all the paths around the house.

Drearily Antonia unfolded the newsheet which proved to be *The Times*. For want of a better occupation, she began to scan the advertisements.

She read aloud: ''To be let for six or twelve months certain, a genteel FAMILY HOUSE, handsomely furnished… A young PERSON about twenty years of age, of respectable connections, wishes for a situation in a ladies' school… A GENTLEMAN, late returned from the East Indies, seeks to LEASE a small country estate within fifty miles of the Capital, comprising both UN-FURNISHED HOUSE and PLEASURE GROUNDS. Apply to Rumbold and Gardiner, Solicitors…''

Antonia laid the paper aside with a sigh. That would be one solution, if only she could bear to see strangers at Rye End Hall. Or, of course, if it were in any condition to be leased.

Donna reappeared from the garden, saying, ''That Jem is a good, willing boy! Show him any task and he sets to with a will. Is there anything of interest in the paper, my dear?''

''I have not yet looked at the news, I was simply running my eye over the advertisements. Listen to this one.'' She read aloud the item concerning the country house required for lease.

''But that is the very solution to our problem!'' cried Donna. ''If you let the house, it would remain in your possession and the rental would allow you to have the repairs done and the grounds set to order.'' She talked on, warming to her theme. ''If it were a repairing lease, it would free you from those costs and you could set the fences and land and the tenants' cottages in order. Then there would be a steady income from those lands as well…''

Perversely, as Donna's enthusiasm waxed, Antonia's waned and she began to see all the disadvantages of the situation. ''How would it appear if I let the house? It would be a clear indication of my penury. And to see strangers in my home? And all the repairs to be done, and the grounds in such disorder—who would look at it? And,'' she added with finality, ''where would we live?''

Donna was prevented from answering by a commotion at the back door. Jem's voice could be heard plaintively protesting, "But, my lord, I'd better tell the mistress you're here…"

"I will announce myself," Marcus Allington replied coldly, stalking into the kitchen as he did so. He was followed closely by his head keeper, Sparrow, who in his turn was holding a man by the collar.

Antonia leapt to her feet, startled by this unexpected eruption of men into her kitchen. "My lord! What is the meaning of this intrusion?"

"I do apologise for disturbing you in your…" he cast a cold eye around the homely kitchen "…living room. But I regret it is necessary to deal with this matter immediately."

He gestured to Sparrow, who pushed his captive forward roughly. "This, I believe, is one of your tenants."

Antonia moved forward, seeing, with some concern that the man had a bloody nose. "Indeed, it is Josiah Wilkins from the cottages at Brook End. Josiah, what has happened to you? Has this person struck you?" She turned angrily on the gamekeeper, recognising him as the one who had so impudently manhandled her. "You! How dare you come on to my land and assault my tenants!"

"Sparrow was on my land, madam, and about his duties for which I pay him." Lord Allington was grim.

Antonia turned a contemptuous shoulder on both master and man and spoke to her tenant calmly. "Tell me what occurred, Josiah, and how you came by your injury."

"Well, miss, it was like this," he began readily enough, although with a wary eye on the keeper. "I was shooting pigeons—got a brace, too, but they came down the wrong side of the brook. I didn't have my old dog with me, see, so I waded across to pick 'em up and this bullying varmint jumped on me.''

''You watch your language—I've got the measure of you, Josiah Wilkins,'' Sparrow threatened. ''Who's to say where you shot those birds? I don't believe a word of it, my lord. All these Wilkinses are a parcel of idle rogues.''

''Hold your tongue, man!'' Antonia snapped, remembering again with a shudder the keeper's insinuating touch on her arm. ''Speak when you are spoken to in my house!''

Sparrow threw her a darkling look and slouched back into the shadows.

''You may not welcome our intrusion, Miss Dane, but I am sure you will agree that I have every right to detain a poacher, and the man is condemned out of his own mouth.''

''I agree you have every right to apprehend a poacher, my lord: however, this man is not a poacher. He was shooting my game, on my land and with my permission. And forgive me, for I imagine my knowledge of the law is not as extensive as yours, but I know he was within his rights to retrieve the birds from your land, providing he did no damage.''

''What nonsense is this?'' Marcus exploded.

''Kindly moderate your tone, my lord! All my tenants have my permission to shoot, trap and fish over my land. In the absence of crops in my fields, I harvest whatever my land yields for the benefit of both myself and my people. You were the one who told me to look to my starving tenants, after all!''

Donna was talking in the doorway to Jem, who came forward to help Wilkins out. ''See that he gets home safely, please, Jem. And see if you can find his pigeons, will you?'' she added, with a vituperative glance at Sparrow.

"Sparrow, leave us," Marcus ordered between clenched teeth.

As the man closed the kitchen door behind him, Antonia remarked conversationally, "I presume, my lord, that you will be placing that man on a charge of common assault for breaking Wilkins' nose?"

"Do not try my patience further, madam," Marcus ground out. "This is madness! Are you so penurious that you must give every ne'er-do-well in the county licence to poach on your lands?"

"My hard-working and deserving tenants are merely harvesting the land as I have explained. They are not responsible for my father's recklessness, but they have to suffer the consequences. I do what little I can to mitigate their poverty."

"And your own," he added quietly. "I do not understand your stubbornness, Miss Dane; I have made you a fair proposal to buy, and I would offer you a fair price— for the house as well, if you would accept it. It would allow you to return to London and to live as a gentlewoman should. Not like this!" His scornful eye once more swept the bare flagged floor, the scrubbed deal table with the shabby chairs drawn up to it.

"Are you suggesting that this household is anything less than respectable, my lord?" Donna had re-entered the kitchen unobserved, her small figure bristling with indignation at the insult.

"Forgive me, Miss Donaldson," he said with a satirical twist to his lips. "I have no doubt that the moral tone of this establishment is as a nunnery. However, it strikes me that Miss Dane might have a better chance of catching herself a husband were she in London."

Antonia had, for the most fleeting of moments, allowed herself to indulge in thoughts of the pleasures of living in Town: shopping in the Burlington Arcade, driving in the Park, congenial evenings at Almack's where she could dance the night away, her card full. But Marcus Allington's crude remarks about her lack of success in the Marriage Mart brought her swiftly to her senses.

"Catch myself a husband?" She pulled herself up to her full height, eyes sparking fire.

Donna, watching from the doorway, thought she had rarely seen her charge looking more magnificent, despite her old gown and simply dressed hair.

"Let me assure you, sir, that a husband is something I regret the lack of not one whit!" Her colour was up, flooding her naturally creamy skin with a warm glow, emphasising the fine strong bones of her features. Her figure was slender but, under the stress of strong emotion, her bosom rising and falling, she looked Junoesque.

Marcus, too, was stirred. "Take it from a disinterested observer, ma'am, a husband to school and curb you would be a most desirable thing! Very well, then, you have made your hard bed—lie upon it. Perhaps after a country winter, you will apply a more reasoned judgement to my offer." He paused to pull on his gloves. "I can wait."

"Then you will wait a long time, my lord. For I intend to lease this house and grounds forthwith to a most respectable tenant."

"Indeed?" Marcus's dark brows drew together. "And supposing you find a person deluded enough to take on this ramshackle estate, where do you intend to live?"

Antonia hesitated, at a loss. He had provoked her into

a wild statement of defiance and now she had no answer to his very pertinent question.

''Why, in the Dower House, of course,'' supplied Miss Donaldson calmly, from the shadows.

Chapter Four

Marcus's hard laugh rang round the kitchen. "A neat device, ladies, I must congratulate you upon your optimism."

"Optimism?" Antonia repeated with dangerous calm. "Why describe a perfectly practical solution so dismissively, sir? Or do you wish me gone from here so much?" She realised, as soon as the words were out, that she wanted to know the answer to that latter question very badly indeed.

"Your whereabouts, Miss Dane, are of little concern to me, provided that you are not inciting your tenants to lawlessness as this episode would suggest." Marcus smiled thinly as he pulled on his riding gauntlets. "I shall watch with interest your attempts to gull some Cit into taking on this…liability of a house. I wish you good day, ladies." He nodded curtly to them both and stalked out.

As the door closed behind him, Antonia clutched the edge of the table to support her shaking legs. The encounter had affected her composure more than she would have thought possible. Marcus Allington was having the most deleterious effect on her equilibrium: she wanted him to like her, to support her efforts to keep her family estates together despite overwhelming odds.

And yet he was so inexplicably hostile. She could only conclude that he disliked her—which, she was honest enough to realise, was a disappointment—but that he wanted her lands badly enough to maintain the connection.

"Well, that was a nasty show of temper," remarked Miss Donaldson as she calmly tidied away the tea things. "But I suppose we should be thankful for, after all, it provoked me into thinking of a solution. Do you truly think it is feasible for us to move to the Dower House?"

Antonia met Miss Donaldson's bird-like eyes, bright with excitement. "But, Donna, I thought that was just something you said upon the spur of the moment to irk his lordship. Were you truly serious?"

"Yes, Antonia, I do believe we could live most comfortably there, for from what you told me it is just of a size for the two of us. However, it grieves me to admit it," she added with a wry smile, "but his lordship is quite correct about this house. How are we to lease it in its present state of repair? We have just agreed we do not have the resources to make it habitable."

Antonia got to her feet and began to pace up and down the flagged floor, her underlip caught in her teeth. Where indeed were they to find the money? She passed her small income and the few pieces of jewellery she had inherited under review. Even with Donna's tiny pension it would not do. There was only one recourse. It came hard, for the example of her late father was ever before her, a man ruined by debt—but she had little choice.

Taking a deep breath, "I shall borrow the money," Antonia announced decisively. "I can put the estate up for security and repay the loan from the rent."

"Oh, dear—" Miss Donaldson creased her brow "—debt makes me so nervous! Only consider your late parent's predicament and what it has cost you to retrieve it."

Antonia remembered only too well the awful moment when their man of law had explained how little remained of the previously substantial family fortune once Sir Humphrey's debts had been quit. But she had little alternative other than to borrow.

She leaned across the table and explained earnestly, "But this is different, Donna. Father borrowed with no intention of repaying the money, unless by gaming! I do not intend to continue borrowing beyond this one contingency; look upon it as an investment, which should soon realise a return. Pass me *Pigot's Directory* and let us see which banks there are in Berkhamsted to whom I may apply."

They scanned the commercial directory together. "There is only one," Miss Donaldson said, running her finger down the column. "Perhaps it would be better if you went into Aylesbury."

"But look—it says here that this bank is an agent for Praed and Company in London: nothing could be better, for they act for Great Aunt Honoria."

"You do not intend to deal directly with the bank, I hope; it would be most unseemly," Miss Donaldson admonished. They may have come to a pretty pass, but for a young lady of breeding to enter a place of business was unthinkable. "You will be writing to your man of business, will you not?"

"No, for it will cause a delay we can ill afford. I shall go the day after tomorrow," Antonia added decisively. "I shall write now to the manager and make an appointment. Jem can take the letter."

Miss Donaldson recognised when Antonia had made up her mind and knew all too well it would be fruitless to argue. "Very well, my dear, if you insist, but I cannot like it. However, needs must: we shall attend to your wardrobe. If you go into town with your kid gloves in the state they are at present, our poverty will be only too evident to all!"

The kid gloves, after much sponging and brushing, were all a lady could desire. Antonia stood on the steps of the Aylesbury Branch Bank wishing her courage were as easily restored, for despite her brave words to Miss Donaldson she was feeling decidedly apprehensive. It was simply not done for ladies of quality to deal with matters of business, and she had neither knowledge nor experience of such proceedings.

Through the discreet veil which Donna had insisted on attaching to her bonnet, she stared at the burnished brass plate that gleamed brightly despite the dullness of the day: Agents for Praed's Bank—James Pethybridge, Manager. Antonia stepped down again and took a few agitated paces along the pavement, glad of its height above the roadway, which was muddy from the day's light drizzle. Even the dismal weather conspired against her courage today.

Perhaps she ought to walk along to the King's Arms and bespeak a cup of coffee in a private parlour… Even as she hesitated, the church tower clock chimed close by. Eleven o'clock, the hour set for her appointment in Mr Pethybridge's reply; Antonia swallowed hard and raised her hand to the knocker.

The clerk ushered her into the banker's inner sanctum with due deference but with a sideways glance that betrayed his surprise at finding her unaccompanied. As she shook hands and sat down, Antonia was gratified to see only a look of polite enquiry on the banker's face, for she had been fearing outright rejection, if not incredulity at the thought of a woman carrying out her own transactions.

Miss Donaldson's assiduous work on her walking dress and frogged jacket had obviously passed muster, and the addition of a new ostrich plume to her bonnet had transformed its appearance. She smoothed down the garnet red cloth of her skirts and smiled back at the banker with a confidence she was far from feeling.

Mr Pethybridge was an amiable-looking gentleman in his early fifties, rotund and greying. His avuncular manner encouraged Antonia as she began to explain her circumstances and the nature of her request, becoming more confident and persuasive as she spoke.

Twenty minutes later, with her optimism and spirits quite dashed, he ushered her out into the main office. "I do hope you appreciate, Miss Dane, the force of my arguments," he said fluently with the air of a man long practised in turning down ill-considered requests for advances. "It would be most unwise for a young lady, circumstanced as you are, to enter into such an arrangement. Indeed, it would be most irresponsible of me to encourage you to take on such a debt at this time..."

He broke off as he became aware that another visitor was speaking to his clerk. "I do beg your pardon, Miss Dane." Mr Pethybridge was flushed with embarrassment at having been caught discussing business in the presence of others. "Allow me to see you out." He ushered her towards the door, bowing deferentially as he passed the newcomer. "Good morning, my lord, I shall be with you directly."

"Good morning, Pethybridge." Antonia started at the

familiar, lazily deep tones and struggled to compose her features as she passed Marcus Allington with a slight inclination of her head. She regretted not replacing her veil.

"Miss Dane, good day. I hope I find you well? May I be so bold as to enquire if your business has prospered?"

There was little doubt that his lordship's business prospered: there was no sign of the angry man in country riding clothes of the previous day. Marcus Allington had obviously driven into town; his multi-caped driving coat was carelessly thrown open over immaculately cut, long-tailed coat and breeches. His boots shone like ebony and had miraculously avoided contact with the mud that, despite her best efforts, had spattered Antonia's kid half-boots.

He had also permitted his valet to trim some of the unruliness from his dark blond hair where previously it had curled unfashionably long on his collar.

Antonia, realising she was staring, swallowed a bitter retort, brought up her chin defiantly, and replied, "It has not prospered, as you will no doubt be unsurprised to hear, my lord."

"Indeed? I am sorry to hear that." Ignoring Antonia's disbelieving expression, Marcus continued, "Perhaps I could offer some assistance? Doubtless with your man of business absent you found yourself at some disadvantage in explaining the circumstances to my friend Pethybridge here."

Thus subtly reminded of the extent of his dealings with his lordship, Mr Pethybridge hastened to usher them both back into his office. "Allow me to send for some refreshment. Do sit down, Miss Dane, and permit me to explore the details further: his lordship is no doubt correct that in your understandable inexperience you have omitted to mention something germane to the case.'' He was all unctuousness now in his desire to please his lordship.

''Doubtless,'' Antonia replied coolly, ''for I am sure his lordship is never wrong.''

To her intense embarrassment, the banker took this as permission to review the facts she had laid before him, thus exhibiting every detail of her financial circumstances to Marcus, who sat at his ease in a wing chair, seemingly unsurprised by what he heard.

Antonia scarcely attended to what the banker was saying, her mind in a whirl of speculation. What was Marcus Allington about, in so promoting her cause? Yesterday he had made it plain he thought her foolish in the extreme—and why should he do anything so prejudicial to his own interests in acquiring her land as to help her to a loan? That was not the way to snap up her property and expand his own...

Her speculation was curtailed by Mr Pethybridge announcing, ''In view of these facts, I see no reason not to advance you the sum you request immediately.''

Antonia was so astonished at this complete about-face that it was as much as she could do to manage the common civilities of thanks. What had Marcus said to sway the man? But she could hardly ask now, thus proving she had paid no attention to the proceedings—the men would think her a perfect fool!

The banker bowed them out with renewed protestations of his desire to assist Miss Dane in any way he could.

Standing on the pavement, drawing on her gloves, she realised that Marcus was at her side. Startled into directness, she demanded, "What game are you about, my lord?"

"What can you mean, Miss Dane?" he enquired urbanely, offering her his arm. "Allow me to escort you to your carriage, the pavements are so slippery."

"You may escort me to the King's Arms where Jem awaits me with the gig," Antonia snapped. "And you know what I mean! Pethybridge had no intention of granting me the loan until you intervened. Nothing, nothing, had changed and yet he reversed his decision, as you knew he would!" The effort of quarrelling in public with a man who retained his infuriating calm only fuelled her anger. "Surely you do not expect me to believe you have no ulterior motive in securing me this loan, my lord?"

"Indeed I have, Miss Dane." The more angry she became, the suaver his manner was.

Antonia was taken aback. "Well, what is it? It seems to me to be an action quite against your own interests."

"I have no intention of telling you that. And you must allow me to judge what my own interests are, Antonia."

"Do not address me so, my lord—and you must tell me! I have no desire to be beholden to you."

"Your desires are not the only ones at issue: and I have no intention of gratifying your curiosity." Marcus glanced sideways at her, a small smile touching his lips. "You were not paying a great deal of attention in Pethybridge's office, were you?"

She flushed at the veracity of his observation, but did not reply.

"That is understandable, for it must have been an ordeal for a lady, and I can understand you being distracted. But it is not sensible to undertake business with only half your mind on the matter."

He guided her through the cobbled entry to the inn. "Ah, your carriage awaits, complete with chickens in a coop and straw upon the boards, I see. Is it too much to hope that you will spend some of your loan on a conveyance more suited to your station in life?"

"Lord Allington, I have never in my life been tempted to strike another human being," Antonia hissed in a low voice, aware of an interested audience of Jem and two lounging ostlers. "But I am sorely tempted now! You are quite the most insufferable, patronising, arrogant individual it has ever been my misfortune to encounter. I must be grateful that you have helped me to obtain the funds I need, but do not think I do not harbour the deepest suspicions as to your motives."

"Your imagination is too vivid, Miss Dane." He steered her to one side as a farmer's gig swept through the yard. "As I observed the other day, your addiction to Gothick novels has much to answer for. I bid you good day, Antonia." Before she could upbraid him for using her Christian name again he had tipped his hat and had gone, striding through the archway into the High Street.

Jem prattled cheerfully as they drove home, very pleased with himself for the bargain he had struck over the coop full of chickens. Antonia made admiring noises, but her mind still dwelt on Marcus's extraordinary behaviour.

What had he meant by telling her she should have paid more attention in the banker's office? Had she missed some vital point? Antonia racked her brains, but in vain. She opened her reticule and unfolded her copy of the paper she had signed: yes, she had mortgaged the house and land against the loan that she had taken out for a maximum term of one year.

She sat and stared heedlessly over the burgeoning hedges already white with May blossom, mentally editing a version of that morning's events for Miss Donaldson. Donna would only say "I told you that you should send a man upon the business" in her most governessy tone, Antonia thought. But that was not what was so irksome about the matter; if her man of business had been easily available, she would have employed him.

No, it was because it was Marcus Allington... She had no desire to be beholden to him for his intervention with Pethybridge! But, more importantly, she did not want Donna to harp endlessly on about his possible motives—why, she would conclude that his lordship was attracted to Antonia. "Too ridiculous for words!" she exclaimed aloud, then had to apologise to Jem, who had taken it as a comment on his commercial triumph and was most put out.

Donna was sitting by the open back door, engaged in turning a worn sheet edge to edge, her work basket at her feet, but she dropped the linen unregarded as she heard Antonia's step on the path. "Well, my dear, back already! Did you have a nice drive?"

Antonia saw at once the anxiety which lay behind the bright words; Donna was steeling herself for disappointment, and was already braced to offer soothing words and encouragement. Antonia put her arms around her companion and hugged her fiercely. "We have the money, Donna! Every guinea we need!"

"Hooray!" Donna threw her pincushion up in the air, seized Antonia's hands and proceeded to jig around the kitchen, much to the consternation of the charwoman who emerged from the scullery, wiping her hands on her apron to see what all the noise was about.

Donna subsided into a chair in a billow of skirts, pink-cheeked and quite unperturbed by the amazement of Mrs Brown, who hastily took herself off to the kitchen garden shaking her head over the unaccountable ways of the gentry. "Tell me all about it—every detail," Donna demanded.

Antonia produced a highly edited version of her interview with Mr Pethybridge, carefully omitting any reference to Marcus Allington, then reached for the commercial directory in search of builders and carpenters.

"I cannot believe the thing was so easily accomplished," Miss Donaldson persisted. "I thought you would have the most enormous difficulty going unaccompanied." She looked beadily at Antonia's betraying flush. "Antonia, why are you looking so conscious? Have you been employing feminine wiles upon Mr Pethybridge?"

"Upon Mr Pethybridge?" Antonia's guilty indignation was fuelled by the knowledge that she had not told Donna the truth. "Really, Donna, as if I would! Why, he is quite an elderly gentleman."

"Hmm…" was the only reply from her perceptive companion who inwardly believed that even elderly gentlemen had an eye for a pretty young woman.

The next few weeks passed in a blur of activity as Antonia began to put her credit to good use. The house seemed full of workmen repairing the roof, reglazing windows, unblocking drains and repainting woodwork neglected for many years. Miss Donaldson thrived amid the chaos. She was in her element supervising the polishing of panelling and staircases and was all for redecorating the entire house from attics to cellars.

"Donna, the bank loan is not bottomless," Antonia cautioned. "And I intend spending some of it reroofing the tenants' cottages, for they are in a scandalous state. Besides, if all is sound and clean, the new tenant will be able to put his own stamp upon the decorations. I have had a most encouraging response from a Mr Blake, the agent for the gentleman who advertised in *The Times*—I shall suggest he comes down to see the house and, should he prove interested, we can discuss such details then.''

Lying in bed that night, kept awake both by the smell of fresh paint and the moonlight flooding in through the window, Antonia stretched luxuriously in the half-tester bed. The two ladies no longer had to share a room and Antonia now occupied one of the chambers at the side of the house overlooking the pleasure grounds. Restlessly, she rose and crossed to the window, admiring the greensward, newly scythed by Old Johnson after much grumbling.

The moonlight was almost as bright as day and even reflected off the river, a curve of which cut across the grounds. It was calm, still and almost unseasonably warm for April and Antonia felt no desire to go back to bed. Her days were very full, but at night, unless she managed to fall asleep at once, her mind kept turning to thoughts of Marcus.

She managed to curb unruly memories of being in his arms, of the touch of his lips on hers, but when she closed her eyes she saw his face as clearly as if he were standing before her. It seemed more than just a few weeks since she had last seen him.

Briskly she shook herself—this would not do! If she could not sleep she should do something useful—or even go for a walk. The light was good enough for a stroll around the lawns, or even to venture as far as the river.

Something her brother Howard had told her years ago when she was still living at Rye End Hall and he was just a schoolboy came back to her; it was better to fish at night, for then the fish rose more easily to the lure. It was a mad idea, but why not try a cast tonight? It seemed a very simple thing when she saw other people do it and she knew where the rods and lines were. How surprised Donna would be to find a nice fat perch on her plate for breakfast!

Hastily dressing in a plain gown and pulling on a stout pair of shoes, Antonia tiptoed downstairs before reason could reassert itself and send her back to her bed.

The rods were in the store-room where she had last seen them; there were several, all different, which was confusing. Antonia tried a couple for weight, then selected the smallest before remembering she would need bait. In the pantry, she cut rind from the bacon, lit a horn lantern, then, feeling quite an old hand at the sport, crept out and across the lawns.

The night was almost completely still; there was no wind and, other than a faint rustling as a night creature slipped through the grass, no sound. Antonia found a patch of dry gravel to stand upon, set down her lantern and attempted to bait the hook. This proved more difficult than she expected: the hook was sharp and the bacon slippery.

Eventually, she succeeded and, throwing her arm right back, cast the line over the water. Nothing happened. Antonia peered at the rod in the lamplight and fiddled with the reel until it was running smoothly, then tried again. This time the bacon shot right across the river and snagged on the rushes on the opposite bank.

After several attempts, Antonia's arm was aching and she was realising that there was more to fishing than met the eye. "One more try!" she muttered. To her great surprise, the line landed plumb in the middle of the river with a satisfying plop.

Despite this triumph, Antonia soon discovered that fishing was a less stimulating activity than she had been led to believe. The silence stretched on, broken only by an owl hooting as it drifted over the meadow. The line hung in the scarcely moving water and Antonia stifled a yawn.

She was just wondering idly what time it was and when the fish were going to start jumping when the rod in her hand gave a jerk and the line began to run out. She had caught a fish! Antonia grasped the handle of the rod firmly and began to reel in the line until the squirming silvery fish was clear of the water. She landed it clumsily on the grass, dropped the rod, then realised she had no idea how to proceed now.

She pounced on the fish, grabbing at it with both hands, alarmed to discover just how slippery and muscular a live fish was. She turned and twisted as the fish leapt in her hands then found herself thoroughly entangled in her own line as it wrapped around her ankles.

"Oh, keep still!" she pleaded with the fish, but it did not oblige, lashing its tail to soak the front of her dress.

"I should have known it would be you!" A voice half-weary, half-amused, sounded almost in her ear.

Antonia shrieked in alarm. As her hand jerked, it freed the hook from the perch, which leapt from her grip into the river. With her heart in her mouth, Antonia spun round to face Marcus Allington. He was quite at ease, leaning against the trunk of a willow that bent over the water.

"Is there no end to your talents, Miss Dane?" he enquired, his mouth twitching with suppressed laughter.

"Do not dare laugh at me," she stormed. "You scared me half to death and you made me drop my fish!"

"A very respectable perch by the look of it; a shame you let it slip through your fingers." The angrier she became, the more amused Marcus appeared.

"*I* let it! If you had not crept up behind me like some thief in the night..." She took a hasty step forward and felt the fine line wrap itself more firmly round her ankles. "Oh, bother this line, it has a life of its own!"

"Stand still and I will untrammel you." Marcus sauntered over and dropped to one knee beside her.

Antonia stood looking down on his bent head, burning with embarrassment at the touch of his fingers at her ankles. She shifted uneasily, awkwardly unsure of what to do with her hands, and he admonished sharply, "If you wriggle you will make it worse! Come," he rallied her, "this is no time for maidenly modesty, Miss Dane— do you want to be here till dawn?"

"Well, hurry up then," she responded pettishly, glad that at least the moonlight would leach the colour from her flushed cheeks. "Can you not cut it?"

"Cut a line?" He sat back on his heels and looked up at her, his eyes glinting in the subdued light. "Really, Miss Dane, I can see you are no true angler. If you had not dropped the hook in the folds of your gown I could be quicker, but I have no intention of running its barbs into my thumb."

"Well, do your best." She subsided, quivering with a mixture of emotions ranging from indignation and embarrassment to a strange excitement and a terrible compulsion to let her hands run through the thick hair on the bowed head before her.

It seemed forever before he rose to his feet, the hook held securely between finger and thumb, the line trailing free on the grass. "There you are—you can begin again now. Where is your bait?"

"Over there, but I think I have fished enough for one night."

"Bacon?" He peered into the dish. "What were you intending to catch with that, for goodness' sake?" The amusement was back in his voice again.

"Perch, of course. Bacon is excellent for perch—as you just witnessed."

"A veritable Izaak Walton," he teased. "Here, take your hook and line."

He held both out to her and the act of stepping forward to take them brought her disturbingly close to him. She held out a tentative hand for the hook, but he shook his head, "No, on second thoughts, you are right, you have fished enough tonight." He secured the hook onto the reel and dropped the rod.

Marcus stood regarding her, musing that, even in the plain, worn gown with her hair awry, the unruly curls falling about her cheekbones, Miss Antonia Dane was quite provokingly desirable, the more so because she was entirely without artifice. Even in the moonlight he could see the clear hazel eyes regarding him steadily, the lashes naturally sooty and curled. The light took the colour from the flawless skin, lending her the appearance of an alabaster statue.

"What are you looking at me like that for?" Antonia asked, her mouth suddenly dry. Encounters with this man in broad daylight were unsettling enough, but under the influence of the full moon she felt anything might happen.

There was amusement in the look he was giving her, but he was not laughing at her expense; rather the look was tender and appreciative and transformed his face, making him seem less harsh, more approachable. "Oh, I was just thinking how charmingly you smell…of fish."

"You…!" She raised a hand in fury, only for him to catch it lightly by the wrist.

"Please, do not slap my face—not covered as you are with fish scales and slime." His voice was warm and insidious as he pulled her gently towards him as if she too were a fish on a line. Antonia found herself moving, unresisting, compliant.

"I really ought to wash my hands," she faltered ridiculously, irrelevantly.

"No need, we can manage if you only keep them at your sides," he remarked dispassionately before bending his head to kiss her.

His mouth was moving around the curve of her upper lip, gently nibbling. Antonia gasped with the intimate shock of the sensation, but made no attempt to break free. When he reached the full softness of her lower lip she capitulated utterly, tipping her face trustingly upwards. His hands still held hers captive at her sides, which made the embrace seem even more shocking and disturbing.

Marcus murmured into her hair, "I must come night fishing again; I would never imagine I would catch such a prize."

"Marcus, I am not a fish!" she protested into his coat front, but it was only the mildest of reproofs. She had no desire to move out of the circle of his arms, away from his warmth and the strength that was evident even through the fine cloth of his coat. Did she feel like this because it was Marcus who was holding her, she wondered, or was it moon madness?

He sighed, his breath stirring the fine hair at her temple. "Agreeable as I find this, we cannot stand out here all night, Antonia. What will the redoubtable Miss Donaldson think has become of you?''

"Nothing, I trust," replied Antonia, trying not to feel disappointed as he turned from her to collect up her fishing tackle and lantern. "She was asleep when I left, and I hope she still is."

He took her arm, guiding her solicitously over the tussocky grass of the still-untamed pleasure grounds. "Then you came fishing on a whim? What an extraordinary young woman you are." The lantern was attracting small moths, which rose from the lawn at their feet so that they appeared to be walking in a small cloud.

"We cannot live on game alone; I thought fish would be a welcome variation." She glanced at him sideways to see how he took this reference to her licensed "poachers".

"I am not going to rise to your bait, Antonia; it is late and I am tired. I am resolved not to mention your poachers again, unless we find any on my land—not that I am happy with the example you are setting. But why do you not set that lad of yours to fishing? He has no doubt been doing it in my rivers half his life."

So, he had decided to let that quarrel lie, she mused. Still, that did not explain why he had so unexpectedly come to her aid with the banker. "It sounds dangerously as if you are resigned to my remaining at Rye End Hall, my lord."

He stopped and looked at her, a glint that was not all amusement in his eye. "Take care, Antonia. You may have a penchant for angling, but do not try to fish for my motives. I told you I would not discuss them, that day in Berkhamsted."

Antonia was not so easily discouraged. "Come, my lord, 'twas less than a week before that that you were violently opposed to our remaining here and wished to buy my lands. Are you no longer interested in acquiring them?''

Marcus tucked her hand under his arm once more and carried on towards the house. ''There is more than one way to skin a cat, Antonia,'' he remarked casually, smiling faintly at her answering snort of exasperation. ''Now, which door did you come out by?''

''The side door—it is unlocked.''

Marcus looked at her in surprise. ''Really, Antonia, have you no care for burglars? You truly are the most extraordinary woman I have ever encountered.''

''If we are to talk of extraordinary behaviours, Marcus, why are you out at this hour? Why, it must be all of half past two.''

''A card party at Sir George Dover's. It was such a pleasant evening I walked over.'' He named a near neighbour of hers whose wife had already made her call of courtesy. ''As you say, the hour is late. Goodnight, Antonia.'' He lifted her hand, kissing the back of her wrist, well away from her fish-scaled fingers, and strode off along the footpath into the moonlight towards Brightshill.

A short while later, Antonia snuggled down in her bed and thought back on that extraordinary encounter. There was no doubting she had behaved most improperly, moonlight or not, but she could not regret allowing Marcus to kiss her.

Her fingers, now mercifully free of fish, strayed to her lips, tracing where his mouth had roamed. Surely he was not simply toying with her affections? There was no denying that her affections were engaged, and he was a gentleman, after all. Yet that casual remark about skinning cats, his refusal to discuss his motives for helping her with the loan—those nagged at the back of her mind. She had refused to sell him her lands—had he now some other ploy in mind?

Chapter Five

"Oh, Donna! Mr Blake writes to say they are most interested in my description of the property and my proposals!"

Antonia waved two sheets of hot-pressed notepaper at Miss Donaldson, who put down her needlework and asked placidly, "Do you refer to your answer to the advertisement in *The Times*? Do stop jigging around the room, my dear, and let me see…"

Antonia, her eyes shining, whirled to a halt on the newly cleaned salon carpet and handed the letter to her companion. "I am so relieved!" she exclaimed. "After putting all this work in hand, I must admit to a severe apprehension that we would not find a tenant willing to take it."

"I, too," Miss Donaldson confessed, smoothing out the sheets to con them again. "After all, it is almost four weeks since you wrote. So much money has been spent—although I must say it is most pleasant to be able to sit in here, instead of sharing the kitchen with Mrs Brown, especially now the weather is so clement."

They both turned to look from the wide bay window across the green swathe of lawn, finally responding to

Old Johnson's frequent scything. The fine weather had allowed the workmen to complete almost all their work on the Hall; tomorrow, they would commence the smaller task of making the Dower House habitable again.

The river glinted in the sunlight, recalling her moonlight encounter with Marcus Allington. Antonia struggled to suppress the nagging feeling of disappointment that struck her every time she thought of that incident. She had honestly expected Marcus to call again, to start wooing her.

She had teased herself, wondering if he was interested in her for herself or her property, and then had felt most disheartened on learning that his lordship had left for London the following day. She told herself that it would teach her not to jump to conclusions, or indeed, flatter herself that a man like Marcus would have serious intentions towards someone with no fortune, no sophistication, no experience…

"Are you attending, my dear?" Miss Donaldson had obviously been speaking for some minutes. Antonia recalled herself and apologised. "I was saying that this Mr Blake states here his intention of calling the day after tomorrow unless he hears to the contrary. I do believe we should send a positive response today, for we are quite ready to receive him."

"You are correct; it would create a good impression and it is important that he convince his principal that this property is right for him."

Antonia felt far from confident that she could negotiate the lease successfully. She had still not told Donna that it was only with Marcus's intervention that the bank loan had been granted. By herself, she had failed utterly with Mr Pethybridge; Mr Jeremy Blake was probably cut from the same cloth. And this time she could hardly call on Lord Allington to negotiate on her behalf, even if he had been at Brightshill.

Two days later Miss Donaldson was flitting around with a duster polishing wood that already gleamed and driving Antonia to distraction. She was nervous enough about their visitor as it was. "Please, Donna, come and sit down. Mr Blake is due at any moment and you are quite flushed. Oh, listen! Is that a chaise I hear now?"

Donna thrust the duster under the sofa cushions and patted her hair firmly under her cap. Antonia smoothed out the folds of her only respectable morning dress and cast a hasty glance in the overmantel mirror. She felt confident her appearance would impress an elderly lawyer: her unruly dark hair was caught back smoothly under a dark ribbon, her high-necked dress was trimmed chastely at collar and cuff with Brussels lace and her only ornaments were a good amber set inherited from her mother.

She turned as their newly appointed maidservant announced, "Mr Blake, ma'am."

A man scarcely older than herself stood on the threshold of the salon. Mr Blake was a pleasant-looking gentleman with a cheerful, plain face, neatly trimmed brown hair and immaculately fashionable, if sober, clothing. A far cry, indeed, from the dessicated lawyer they had been expecting. And if the ladies were surprised, so too was Mr Blake. He was not quite quick enough to conceal the look of, first, surprise and then pleasure as he took in the striking young lady stepping forward to greet him.

From the cool formality of the letter Miss Dane had written him, Mr Blake had expected to find a formidable spinster of indeterminate age. Instead, he was confronted by an elegant young woman dressed with stylish severity. She was not quite in the established mode, being too tall and willowy, to say nothing of being a brunette when the fashion was for blondes, but to him she appeared entirely admirable.

He schooled his face and took her proffered hand as she greeted him. "Good day, Mr Blake, I trust you had a pleasant journey from Town."

"Thank you, ma'am. I spent the night in Berkhamsted at the White Hart in tolerable comfort."

"May I present my companion, Miss Donaldson."

This lady was more in the style Jeremy had been expecting. He exchanged polite bows with Donna and accepted both the seat and the cup of tea that were offered.

"I realise you have only had the most cursory of first impressions of Rye End Hall," Antonia said, attempting to sound unconcerned, "but may I ask if this is the sort of property your principal is seeking?"

"Yes, indeed," Mr Blake said warmly, then recollected himself, adding more coolly, "That is to say, the location is precisely what Sir Josiah desires, and the house appears charming."

"Sir Josiah?"

"I think there is no harm in my revealing that I represent Sir Josiah Finch, who returned from the East Indies some twelve months ago and is now desirous of settling in this area from whence his family originated."

"How very interesting; no doubt he will find the countryside hereabouts a great contrast to the Indies!" They continued to exchange pleasantries whilst the tea was drunk. Antonia talked on, not showing by a whit her instinct that Mr Blake was not only very favourably disposed towards the Hall, but also towards herself. It was very gratifying to feel one was admired, and she was enjoying the respectful admiration in Mr Blake's eyes.

"Another cup of tea, Mr Blake? No?" Antonia rose to her feet. "Then may I conduct you on a tour of Rye End Hall?"

As they crossed the hall, Antonia paused to allow him time to observe its proportions before she asked, "Are you well acquainted with Sir Josiah?"

"Indeed, I am, Miss Dane, we are related by marriage."

"I asked, for I was wondering if he intended bringing his family; there is ample accommodation."

"Sir Josiah is married—Lady Finch is my aunt—but alas, they are without surviving children; the Indies are a cruel place for those of tender years."

Out of the corner of her eye, as she murmured words of regret, Antonia was aware of Donna slipping back into the salon, no doubt to peruse the pages of *Burke's Landed Gentry* for the records of the Finch family. Such a connection would explain Mr Blake's air of easy good breeding. And, Antonia mused, it should also make negotiations much simpler; no doubt he was fully in his uncle's confidence and would be able to make decisions without constant reference to his principal.

Mr Blake proved to be an undemanding visitor, although he made frequent notes in his notebook. He admired the number and proportions of the rooms, commented favourably upon the domestic arrangements and was fully in accord with their decision not to decorate extensively.

"Sir Josiah will be bringing a considerable collection of Oriental furnishings and art works," he explained as they descended the staircase. "And he will wish to hang some very fine Chinese wallpapers, if that is acceptable to you, Miss Dane?''

''Oh, certainly, I would have no objection. You sound as though you have already resolved to recommend Rye End Hall to Sir Josiah,'' Antonia commented, attempting to conceal the eagerness in her voice.

''I think it would suit them admirably,'' Mr Blake began, ''but the final decision is, of course, Sir Josiah's,'' he added with a sudden return to lawyer-like caution.

''Would you care to take a little luncheon before seeing the pleasure grounds and Home Farm?'' Antonia offered, determined to remain cool and businesslike, but quite unable to hide the pleasure and relief that flooded through her at his positive words.

Jeremy Blake blinked at the radiant smile which illuminated Antonia's face, transforming her from a cool and severe lady into a charming and vivacious girl. There and then he determined that not only was Sir Josiah going to lease Rye End Hall, but that he would make every effort to provoke Miss Dane into smiling at him like that again.

Miss Donaldson had left off from her scanning of *Burke's* long enough to order up a light collation to be served in the breakfast room. Antonia would have wished that the smell of beeswax polish was not quite so obvious, bespeaking as it did all the hard work and hope which had gone into preparing the house for this visit. Fortunately, Mr Blake seemed oblivious to such details of housekeeping.

''Most eligible…extremely well connected,'' Donna hissed excitedly in Antonia's ear as they entered the room. ''I have marked the page…''

"Donna…shh! Do take this seat, Mr Blake, it affords a fine view down to the river."

"That puts me in mind of another question I must ask—thank you, ma'am, cold pigeon would be most acceptable—is the fishing good? And do you intend to retain the rights?"

To both his, and Miss Donaldson's, astonishment, Antonia blushed to the roots of her dark hair. Mr Blake frantically scanned his memory to find what he could have said to produce such a reaction while Antonia recollected herself hastily. "I believe there are perch, but I really cannot say. I have no intention of keeping the fishing rights, none at all."

Her vehemence was as puzzling as her confusion and she was very aware of Miss Donaldson's beady regard. She must pull herself together, stop falling into daydreams and reveries every time anyone mentioned the river. A sensible woman would conclude that, despite his dalliance on the river bank, Lord Allington's absence was a clear signal that the incident meant nothing to him. She became aware that Mr Blake was speaking again and remarked hastily, "And no doubt pike are common."

"In the stables?" Miss Donaldson interjected. "Antonia dear, you have lost the thread of the conversation, we were speaking of accommodation for Sir Josiah's carriage horses."

"I am so sorry. A syllabub, Mr Blake, or can I tempt you with a jelly?"

"Either, Miss Dane," the lawyer responded warmly, causing Donna to cast up her eyes. The man appeared to be highly attracted to dear Antonia, which, considering his most eligible connections, was not to be discouraged. On the other hand, she had entertained hopes of Lord Allington, but that unfortunate disagreement over the poaching appeared to have driven him away...

An hour later, only the stables remained to be inspected. Mr Blake expressed his intention of setting forth immediately and set his groom to hitching up his pair while he looked around.

"I hope to regain London tonight and speak to Sir Josiah tomorrow morning," he explained as they emerged from the carriage house into the sunlight once more.

"You will be very late, surely?" Antonia queried.

"I shall change horses at Stanmore and expect to make good time. Sir Josiah is impatient when it comes to matters of business—he will expect a prompt report."

"May I enquire if you are still of a positive mind in recommending this house to Sir Josiah?" Antonia crossed her fingers in the folds of her skirts as she ventured the question.

"Let me just say that I shall ask the name and direction of your man of business before I leave," Mr Blake replied, pencil poised over his notebook.

Antonia dictated the details and London address, making a mental note to write with all dispatch to Mr Cooke at Gray's Inn, who would otherwise be deeply confused to receive such an approach from Mr Blake.

She was slightly taken aback at the sight of Mr Blake's conveyance, a rakish sporting curricle pulled by a pair of handsome matched bays. She had expected a lawyer to be driven in a closed carriage, not to be tooling himself down the highway. But then, Mr Jeremy Blake was most unlawyerlike in many respects.

"Well, I must thank you for your hospitality, Miss Dane, Miss Donaldson," Mr Blake began, taking Antonia's hand in his and looking into her hazel eyes warmly. "And I hope to be able to give you an answer within a few days…"

He was in mid-sentence, Antonia's hand still clasped in his own, when, with a flurry of hooves on the gravel, Marcus Allington cantered into the stableyard astride a rakish chestnut. He reined in hard, but not before the carriage horses shied in alarm, the groom running to their heads.

Mr Blake immediately stepped between the ladies and the horses, glaring with unconcealed annoyance at the source of the intrusion.

Antonia's heart leapt in her chest as she stood there, a prey to mixed emotions. She was glad to see Marcus again after so many days, annoyed at herself for caring that he had not called, and acutely conscious of how they had last met. Her eyes flew to his face, searching for some glance, some acknowledgment of their encounter by the river.

Marcus had calmed the chestnut, but made no attempt to dismount, staring haughtily down at the stranger. Mr Blake squared his shoulders in his admirably cut coat, drew his brows together in an expression of some severity and remarked coldly, "Sir, you have alarmed the ladies."

It was as if he had not spoken. Marcus looked over his head, bowed slightly and greeted the ladies. "Good day, Miss Dane. I trust I find you well, Miss Donaldson."

Mr Blake, who had had more than his fair share of experience in dealing with arrogant aristocrats and who had a very good sense of his own breeding and worth, was not to be bested. This carelessly dressed man on the superb horse was obviously known to the ladies; none the less, that did not excuse his abominable bad manners.

He turned his shoulder on the rider, bowed slightly to Antonia and continued with his farewells as though Marcus Allington did not exist. "Thank you again for your hospitality, Miss Dane; I hope to return to Rye End Hall very shortly. I will, of course, write at the earliest opportunity."

Consoling himself with the thought that his carriage horses would pass muster with the most critical of horsemen, Jeremy Blake mounted his curricle, looped the reins neatly and set his pair in motion, sweeping past Lord Allington as if he were not there.

Antonia waved energetically at the departing carriage, noting with some pleasure the set expression on his lordship's face. She squeezed Donna's hand warningly, although it was unlikely that her companion would prattle of the lawyer's identity or purpose. It was too much to hope that this display of displeasure was jealousy because his lordship felt some partiality for her; on the other hand, it would do no harm to keep Marcus Allington guessing about her visitor.

Antonia stepped forward with a cool smile. "Lord Allington, good day." She might entertain warm—even romantic—feelings about him when he was absent, daydream about the pressure of his lips on hers, speculate about his intentions but, faced with the man himself, she found herself provoked by his arrogance. "A very fine day, is it not? One really feels that summer is around the corner."

Marcus dismounted, tossing the reins to a groom as he did so. "Oh, a visit! How nice," Antonia prattled brightly. "I had assumed you were merely passing. What a pity we have just finished luncheon."

"I have eaten, ma'am, some time ago. I would not have intruded if I had realised you were entertaining company." Marcus was chillingly polite.

"Of course you would not," Antonia replied with what she hoped was maddening complacency. At that moment Miss Donaldson gave up all hope of Lord Allington as a suitor, made a hasty excuse and left. Antonia glanced sideways at Marcus's unsmiling face. "You seem out of sorts, my lord."

Marcus met her eyes steadily, then suddenly smiled, his brow clearing. Antonia had the distinct impression she had overplayed her hand. "Not at all, Antonia. I merely called to see if you had experienced any more difficulty with the bank while I have been in Town."

"Oh, have you been away? Now that I think of it, I do believe one of the servants mentioned that you were not at Brightshill. Have you been absent long? For ourselves, we have been so busy that time has just flown by. Thank you for enquiring, everything has proceeded most smoothly."

They were strolling towards the house as they spoke. Antonia was very conscious of his nearness. From the very beginning, she had found him a dominating physical presence, but since experiencing his kisses she found herself acutely aware of his hands, of the breadth of his shoulders, of the very scent of him. It was most unsettling to find the sensations she had experienced under the moonlight recurring now in full daylight. There was no excuse for it, going as it did against all proper behaviour!

They had now arrived at the front door, which still stood open. "Would you care to see the work we have had done?" Antonia asked, feeling that some conciliatory gesture was owing, considering that Marcus had been instrumental in obtaining the necessary funds for the work for her.

It became obvious as they walked through the house that he must take a personal interest in the practical details of his own estate. The questions he asked the plasterers and roofers who were putting the finishing touches to the attic rooms were informed, and Antonia was surprised by the easy demeanour he showed with the men.

It was partly explained when the plumber said, ''If you care to take a look at the roof, my lord, you will see we used the same way of fixing the leadwork as we did at Brightshill.''

Antonia stepped back into the shadows and watched Marcus talking to the men. They were deferential, she realised, not entirely because of his rank, but because in him they recognised someone who understood the needs of a big estate and of their place within it.

His face as he talked had lost all its severity and his whole frame was relaxed as he handled a damaged piece of leadwork handed to him by the plumber. Here was a far cry from the magistrate punishing a poacher, or the brusque landowner ordering his gamekeepers.

William Hunt the plumber was pointing at something out on the leads. To Antonia's astonishment, Marcus stripped off his jacket, rolled up his shirtsleeves and swung easily out of the cramped dormer window on to the flat section of the roof.

When the plumber and his mate had followed him out, she strolled across to the window and watched them. To her alarm, Marcus was leaning dangerously over the parapet, prodding at brickwork and throwing comments over his shoulder to Hunt. Incomprehensible remarks about flashing, downpipes and rain hoppers floated back to her.

Gradually her alarm abated. As Marcus got to his feet, Antonia found her eyes drawn to the play of strong muscles under the fine linen the breeze was flattening to his back. He stood, one foot on the parapet, looking out over the grounds; as he turned to toss a remark back to the plumber, the wind caught his hair, blowing unruly blond locks into his eyes.

"I agree, you had better talk to Miss Dane about those downspouts. A decision must be made one way or another," he was saying prosaically as he pushed back the hair and met her eyes.

Across the space their gazes met and locked, his eyes holding a question she could not decipher. As she searched his face, Antonia realised with a jolt that she was falling in love with Marcus Allington and that if he made any answering sign of partiality she would run to his side, however many workmen were present, however inappropriate the setting.

The moment seemed endless, but only a few seconds could have passed for Hunt was saying to her, "It's like this, ma'am; the weight of rainwater coming down off this roof is too great for the size of hopper, it's difficult to explain without you seeing it…" He scratched his head, at a loss for the words that could better explain the situation to a lady who could not hope to understand technical matters of this sort.

Marcus strode across to where she stood at the window and extended his hand. "Come, Miss Dane, you will be safe in my care. It is quite flat for the most part."

Willingly, Antonia let Marcus take her hand. His grasp was warm, firm and sure and she experienced no fear as she stepped up on to a box, then stooped to climb over the window ledge.

"Thank you, Hunt," Marcus said to the plumber. "I

am sure you want to be getting on inside: I will show Miss Dane the problem.''

''Oh, look, you can see for miles,'' Antonia exclaimed, gazing out over the greening Hertfordshire countryside and the great beech woods rolling over the scarp edge of the Chilterns towards the Vale beneath.

She leaned on the brick parapet, her eyes fixed on the distant horizon, happily unaware of the height until she made the mistake of looking downwards. The paved terrace four storeys below seemed to swim up to meet her as she recoiled with a gasp of terror.

Marcus took her in his arms and spun her round so that his body shielded her from the drop and she was held hard against him.

Antonia's eyes were tight shut; she had never been at such a height before with so little between her and the ground. Her heart was beating sickeningly, her breath tight in her chest.

''You are not going to faint,'' he informed her firmly. Antonia felt rather than heard the command as her ear was pressed against his shirt front. The breeze had cooled the linen, but through it she could feel the heat of his body. He smelled faintly of cologne, leather and something which was indefinably Marcus.

''Are you certain?'' Antonia quavered. She had never fainted before, but the mixture of sensations she was now experiencing made her feel she might do so at any moment.

''Quite certain,'' Marcus assured her. He set her firmly at his side, his body between her and the drop, his arm still protectively about her shoulders. ''You see, you cannot possibly fall. Come, over here and sit down away from the edge. You cannot go in until I have explained the deficiencies of your rainwater system or Hunt will be quite unable to proceed.''

Antonia glanced up, wondering at his mood, and caught the glint of amusement in his dark eyes. ''Do you truly understand these matters?'' she asked as he handed her to a low brick wall safely away from the edge.

''But of course, and so should you. I trust you also understand about the correct dimensions to ensure a chimney draws properly and the desirable fall of drains away from the house…''

''I find nothing desirable about drains under any circumstances,'' Antonia stated firmly, trying not to wish he would put his arm around her again.

As though answering the thought, Marcus sat down beside her and almost casually tucked her arm through his. The thought of protesting at the familiarity flickered through her mind, only to be dismissed. It was certainly most improper, but then, who was there to see it? And it was broad daylight; he had kissed her in the moonlight yet had taken no further liberty. This was safe enough for propriety, Antonia told herself, although it was wreaking havoc with her sensibilities.

''Those are fine chimneys on the Dower House,'' Marcus remarked, pointing them out through the trees. ''Have you decided what you will do with it?''

''The men have begun work on it this week, although there is little amiss with the structure. Donna and I will be quite comfortable there.''

''Then you will be selling this?'' He half-turned to face her, evidently surprised. ''You have changed your mind since I made you an offer for it?''

''Indeed, no, I have no intention of selling Rye End Hall, it is my family home. I am to lease it. Do you not recall? You were most slighting about the suggestion. I am grateful that, thanks to your intervention, I have the capital with which to do the work here: I assumed you knew why I wanted the money. I was quite clear about it, I believe.''

''I had thought those just hot words thrown at my head.'' Marcus smiled at her. ''We were, after all, somewhat intemperate in our discussion of the matter, and I must admit I did not take your scheme seriously.''

Antonia turned a puzzled countenance to him. ''But what did you believe I wanted the money for, if not to renovate the house in order to lease it?''

''Why, to live in moderate comfort as is befitting of your station.''

''So you influenced the banker solely out of concern for my comfort? You must have wondered how I intended to repay the loan,'' she exclaimed in a rallying tone. But underneath she felt a sudden surge of hope that he may have acted to keep her in the neighbourhood because he had a partiality for her.

''I would hope that I always act for the comfort of others,'' Marcus replied drily. ''But there is an overriding consideration…''

Antonia could scarcely breathe waiting for him to finish the sentence.

''…it is of great concern to me, and our neighbours, that a fine estate such as Rye End Hall should not fall into rack and ruin. It leads to poverty, which in its turn brings about lawlessness and want.''

''If your motives are so altruistic, sir, I am amazed you felt unable to air them the other day when I asked you directly why you had secured the money for me!'' Really! Just when she found she was liking the man— she could not bring herself to even think the word love—

he said something insufferable. "You will be pleased to hear that I am in hopes of securing a most respectable tenant for the house and the Home Farm," she added stiffly, spots of colour touching her cheekbones.

"Ah, I thought I smelt a clerk this morning!" Marcus seemed quite unaware of her discomfiture. Antonia sensed only his satisfaction at placing Mr Jeremy Blake.

"No clerk, sir! Mr Blake is a lawyer with the highest connections. I am most hopeful his principal—and uncle—will take the Hall."

"You are warm in your defence of—what is his name, Black?"

"Blake. I found him a most amiable and intelligent person to do business with. And, of course," she added slyly, recovering her equilibrium, "such a gentleman. It would be a considerable asset to our social circle locally if he were to accompany his uncle here."

"I shall look forward to making his acquaintance," Marcus said politely. "But we stray from the point— you intend taking up residence at the Dower House?"

"Certainly. Both Miss Donaldson and I expect to be most comfortable there. It is entirely the right size for two unattached ladies, the gardens can be made charming..."

"So you intend to dwindle into respectable spinster-hood there, do you? No doubt you will be able to devote many fascinating hours to constructing a shell grotto in the grounds or perfecting your tatting."

Antonia was taken aback by his sarcasm, then recol-lected that he must be disappointed that she had not cho-sen to sell the property to him. "Dwindle! Indeed not! We have every intention of entering fully into the social life of the district as soon as we are established at the Dower House. I have retained control of the lands other than those attached to the Home Farm, so I shall have tenants to oversee…indeed, I have every expectation of being rushed off my feet.''

''I am reassured to hear it.'' His brow quirked with what Antonia had come to recognise as hidden amusement. ''May I hope you will visit Brightshill? I have a houseparty assembling soon—we may even muster enough couples to get up a dancing party on occasion.''

''I should like that very much,'' Antonia responded formally, although the thought of finding something in her wardrobe to match the London gowns of his guests was somewhat daunting. The light breeze suddenly strengthened and Antonia shivered in her light gown. ''We should go in, Donna will be wondering what has become of me.''

Marcus took her hand to help her across the roof, but at the window ducked through it, before turning and holding up his arms.

''I can climb down by myself, thank you,'' she said, blushing at the thought of so close a contact.

''Antonia, there are two ways of doing this; either I turn my back while you scramble down, doubtless tearing your gown in the process, or I lift you down—in the most respectful way, of course!'' Laughter danced in his eyes. She knew he was laughing at her, but suddenly she did not care. She would be in his arms, however briefly, would feel his strength keeping her safe.

Wordlessly she reached down to him and found herself swung effortlessly over the sill and into the attic. Marcus held her for a fraction longer than was needful, before setting her down on the dusty floor. ''Tell me,'' he began, looking down at her.

''Yes?'' Antonia faltered, lifting her eyes to his, noticing a smudge of whitewash on his cheekbone, a cobweb caught in his unruly dark blond hair and ruthlessly suppressing the urge to brush it away.

"Have you retained the fishing rights?" He smiled, teeth white in the gloom.

So, standing here so close to each other evoked the same memories in him, too. "No, I am convinced I would never make a good fisherwoman, no matter what," she said with a shaky laugh.

"Practice is what you need, Antonia," he murmured, his eyes warm on hers. "You must come to Brightshill and let me teach you." He put up one hand as if to touch her face, but dropped it as heavy boots sounded on the floorboards outside. By the time William Hunt joined them, there was a clear five-foot space between them and Marcus was commenting on the state of the plaster-work.

Marcus took his leave soon after and Antonia drifted back to the small salon, half-excited, half-irritated with herself. She had been out for several Seasons, had en-gaged in elegant flirtations with eligible men at balls and dinners: why did Marcus Allington have this effect on her? Her heart told her she was in danger of falling deeply in love with him, yet her head told her it was impossible.

She had been thrown into his company in the most extraordinary circumstances, hauled up before him as a common criminal. And their meetings since then had been characterised by an intimacy which was most un-seemly. Antonia told herself firmly that it was this im-proper proximity that was fascinating her. And as for Lord Allington, he no doubt flirted with any lady willing to indulge him, and her circumstances were perhaps un-usual enough to have piqued his interest.

By the time she rejoined her companion she had the

satisfaction of having her unruly emotions firmly under control, or so she believed. Miss Donaldson, however, missed very little.

"His lordship has gone?" she enquired, putting aside her needlework.

"Some minutes ago," Antonia replied indifferently. "He and Hunt appear to have settled a most difficult question to do with the downspouts."

"Indeed. And that necessitated you romping all over the leads?"

"Hardly romping." Antonia laughed lightly, flicking through the day's post. "The height is most disconcerting, although the view is wonderful."

"So you spent the entire time up there discussing drainage and the view?"

"Oh…we spoke of our plans for the Dower House. And his lordship was kind enough to extend an invitation to Brightshill shortly—he is assembling a houseparty."

"Then I am not entirely without hope," observed Miss Donaldson archly.

"Hope?" Antonia turned to regard her companion. "Of what?"

"Of your moving in Society, of course, as is fitting." Miss Donaldson kept her countenance schooled, but Antonia had the distinct impression that that was not her meaning.

Chapter Six

"My dear Antonia!" Miss Donaldson exclaimed. "If you cannot find any rational occupation within the house, then please go out and take the air—for I declare you are quite fraying at my nerves with this incessant fidgeting!"

The uncharacteristic sharpness of her companion's tone startled Antonia. "Am I fidgeting? I am so sorry, I was not aware of it."

"You have done little else the past two days," Donna replied more kindly. "You have embroidered two flowers on that scarf, only to pull both out again; the pages of that new volume of Shelley's poetry are still uncut; there are two letters awaiting reply from your cousin Augusta…"

Antonia put up her hands to stem the flow. She knew Donna was right, but she felt she could not settle to anything now the workmen had left and the big house stood ready for its new tenant. Outside the windows, the trees were heavy with fresh greenery, the newly planted pleasure grounds were breaking with new growth and the very air was heavy with the promise of summer just around the corner.

"If only we knew what was happening—whether Sir Josiah has decided to take Rye End Hall! It is a week now since Mr Blake's visit—I had expected to hear from him several days ago." She paced restlessly across the drugget protecting the newly laid carpet, then burst out, "Oh, Donna, what if Mr Blake has failed to persuade his uncle! What shall we do then with all this money laid out and no way of repaying it?"

Miss Donaldson came to put her arm around her young companion. Knowing Antonia as she did after nearly a decade together, she recognised the strain she was under. A surge of real anger shook her normally well-schooled emotions. This was all the fault of Sir Humphrey Dane and his son! How could Antonia's father and brother have been so feckless, so selfishly uncaring as to leave her the sole inheritor of debt and disarray!

"It is only a week, dear," she began soothingly when the sound of hooves crunching on gravel caught their attention. "Ah! No doubt that is Lord Allington come to call. Now that I think of it, it must be a week since we last saw him. The diversion of a visitor will turn our minds from these worries." Miss Donaldson spoke brightly but was precisely aware of how long it had been since his lordship had been at the Hall, and had been feeling quite cast down at his lack of attention to Antonia. She had entertained such hopes of the pair of them...

"Mr Blake, ma'am." Anna the housemaid was bobbing a curtsy in the open doorway.

"Why, Mr Blake! We had not looked to see you in person—what an unexpected pleasure." All the relief Antonia felt—for surely he would not have come in person to give her an answer in the negative—was in Antonia's radiant smile as she offered him her hand.

Jeremy Blake shook the proffered hand and bowed to Miss Donaldson, whilst reflecting that his arrival on business was not normally greeted with such warmth. His eyes lingered on Miss Antonia Dane: her slender figure was enhanced by the simplicity of the muslin gown she was wearing. He could scarcely believe, for he was a modest young man, that it was his appearance that had prompted the sparkle in her dark eyes or the warm colour heightening her creamy complexion, but he was susceptible enough to appreciate it none the less.

"Do, please, take a seat, Mr Blake. May we offer you some refreshment after your journey? Anna, bring the decanters." Antonia sank down gracefully on the sofa, prey to a sudden fear that he had bad news and was kind enough to bring it in person. "Have you ridden over from Berkhamsted this morning?"

"No, ma'am. I have taken rooms at the Green Man in Tring. It is rather more conveniently situated for riding here daily, which I hope you will permit me to do, for there are many practical details to be settled…"

"Then Sir Josiah is minded to take Rye End Hall?" Antonia could hardly contain her excitement and relief in order to speak calmly.

"Indeed yes, Miss Dane. He was most happy with my account; both he and my aunt feel this will be the ideal country establishment for them."

"You must feel very gratified that Sir Josiah and Lady Finch place so much trust in your judgement as to take the house unseen," Antonia responded warmly. "And I must thank you for your persuasions on our behalf. It is such a relief to know that Rye End Hall will be let to such a notable person as Sir Josiah and will regain its place amongst the estates of the area.''

Mr Blake flushed slightly at the compliment. ''I thank you, ma'am, but I assure you that once presented to him, the merits of the estate were such that Sir Josiah needed little persuasion by me. And it is you and Miss Donaldson who should be congratulated on the taste and propriety of the renovations.''

Setting his glass on one side, Mr Blake removed some folded papers from his breast pocket and handed one, closed with a seal, to Antonia. ''I act as messenger from your man of business whose letter you have there. Between us, we have drawn up a contract which I trust you will find acceptable: may I hope you could give me an answer upon it if I return tomorrow?''

''But surely we can close on this today!'' Antonia exclaimed. ''If you will allow me an hour to peruse it before luncheon, then, unless I have any questions, I can sign it and the deed is done. You will stay for luncheon, Mr Blake?''

''That would be most acceptable, ma'am, thank you.'' Mr Blake got to his feet. ''With your permission, I will use the time until luncheon to ride around the estate: there are some notes Sir Josiah has charged me to make, and it is a most beautiful day.'' He bowed to the ladies and left.

Antonia seized Donna's hands and danced her round the room in a jig of joy and relief. ''We've done it, we've done it, we've done it!''

''Antonia, dear! What if Mr Blake should see us!''

''He has gone—and what if he does see us? I do not care!''

''Antonia, please, I am quite breathless. And this is most indecorous!'' But Donna was smiling.

When Mr Blake rejoined them for luncheon Antonia greeted him with the words, "I am most happy to sign this contract. My man of business recommends it to me, and I am more than happy to vacate the Hall by the date specified."

A look of anxiety crossed Mr Blake's pleasant features. "I had feared that a date only two weeks hence might be too precipitate for you. Are you quite certain it is convenient?"

"Let us discuss it over luncheon." Antonia led the way through to the breakfast-room, which served them as a small dining-room. "Please sit here, Mr Blake: will you carve the ham? I tell you truly, Miss Donaldson and I would be ready to move to the Dower House within the week. All the building work there is done: it only remains to hang the curtains, make up the beds and remove our personal possessions."

"I am most relieved to hear you say so, Miss Dane," he rejoined, passing a platter of carved ham to Donna as he spoke. "If I may, this afternoon I had hoped to ride over and see your tenant at the Home Farm. I will need to spend one or two days with him this week, and then there are numerous measurements Lady Finch has charged me to make in the house, if that will not be inconvenient to you."

"Not at all," Antonia assured him warmly. "I will give you a note of introduction to Thomas Christmas at the farm, and as to the measurements, you are to make yourself quite at home and not stand on ceremony. Come and go as you please."

The rest of the meal passed most pleasantly for the ladies as Mr Blake proved to be an unexpected source of anecdotes about London Society. It was obvious he mixed freely with the Quality and Antonia could well imagine him gracing the floor at Almack's. She felt he perhaps viewed life a little too seriously—a product of his profession, no doubt—but he was most agreeable company.

"Are you frequently away from home upon Sir Josiah's business?" Miss Donaldson enquired. "I only ask because, for a young man such as yourself, absences must put a strain upon domestic harmony."

Antonia flinched at what was, to her ears, an obvious attempt to discover whether he were married or not. Mr Blake, however, showed no sign of discomfiture at the probing.

"Fortunately, ma'am, I have my own apartments within Sir Josiah's London residence and come and go as I please with no inconvenience."

An expression, which Antonia recognised as the nearest Donna ever came to smugness, crossed her birdlike features. So, Mr Blake was not married and was even now being added to Donna's mental list of suitable suitors for Antonia.

Jeremy Blake, mercifully unaware of his hostesses' thoughts, soon took his leave, taking the signed contract and a note for Thomas Christmas from Miss Dane urging the farmer's complete co-operation with his new landlord.

Antonia stood on the sunwarmed steps watching as he cantered off towards the Home Farm. Halfway down the driveway, he encountered another rider. Both gentlemen doffed their hats as they passed one another and Antonia recognised Marcus's blond locks in the sunlight.

He dismounted at the front door, tossing his reins to the groom who was riding at his heels. "Ten minutes, Saye," he ordered. "Keep them walking, this breeze is fresh. Good afternoon, Miss Dane.'' He bowed slightly to Antonia. ''I trust I find you well?''

''Very well indeed, my lord. You find me on my way to the flower garden. Would you care to accompany me and protect me from Old Johnson, who refuses to believe any of his blooms are for cutting?''

Marcus strolled alongside her, wondering what had occurred to put her in such high spirits. For, though Antonia's manner was controlled, her eyes were sparkling and her whole figure seemed animated with suppressed excitement.

''Did I recognise that London clerk visiting again?''

Antonia hid a smile at his apparently casual probing. It seemed Mr Blake piqued his lordship's interest, which could only be flattering to herself. ''Indeed, it was Mr Blake. I see no reason why I cannot tell you now that his principal, Sir Josiah Finch, has decided to take Rye End Hall. I expect Sir Josiah and Lady Finch—she is Mr Blake's aunt, by the by—will be in residence here within the fortnight.''

''I congratulate you!'' Marcus pushed open the wicket gate into the garden and held it for Antonia to pass through. ''You appear to have scored a veritable triumph with your tenant: a very notable nabob, indeed.''

Antonia scanned his face, looking for signs of sarcasm, but saw only genuine admiration for her business acuity. ''You know Sir Josiah?''

''No, but I have heard of him. I believe he has been returned to this country from the Indies for almost a year, and the *on dit* is that he has amassed a great fortune in his years in the East. He and Lady Finch do not go much into Society, although she, of course, is widely connected with some of the best families. He, I believe, is a self-made man...''

"And none the worse for that," Antonia exclaimed hotly.

"I had intended no slur on your nabob. I am sure he is a most excellent man and will adorn our local society."

Antonia was surprised. She had expected Sir Josiah's origins in trade—however exalted—would be despised by an aristocrat such as Lord Allington, as they would certainly have been by her own father.

"You do me an injustice," Marcus continued evenly, "if you believe I would condemn the man for such a reason. If he proves a bad landlord, I may revise my opinion."

Antonia suspected there was a veiled hint about her "poachers" in that last remark but, warmed as she was with her success and the admiration of Mr Blake, she chose to ignore it, not wishing to provoke an argument.

Old Johnson greeted them with a look of deep suspicion and a grunt. When Antonia asked him for a basket he produced one with bad grace. "And some scissors, please, Johnson," she requested firmly, knowing how the old man hated her to pick "his" flowers.

"Ain't got none," he muttered, but was foiled by Marcus producing a pocket knife.

Marcus held the basket while Antonia snipped her selected blooms, wandering up and down the paths under the old man's hostile eye. "He appears to have taken a great dislike to me, as well as to your flower picking," Marcus observed.

"Small wonder," Antonia responded crisply, "as you are the cause of his son's present condition."

"I? And what condition might that be?" He looked down into her indignant eyes, noticing for the first time that in their hazel depths there were flecks of green.

"He is languishing in Hertford gaol, sent there by you for poaching, and meanwhile his old father must support his family!"

"I remember him now—and I doubt his father is supporting his family, which consists of numerous by-blows scattered from here to Berkhamsted. The son is a ne'er-do-well who has never done an honest day's work in his life and who crowned a career of poaching, thievery and wenching by clubbing a keeper so savagely the man lost the sight of one eye. No, ma'am, save your sympathy for those who better deserve it."

Antonia shivered at the chill in his voice and in his eyes. "I am sorry," she stammered. "I should not have spoken without knowing the full facts. Was the injured man one of your keepers?"

"Yes," Marcus replied shortly, then seeing her stricken face, relented and explained. "He is the younger brother of Sparrow, my head keeper. He works in the stables now, for his sight is quite poor at night."

Antonia remembered Sparrow's rough grasp. "No wonder Sparrow is so hard on poachers."

"Indeed, Miss Dane. It is as well to remember that not every picture is painted in black and white."

She stooped to snip off some greenery, averting her face from his. "I accept your reproof, my lord. I acknowledge that I become so passionately engaged sometimes that I fail to see the shades of grey."

Marcus put one hand under her elbow to help her upright. Even through her gown and the leather of his glove she could feel the warmth of him. "I would not wish to see you any less passionate about anything, Antonia," he murmured.

She could not meet his eye, glancing away in confusion, to encounter instead the rheumy regard of the old gardener. This was no place to engage in...whatever was occurring between her and Marcus. Was he flirting with her, or merely teasing her? She could hardly tell, and her growing partiality for him was clouding her own judgement.

"I have filled my basket as full as I dare," Antonia said lightly, nodding to Johnson as she led the way out of the garden. "Donna will be wondering what has become of me, for she wanted to fill the vases in the hall."

Marcus took the basket from her and they strolled back towards the house in companionable silence. At the front door he handed her the flowers and remarked, "I had almost forgot the purpose of my call. I am assembling a houseparty at Brightshill next week—I believe I mentioned it before—and I hope Miss Donaldson and yourself will do me the honour of joining us for dinner on Tuesday evening."

"I would be delighted, my lord, as, I am sure, will be Miss Donaldson." Antonia spoke calmly but inside her heart had leapt at the thought of mixing with society again after so many months. And to see Marcus in his own setting, to see Brightshill in all its glory, filled with people...

But those people, she suddenly realised, would be of the height of London Society, fashionably dressed, *au fait* with the latest gossip and news. She had neither the gowns nor the gossip to mix comfortably with such a set; what would Marcus think when he saw her in such a company? He might find her amusingly unconventional now, but what appeared refreshing as a country diversion would seem gauche and soon lose its charm set against Town polish.

"Antonia? Is anything wrong?" Marcus appeared preternaturally alert to her mood today.

"Oh, no…I was merely woolgathering."

"Forgive me, you must have much to be doing and thinking about. I shall leave you to your housekeeping and look forward to your company next Tuesday."

Antonia held out her hand to shake his and was startled to find him bending over it to brush the back of her knuckles with his lips. "Adieu, Antonia."

She watched him, unconscious of bringing her hand up to her cheek as she did so. Saye came up with the horses and the two men were trotting off down the driveway before she recalled herself.

"Donna, Donna!" she called, running up the steps.

"There you are with the flowers." Miss Donaldson emerged from the salon, a vase in each hand. "What an age you have been, Antonia, I could not imagine what was detaining you."

Antonia recognised the teasing note in her voice. "You know full well Lord Allington called! Oh, Donna, he has invited us to dinner at Brightshill next Tuesday. His house party will be assembled—what are we to wear?"

"I shall wear my garnet silk, of course," Donna replied composedly. "It is perfectly suitable, and my attire will not in any case signify. No, my dear, the real question is, what are you to wear?"

Antonia dumped the flowerbasket unceremoniously on the side table and wailed, "I have not a notion! I do not even know what is the latest mode—although you may be certain that not a garment that I own will be in it!"

"Then we must set to work immediately. Anna can arrange these flowers; we must review our wardrobes and see what will pass muster. Now," she began, ticking items off on her fingers as she ascended the stairs. "Gowns, those must be new, then there are your stockings, gloves, slippers… Anna! Where is that girl? We must see if there are any of your old gowns that will cut up…''

Antonia hurried after her companion, bemused that for once Miss Donaldson was not taking the opportunity for remarks on the folly of fashion and the impropriety of a mind set upon adornment.

An afternoon spent in turning out both their wardrobes swiftly passed. At length, they sank down gratefully with a cup of tea and reviewed their findings.

''It is as I feared,'' Antonia said gloomily. ''We each have one pair of respectable evening gloves, there is enough ribbon to furbish up your gown and your slippers are presentable. But our stockings are woeful, my evening slippers unwearable and not a single gown of mine is in such a condition that I could either wear it or cut it up to make another with any pretensions to style.''

''None of this is insurmountable,'' Miss Donaldson said firmly, setting down her cup and raising her voice. ''Anna!'' The girl hurried in, only to be dispatched to find Jem and order his presence with the gig the next morning. ''We can try what Berkhamsted has to offer and go further afield if necessary.''

''But, Donna,'' Antonia protested, ''we cannot afford to shop for any of this!'' She was utterly bewildered by Miss Donaldson's enthusiasm.

''Nonsense! You have money left from the loan; look upon this as an investment.''

''You cannot be suggesting that I use that money for husband-hunting!''

''I did not say anything of the kind. But you cannot go into Society attired like a milkmaid. And if you are not to go into Society, pray tell me why we have been wasting so much time and money to establish ourselves in the Dower House?''

"Oh, very well," Antonia conceded, knowing there was no gainsaying her companion in this mood. "But we only have a week in which to prepare."

"It will suffice. If luck is with us, we shall be able to obtain copies of the *Ladies' Intelligencer* in Berkhamsted, which will give us an inkling of the current mode. I have already found an excellent shop for haberdashery—I told you of it when I bought the linens last month—and there are several drapers. One, at least, must have some acceptable silks."

"But we do not know which dressmakers to trust," Antonia protested.

"Dressmakers? No time, my dear—we will sew the garment ourselves. With my skill—for I believe I do not flatter myself—in pattern cutting, and your fine stitchery, we may save several pounds and no one be any the wiser. Now, let us have some supper and retire early: we have a busy day before us tomorrow."

"Now this will become you very well," Donna said with satisfaction, holding up the dull gold silk against Antonia's creamy skin. "That subtle counter-stripe in the weave quite picks up the brown of your hair."

"Indeed yes, ma'am," Mrs Mumford the linen draper hastened to add her voice. "If you intend to make this gown here—" she gestured to a striking fashion plate open on the counter "—I can think of nothing that will cut and drape better."

"It is very expensive," Antonia demurred, wistfully fingering the soft sheen.

"Quality will out, madam, if I may make so bold an observation."

"Quite right," Miss Donaldson declared. "We will take a dress length of this, and the lining we had already agreed upon. Now, trimmings…"

Another delightful half-hour was passed deciding between the rival merits of mother-of-pearl buttons or covered silk ones, floss edgings or corded ribbon and whether to add a sprig of artificial flowers at the neckline or an edging of fine lace.

"And will you be bringing in your slippers for dyeing, ma'am?" Mrs Mumford enquired as the girl made up the parcels. "I can recommend Thomas Hurst in the High Street for kid slippers, but his dyeing isn't all it ought to be."

After negotiating with the shoemaker to send the new slippers to Mrs Mumford, they retired to a private parlour overlooking the inn yard at the King's Arms and sent for coffee and biscuits. Antonia made herself comfortable in the window seat and surveyed the bustle below. "Oh, Donna, do look at Jem. He is sitting up in the gig with his arms folded, aping the groom in that curricle over there."

"He is a good lad," Donna remarked with a smile. "I am glad we are able to give him employment. The yard is very busy, is it not? Here comes another post chaise—and I do declare, is that not Lord Allington coming out of the inn?"

It was, indeed. Antonia, from her vantage point, could look down on Marcus as he strolled out into the sunlight and stood waiting for the post boys to let down the steps of the chaise. Although he was wearing riding dress as usual, Antonia noticed he was more carefully attired than normal. As he lifted his tall hat, she saw he had submitted his tawny locks to the attentions of his valet, for the nape of his neck, newly shorn, showed paler against skin tanned by outdoor pursuits.

The door of the chaise swung open as soon as the vehicle came to a halt and, without waiting for the steps to be let down, a boy of about nine years tumbled out. For a moment Antonia thought he was about to throw his arms around Marcus, then he checked himself, pulled himself to his full height and with great dignity thrust out a small hand. Lord Allington solemnly shook it, then bent and scooped the boy into his arms.

The lad's face broke into a huge grin which persisted as Marcus set him on his feet again just as a small blonde whirlwind threw herself at his lordship's knees. Marcus rocked slightly, then stooped again to pick up the child who snuggled her face into his neck and clung firmly.

Antonia drew back slightly against the drapes, feeling excluded from the affectionate reunion.

Still holding the child, Marcus stepped up to the carriage door and held out his hand to assist the young matron who had one foot on the steps. She was laughing up into his face as he bent and allowed his cheek to be kissed and Antonia realised, seeing the two dark blond heads together, that they must be brother and sister.

"What an elegant ensemble," Donna remarked approvingly, her eye on the lady. "That moss-green pelisse and bonnet set against the paler green of her skirts—so tasteful and understated!"

"And so flattering to her colouring," Antonia commented. "I had no idea Lord Allington had a sister—as indeed she must be, for they are so alike—and certainly not that he was an uncle."

His sister was saying something to Marcus that caused him to set his little niece down and step once more to the post chaise. Another lady was hesitating prettily on the top step, almost as if the unaided descent was too much for her fragile frame.

"Well! That is most certainly not a sister, and possibly not even a lady!" Donna remarked tartly, disliking the woman on sight.

"She is very pretty," Antonia said, seeking to be fair in the face of Donna's hostility.

"Artifice, pure artifice. She owes a great deal to the arts of her modiste and coiffeuse, and no doubt to the rouge pot!"

"Donna! We are too far away for you to know that. How uncharitable you are this morning!"

They both fell silent as the lady allowed Marcus to hand her down, swaying towards him with one hand to her brow and a brave smile trembling on her lips. "Huh! Showing him what a dreadful headache she is suffering, but how brave she is being despite all," snorted Donna.

The apparition was swathed in madder rose silk with a velvet pelisse, cut with fluttering edges, each trimmed with a gold tassel. She was poised carefully on the cobbles, as if reluctant to place her dainty kid boots on the horse-trampled ground.

"She is tiny," Antonia observed, and indeed, as she stood, one hand firmly on Marcus's arm, the stranger stood no higher than his shoulder. "No doubt another member of the houseparty, yet if I am not mistaken, Marcus is surprised to see her."

"Do you think so? Well, you know him better than I, my dear."

It might not be apparent to Donna, but to Antonia, whose mind's eye was so often full of every nuance of Marcus's tall figure, a certain rigidity in his shoulders and an expression of bland politeness showed a change of mood.

The party was returning to the carriage, the post boys in their big boots swinging up on to the horses' backs, and Saye was leading out Marcus's mount. In a flurry of hooves the carriage and the two riders turned and were out of the yard, leaving it strangely empty to Antonia's watching eyes.

Donna got to her feet and summoned the parlourmaid, giving her instructions to carry their parcels down to Jem. "Tell him we will be at least another hour," she ordered, "and send him out some bread and cheese and ale."

"Donna? Why are we not returning home?" Antonia demanded as she found herself being hustled down the stairs and into the High Street once again.

"We are going back to Mrs Mumford's shop," her companion announced firmly. "We are going to buy several ells of ribbon to furbish up your russet walking dress, some velvet for a new pelisse, a new bonnet and," her gaze fixed on Antonia's sensible walking shoes, "some kid boots."

"That is dreadfully extravagant!" Antonia protested as they passed St Peter's church.

"No more than you deserve," Donna riposted.

"This is not a competition," Antonia said drily, recognising the source of her companion's sudden burst of extravagance.

"Is it not?" Miss Donaldson's lips compressed with finality.

Mrs Mumford was almost overcome to receive further patronage from the ladies of Rye End Hall. She was commenting effusively on the elegance of taste shown by their selections while the assistant tied the parcels, when the shop bell jangled and in walked Mr Jeremy Blake.

"Ladies!" He doffed his hat and bowed politely, an expression of pleasure on his amiable features. "I trust I find you well?" Although, looking at Miss Dane's glowing complexion and sparkling eyes, he could not doubt it. "May I be of assistance to you with your parcels? I have only a small commission—some cravats, if they can be furnished—and then I am at your disposal."

The ladies accepted gratefully—Donna, because she could never reconcile herself to her charge going out without a footman to carry her parcels, Antonia simply because she found Mr Blake's company so congenial.

The cravats were soon added to the pile of purchases and the party made its way back along the High Street towards the King's Arms.

"I was intending to call upon you tomorrow," Jeremy observed as they crossed the street. "But as we have happily encountered one another, I wonder if I might raise the matter now."

"Please do so Mr, Blake. Have you heard from Sir Josiah?"

"Indeed I have, ma'am. I would find it most helpful to know when I may order the paperhangers to begin. But," he added hastily, "I would not want to inconvenience you in the slightest."

"Thank you for your consideration. It must be an object with us to oblige Sir Josiah and Lady Finch in any way that we can." Antonia turned to Miss Donaldson. "I believe we can undertake to have vacated Rye End Hall by today week, could we not, Donna?"

"The Dower House is already cleaned and aired. All we need to do is remove our personal possessions, and that is but the work of a day. I am sure we can oblige Lady Finch."

"I am most grateful. Is there any assistance I can lend you in your removal?"

The ladies assured him that they had matters well in hand and thus they parted, Mr Blake on some further errand in the town, the ladies to rejoin Jem and drive home.

"Well, my dear," Donna said briskly as the gig bowled past the castle ruins, "we shall be busy indeed! What with establishing ourselves in the Dower House and undertaking all that dressmaking, we shall scarce have a minute to spare. But we will prevail!"

"You are enjoying the prospect, are you not, Donna?" Antonia enquired drily.

"I am, indeed. We have the prospect of a change of scene, of congenial company in Sir Josiah and Lady Finch and the house party at Brightshill, and some hard but rewarding work ahead. How far we have come from our first dismay at seeing Rye End Hall in March!"

"How far, indeed," Antonia agreed, musing that her life had indeed changed greatly since that first, singular, encounter with Marcus.

Chapter Seven

Lord Allington leaned negligently against the frame of the parlour door at the Dower House and crossed his booted feet at the ankles. Having found the front door standing open and no servant to announce him, he had strolled through, tossing his hat and riding crop on to the hall chest, before hearing the sound of a chair being scraped across wooden boards in the front parlour.

Antonia was standing upon the chair before the window, stretching up to catch a length of muslin on hooks. She was so absorbed in her endeavours to achieve a pleasing drape she was quite unconscious of being observed from the doorway.

His lordship was in no hurry to attract her attention. He was used by now to finding pleasure in the sight of Miss Dane, but she was looking more than usually striking that morning. Her luxuriant hair was caught back simply by a black velvet ribbon, she was clad in a plain gown which showed off her figure to advantage, and her movements had a natural grace as she reached up to the window.

She stretched further, then the muslin slipped from her

fingers and dropped to the floor, remaining suspended only by the far corner. "Oh, bother!"

"Allow me." Marcus stepped forward.

Antonia spun round on the wooden seat, which tipped precariously, precipitating her into his lordship's arms, which were very ready to receive her. "Oh! My lord…you quite startled me."

"My fault entirely, Miss Dane." He smiled down at her, causing Antonia's heart to flutter uncomfortably. "We are being very formal this morning, are we not? However, I feel I must mention that something appears to be stabbing me in the right shoulder."

Antonia hastily dropped her hands, which had been clasping his lordship's coat. "It is my pincushion—see, I have it tied to my wrist."

She held up her hand to show him, and blushed when Marcus caught her wrist between his fingers and bent his head over the velvet pad.

"Marcus, you are tickling me!"

"I am sorry, I have never appreciated the complexity of needleworking devices."

"Now you are laughing at me."

"Not at all, but I must wonder why the mistress of the house is scrambling about on chairs when she has servants to do this sort of thing." He released her hand and strolled across the parlour, surveying it as he did so. "You have made a great difference here in a short time—I should never have believed this place could look so elegant."

"Hardly that, although I flatter myself we have made it tolerably comfortable and homely. I have no fear of headless ghouls now." Antonia cast him an arch look from under her lashes, but failed to provoke any response other than a slightly raised eyebrow. "And as for the servants, they are assisting Donna with our trunks."

"In that case, allow me to assist you." He stopped to right the fallen chair and set it to one side. "I believe I can reach the hooks if you will direct me how you desire the fabric to hang."

Antonia, surprised that his lordship would stoop to such trifles, hesitated briefly before gathering up the muslin and handing it to him. "I am trying to achieve a soft curve across the top of the window…a little more…a little more fullness on the left—perfect! If you can just secure it there…"

They stepped back together to admire the finished effect. "Now, what is the next task?" Marcus asked agreeably.

"My lord…I am certain you did not come here to hang curtains! I really cannot trespass on your time, especially when you have a house party assembled at Brightshill to claim your attention."

Marcus appeared not to have taken in a word she had said, for he was gazing at her in an abstracted manner, a slight smile on his lips.

"My lord?" she prompted.

"I do beg your pardon, Antonia, I was quite some distance away. I was in fact in contemplation…"

"That much was plain, my lord," Antonia responded somewhat acidly. "Might I enquire what it was you were contemplating?"

"Mm? Yes, of course you may. Matrimony."

"Matrimony!" Antonia's eyes flew to his face. "What can you mean?"

"I mean that I am intending to make an offer of marriage, Antonia."

Her heart sank towards her kid slippers as the image

of a fragile blonde figure emerging from the post chaise filled her mind. With a great effort of will, she forced a small smile to her lips. "I am flattered that you regard me as a friend to be confided in on such a delicate matter."

He took her hand in both of his and looked straight into her troubled eyes. "I do not make myself plain, Antonia, and perhaps I should not have approached you thus; although, in the absence of either father or brother…in short, Antonia, will you do me the honour of becoming my wife?"

Antonia felt as though all the breath had been sucked from her lungs by the shock of his declaration. She knew he found her attractive—his kisses had left her in no doubt of that—but she had never allowed herself to hope that anything more would come of it than a light-hearted flirtation.

She wanted to say "yes, with all my heart", but her common sense held the words back. After all, he had made her no declaration of love, but in the past he had made a declaration of another strong motive for an alliance—his desire for her lands. A young lady of her class would be expected by Society to marry for position, yet she had seen at first hand the destructive sadness of a marriage where the love of one partner—her mother—had not been returned by the other.

His hands were warm and strong holding hers, she felt his eyes on her face but could not raise hers to meet them, for if she did she knew she would lose all level-headedness. She swayed towards him, wanting to bury her face in his coat front, drink in the scent of him, give herself up to him.

Instead Antonia took a deep breath, gently freed her hands and sat down in the chair. "I am very sensible of the honour you do me, my lord,'' she began, surprised to find her voice so steady when her pulse was leaping.

"But—you are going to refuse me, are you not?'' Marcus's voice was equally steady.

"Oh, no!'' She did look up then, searching his face for emotion and finding none. "I must…my lord, I must ask for time to consider my answer.''

"I see. You would advise me not to give up all hope, then?'' he enquired drily. "How long would you require to make your decision?''

Chilled by his lack of ardour, Antonia's reply was equally cool. "A few days…a week at most.'' He could at least have seemed disappointed!

"Then we are agreed: I will raise the matter again a week from today, and until then, we will not refer to it. I trust you will still feel able to dine at Brightshill tomorrow. My sister is much looking forward to meeting you.''

"Your sister?'' Antonia was grateful for the change of subject. "Is she married? Is she accompanied by her family?''

"Yes, Anne is the wife of Charles, Lord Meredith. He will join us later today, but my nephew and niece accompanied their mother.''

"It must be pleasant to have children about the house.'' They must have been the charming children she saw arriving at the inn, greeting their uncle with so much affection.

"Indeed: young Henry has already dug holes in the lawn for his cricket stumps and his little sister Frances appears to regard me as an endless source of sugar plums.''

Antonia laughed, remembering the little girl clinging tightly to Marcus's neck in the yard. "You pretend to

be severe, my lord, but I can tell you are a fond uncle!''
They both seemed relieved that the tension between
them had passed. "And do you have many other
guests?"

"My sister was accompanied by a friend of hers, Lady
Reed. She comes alone; her husband is at Brighton, commanding a regiment of foot."

A friend of his sister's, indeed! Antonia remembered
the sharp little feline face smiling up into his with a great
deal of warmth and felt a deep stirring of unease.

"Two friends of mine are also with us already, and
my sister is chaperoning a Miss Fitch. Her mother and
mine have some matrimonial enterprise in hand, but who
the lucky man is to be, I have no idea as yet."

"You, perhaps?" Antonia asked lightly.

Marcus laughed. "Good lord, no! I have it on good
authority that she considers me to be almost in my do-
tage."

Antonia looked at the tall rangy figure, the thick blond
hair, the firm set of his jaw and wondered if Miss Fitch
was in need of an oculist. No, Marcus Allington was in
his prime… Swiftly burying these thoughts she cried,
"Unkind, indeed! Why, you cannot be more than five
and thirty, my lord."

"I am thirty, Miss Dane. However I am flattered you
consider me so mature." His tone was severe, but his
eyes were twinkling with amusement at her teasing.

"Antonia dear, this hem… Oh! My lord, forgive me,
I had not realised you were here." Miss Donaldson had
her arms full of dull gold silk which she was trying to
conceal without crushing it fatally.

"I was just leaving, Miss Donaldson, I would not
dream of intruding further as you are so much engaged
with domestic affairs. Good day, ladies." He paused in

the doorway. "I look forward to your company tomorrow evening. I shall send the carriage at seven, if that is convenient."

As soon as he was gone, Donna spread the dress out over a chairback, tutting over the creases.

"Donna, what are you about with my new gown?"

"I came down for your advice on the length of the hem. But I was so put about by finding his lordship here, I fear I have creased it," her companion twittered. "Do you think he will recognise the dress when he sees it tomorrow?"

"What if he does?"

"I would not have him know you are reduced to making your own gowns." She smoothed it down anxiously. "There, after all, it is not too badly crushed, it will steam out."

"I doubt whether Lord Allington, in common with most of his sex, would remember such a thing from one day to the next." Antonia was sorely tempted to tell her companion of Marcus's declaration, but swiftly thought better of it. Miss Donaldson would see no obstacle to acceptance—indeed, would regard it as the height of her ambitions for Antonia, and would never enter into a rational discussion of Antonia's misgivings on the matter. "Now, let me see what remains to be done with this gown, and while we work I will tell you what Marcus told me of his guests."

"It seems strange to be setting out in evening dress when it is so light," Antonia remarked as they settled themselves against the luxuriously upholstered squabs of the carriage Marcus had sent as he had promised.

"Not so strange when you consider it is but a few weeks from the longest day," Miss Donaldson observed prosaically. ''But for me the strangeness lies in going out into company at all—it must be quite nine months since we last put on long gloves!'' She looked down complacently at her own, and adjusted a pearl button.

Antonia smiled back, thinking how like a neat little bird her companion was in her elegant dark garnet-shot silk with its modest infill of lace at the bosom. Miss Donaldson had never been a beautiful woman, even in the first flush of youth, but now, in her mid-forties, she had character and style and a surprising taste for fine fabrics and Brussels lace.

''How pleasant it is to travel in such comfort,'' Antonia observed, running an appreciative hand over the seat beside her. ''One would hardly credit that this is the same track over which we are wont to jolt with Jem in the dog cart.''

The observation started a train of thought in Miss Donaldson's mind. ''It would be such a relief to me to see you settled into a mode of life suited to your breeding,'' she sighed.

''Mmm?'' Antonia pretended not to hear. ''Oh, do look at the setting sun on the west face of Brightshill, turning the grey stone pink! How very pretty.''

Marcus came out onto the steps as the carriage pulled up, sending Miss Donaldson into a flutter by handing her down with a bow. Antonia, waiting until Donna was safely out, had the leisure to observe his lordship. She reflected that his rangy figure and long well-muscled legs could bear the fashion for tight trousers better than most. His coat of dark blue superfine set superbly across his broad shoulders and his shirt front gleamed white in the now-lengthening evening shadows.

His glance as he handed her down was openly appreciative and his fingers found, as if by chance, the gap between the pearl buttons at her wrist, lingering caressingly on the smooth flesh there. Antonia shivered and met his eyes. There was banked fire behind the bland politeness of his expression, a danger she had only glimpsed before when he was angry. But he was not angry now. Antonia, recognising raw desire for the first time in her twenty-four years, dropped her gaze and swallowed hard.

It was only a few minutes later when, still shaken, she was following Lady Meredith's maid to a bedchamber to divest herself of her cloak, that she wondered why he had not shown those feelings when making his declaration. How could she have resisted him then?

Donna, observing Antonia biting her lip, came over and pinched her cheeks, saying, "Indeed, yes, you do need a little colour, you have gone quite pale, my dear."

The butler was waiting at the foot of the stairs. Not by a flicker of his well-schooled features did he show that he had ever set eyes on Miss Antonia Dane before, although it had been a scant three months since she had been manhandled through this very hall by two burly gamekeepers.

"Miss Dane. Miss Donaldson," he announced, throwing open the salon doors with a flourish.

Antonia, summoning up all the poise necessary to confront the patronesses of Almack's in critical mood, straightened her spine, took a deep breath and sailed into the room.

The men sprang to their feet, but Antonia was conscious only of Marcus's eyes upon her.

Lord Allington was accustomed to considering Miss Dane an exceptionally handsome young woman, but he had never seen her in anything other than plain, workaday gowns with her hair dressed simply. Tonight she was resplendent in dull gold silk, her bare shoulders rising creamily above the seductive slopes of her bosom revealed by the cross-cut of the bodice.

Diamond eardrops trembled against the bare column of her throat and her hair had been caught up severely and allowed to tumble from the crown *à la* Dido.

Marcus stepped forward, ruthlessly suppressing the desire to sweep her into his arms and kiss her insensible. "Miss Dane, welcome to Brightshill."

"Thank you, my lord." Antonia dropped a curtsy, thrilling to the knowledge that this man desired her. "It is not, of course, the first time I have visited here." She had the satisfaction of seeing his eyes narrow warily, before adding, "I have a vague memory of coming here with my grandfather, many years ago."

He turned to greet Miss Donaldson, but not before Antonia caught the hint of a sensual smile of recollection on his lips. It heightened her recollection of that audacious kiss in his study and her colour was becomingly warm when he turned to her again.

"May I make you known to my sister, Lady Meredith and to her friend, Lady Reed." The two ladies rose and exchanged curtsies with the new arrivals, Anne Meredith with a warm smile, Lady Reed with a speculative glance that was not lost on Antonia. "Miss Fitch…" The young lady, only just out of the schoolroom, blushed charmingly at being the centre of attention and retreated hastily to her place beside Lady Meredith.

"May I also present Lord Meredith… Mr Leigh… Sir John Ollard." The gentlemen bowed in their turn.

Antonia found herself seated next to her hostess, who was making polite enquiries about the move to the Dower House. Within minutes she felt herself quite at her ease with Marcus's sister, who appeared to have none of her younger brother's hauteur.

As Antonia had observed in the inn yard, Anne Meredith shared Marcus's colouring and bone structure, making her a handsome rather than a pretty woman. She made the best of her looks by dressing *à la* Turque in dramatic jewel-coloured silks and a turban-like headdress. The regard of her husband was amply demonstrated by the very fine suite of emeralds at her neck and ears and Antonia admired the manner in which she carried off the entire ensemble.

They were comfortably moving on from the perils of house removal to the best way of approaching the layout of a small pleasure garden when Antonia became aware that someone was watching her intently.

Lady Reed was quite openly assessing Antonia, her chilly blue eyes moving from the diamond eardrops to the little kid slippers, so newly dyed bronze to match the stripe in the silk. Antonia felt uncomfortably as though she was being priced on a market stall—and being found wanting.

Nettled, Antonia turned with a chilly smile, determined to outface the older woman. But it was too late; Lady Reed got to her feet and strolled, with maximum effect on the onlookers, to talk to Mr Leigh.

Donna had been making small talk with Miss Fitch, an uphill battle with so shy a child. "Is not Mr Leigh the younger son of the Earl of Whitstable?" she enquired.

"Yes, he is the Honourable Richard," Sophia confided, blushing rosily.

Ah ha, Donna thought, so that's the way the land lies, amused to see Miss Fitch casting a dark look at Lady Reed.

The young man in question appeared less than comfortable at being the target for her ladyship's attention. She was resting one small white hand confidingly on his sleeve, her little face upturned to his, her eyes big and appealing as she hung on his every word.

Antonia caught Donna's eye and almost collapsed into giggles as Miss Donaldson cast her gaze ceilingwards. Still amused, she glanced round and saw Marcus watching the tableau stony-faced.

She was speculating upon his thoughts when the butler announced that dinner was served. Lord Meredith offered her his arm and the entire party made its way through to the dining room.

Antonia blinked in the dazzle of light from the two magnificent chandeliers suspended over the table. Despite having had three of its leaves removed to accommodate a party of only nine, the table still dominated the room with its burden of crystal, fine china and decorative pieces.

With five women and four men the seating plan at the table was, of necessity, unbalanced. Lady Meredith, as hostess, had sought to overcome this as best she could: she and Marcus faced one another down the length of the board. He had Lady Reed to his right and Antonia on his left. Lord Meredith on Antonia's left faced Miss Fitch and Miss Donaldson and Lady Meredith was flanked by Sir John and Mr Leigh.

Conversation was at first general as servants poured the wine. Antonia chatted lightly to Marcus of the originality of the display of flowers down the centre of the table.

"Yes, the hothouses are producing particularly well this year," Marcus replied. "You must allow me to conduct you round them one day soon, Miss Dane. I would value your opinion on any improvements we might make.''

Antonia's heart leapt at the use of the word ''we''. But no, she was reading too much into the word; doubtless he meant his gardening staff and not the two of them as man and wife.

The ambiguity had not been lost upon Claudia Reed either. Across the table, she glanced sharply from Antonia's flushed cheeks to Marcus's inscrutable expression and immediately began to talk to him of mutual acquaintances in London. ''I do declare, Marcus,'' she drawled, touching his sleeve, ''your hothouses are now far superior even to Lord Melchitt's. I remember so clearly the advice you gave to him when we were in Bath last spring.''

She looked at Antonia as she spoke, her blue eyes signalling quite clearly the message that she and Marcus had a history, shared not only friends, but experiences, too.

Antonia smiled sweetly back, refusing to be drawn, and began to converse with Lord Meredith, who was offering her the dish of poached turbot. Marcus's chef had excelled himself: the fish dishes were followed by elaborate entrées of truffled roast chicken, glazed ham and roast larks in pastry cases.

Antonia caught Donna's eye across the table and smiled at her companion's carefully schooled expression. After months of frugal housekeeping and good, plain fare culled from the land or their garden, this sumptuous menu with its rich sauces was almost overwhelming.

Lord Meredith proved to be genial and entertaining. Antonia guessed that he was less intellectual than his wife, and more concerned with his estates than with the arts or politics. He cast fond glances at his spouse, who appeared to be discussing the state of the Whigs with Sir John.

"Intelligent woman, my wife," he confided in Antonia with immense pride. "Don't understand why she finds politics so interesting—rather go hunting, myself—but I like to see her enjoying herself."

Antonia followed his gaze and thought how magnificent her hostess looked, her strong features animated by intelligence as she rallied Mr Leigh on his views on the government.

She was guiltily aware she had been talking far too long to Lord Meredith and should be devoting some of her time to Marcus. It was an effort to turn back into Claudia Reed's glittering sights, but she did so.

"Might I trouble you for the powdered sugar?" Marcus enquired, taking it and passing it to her ladyship who began to dip early strawberries into it before pressing them to her lips with little cries of pleasure.

Antonia regarded the spectacle with carefully veiled distaste, wondering exactly what was, or had been, the relationship between these two. Could she have been his mistress? Such things were not uncommon in polite society, she knew; after all, Marcus was no stripling. She could not, however, admire his taste.

And, if Claudia Reed were his mistress, what was she doing here when he was courting Antonia? Was he motivated simply by his desire for her lands and a degree of attraction to her? Antonia acknowledged that her breeding, if not her present circumstances, made her an acceptable match. But she was never going to be able to employ the wiles and artifice of such a highly finished piece of nature as Lady Reed.

"Marcus tells me that you and Miss…er… Dickinson

have set up housekeeping in some quaint Tudor ruin,''
Lady Reed smiled sweetly with her lips, but her eyes
remained cold. ''How quixotic of you!''

''Miss Donaldson,'' Antonia corrected evenly. ''And,
indeed, it would be most quixotic if the Dower House
were a ruin, but in fact it is a most charming place,
requiring only a little care and attention to make it a
comfortable home once again.''

''And that despite the headless ghoul,'' Marcus added
with a shared smile towards Antonia.

''Will you never stop teasing me about my foolishness—'' she began to reply but was interrupted by a
squeak from Claudia.

''A ghost! Oh, Marcus, I am so relieved to be staying
here at dear Brightshill! I know from past experience,''
she added to Antonia, ''that there are no spectres here
and, even if there were, I know Marcus would protect
me.''

Only the memory of her own folly in flinging herself
into Marcus's arms saved Antonia from making an acid
rejoinder. Claudia's intention was quite plain: she had
established that she had been a guest at Brightshill before—and perhaps more than just a guest. She spared a
passing thought for Sir George Reed, drilling his troops
at Brighton. What was the man about to leave his wife
to her own devices? Surely he must know her for what
she was?

''Ladies? Shall we?'' Lady Meredith was on her feet,
gathering the attention of the female guests. ''I suppose
we must leave these wretches to their port, and what they
always assure us is not gossip but a serious discussion
of affairs!''

In the drawing-room, Anne Meredith linked arms with
Antonia and began to stroll up and down the length of

the room. "What a charming gown, my dear. May I ask who your modiste is—surely not a provincial dressmaker?"

Antonia was just deciding whether to be frank or to turn the question when she was saved by the intervention of Lady Reed. "Yes, charming simplicity—almost naïve, is it not? And that gold is such a difficult colour unless one is somewhat swarthy! For myself with my porcelain skin, I have to choose only the purest colours."

Antonia suppressed the desire to grind her teeth in the face of such comprehensive spite and replied, "How trying for you." Really, she fumed inwardly, men could be such fools. What did Marcus see in her? Then she looked at the perfect figure, the pert bosom displayed by expensive dressmaking, the pouting red lips and told herself not to be such an innocent. And with Sir George so safely out of the way in Brighton it would not be ghosts wandering the corridors of Brightshill at midnight...

Antonia's first instinct was to have no more to do with Marcus. If he thought she was so complacent—or such a fool—as to tolerate his mistress, then he had sadly misjudged her character. Then the doors opened and the gentlemen rejoined the party and she looked across the room and saw him.

Marcus was standing in the doorway, regarding her without expression. Haughtily Antonia raised her brows; in reply, his lips curved into a smile so intense, so full of promise that her resolution melted and her heart lurched with love for him. She smiled back into his eyes, seeing only him, conscious only of him, the sounds in the room fading into nothingness.

She was still arm-in-arm with her hostess and was jolted back to the moment by Anne exclaiming, "Ah, good! The gentlemen! What say you we make up a table or two of cards? Mead, set up the tables over here.''

As the butler directed the footmen, Miss Fitch protested softly that she had no head for cards. ''I am very foolish, I am afraid,'' she confessed.

''Never say so!'' Richard Leigh protested. ''Will you not play for us, instead? I would be delighted to turn the music for you.'' He waved aside her blushing protests, lifting the lid of the pianoforte and adjusting the stool for her. ''What piece shall we start with?'' he asked her, coaxing her out of her shyness.

After a moment, under cover of the first bars of a Mozart air, Lady Meredith remarked, ''How charming! The child really does play beautifully.''

''If one has a liking for the insipid,'' Lady Reed commented. ''It is as well she has some talent to attract, I suppose, for she is otherwise unremarkable. So gauche!''

''No more so than any debutante of her age,'' Antonia retorted. ''I find her refreshing. But then I have always preferred the natural to the contrived, and it would appear that I am not alone in my opinion.'' She nodded towards Mr Leigh, who was assiduously turning the pages, his dark head bent close to Sophia's soft brown curls.

Lady Meredith skilfully turned the conversation, but not before Antonia had caught a gleam of approbation in her eyes. It seemed to Antonia that her hostess had no more liking for Claudia than she, which made it even more obvious that the woman was there not at her invitation but at Marcus's.

''Now, let us set to partners,'' Lord Meredith exclaimed, tearing open the seal on the first pack of cards. ''Miss Donaldson, do you care to play?''

"Well, my lord, I must confess a distinct partiality for whist," Donna admitted.

Antonia laughed. "I warn you, my lord, she is a demon player!"

"In that case," Lady Meredith declared, "I shall claim her for my partner."

"Then I will partner you, Meredith," Sir John offered, "unless either of you ladies, or you, Allington, wish to take my place. No? Very well then, Meredith, I am with you and we must hope the ladies will be gentle with us!"

Antonia moved to a sofa where she could listen to the music and watch the card players. Lady Reed, sighing heavily, drifted off to the other end of the room where she posed decoratively against a table and began to turn over the pages of an album of engravings.

Marcus was turning towards Antonia when his sister called to him. "Marcus, I need you! This hand is beyond everything—if I do not have your assistance, I must throw it in immediately."

To cries of "Unfair!" from the men, Marcus pulled up a chair and sat at his sister's side.

Antonia sat, the intricate melody on the edges of her consciousness, her eyes on Marcus as he teased his sister, dropping his head into his hands as she played a disastrous card. He was totally natural and at ease, his good humour and his affection for his sister evident.

Antonia had known for some time that she was in love with him, but seeing him like this, all his coldness and arrogance gone, she realised she liked him very much as well. And she could not deny that she could imagine herself mistress of Brightshill…

She sat there, warmed by her thoughts, dreaming a

little, unheeding of time when she was brought back to the present by laughter at the card table.

Lord Meredith was totalling points and saying teasingly to his wife, "My dear, you and I will play the next rubber together and permit Miss Donaldson a partner more worthy of her skills!"

The table broke up and resettled itself amid Miss Donaldson's laughing protests and Marcus got to his feet, strolling over to the sofa where Antonia sat.

"Antonia, I feel in need of some fresh air. Will you join me on the terrace? It is quite warm."

"Yes, I would like that." She looked up into his face, her dark eyes meeting his frankly. She saw his face change, soften, as he extended his hand to her and led her towards the long windows, which were open on to the balmy night. He handed her across the low threshold, then, when they were both standing on the flagstones, tucked her hand under his elbow and strolled towards the balustrade.

Antonia watched their shadows precede them across the terrace, lengthening as the light diminished behind them. Her heart beat strong but steady and her certainty grew that Marcus would take her in his arms as soon as they were out of view.

He led her round the corner of the terrace, into the moonlight that bathed the garden. Moths fluttered around and the perfume of night-scented stock hung heavy on the warm air. Neither of them spoke. Antonia rested her hands on the cool roughness of the stone balustrade, quite content to wait for what would come.

The fine cloth of Marcus's sleeve brushed against her arm, and so aware was she of him that it felt like his touch. After a long moment, he put his hands on her shoulders and gently turned her to face him. Antonia tipped up her face trustingly, inviting his lips. When the kiss came she returned it with ardour, melting into his embrace.

She was very conscious of his body hard against hers, of his breathing, of his desire for her. Finally he freed her mouth and looked down at her. His face was shadowed, but she could still read the question in his eyes.

"Yes, Marcus," she said simply.

"Yes?"

"I will be your wife."

He raised her hand to his lips, kissing her fingertips. "You have made me a happy man." It seemed as if he were about to claim her lips again, but he checked himself, glancing over her shoulder towards the house. "Come, let us rejoin the others, I would not have our absence remarked upon."

Despite her happiness, Antonia felt a tiny chill at his correctness, his formality. She wanted him to sweep her up, cover her face with kisses, say how much he loved her...

As they rounded the corner of the terrace, Antonia glimpsed a figure slip back through the far windows and recognised Claudia's flounced skirts.

Perhaps that was why he was being so restrained—he wanted to protect her from Lady Reed's acid tongue. There was time enough to talk of love when they could be sure they were alone.

Chapter Eight

Antonia felt she was floating across the threshold, hardly needing Marcus's guiding hand on her arm. She was so suffused with happiness that she felt everyone in the room must be aware of it the moment they looked at them. It seemed they had been gone for hours, yet the card game was still in progress, Miss Fitch was still playing her pretty airs on the pianoforte and the clock on the mantel was just chiming eleven.

"Shall we tell them now?" Marcus whispered in her ear.

"Oh, yes, I want everyone to share in our happiness," she whispered back, glowing.

Marcus pressed her hand, gazing deep into the luminescent hazel eyes that promised him so much. He looked round the room at his friends, who were now becoming aware of their re-entrance, opened his mouth to speak, then was forestalled by a quavering cry.

"Ohhh…" On the chaise-longue, Lady Reed raised a trembling hand to her brow, moaned again, and slid gracefully from the low silk seat to the carpet where she lay motionless.

At once Marcus and Antonia were forgotten in the

rush to the swooning woman's side. Lady Meredith was there first, kneeling on the carpet, her hand under Claudia Reed's head. Donna knelt beside her, chafing one small hand between her own capable ones.

"My dear," Lady Meredith commanded over her shoulder to her husband who was standing somewhat helplessly behind her, "pray, ring for Mead. I fear we may need to call for the doctor, and we must certainly have her woman here."

"I shall do it, ma'am," Sir John rejoined, striding to the fireplace and tugging hard at the bell pull.

Miss Fitch had started up from the piano stool in alarm and now stood clutching her throat, almost as pale as Lady Reed. Antonia, seeing her distress, crossed swiftly to Mr Leigh and whispered, "See to Miss Fitch, or we will have another patient on our hands. Why not take her out on to the terrace—the fresh air will revive her."

"Willingly, Miss Dane, but do you think it entirely proper that I should do so in the absence of her chaperon?"

"Indeed, yes!" Antonia was losing patience with such a backward lover. "I can see perfectly well from here if you just step outside the window." She gave him a gentle push, and with a grateful look he put one arm protectively around Sophia and ushered her out of the window.

Marcus had stepped across to speak to the butler, who turned and hurried from the room to summon his minion. Antonia cast a tolerant glance at the young people on the terrace before strolling across to the chaise-longue.

She felt no great concern for Lady Reed, convinced she was merely playacting, but, standing next to Lord

Meredith and looking down at the prone figure, she began to have doubts for the first time.

Claudia was as pale as marble, the blue veins visible on her eyelids, her lips pinched and chalky. She was lying in what must have been an exquisitely uncomfortable position without a sign of movement and appeared unresponsive to Lady Meredith's ministrations. "Oh, she is very convincing," Antonia muttered to herself, not quite under her breath.

"I beg your pardon, ma'am? Did you speak?" She had forgotten Lord Meredith at her side.

"I said, 'I fear she is sinking'," Antonia extemporised hastily. "Where can her maid be?"

At that moment the woman hurried into the salon, vinaigrette in hand, and bent over her mistress to administer the smelling salts. Despite the strength of the salts, the only effect was a low moan and a brief fluttering of eyelids before they closed again. All Antonia's concern vanished as she caught the swift assessing glance around the tableau of helpers that Claudia made in that moment.

She was looking to see where Marcus was, the devious baggage! All this was a device to divert his attention from Antonia. Well, we will see about that, Antonia thought grimly. "Oh, dear," she declared out loud in a voice of deep concern, "I fear such a long lasting swoon must surely be injurious to her health. We must revive her!"

As she spoke, she picked up a glass of water from the table that had been placed beside Lady Meredith as she sat at cards. With one swift movement, she dashed it into the face of Claudia Reed.

With a shriek Lady Reed came to, sitting up so swiftly she almost overturned the women kneeling beside her.

Her mouth was opening and closing with shocked outrage while the water trickled down her face, turning her blonde curls into rats' tails and sending the cunningly applied lamp black on her lashes running down her cheeks.

"You...you..." she began to splutter, turning venomous blue eyes on Antonia.

"No, do not thank me, I am only relieved that my actions have restored your senses!" Antonia hastened to assure her.

The men had tactfully turned away and Anne Meredith and Donna, assisted by the maid, helped Claudia to the chaise. Donna glanced up, catching Antonia's eye, her expression a mixture of amusement and censure.

The maid began mopping her mistress's cheeks. When Lady Reed saw the black staining the cloth, she gave another shriek and demanded to be taken to her chamber. "Give me your arm, you stupid girl!" she railed at the unfortunate maid. She stumbled from the room, Lady Meredith in attendance, leaving a stunned silence behind her.

"Poor gel!" Sir John Ollard commiserated clumsily after a moment. "Quite understandable, though, that she should swoon. It is a devilish close night. Very quick thinking on your part, Miss Dane, I have to confess I was becoming anxious myself."

Antonia, who by this time was feeling thoroughly ashamed of herself, merely coloured and glanced uneasily at Marcus. His face was impassive as he tugged on the bell pull again, but Antonia thought she could detect a hint of a smile at the edges of his lips.

Mead appeared with his usual quiet calm. "My lord?"

"Please ascertain from Lady Meredith whether she requires you to send for Dr Rush."

"I have already done so, my lord, and James has taken the gig to collect him."

Antonia's conscience was still pricking her. "Does Lady Meredith require any assistance, do you know, Mead?"

The butler turned to her with his usual gravitas. "I believe not, Miss Dane. However, I will enquire."

Another short silence ensued, broken this time by Miss Donaldson. "When it is convenient, my lord, I do believe it is time Miss Dane and I returned to the Dower House. Pray bid goodnight to Lady Meredith for us."

At that moment Miss Fitch, becomingly flushed, was helped across the threshold from the terrace by Mr Leigh. Donna gave the young woman a somewhat beady look and said in a tone she had often used to Antonia, "My dear Miss Fitch, perhaps it would be better if you too retire now." Blushing, Sophia complied, whispering her goodnights and hurrying from the room.

Marcus turned from holding the door for her. "I believe I can hear the wheels of the carriage on the drive. Let me accompany you to the front door, Miss Dane, Miss Donaldson."

He took advantage of the slight flurry whilst Miss Donaldson settled herself in the corner of the carriage to say, low-voiced, "I will call on you tomorrow morning, my dear."

Antonia pressed his hand responsively and let him hand her into the carriage. It took all her social training and self-control not to lean out of the window for a last glimpse of him as they turned the bend in the drive.

Donna was uncharacteristically silent. Antonia, braced for an inquisition, found it hard to tolerate and finally broke into speech herself. "I wonder what can have been the matter with Lady Reed," she mused disingenuously.

"Admittedly, the evening is warm, but she could hardly be said to be overdressed."

It was difficult to descry Donna's expression in the gloom of the carriage, but when she spoke her voice was dry. "I doubt it was anything to do with the heat." She paused, then added, seemingly changing the subject, "You were out alone on the terrace with his lordship for a long time, my dear."

Antonia knew her companion too well not to catch her drift. The temptation to tell Miss Donaldson of her acceptance of Marcus's suit almost overcame her, but then she thought better of it. Donna would be full of questions, none of which she could answer. No, better wait until Marcus had visited her tomorrow and then she could give her the glad news and a date for the marriage.

"The air was very pleasant, quite refreshing," she said lightly. "Did you not observe how completely it revived Miss Fitch?"

"Hmm!" Donna snorted. "What revived that young lady was having Mr Leigh hold her hand for twenty minutes! I am sure Lady Meredith would not approve—I was in two minds whether to go out there myself."

"Why did you not?" Antonia encouraged, happy that the conversation had turned from her own sojourn on the terrace.

"Because I was more concerned with what you were about!" Donna was tart as she leaned forward to look into Antonia's shadowed face. "To dash water into Lady Reed's face in that way was quite outrageous!"

"It did revive her most effectively."

"Do not seek to be so disingenuous with me, Antonia—I can read you like a book. No, it is not Lady Reed's health that causes you concern, and well I know it."

"Do you think she was Marcus's mistress?" Antonia enquired daringly.

The improper question had the desired effect of completely distracting Miss Donaldson from the scene in the salon. "Antonia! What an unseemly question! You should know nothing of such things…I am sure his lordship would not…"

"His lordship is thirty years old," Antonia retorted tartly. "He has hardly lived as a monk, and Lady Reed is an attractive woman—even if she does black her lashes—with a complaisant husband hundreds of miles away."

"Antonia, stop it—you should not have such thoughts! Well, at least, if you do, you should not voice them aloud. A well-bred young woman pretends not to know how men go on."

"Oh, stop this pretence, Donna, we both know what goes on!" Her voice dropped and trembled slightly. "Do all men have mistresses, Donna, even after they are married?"

"Some do," Donna admitted, then rallied with a happy thought. "But those who have married for affection and who retain their feelings for their wives do not—why, look at Lord Meredith, can you imagine him keeping a mistress?"

Antonia leaned back against the squabs with a sigh, looking out at the silent countryside now bathed in moonlight. She was suddenly very tired, all the excitement of the evening, of Marcus's declaration, ebbing away to leave her feeling somewhat low.

Entering the Dower House, she was glad of Donna's silence and bade her goodnight on the landing with only a few words.

She had been certain she would fall asleep as soon as

her head touched the pillow, but in the darkness the foolishness of her behaviour came back to haunt her. How could she have thrown that water at Lady Reed? And in doing so, had she not behaved just as badly as the other woman?

Miserably, Antonia could not but fear that Marcus would think less well of her because of it, for she knew he had not been gulled by her expressions of concern for Claudia. She loved him, wanted to appear wholly admirable in his eyes. In the darkness she tossed and turned, scourging herself with reproaches. A lady would have behaved with dignity: after all, she was the one whom he had asked to marry. Why then descend to such jealous behaviour?

The night seemed endless, sultry and oppressive. When Antonia finally slipped into sleep it was only to dream vividly of Marcus—his lips hot on her throat, his arms binding her tightly to his body. When she woke it was to find the sheets tangled round her, her hair damp and tousled on the pillows.

Consequently, it was a wan-faced and subdued Antonia who faced Donna across the breakfast table the next morning.

"My dear, you look quite pulled down," her companion said anxiously, scanning her face. "I am sure this weather is unhealthy. Shall I send for Dr Rush after breakfast? You must go and lie down with a nice cup of tea…"

"No, please do not concern yourself, Donna. It was so close last night, I felt I was stifling. When I did sleep, it was very fitful and has done me no good." Antonia listlessly spread some butter on her bread, looked at the conserves and found the decision between honey and jam quite beyond her.

Donna was still worrying on. "I think you should return to bed. I will make you a tisane—"

She broke off as Anna the maidservant bustled in with a tray and fresh tea. "Anna, please go directly and make up your mistress's bed and open the windows wide. It is fresher this morning, my dear, I am sure there will be a breeze and you will sleep more easily in the cool."

"Thank you, Donna, but I am expecting Lord Allington to be calling on me this morning. Perhaps I will lie down when he is gone." What he would think when he saw her wan face and the dark shadows under her eyes she could not imagine. The comparison with the exquisite Claudia Reed could only be unfavourable.

Antonia sighed heavily. She wanted to see Marcus again so badly, to be in his arms, hear him at last tell her he loved her. Yet she felt so drained, so guilty that she had behaved badly the night before. She was ashamed of being jealous, ashamed of thinking ill of Marcus. And in some far less worthy part of her mind, she acknowledged that she had shown her hand to the other woman. If Claudia Reed had been in any doubt about Antonia's feelings for Marcus, the incident last night would have made them crystal clear.

By her own actions, she had given that unscrupulous female the upper hand—and Claudia was living under the same roof as Marcus. She was a married woman, entirely unconstrained by the strict social rules that governed Antonia in her dealings with Marcus.

"You do not seem very pleased that Lord Allington is calling this morning," Donna observed. "Is something amiss? He appeared most attentive last night as he saw us to the carriage."

Her eyes were beady with pleasurable curiosity. Surely he could only be calling in order to make dear Antonia a declaration! The foolish child had been tossing and turning all night in anticipation. No wonder she was feeling so enervated.

"If we are expecting a visitor, it would certainly not do for you to retire to your bedchamber," she continued briskly, biting back the torrent of questions which filled her mind. What had Lord Allington said to her dear Antonia last night? She had had to overcome all her instincts as a chaperon to allow them so much time alone together on the terrace, but it appeared to have paid dividends.

Antonia found herself being steered firmly out of the breakfast parlour and up the stairs to her bedchamber. "If we brush out your hair—really, tying it back so tightly makes you appear quite schoolmarmish!—and I think we can conceal those dark shadows with just a touch of rice powder…and your new jonquil muslin is most becoming…"

Donna bustled round the room as she spoke and Antonia passively allowed herself to primped and preened. But she had to admit, looking in the mirror afterwards, that sitting in the cool room had refreshed her, and Donna's ministrations had transformed her into some semblance of her usual self.

Her skin was still pale, without its normal glow of health, but it was flawless. Her abundant brown hair clustered in a tumble of curls on the shoulder of the pale jonquil gown and her eyes were clear, although the heavy lids still spoke of her sleepless night.

"There!" announced Donna with satisfaction. "You look quite yourself again. I am sure his lordship will notice no difference."

Antonia smiled back at her companion, her spirits rising. How strange that one sleepless night could put things so out of kilter, disturb the balance of her emotions so! It was she Marcus wished to marry, and today when he came to her he would tell her that he loved her. Now he was betrothed, some former associations would inevitably cease.

Hoofbeats sounded on the gravel drive. Both women hurried to the low open casement and looked out, but the rider below was not Marcus.

"It is Saye, his lordship's groom," Antonia observed as the man reined in his black cob and leaned down to hand a folded paper to Anna, who had run out at the sound of his arrival.

The girl slipped the note in her apron pocket, but made no move to go back into the house. She was looking up at the sturdy young man with coy admiration, her cheeks pink. Antonia could not catch what the groom was saying, but the two appeared to know each other well, for he was laughing and chatting easily to the girl.

He gathered up the reins to leave, but bent down at the last moment and snatched a quick kiss from the maid before cantering off down the drive. Anna stood looking after him, her fingers straying to her cheek.

"Anna!" Donna's voice came sharp on the morning air. "Stop standing there like a moonstruck calf and bring that note in at once!"

The girl started and stared upwards in alarm. "Yes, ma'am, sorry ma'am."

She was still very pink as she handed over the missive to Antonia. "And just what are that young man's intentions?" Antonia demanded. "I am not aware you have asked Miss Donaldson's permission for a follower to call."

"Intentions? I don't know what you mean, miss," the girl stammered. "I've known Josh Saye all my life—friend of my brother's, he is, miss."

"Indeed," Miss Donaldson observed coolly, but not unkindly. "I am sure if he is one of his lordship's men he is respectable, but even so, if he is to call on you, then I must know and you can both sit in the kitchen in a proper manner. And," she added, "no dallying on the front doorstep!"

"Yes, ma'am, thank you, ma'am." The girl scuttled from the room, relieved to have got off so lightly.

"Oh!" Antonia said blankly, scanning the letter.

"Why, what is wrong, my dear?"

"His lordship writes that he is unable to call this morning after all. It seems the parish constables have brought a most complicated case before him and he must sit—perhaps all day—to hear the evidence against them before committing the men to the County gaol."

She could have handed the letter to Miss Donaldson without a qualm, for the businesslike lines in his firm black hand contained nothing beyond the simple message, his formal regrets and his intention to call later that evening.

Antonia was conning the household accounts after luncheon when Jem was admitted to the small parlour.

"I've brought the post, miss." He held out the papers in one slightly grubby hand and hesitated, looking hopefully at Miss Donaldson, who was ensconced in the window-seat stitching a pillowcase.

"Have you eaten, Jem?" she asked, just as he had hoped.

"Not since a bite of bacon at breakfast, ma'am. Long

time ago, that was,'' he added, managing to sound half-starved.

"Then go to the kitchen and tell Anna I said you were to have a bowl of soup and some bread. And when you have finished, go to the kitchen garden and see if there is any weeding you can do for Johnson.'' The lad grinned and dashed off.

Antonia spread the handful of letters on the table. "There is a note from Great-Aunt Granger—that is a hopeful sign, her handwriting seems much firmer. And a bill from the corn chandler for the chicken feed. Oh, I think this is from Mr Blake.'' She broke the seal and spread out the crackling sheets. "Yes...he writes that Sir Josiah and Lady Finch will be arriving at Rye End Hall the day after tomorrow.''

"How interesting.'' Donna put down her sewing and gave Antonia her full attention. "How soon do you think we should call? We must not be backward in paying our respects to our new neighbours; yet, they will no doubt be fatigued after their removal and one would not wish to intrude.''

"Then let us leave our cards in four days' time.'' Antonia finished scanning her great aunt's letter and handed both it and Mr Blake's note to Donna. "Great-Aunt does indeed seem more like her old self, I am glad to say.'' She pushed the ledger away and stood up. "These figures are giving me a headache. I think I will go for a walk. Will you accompany me?''

"No, thank you, my dear, I think I will remain here and finish this linen. Keep to the shade and do not forget your hat,'' she called after Antonia.

Antonia strolled along the river bank, idly swinging her broad-brimmed straw hat by its ribbons and taking deep lungsful of the warm air. Above her, skylarks sang in the clear sky without a hint of cloud. The river glinted in the sunshine as it hurried along, its surface disturbed as fish rose to take flies from the surface.

She paused to pick dog roses as she went, sucking her finger as she pricked it on the thorns. Her spirits were rising as she walked and she began to sing under her breath. The trees closed in over the river in a green tunnel and she strolled beneath them, grateful for the shade and uncaring how far she had walked.

It seemed to her that she had her heart's desire: she was in love with a man who wished to make her his wife, whose every action showed his desire for her. She had secured her family home from ruin and by her actions in the neighbourhood had made the name of Dane respected once more. To have found a husband so close to home was an added joy, for she had grown to love the rolling beauty of the countryside, to value the good relations she felt she had forged with her tenants.

With a start she realised how far she had ventured. Although she had never walked so far along this path before, she guessed she was on Brightshill land. In fact, she calculated, if she walked on around that bend, she might be able to glimpse the roof of the house where Marcus was. The evening, when he would come to her, seemed a long way away…

The turn of the river revealed a summerhouse built as a small classical temple on shorn grass. The lawns swept up towards the house, almost hidden by the rise of the land. All seemed deserted, shimmering in the heat of the afternoon. Antonia gazed towards the house for a long moment, hardly believing that she would be mistress of it, perhaps before the year was out.

The classical portico of the temple was casting tempting shade; Antonia realised just how far she had to walk back and decided that a few moments' rest would be welcome, for if anything the day was getting hotter. She sank gratefully on to a wrought-iron bench and fanned herself with her hat. Through gaps in the trees she could see the sky was no longer cloudless and great thunderheads were building, threatening a storm later.

Antonia got to her feet and decided to set out again before she was caught in the rain.

''What are you doing here?'' Marcus's voice enquired from behind her.

She whirled round, her heart beating with delight at the sound of his voice, then found she could not see him. Puzzled, she descended the short flight of marble steps and rounded the far corner of the summerhouse.

Trees had been planted to surround a grassy glade where the wild flowers had been allowed to grow unchecked in the natural style. A semi-clad goddess in marble gazed out to the river with unseeing eyes, a docile fawn recumbent at her feet.

For a moment Antonia stood, enchanted by the tranquility of the spot, then she saw Marcus. A hammock had been slung between two trees, providing a shady resting place, and he was lying, coat discarded, shirt open, a book and pitcher on the ground beside him.

Whoever Marcus had spoken to, it was not Antonia. His gaze was fixed on someone within the grove of trees, someone who at that moment emerged.

For a dizzy moment Antonia believed the statue had come to life and descended from its plinth, then she realised it was Claudia. Her hair was caught up in classical ringlets, her form molded by the diaphanous muslin of a white gown. The garment, confined only by a crisscross of ribbons at the bosom, was to Antonia's horrified eye, quite outrageous.

Claudia skirted the foot of the hammock to stand at Marcus's side, her back to Antonia. As the sunlight caught the gown, the wearer's limbs were clearly defined beneath skirts that must have been dampened.

They were talking, low-voiced. Antonia, frozen to the spot, was unable to hear what passed between them, but she could clearly see Claudia reach out to brush the hair from Marcus's forehead before leaning down and fastening her lips on his.

Surely he would rebuff her, push her away! Then, before Antonia's startled eyes, his arms encircled Claudia, pulling her into his embrace. The hammock swayed wildly, the slender trees supporting it bent inwards and Claudia, ever graceful, subsided on to Marcus's broad chest.

Seconds later the hammock tipped, tumbling them both onto the grass sward, where they lay in a tangle of limbs, lips still joined.

With a sob Antonia whirled round and ran blindly back along the river bank, stumbling over roots, briars catching at her skirts.

Behind the summerhouse, Marcus freed his lips from the voracious, experienced mouth above him and pushed Lady Reed from his chest with more force than gallantry.

He raised himself on his elbows, panting slightly, and glowered at Claudia, who still sprawled enticingly at his side.

"Damn it, woman! Have I not told you to behave with more circumspection? Anyone could have seen you."

Claudia pouted prettily. "Why so hot for respectability, my love, when you used to be so hot for me?"

He snorted, pushing himself into a sitting position.

"When was I ever your love, Claudia? Admit it, you love only yourself."

"And you, Marcus? I suppose you are going to tell me now that you love that…female. What is it that attracts you, my dear? It surely cannot be her clothes, her lack of style and connections? She is all ungainly legs and country complexion." Her drawling tone did not quite disguise the malice behind the words.

Marcus got to his feet in one easy movement. "Enough." He stooped to take Claudia's hand and help her up. "I intend to marry Miss Dane. It is an entirely suitable match."

"In terms of land, I suppose it is wise," Claudia conceded. "For I can see the advantages of connecting the two estates, they march together so well. I am quite fatigued, my dear, and bored with talking of your little country mouse." She slipped her hand through his arm, "Let us go back to the house and take tea."

As they began to stroll up the long sloping lawns, Antonia had reached the last stretch of river before the Dower House. She had sobbed as she ran, and now, breathless and dishevelled, sank to the bank edge.

She could not go into the house like this, unless she was prepared to tell all to Donna. Antonia bent, scooping up cold water to splash on her hot eyes, and eventually felt calm enough to return home.

In the parlour Donna was sipping tea, the mended linen in a basket at her feet. "My dear!" She started up at the sight of Antonia's flushed face and heavy eyes. "Come and sit down. You have walked too far, undone all the good work of this morning. I do hope you are not sickening for something."

"I think it is the weather." Antonia was surprised at the matter-of-factness she could achieve, although her heart felt as though it were breaking. "See, the clouds are banking up, we will have a storm soon." Despite the heat, she felt as though something had frozen inside her. It was as though she had known all along that he did not love her, that he had offered only for her land, not for her love.

You fool, she told herself, as she mechanically drank the tea Donna passed her. You have been living in a fool's paradise: after all, he had never spoken of love. She could not fault him in that. It was all her own foolishness, her own romantic daydreaming. Her own inexperience had ensnared her, leading her to believe that a man's passions were all allied to love. But men, she was learning, could desire a woman with their affections entirely unengaged. And, it seemed, could feel that desire for more than one woman at a time.

And several hundred acres of land were, no doubt, a powerful inducement to desire.

She was still more despising of herself than angry with Marcus when, an early supper eaten, she sat waiting for him in the garden. Donna, in obvious expectation of a proposal, had tactfully made herself scarce.

The air was heavy with a threatening chrome yellow tinge to the banked clouds. Lightning flickered over the Vale and thunderflies swarmed above the flowerbeds. Antonia, despite the light summer gown, felt as if she were wearing furs, so oppressive was the heat.

She was fighting to keep calm, rehearsing the dignified, frigid speech with which she intended to withdraw her acceptance of his offer. She had no intention of bringing Claudia Reed's name into it. No, she would say in measured tones that she had thought better of it, that they would not suit. After all, she could never admit she had seen them that afternoon.

The old longcase clock from the hallway struck seven, the sound echoing faintly across the garden from the open casements, set wide to catch what little breeze there was.

Where was he? The longer she waited, the harder it became to maintain her fragile composure. Then she heard the hoofbeats and started to her feet, her heart beating painfully.

Marcus, trotting up the driveway, saw the tall, slim figure in the pale yellow gown against a rose bush and turned his horse's head. Tossing the reins over a branch he strode across the lawn towards her, a smile warm on his lips.

Antonia knew her face was set—try as she might, she could not arrange her features into any semblance of welcome. As he neared her and saw her expression his changed, too, into a look of questioning concern.

"Antonia, what is wrong?" He took her hand in his, raising it to his lips.

Antonia pulled her hand away, her legs suddenly weak with longing for him, for his touch. She could not allow herself to falter, weaken, or she would be lost, loving him as she did.

"My lord," she began formally, her lips stiff. He began to speak, but she held up her hand to forestall him. "My lord, I have to tell you that, flattering as your offer to me yesterday was, I feel my acceptance of it was mistaken. Upon mature reflection…" her voice wavered slightly as a frown gathered between his brows, but she pressed on bravely "…upon reflection, I must decline your proposal, sensible though I am of the honour you do me. My lord, we should not suit," she finished baldly.

This was as far as she had gone with her prepared speech. Her imagination had not allowed her to envisage Marcus's reaction.

"Should not suit!" His voice was incredulous. "Antonia, what can you mean?" She was having an attack of maidenly vapours, no doubt, although he had not thought it of her.

Antonia drew herself up and took a steadying breath. "I mean what I say, my lord. We should not suit. I am only grateful circumstances were such that we made no announcement last night."

He let out a short bark of laughter. "We may have made no announcement, but our friends know what to expect."

"I have done nothing to lead them to draw conclusions," she said stiffly. "What you have done, my lord, is your affair."

"Damn it, woman, will you stop calling me 'my lord'!"

"How dare you use such language to me!" The thunder cracked and rolled overhead, causing Antonia to start nervously.

Marcus did not hesitate. He seized her in his arms, fastened his mouth on hers, feeling its hard resistance soften and yield beneath his lips. Antonia felt close to swooning, the pounding of her heart finding echo in the skies above. His hands were roaming tantalisingly, finally settling on her shoulders, hot on the bare skin exposed there.

She wanted him so much, and when his tongue invaded her mouth she opened to him, welcoming the intimacy. Her hands tangled in his hair, and as they did so a picture of Claudia flickered against her closed lids.

Antonia stiffened in his arms. It was as though she

could taste the scent of the other woman on his lips and it repelled her. With a gasp, she wrenched herself free of him.

"My God, Antonia," he exclaimed, running his hand through his disordered hair. "How can you claim we do not suit? I have never known a woman respond so, with such passion…"

"And you have known so many, my lord," she riposted, her colour high, her bosom heaving.

So that was what it was all about! Damn Claudia. This was what he feared would happen when she had turned up uninvited and against his wishes. He had implored her to be discreet, not flaunt their relationship. But he should have known that the slightest hint of competition would drive Claudia to a display of ownership as provocative as it was indiscreet.

"If this is about Claudia—" he began, with fatal misjudgment.

"About Claudia! You have the effrontery to invite your strumpet to your home at the very time you make me a proposal and you wonder that I reject you? I had a better opinion of your understanding than that, my lord!"

Heavy rain drops began to fall, plopping weightily on the dusty earth. Neither heeded the wetness, so caught up were they in their battle.

"Strumpet! That is fine language for a lady to use! And Claudia Reed is not my mistress, if we must speak plainly of such things." His eyes were narrowed in the failing light, but she could still see the angry glitter through the rain that now lashed down.

"Do not lie to me!"

"How dare you!" His voice was like the thunder above.

"I dare because I speak the truth! I cannot deny the evidence of my own eyes!" As soon as she uttered the words Antonia realised how she had betrayed herself.

"What evidence? What are you speaking of?" The water was running down the hard planes of his face, his hair was as sleek and dark as an otter's.

"I saw you this afternoon," she cried out. "I saw you behind the summerhouse with your wh—" She almost used the shocking word, but some vestige of restraint held her back.

"Those who creep about spying should expect to see unpalatable sights, madam." Marcus's cheeks were flushed, although whether from anger or shame she could not tell.

"You do not deny it, then?" she accused hotly.

"I am not going to justify myself to you, Antonia. If you are not prepared to take my word, then you are correct: we would not suit." He bowed stiffly, clapped his hat back on his sodden head and strode to where his horse sheltered miserably under the tree.

She stood, unheeding of the torrent, until she could no longer discern the sound of hoofbeats, then, her gown winding wetly about her limbs, she stumbled back towards the house.

Chapter Nine

The heavy rainstorm of the night before had ruined all but the most sheltered roses in the Dower House gardens. Antonia lifted up the water-weighted branches to try and find some buds fit for cutting, grimacing in distaste as the pulpy petals clung to her hands.

The storm had cleared the air: the morning had dawned bright and fresh and a slight breeze was fast drying the gravel paths. Antonia was resolved to keep herself occupied, but her mind felt numb. Her thoughts flickered to the events of the day before, then flinched away as though she had touched a burn. She could not bear to think of Marcus and of what she had lost by spurning him…

Hoofbeats sounded in the lane beyond the high quickthorn hedge and she dropped the basket, her hand flying to her throat. ''Marcus!'' she said out loud as the hoofbeats slowed and the rider turned into the carriageway of the Dower House.

It was Marcus…her eyes strained against the bright sunlight, then the silhouetted rider became clearer. The man was shorter than Lord Allington, his hair a neatly barbered brown and the horse he was riding obviously a hired hack.

Antonia bent to hide the dismay on her face, righting the basket and dropping the scissors in beside the roses. By the time she was ready to face Mr Jeremy Blake, she had composed herself. He had dismounted and was waiting politely for her to notice him, the reins looped over his arm.

"Mr Blake, what a pleasure to see you again. I must thank you for your letter; we are looking forward greatly to meeting Sir Josiah and Lady Finch. May I offer you refreshment?"

Antonia called to the maidservant, as the girl, warned by their voices, threw open the front door. "Anna, please show Mr Blake where he can leave his horse and then bring some refreshment to the drawing-room."

She entered the house, placing the basket of roses on the hall table before examining her reflection in the glass. How was it possible to feel so unhappy and yet for it not to show on her face? True, there were smudges of purple under her lashes and she was paler than usual, but she looked quite composed in her fresh sprigged muslin, her hair tied back in a simple ribbon.

Hearing noises, she went in search of Donna and found her, as she had expected, sewing in the small parlour. "Mr Blake is come. I have told Anna we shall receive him in the drawing-room."

Donna laid aside her work, and her worries about his lordship's failure to call yesterday as expected, and hastily patted her already immaculate hair into place. She approved of Mr Blake: a most well-mannered and well-bred young man, although not, of course, such a catch as Lord Allington would be...

Consequently she beamed upon the young man as he

was shown into the drawing-room by Anna a few minutes later. It would do no harm, she reflected, to encourage Mr Blake in his association with them. His lordship was showing alarming signs of taking her dear Antonia for granted—a rival to pique his jealousy was all to the good.

Jeremy Blake found himself greeted, therefore, with a distinguishing degree of warmth by both his hostesses. Miss Dane, smiling though she was, seemed to him to be almost wistful behind her welcome. What could have put her out of countenance? He could not conjecture, but resolved to defend her against whatever had caused that slight crease between her pretty brows, the shadows beneath those soft hazel eyes.

He sat in the proffered chair, flicking up the tails of his new riding coat, pleased he had decided to wear it that morning. Crossing one leg over the other, he was conscious that, although his valet might not use champagne in the blacking, he still achieved a most creditable appearance to his master's boots.

Fortified by the fact that he was appearing at his best, and by the sip of Canary from the glass at his side, he turned his mind to the matter in hand. "I am charged with messages from my principal and his good lady. Sir Josiah wishes me to say how obliged he is at the expedition with which you have instructed your man of business to proceed and Lady Finch asked me to present her compliments and to hope that you both will call upon her at Rye End Hall at your earliest convenience."

Donna beamed upon him, feeling that these formal attentions were entirely in keeping with how her dear Miss Dane should be treated. It was a scandal that she had had to endure poverty and social obscurity because of her father's outrageous behaviour. Now at last, received at the two great houses of the neighbourhood, she was moving in circles appropriate to her breeding.

She recalled herself from dreams of social advancement for her protégée to find that Mr Blake had moved on to less formal matters. ''And in the carriage house, right at the back, I found a whisky. Just a one-horse carriage, of course, but in very good condition and eminently suitable for a lady to drive in the country. The terms of the lease do not include any vehicles other than the farm carts, so, of course, I had intended sending it round to you. I thought perhaps you had overlooked it…''

''How delightful,'' Antonia cried. ''As you say, it is just the thing.'' Then her face fell. ''But no, it would not be practical, for we have no horses, and to purchase one simply for this purpose would be profligate indeed.''

The room fell silent for a moment, then Mr Blake brightened visibly. ''I believe I may have a solution, ma'am, if you would not object to performing a favour for me. I shall be bringing up my riding and carriage horses from London, and Sir Josiah is most willing to stable them for me as I shall be here so much in future.''

The ladies nodded in comprehension, Antonia concealing a small glow of pleasure at the thought of furthering their acquaintance with such a congenial gentleman. ''However, I have one carriage horse for which I no longer have a use as I only drive a team these days. I am reluctant to sell it, for I have had it for many years, yet I do not feel I can pension it out on Sir Josiah's land. It is most suitable for a ladies' carriage. If you could give it pasturage, I would be delighted for you to have the full use of it.''

Mr Blake leaned back in his chair, pleased with his tactful solution. He wondered if Miss Dane could drive.

Pleasant fantasies of long summer afternoons teaching her to handle the reins flitted through his mind.

"How very generous and thoughtful," Antonia began, then commonsense reasserted itself. "But we have no groom."

Donna hastened to interject. "My dear, we were only speaking of this yesterday. Did we not agree that we needed a man to assist with the heavier work about the place? Jem is too young and Old Johnson too infirm. There must be a suitable and honest youth in the village looking for employment."

"If you will permit me, ladies, I will speak to the estate manager and ask him to recommend a reliable man and send him over for your approval."

The matter thus satisfactorily concluded and his messages delivered, Mr Blake rose to go. Antonia waited for him at the front steps while he rode round from the yard. He reined in, doffing his hat and leaning down as he realised she wished to speak to him.

"Mr Blake." She held out her hand and he took it, holding it as he looked down at her. "I must thank you again for your kindness. We would be happy if you would call again—please do not stand on ceremony." She smiled up at him, her hand feeling safe in his. He seemed so uncomplicated and honest and his admiration warmed her chilled heart.

At that moment, another rider passed the gate, slowing almost to a standstill. Jeremy's mount tossed its head at the presence of another horse and they turned to see who it could be. Lord Allington, sitting tall and erect on his rakish hunter, regarded them coldly for a moment, then clapped his spurs to his horse's flanks and cantered off.

"His lordship appears out of humour again," Mr Blake remarked more laconically than he felt.

"Indeed, yes," Antonia agreed with a small sigh.

So that was how the land lay, Jeremy mused as he trotted down the drive and turned towards Rye End Hall with a last wave of his hand. Lord Allington was the cause of Miss Dane's unhappiness, was he? He had seen more than enough in London of eligible aristocrats playing fast and loose with the affections of young ladies without the protection of watchful male relations. He would have a quiet word with his aunt, Lady Finch. Without daughters of her own, she would be charmed to take Miss Dane under her wing.

Antonia drifted back into the house, her pulses still racing from the unexpected sight of Marcus. Had he been intending to call and been deterred by the presence of the other man? Unconscious that her thoughts were chiming with those of Jeremy Blake, she told herself that she may be Miss Dane of Rye End Hall, Hertfordshire, but she was still dowerless and unprotected.

Antonia felt she had been naïve: Marcus had proposed for her lands, expecting her to be a complaisant Society bride, willing to overlook his mistress—and no doubt his gambling and sporting entertainments—in return for a title and an establishment. Like any foolish village girl, she had expected love and courtship and fidelity.

Well, foolish she might be, but she was not willing to settle for less. How much better to have discovered this now than to have married Marcus and faced humiliation and disillusion when she had no escape!

Borne up by a new sense of resolution, Antonia went to find Donna. The latter was arranging the battered roses in a pewter jug in the small parlour, a frown on her face.

"Was that Lord Allington I saw just now riding past?" her companion enquired bluntly.

"It was." Antonia fiddled with a discarded stem, rolling it between her fingers, unwilling to meet Donna's eye.

"Antonia, what is afoot? I thought the man was coming to propose to you." Donna regarded her beadily. "Is he playing fast and loose with you, because if he is…?"

Antonia knew she had to stop Donna's speculation before she confronted Marcus and demanded to know what his intentions were. "He proposed to me and I have refused him," she announced flatly, subsiding wearily onto a bench.

There was a moment's shocked silence, then Miss Donaldson repeated slowly, "You have refused him!" She, too, subsided into a chair, too amazed to stay on her feet. The scissors dropped unheeded to the floor. "But why, Antonia? He is the most eligible man, and I was certain you were in love with him. When you came in from the terrace the other night, your happiness was almost palpable…"

Antonia swallowed down the lump in her throat at the thought of that happiness, of how much she still loved Marcus. "I have discovered that his moral character is not such as I could tolerate in a husband. I must be able to respect the man I marry."

As she had expected, this completely persuaded Donna. Moral instability was one thing she would never tolerate—and one subject on which she would never feel able to question Antonia further.

Donna got to her feet and began to pace the room, her small frame a-quiver with indignation as she spoke. "Well, my dear, it is indeed fortunate that you discovered how deceived we were in his lordship. We will cut him, of course—he will not be welcome in this house again, that is for sure! It is a lesson, is it not, how one may be taken in by a handsome face and an air of breeding!''

Despite everything, Antonia could not help but be amused at the thought of the redoubtable Miss Donaldson making her displeasure clear to Marcus at their next meeting.

Donna was employing her happy knack of finding a silver lining in even the blackest cloud. ''And the arrival of Sir Josiah and Lady Finch could not be more providential, for we shall not lack congenial company. And if Mr Blake is to be residing here—'' she glanced at Antonia under her lashes ''—no doubt parties of younger people will frequently be present.''

Any further speculation was interrupted by the unceremonious arrival of Jem into the room. ''Begging your pardon, miss, but come quick, Old Johnson's having a seizure in the rhubarb patch!''

The ladies hastened after the small figure as Jem scuttled out through the kitchen and into the back yard. The old gardener was indeed visible, slumped on a log, his face ashen, his gnarled hands wringing the hem of his smock.

''Johnson! Are you ill?'' Antonia turned to Donna. ''Could you fetch him some of the port wine?''

The old man struggled with his emotions and finally found his voice to utter a string of curses which caused Antonia to clap her hands over her ears. Seeing her reaction, he controlled himself with difficulty and growled, ''Begging your pardon, ma'am, but it's more than flesh and blood can stand, that it be!''

Donna hastened up with a tumbler of wine which the old man swigged back in one, wiping the back of his hand across his mouth. ''God bless you, ma'am! Real gentry, you are, not like that bastard up at Brightshill.''

"*Johnson!* Mind your language!"

Jem, seeing the look of bewilderment on Antonia's face as Donna continued to remonstrate with the gardener, hastened to explain. "He's had a shock, see. It's his other three sons, ma'am. They've been sent to Quarter Sessions by his lordship for fighting with his keepers. And they'll be transported, sure as sure, to Botany Bay—and that's miles away, Essex at least!" Jem's eyes were huge with the wonderful horror of it all.

"And our Sim withering away in Hertford gaol these last three months," the old man moaned, "and all due to his lordship's terrible hardness. Now he's took all my boys. Starve, I will, and their wives and little ones along'a me!"

"No one is going to starve," Antonia declared robustly, her mind trying to place the Johnson families amongst her tenants. "Are there many children?"

"Fifteen at the last count, ma'am," Johnson said gloomily, "and young Bethan in the family way, I'll be bound."

"That's one of his granddaughters," Jem supplied helpfully. "I expect the father'll be Watkins up at Brightshill."

"Well, he will just have to marry her," Antonia said firmly.

"His wife'll have something to say about that—he's married already with six children," Jem replied helpfully.

Antonia's brain reeled. There were ways and means of keeping the families from starvation, but they needed their menfolk home as soon as possible. Really, she could not comprehend how Marcus could be so harsh, all for the sake of a few pheasants! Obviously the men were in the wrong to have gone on to his land, but she

knew only too well how ready his keepers were to attack. Look at the way she had been manhandled!

"Those brutes of keepers!" she exclaimed. "I am
sure your sons were only defending themselves. I shall
speak to his lordship directly. Jem, help Johnson home
and go by the kitchens with Miss Donaldson on your
way, I am sure there is some food you can take for the
children."

Antonia swept inside on a tide of high dudgeon, calling her maid. No doubt the Johnson clan were among
the more feckless of her tenants—there had to be a few
in every village—but if they were kept in poverty, they
were bound to be tempted into crime!

An hour later, attired in her best walking costume,
parasol tilted against the sun, she ascended the steps to
the front door at Brightshill and pulled the bell handle.

"Miss Dane." Mead the butler bowed respectfully as
he held the door for her. "How may I be of assistance?
I believe her ladyship is at home. A warm day, is it not?
Most clement." Miss Dane appeared more than a little
heated, her hair was coming loose under the brim of her
bonnet and the colour was high on her cheekbones. Not
that her spirited looks were in any way marred, he
thought appreciatively.

"I wish to see his lordship." Antonia was in no mood
for polite chit-chat about the weather with his lordship's
upper servants.

"I will ascertain whether his lordship is at home,
ma'am. Would you care to step into the white salon
while you wait? I will send refreshment in." He ushered
her into a cool, high-ceilinged chamber and bowed himself out.

Antonia was not inclined to admire the charm of the

room, a feminine confection of white picked out in gold with ormolu enhancing the delicate French furniture. During the hot walk up to Brightshill, she had decided angrily that not only could she do without the responsibility for three wives, fifteen children and an old man—not to speak of the unfortunate Bethan's predicament—but that Lord Allington was entirely responsible for the entire sorry coil.

By the time his lordship joined her, she had quite forgotten all her embarrassment at meeting him again. He closed the door behind him, and walked slowly towards her, a look of quizzical tenderness softening his face. "Antonia…" he began to say, then must have seen the stormy expression on her face, for he stopped, his brows drawing together into their familiar hard line.

"Don't you Antonia me," she snapped. "I have come to demand that you release my men immediately."

"Your men?"

"Job, Boaz and Ezekiel Johnson, the men you have had dragged off to prison, leaving their families to starve!" Marcus was regarding her with astonishment. Antonia stamped her foot in exasperation. "Come, sir, it was only yesterday! Do you sentence so many men that you have forgotten them already?"

"Please sit down, Miss Dane." Antonia sank gratefully onto a sofa, her legs suddenly weak with reaction. He appeared about to speak again as he pulled up a chair opposite her, but he was forestalled by the entrance of a footman with lemonade and orgeat.

By the time the servant had left, Antonia was calmer, but as she sipped the cooling drink her hand was shaking and her bosom rose and fell with emotion.

"Now, Miss Dane, perhaps you can explain to me

why it is a matter of concern to you that three violent rogues are about to receive their just desserts?''

Antonia met the hard eyes, remembering with a shiver the day she had been dragged before him as a poacher. ''Just because they had a set-to with your keepers—who are all too ready to use violence themselves—does not make them violent criminals! These men have families to support: why can you not relax your implacable opposition to a little local poaching? You do not need all those birds, and this is a time of such agricultural hardship.''

''The law is the law, ma'am, and should be observed. You do no good with your meddling. I am sworn to uphold His Majesty's peace—what would you have me do when it is broken?''

''Meddling! Can you show no mercy? You may uphold the letter of the law, but there are moral laws as well—I hold you entirely responsible for Bethan Johnson's predicament.''

''And what might that be?'' he enquired, only the whiteness around his mouth betraying the mounting anger within him.

''She is with child.''

''I assure you, ma'am, I am not the father. I have no recollection of the wench, and whatever your opinion of me, I can assure you I always ask their name first before seducing village virgins.''

Antonia leapt to her feet, her cheeks burning. ''How dare you speak of such things to me!''

Without answering, Marcus strode across to the fireplace and tugged the bellpull sharply. Antonia turned away from him to hide her flushed cheeks and stared out stormily across the tranquil park. Behind her she heard him order, ''My curricle, at once, with no delay!''

A furious silence hung in the room until they heard the crunch of gravel beneath hooves. Marcus took her by the elbow in no gentle grip and marched her out of the door and down the steps to the curricle.

"Where are we going?" Antonia demanded when she found herself seated on the high-perch seat. She had not struggled with him in front of the servants, but she had every intention of demanding he let her down the moment they were out of sight of the house. "How dare you manhandle me so! Stop and let me down at once!"

"No, there is something you should, and will, see." All she could see of Marcus's face was his grim profile.

"If you do not let me down, I will jump," Antonia threatened, gathering her skirts in readiness.

In response, he transferred all the reins and the whip to his right hand, throwing his left arm across her to pinion her to her seat. The horses, unsettled by the sudden shift of balance, plunged in the shafts and broke into a canter. Antonia felt herself thrown back against the seat, his arm like an iron bar across her. "Do not be such a damn fool," he snarled, controlling the horses one-handed. Even in her distressed state, Antonia could not help but admire his mastery.

It was only a few minutes before he drew up in front of a neat lodge at one of the side gates into the park. Another vehicle, a modest gig, was standing outside; as Marcus handed her down, Antonia recognised the local doctor emerging from the back door of the lodge.

"My lord, Miss Dane, good day to you. A bad business this, but he is young and strong and will come to no harm in the end. I will call again tomorrow."

"Thank you, Dr Rush. Whatever he needs, he must have. You will send your account to me."

The doctor mounted into his gig and drove away with

a polite tip of his whip. "Why have you brought me here?" Antonia asked, a strange feeling of apprehension gripping her.

"To see the handiwork of your innocent and starving tenants," he replied tautly, pushing open the door without knocking and ushering her through.

Antonia found herself in a small but neat kitchen. A little girl was rocking a cradle by the hearth. She turned a tear-stained face towards them and Marcus patted her gently on the head. "Are you being a good girl and helping your mother, Jenny?" The child, no more than four, nodded mutely. "We will just go and see your father; the doctor says he will soon be well, so don't you cry now."

In the back room, a woman was spooning water between the lips of the man laying on the bed. When she saw Marcus, she put down the spoon and laid the man gently back against the bolster. "Oh, my lord…"

"Do not get up, Mrs Carling. How is he?"

Antonia saw with horror the white face of Nat Carling the underkeeper. His head was swathed in bandages, his eyes black and blue and his nose askew. He seemed barely conscious, except for a faint groan which escaped his lips every time he breathed.

"In a deal of pain, my lord. The doctor says his ribs are broke, but his skull's not cracked, thank the lord."

"What has happened to him?" Antonia gasped in horror, although with a sinking heart she could guess.

"'Twas them Johnsons, the whole pack of them, miss. Set upon him last night as he came home from the alehouse. Three against one, it was," the woman added bitterly. "And them with cudgels. If Vicar hadn't have been coming back from Berkhamsted and disturbed them, my Nat'd be dead now."

"But why?" Antonia asked, appalled, staring down at the bruised face on the pillow, the stubble stark on the deathly face.

"He'd reported them to his lordship for poaching again, ma'am. Setting snares all through his lordship's Home Wood, they were, 'tother night, bold as brass. Ran off when Nat and his old dog disturbed them, but he could see 'em by the moon."

"But to beat him so…"

"And kick him, too," Marcus said grimly. "Let me have a look at those ribs, Nat lad." He eased back the coarse sheet with infinite care and Antonia gasped at the sight of the man's ribs, covered in bruises with the clear marks of hobnails on the flesh.

Antonia turned away, her hands pressed to her mouth, nausea rising. She heard Marcus behind her, talking low-voiced to the woman, assuring her the doctor's bills would be met and promising that the housekeeper would send down food and cordials from the house daily. "One of the stable lads will come down and sleep in your shed, Mrs Carling. He can do the heavy work and help you with Nat. Now do not fret, he will mend soon."

Outside Antonia gripped the side of the curricle, taking great gulps of the warm dusty air. Marcus took her arm and began to walk back into the park, leaving the horses standing. "You are not going to faint," he stated coldly.

Antonia looked up at him, startled by his frigid tone. "What has happened to that man is terrible!"

"Indeed it is, and much to your discredit."

"Mine! What have I to do with it?"

"You have coddled and encouraged not only the deserving and unfortunate amongst your tenants, but the rogues also. They laugh at you for being so gullible!

What did you think you were about?'' His voice grew harsher as she turned hurt and bewildered eyes to his face.

"But they were starving. I only sought to feed them."

Marcus took her by the shoulders and shook her. "You fool, all you did was to teach them to steal. You have undermined the right of the law. Why did you not employ your own keepers? You could have instructed them to take the birds and distribute them to the deserving and those in genuine need and you would have given the keepers respectable employment besides."

"Why did you not tell me sooner?" Antonia stammered. "I never thought to employ my own keepers. I thought I was doing good, helping my tenants…"

"I did not know myself the lengths to which you had gone. Sparrow only told me today what has been the talk of the alehouses for weeks. I was coming to tell you of it this morning, but you were otherwise engaged."

"Why did not Sparrow speak to you sooner? I so wish he had…I have misjudged the man."

There was an uncomfortable pause before Marcus replied, "He felt there was a degree of attachment between us that would make it impossible for him to speak critically of you without offending me."

"How foolish of him," Antonia replied between stiff lips.

"Indeed," Marcus replied, dropping his hands from her shoulders.

She shivered, feeling bereft without his touch. "Can you recommend a suitable man to act as keeper for me? And is there any other foolishness of mine which you should draw to my attention before I do any further damage?" she added, bitterness in her voice.

"I will find someone for you, if that is what you wish.

As to your…foolishness, perhaps you will remember that I recommended you to return to London. It would have been as well for all of us if you had taken that advice.''

Antonia turned her head away so he could not see the tears starting in her eyes. He could not have put it more plainly: he wished rid of her, and his instincts from the beginning had been correct. Marcus, having failed to secure her lands, now wanted her out of his sight.

''I must thank you for an instructive afternoon, my lord,'' she said, her head still averted. ''I trust you will let me know if there is anything I can do to assist Mrs Carling and her family. Good day.''

''Let me drive you home, Antonia.'' Marcus put a hand on her arm, but she shook it off angrily. ''We should not part like this. I spoke harshly in my anger, but we can deal better together than this.''

''Sir, I am grateful for your concern, but we are neighbours, nothing more.''

''We have been more than that, and could be again.'' He put his fingers under her chin, turning her face to his. Before she could protest he bent his head and kissed her lightly on the lips, then turned and walked away.

Chapter Ten

"I can hear a carriage," Donna remarked, leaving a pile of linen unfolded as she hurried to peep discreetly from the bedroom casement. "I wonder who that can be? I do not recognise the barouche."

Antonia joined her, attempting to descry the crest on the carriage doors. "I do believe it is Lady Finch. How very gracious of her to return our call so promptly!"

The ladies abandoned their work and hastened downstairs to greet the visitor. They had called at Rye End Hall two days previously to leave their cards and had been gratified to be received by Lady Finch herself. Sir Josiah, she had explained, was not with her because he had been detained in London on business, but was expected daily for he was most eager to establish himself in his new home.

Since their visit to their old home, Donna and Antonia had found much to talk of. Lady Finch had proved welcoming and open, delighted to make their acquaintance and full of praise for Rye End Hall and their preparations. She was obviously very well bred, but years abroad had lent a refreshing informality to her manner that captivated Donna particularly.

Antonia had noticed the ready affection that Lady Finch evinced for her nephew: a pastel sketch of him was one of the few pictures that had already been hung. "I do hope dear Jeremy has been able to accommodate all your wishes in the arrangements," Lady Finch had said. "He is generally such a thoughtful individual, but you must appraise me immediately if anything has been overlooked." The warmth and pride that tinged her voice when she spoke of Mr Blake indicated that she regarded him more as a son than a nephew.

"Lady Finch," Anna announced, showing the older woman into the drawing-room.

There was a flurry of greetings and curtsies before the three were seated, tea poured and macaroon biscuits offered. "What a charming old house," Lady Finch enthused. "After so many years in the Indies, it is such a pleasure to see a fine example of the antique English style. Are you comfortable here? It has a welcoming and homely atmosphere."

Both Donna and Antonia found it easy to talk to Susan Finch and the half-hour visit quite flew by. At length, their guest stood up, drawing on her gloves, and looking out over the garden as she did so.

"What magnificent roses, Miss Dane. I hope you will allow Sir Josiah to visit your garden, for he has lately developed a keen interest in gardening. It is such a struggle to maintain a truly English style in a hot climate: there must be constant irrigation and all one's favourites just wither and die. I confess that, after a few false starts, we simply gave up."

"I would be delighted, for gardening is one of my joys also—" Antonia began to say when they were interrupted by the sound of carriage wheels on gravel.

"I must bid you farewell, for you have other visitors,"

Lady Finch was saying when the newcomers came into view, trotting up the drive in a neat curricle. "Why, it is my husband and Mr Blake!"

The two men were ushered in by Anna, flushed with importance at receiving so many guests in one morning.

"Sir Josiah!" his lady cried. "I had not looked for you until tomorrow." She held out her hands to her husband and Antonia was touched by the unfashionable warmth with which Sir Josiah kissed his wife.

"Miss Dane, I must make my husband known to you." Antonia curtsied, liking Sir Josiah on sight. Where his wife was thin, her complexion made sallow by years of heat, he was rotund and still tanned on the top of his bald head. His shrewd eyes twinkled cheerfully in his open face and Antonia knew instinctively that she was meeting an honest man.

The enlarged party settled again, Sir Josiah accepting a dish of Bohea while he explained that his London business had been accomplished with more expedition than he had expected. He had hastened down, eager to view his new demesne, to be greeted by Mr Blake with the news that his wife was visiting Miss Dane.

"Naturally, I could not hesitate to make your acquaintance, ladies. My nephew has told me of your gracious assistance in rendering the Hall all that we would wish it to be." The shrewd eyes slid sideways over the top of his tea cup to catch the slight flush on Mr Blake's cheeks.

Sir Josiah, tragically deprived of heirs of his own, was of a strongly dynastic turn of mind and was deeply fond of his nephew by marriage whom he intended making heir to his considerable fortune. Mr Blake had been admirably discreet on the subject of Miss Dane, but Sir

Josiah knew enough of his nephew to recognise a man with a marked partiality.

Miss Dane was chatting easily to his wife and Mr Blake, allowing Sir Josiah to observe her whilst exchanging pleasantries with Miss Donaldson. A very handsome and prettily behaved young woman, he concluded. Somewhat tall, perhaps, and not dressed in the first stare of fashion, but unmistakably well bred.

Accustomed to assessing fabrics with the eye of a merchant, he approved of the jonquil muslin gown, but could not help but imagine Miss Dane gowned in one of the more striking shot silks his warehouse had recently imported. He must mention it to Susan; perhaps the opportunity for a small gift might arise...

His wife rose, catching his wandering attention. "My dear, we must not impose on Miss Dane and Miss Donaldson's time further this morning. However, I have secured a promise from Miss Dane that she will show you her roses before much longer."

"Capital! A fellow gardener—I could not have wished for better. Lady Finch, tell me, what is the state of our kitchens? When can we hope to entertain, for I would wish to hold a dinner party for our good neighbours as soon as may be?"

"Thanks to the perfect order in which all was left, I believe we could name this Saturday—that is, if you are free, ladies?"

Miss Donaldson coloured with pleasure at the compliment to her housekeeping and hastened to accept the invitation. The Finches departed, Sir Josiah begging the honour of sending his carriage over to collect the Dower House party on the appointed evening.

Donna was obviously burning to discuss their visitors

but Mr Blake, by remaining when his aunt and uncle had gone, forced her to silence.

"I wished to ask if the groom the estate manager sent down met with your approval," he enquired. "If so, I will arrange to have my carriage horse sent over immediately with the whisky."

"Indeed, Fletcher appears a most respectable and willing man," Antonia approved warmly. "He has righted a stall in the old barn, so we can house both horse and carriage suitably."

"Then would you wish me to drive the whisky over tomorrow?" he asked, his eyes smiling into hers. "And perhaps it would be wise, with a horse that is unfamiliar to you, if I were to accompany you on your first drive."

"But Antonia, dear," Donna intervened hastily, "have you not told Mr Blake that you never learned to drive?" Antonia knew all too well that Donna, having consigned Lord Allington to the ranks of Unsuitable Suitors, was already looking to Jeremy Blake to replace him.

"But you must allow me to teach you," he cried enthusiastically. "It would be my pleasure, for I am sure you will prove an apt pupil." Antonia accepted, but in restrained tones. She liked Mr Blake—he was congenial and pleasant and good company—and she wanted to learn to drive, but Donna's unsubtle encouragement of the young man was unwelcome.

The parting from Marcus was still bitter. She loved the man, still dreamt of him at night, still longed to see his eyes smiling into hers with that unspoken promise. Donna could switch allegiance for her at the turn of a card, not knowing how strongly her affections were engaged, but her own heart was not so fickle, nor did she wish to give Jeremy Blake false encouragement and perhaps to hurt him.

Jeremy Blake was as good as his word: a groom delivered a note the next morning proposing a drive later that day and containing an invitation from Lady Finch to Miss Donaldson to take tea.

"She says here that, unless she hears to the contrary, she will send the carriage at three for me." Donna's sallow cheeks were flushed with pleasure at the invitation. "How kind her ladyship is, to consider my entertainment while you are engaged."

"I am sure she is most considerate," Antonia responded, "but I am certain she also wishes to become better acquainted with you. After all, you have much in common. Was your father not stationed in several of the places in India she spoke of yesterday?"

"Indeed, he was. What a pleasure it will be to hear her descriptions of those scenes! I wonder if she has any sketch books?"

Mr Blake arrived at the appointed time, but Donna was not downstairs to admire the whisky and the neat bay horse he was lending them. She was still in her chamber, dithering over the choice between her three decent day gowns, a most uncharacteristic way for her to carry on.

Although thinking Miss Donaldson a pleasant woman, Jeremy Blake felt no chagrin at her absence—it allowed him free rein to admire the picture Miss Dane presented. She was sensibly dressed for driving in a pale fawn muslin gown with jonquil braid about the hem and a neat bonnet shading her eyes. He stood in the hallway admiring her elegant figure as she pulled on a pair of tan gloves and called up the stairs, "I am leaving now,

Donna! I will see you later, please give Lady Finch my regards.''

"Where would you like to go, Miss Dane?" Jeremy enquired as he handed her up into the little carriage and gathered up the reins. "It is a very warm day, and the flies are so bad in the park, I wondered if you would care to drive out onto the Downs. There will be a breeze, and a fine view and I found a trackway the other day where you can take the reins without fear of other traffic.''

"That would be delightful," Antonia agreed. "I think I know where you mean, and I had intended to go there myself, but the weather has turned far too hot for such a long walk.''

"You would not consider such a long distance on foot, surely?" Jeremy's eyebrows shot up as he turned left into the lane. "It is all of three miles in each direction: you are a most energetic walker, Miss Dane, if you considered such an expedition.''

"Why so surprised, Mr Blake? Did you think me a drawing-room miss who would never deign to do more than stroll around a pleasure garden? I must confess to enjoying vigorous exercise. Why, if I thought Donna would permit it, I would even dig the garden!''

Jeremy Blake looked at her sideways and said warmly, "I never thought you a conventional young lady, Miss Dane. Making your acquaintance over the past few weeks has convinced me that you are quite out of the ordinary. Ah, here is the start of the track. Would you care to take the reins now?''

"Yes, please. I have been observing how you handle the reins and I believe I can manage, if he only walks to start with…''

Jeremy pulled up and transferred the reins into Antonia's gloved hands. "It is not so very different to riding when you are driving only one horse: there, you have got it just right." There was a fleeting pressure of reassurance from his fingers through the fine kid of her gloves.

Antonia clicked her tongue and shook the reins and the obedient bay walked docilely forward, little puffs of chalky dust rising as his hooves struck the hard ground.

The hot air was full of the vanilla scent of gorse blossom. Overhead larks sang and spiralled out of sight in the cloudless blue sky and chalk blue butterflies and fritillaries danced away from the horse's progress.

The track rose gradually as they climbed to the top of the Downs. Antonia's spirits rose with their progress; the feeling of freedom was so intoxicating. As they came out onto the short cropped grass and saw the view of the whole Vale stretched out before them, still and shimmering in the heat, she reined in instinctively.

"That is very good," Jeremy encouraged. "You have a very light hand on his mouth—see how well he goes for you. I do believe you are ready to trot."

"Oh, let us just stay here a moment!" Antonia begged. "It is so lovely here—so wide and open and the breeze is fresh. When I am here, I do not miss London one jot!"

"You must have many friends and acquaintances in Town who miss you, however," he said gallantly.

"We had a wide circle of acquaintances when I lived with my great-aunt," Antonia acknowledged. "But it was quite remarkable how quickly they fell away when we had to move to less fashionable lodgings." She turned luminous hazel eyes on Jeremy and spoke with emotion. "I will not attempt to hide the truth from someone who knows our circumstances as well as you: after the death of my father, we were in most straitened circumstances.''

There was a small silence as they both gazed across the tranquil vista beneath them, then Jeremy spoke carefully. ''I will be equally frank and say I much admire the courageous way in which you have retrieved your fortunes. Now, shall we try trotting?''

As the bay responded to Antonia's tentative signals with a neat trot, the young lawyer reflected how easily he could find himself in love with Antonia Dane. And that was not part of his plan: he had his way to make in the world, and he could not yet afford the financial—or emotional—burdens of domesticity. One day he would inherit Sir Josiah's fortune, but he was too proud a man to wile away his days as his uncle's pensioner.

Jeremy indulged himself by putting a restraining hand on Antonia's slender wrist as the bay's stride lengthened. A small sigh escaped his lips. A sensible plan and laudable ambitions and hard work were all very well, but Miss Dane was a delight to be with and to look at.

He wished he could ask her about Marcus Allington, but that, of course, was out of the question.

There was a fine stand of perhaps a dozen beeches ahead, casting a broad swathe of shade over the turf. ''The track goes around that copse,'' he directed. ''Try taking the bend at a steady trot—you are doing so well on the straight, it should give you no trouble.''

As they rounded the curve, they found themselves almost on top of a picnic party assembled under the shade. There was a welcoming cry of ''Miss Dane! Please stop and join us!'' and Antonia recognised Anne Meredith waving from a rug spread on the grass.

''Why, it is the houseparty from Brightshill! Do you have any objection to our stopping a while, Mr Blake?''

"Not at all, although you must introduce me, for I know only Lord Allington in the party."

The picnickers had apparently arrived in two open carriages, which were drawn up some little distance away; as Antonia turned the bay's head towards the group, a groom hurried down to take its head.

Jeremy Blake helped her down from the whisky with rather more care than the modest height of the little vehicle demanded. He despised himself for permitting his hackles to rise whenever he came across the arrogant Marcus Allington, but he could not curb the desire to stand between Miss Dane and the man he was sure was playing fast and loose with her affections.

The picnic party had thrown all formality to the wind in the heat of the day. The gentlemen had cast aside their jackets and loosened their cravats and the ladies were reclining languidly against heaps of cushions on the ground. Only the children were unaffected and were playing hide and seek in the bushes, sun hats bouncing on the ends of their ribbons despite pleas from their mother to cover their heads.

Marcus, who had been lying stretched out at his sister's feet, a book open in one hand, his chin propped on the other, dropped the volume and got to his feet with an easy grace that belied his height.

Antonia swallowed hard and fought for composure as he strolled towards them. They had last met, and parted, in anger, but her feelings for him still burned as strong as ever. Marcus's eyes were fixed on her face and she lowered her chin so that the brim of her hat shadowed her expression.

The glimpse of bare skin where his shirt fell open, the play of muscles as he walked, the sun glancing off that tawny head, all conspired to rob her of her breath, of her senses. She remembered that last puzzling kiss and yearned for the feel of his lips again.

This was madness! She had made her decision, rejected him. Where was her pride that she could long for him so, knowing what his relationship was with Claudia Reed? Antonia made no effort to free herself from Jeremy's light grasp on her elbow; let Marcus think what he might!

Her chin came up and she faced him out, her colour high, but her eyes wide and sparkling. "Lord Allington! Good afternoon. What a very pleasant spot for a picnic. You know Mr Blake, of course? He is teaching me to drive. Is that not kind of him?"

Antonia did not wait for a reply but sailed past Marcus, leading Jeremy to where Lady Meredith was sitting up and straightening her hat. "Lady Meredith, may I make Mr Blake known to you? Mr Blake is the nephew of Lady Finch, our new neighbour."

"Miss Dane, what a pleasure to see you again. Good afternoon, Mr Blake—do please excuse our informality. Will you not sit down and have some lemonade? I will introduce you."

Mr Leigh helpfully piled up some cushions for the newcomers while Miss Fitch poured lemonade and the rest of the party was made known to Mr Blake. Antonia saw his eyes widen as Claudia languidly raised herself from a nest of pillows, revealing a scandalously flimsy and low-cut gown and an outrageously large straw hat.

"Mr Blake, how do you do?" she purred, her eyes narrowing as she took in the lawyer's well-cut clothes and handsome figure. He bowed formally, but to Antonia's delight made no move to approach Lady Reed, seating himself beside Antonia and Lady Meredith.

Marcus sat down again, not beside Antonia, but next to Jeremy, whom he began to engage in conversation.

"Neat little bay, that, not too long in the back," he observed pleasantly.

"A little long in the tooth now, my lord, but it is a nicely bred animal and ideal for a lady learning to drive." Jeremy was polite but guarded.

"Ah, so it is yours, then? I wondered if Miss Dane had made a fortunate purchase."

"Yes, it is mine, but Miss Dane is kindly stabling it for me." Jeremy began to relate the tale of discovering the whisky and engaging Fletcher the groom for the ladies and the men began to fall to a general discussion of horseflesh, the others rousing themselves to participate. Lord Meredith, Mr Leigh and Sir John all had tales of difficult beasts and astute purchases to exchange and the ladies were soon quite forgotten.

Lady Meredith leaned over and touched Antonia lightly on the arm. "Well, we have lost their attention for a while! Once men start talking of horses, I declare it would take an earthquake—or their dinner—to divert them."

Anne Meredith glanced around. The men were oblivious, Miss Fitch had taken up Marcus's book and was engrossed and Claudia Reed appeared to have fallen into a light doze against an abundance of cushions. Although how she managed to sleep with her mouth set in such a pretty pout was beyond her hostess's comprehension.

Marcus's sister had liked Antonia on sight and had entertained strong hopes that her exasperating brother had finally met his match in all senses of the term. Miss Antonia Dane was no vapid debutante, but refreshingly different, and Anne had had high expectations of an announcement.

But something had gone wrong, something had passed between Antonia and Marcus. Marcus had been like a bear with a sore head, even though he managed to hide it from everybody else. But she knew her elder brother—and she could guess the cause of the trouble. She glanced at Claudia and, in doing so, caught Antonia's eye.

"It is remarkable how that woman manages to cast her lures at every man she meets," Anne whispered.

"And sometimes makes a catch," Antonia murmured in return.

Ah ha! This remark was not lost on Lady Meredith. So that was how the ground lay! Anne knew there had been a discreet affaire some months ago—her brother, after all, was no monk—but she had believed it at an end. She had been surprised when Claudia had inveigled her way into the houseparty at Brightshill, discovering too late that Marcus thought she, Anne, had invited her, when she had believed Claudia was there at Marcus's behest.

Somehow Claudia had managed to poison the relationship between this delightful young woman and her beloved brother, but what could Anne do about it? Anne brooded thoughtfully. She could hardly eject the woman from Brightshill—it would cause a scandal. No, there had to be some other way to clip her wings. She would write that evening to Colonel Reed, inviting him to join the party, providing the regiment could spare him. Marcus would not like it, but he could not refuse to honour her invitation—and she could manage her brother!

Antonia wondered what had promoted the small smile of triumph that suddenly curved her hostess's lips, but her thoughts were interrupted by the children tumbling onto the rug beside them, hot and thirsty.

Mr Blake, obviously unused to boisterous children,

shied away and broke off from a discussion of Tattersall's prices to suggest to Miss Dane that it was time they returned to Rye End Hall.

Antonia responded very promptly to Mr Blake's urgings with a pretty, biddable air that caused his lordship to raise an eyebrow, but he did nothing more than get to his feet politely as they left.

Mr Blake was assiduous in his daily lessons and by the end of the week Antonia was confidently taking gateways at the trot and even able to back the whisky for a short distance. Their drives had to be taken earlier and earlier during the day as June moved into July and the heat became oppressive by noon.

Antonia slept fitfully, her dreams full of Marcus, but by day she managed to push him to the back of her mind, enjoying Jeremy's undemanding company. She was certain now that he had no romantic intentions, although it was obvious that he admired her still and enjoyed her company in turn.

She would have felt less complacent if she had been aware of the conversations his aunt and Donna were having about them, for the ladies found one another's company so congenial they met almost daily and were soon on terms of the utmost confidentiality.

"What a match it would be, my dear Miss Donaldson!" Lady Finch opined, pouring more tea for her guest. "He has such a good nature, nothing ruffles him—so like my dear sister. And he is certain to achieve great things in his profession—I declare he would be most eligible, even if he were not our heir."

"He is everything I had hoped for my dear Antonia," Miss Donaldson confided. "A steady, good, high-principled man. Not some flighty aristocrat who thinks his position allows him to toy with a young woman's affections.'' This was said with a darkling look in the general direction of Brightshill, which Lady Finch had no trouble in interpreting.

The ladies were comfortably ensconced in the deep shade of a magnificent old cedar of Lebanon where they had spent the entire afternoon in pleasurable gossip. They were interrupted by the arrival of Sir Josiah who, broad straw hat on head, had been touring his gardens, a reluctant Old Johnson at his heels.

''Ladies! A fine day, is it not?''

Donna, fanning herself against the intense heat, moaned faintly. ''I fear it is just a little warm for me, Sir Josiah.''

''Reminds me of our days in the Indies!'' He sank down, fanning himself with his hat and gratefully accepted a cup of tea from his wife. ''And what are you ladies plotting?'' he enquired archly.

''Sir Josiah!'' his lady protested. ''What a suggestion! Miss Donaldson and I were just discussing…er…''

In the face of the scepticism on her husband's face, she faltered. ''Well, if you must know, we were speaking of dear Jeremy and Miss Dane.''

''Ah ha! So that is how the land lies!'' The nabob contemplated his cup for a few moments. ''I cannot pretend I am anything but delighted.''

Miss Donaldson, flustered by this frank speaking, hastened to set the story straight. ''Sir Josiah, please, I believe you run a little ahead of us! Nothing has been said between the young people.'' She broke off, looking pensive. ''At least, I believe not—Lady Finch and I were merely speculating upon the desirability of the match.''

''Well, well.'' Sir Josiah was unperturbed. ''We shall see. But I have every hope…two handsome young peo-

ple thrown together... Nature has a way of dictating
events..." He tipped his hat over his nose and dozed
off, leaving Miss Donaldson tutting in horror at the unseemly notion of Nature, and Lady Finch hiding her
smiles behind her fan.

The two handsome young people in question had
spent the morning bowling along the dusty country roads
in perfect harmony, happy in each other's company, but
without a romantic notion in their heads.

Mr Blake, no fool, had drawn his own conclusions
about Miss Dane's feelings for Lord Allington. However
unsatisfactory he considered her choice to be, he was far
too pragmatic a man to waste time pining for what could
never be his.

Miss Dane, too honest to mistake liking for love, was
content to enjoy Jeremy's company. The attraction to her
that she had sensed in him on their first meeting had
tempered to liking and mutual respect and if she could
not—would not—have Marcus, then she would settle her
mind to being an old maid...but one with many good
friends.

By one o'clock the next morning, with the moonlight
flooding across the bedchamber floor as bright as day,
Antonia's resolution to be a happy old maid had quite
deserted her.

Marcus had filled her dreams and now, fully awake,
she could not shake his image from her mind. She was
also very hot, the low-ceilinged room seemed oppressive
and suddenly she had to be out in the fresh air.

Antonia pulled on a light muslin gown and kid slippers and slipped quietly out of the house, across the lane

and into the pleasure grounds of Rye End Hall. But even here the air felt sultry and still.

Only down by the river did there seem to be a faint breeze stirring the willows. Antonia walked slowly along the river path, yawning and wishing she could sleep.

The moonlight silvered the willow fronds as they flickered in the cooling zephyr and she was suddenly transfixed by the bubbling beauty of the nightingale's song. It was an exquisitely lovely noise, yet melancholy and did nothing to soothe Antonia's heartache.

Ahead, beyond the curve of the river, she heard a splash. Probably fish leaping for the flies that danced over the surface of the water, she mused. What was she about, wandering around at this time of night? Antonia chided herself. All she was achieving was to deepen her gloom…on the other hand, just around the bend there was a shelving beach of gravel and a wide pool of water. She could take off her slippers and paddle a little. It would be so cooling.

Silent as a moth, she padded down to the water's edge, cast off her shoes and stepped into the rippling water. Oh, it was so good! Even the soft mud insinuating itself between her toes was cooling. The moon went behind a cloud momentarily, and as it did so she heard another splash, then another.

Alarmed, Antonia peered across the pool, seeing a dark, sleek object appear around the bend. An otter! How wonderful to see the shy animal, she thought, standing very still. Then the moon was unveiled again, the pool suddenly flooded with light, and she saw it was no creature, but a human swimmer, lazily drifting on his back with the current.

Antonia was transfixed with horror at the mortification of being found by one of her tenants, barefooted and unescorted at this time of night. And then the realisation that at any moment she might be confronted by a scarcely clad—even naked—man, sent the colour scalding her cheeks.

She turned to run, but at the same moment the man twisted in the water, his body breaking the surface, and stood up. Antonia's gasp was clearly audible in the still, sultry air. This was no tenant, this was Marcus, water cascading from his sleek dark hair and off the naked planes of his body.

After one startled, horrified, downwards glance Antonia averted her burning face and stood helpless. Moving, saying anything, even running away, were quite beyond her powers.

She was aware of him wading ashore and moving about on the bank, but then to her horror she heard him splashing through the shallows behind her.

''Antonia?'' He was close enough to send ripples lapping against her ankles, drenching the hem of her muslin skirts. His breath was warm on her neck and even though he said no more, that one word was full of amusement.

Furious, Antonia spun round, stumbling in the mud, unheeding of Marcus's state of undress, and found herself confronting him. He had pulled on his breeches and shirt, but the fine white lawn was unfastened and clung to his damp body and his wet hair was slicked back from his forehead.

''Sir…I…this is not seemly!''

''Indeed it is not. Really, Antonia, you shock me. Do you make a habit of haunting the local bathing pools at night? I was most embarrassed.''

''You! Embarrassed! How dare you imply that I was spying on you!'' He was so close that she could see the glitter in his dark eyes, part mockery, part something far more disturbing. His mouth was curved with amusement and a deep sensuality.

"Were you not? Then what were you about out here at this time of night?" He was closer now, his voice husky.

"I was too hot, I went for a walk!" He was overwhelmingly close, his part-clad body disturbingly different, his eyes now openly travelling the length of her frame to where her feet glinted white through the water. Antonia raised both hands in a futile gesture of denial and found her wrists caught lightly in his hands.

Marcus pulled her gently towards him and she went, oblivious to the water splashing to her knees, oblivious to everything in her desperate craving for the touch of his lips. His mouth was burning on hers, his hands cold on her shoulders and the bare skin of his chest wet against the sensitive curves of her breast above her low-cut bodice.

His mouth opened on hers, his tongue gently invading, inciting, tormenting her until she responded, tentatively at first, then with growing abandon, the shock of the intimate intrusion rousing feelings of desire she was not aware she was capable of.

Marcus's strong arms enfolded her, then he picked her up effortlessly without breaking the kiss. Antonia clung to him, unconcerned that he would drop her, only anxious that he never stop kissing her, possessing her like this…

Marcus strode up the beach and laid her gently down on the grass slope of the bank. "Antonia, darling…" he murmured huskily, his hands brushing the soft skin at the edge of the bodice, before reaching up to shrug off the clinging fabric of his shirt.

Antonia, looking up into his face as he bent over her,

lifted one tremulous hand and traced her fingers over the cool skin of his chest, gasping as his nipple hardened under her fingertip.

Marcus moaned, deep in his throat and stooped to press his mouth to hers again, the weight of him thrilling against the length of her.

The nightingale whistled a few bars, almost beside them, then Antonia realised it was not the bird, but a human, imitating the song. She gasped and pushed against Marcus's chest, but he responded only by tangling his fingers in her tousled hair.

Then the silence was broken by the sharp crack of a twig on the path and Marcus sat up, his eyes narrowed as he searched the shadows. He stood, pushing Antonia behind him and called sharply, "Who is there?"

Antonia cast around wildly for a bush to hide behind, found none and prayed that the newcomer would take alarm at the challenge and turn tail. She pulled the edges of her gown up, pushing the hair from her face and tried to still the tumultuous beating of her heart.

"I am Jeremy Blake of Rye End Hall! And who the devil might you be, sir, on my uncle's lands?" came the sharp response as Jeremy stepped out of the shadows cast by a willow onto the cropped grass of the little bay. "Allington! Damn it, man, you gave me a start! I thought you were a poacher after my uncle's trout."

"Blake, yes, indeed, it is I. I came down for a swim, it is so infernally hot. I had not looked to see anyone else about at this hour. Are you also intending to swim? It is a good safe bottom here, if you are." His lordship spoke easily. Antonia admired his sang-froid and the way in which he resisted any temptation to glance behind him to where she stood.

"No, I...er..." Jeremy faltered. In truth he had woken

and, hearing the nightingale, had decided to stroll along the river bank to find out if any more were about. He had a keen interest in matters ornithological, but felt his lordship would consider it an unmanly occupation. However, he was conscious that he sounded evasive in the extreme and was about to say something about seeing how the fish were rising when he caught a glimpse of something pale beyond Marcus's shoulder.

So that was what had brought his lordship out at this time of night. Mr Blake was not sure he approved of liaisons with village maidens, but neither did he feel that now was the time to take a moral stand. "Allington! You should have said I was intruding. I will bid you good night!"

Antonia saw him turn to go and stepped forward to Marcus's side in relief, only to freeze in horror. Just as she stepped into the moonlight Jeremy turned again. "You may rely on my discretion, my lord... Good God! Antonia!"

Chapter Eleven

"Antonia?" Jeremy Blake said again on a note of rising disbelief. Antonia saw herself through his eyes; hair tousled, gown damp about her ankles, her bodice awry. She felt ready to sink through the ground with the sheer mortification of being found in such an embarrassing position.

"Jeremy," she began, imploringly, desperate to explain to her friend how she came to be so deeply compromised.

Mr Blake, hearing the anguish in her voice, seeing the deep distress on Antonia's face, leapt at once to the conclusion that Lord Allington was hell bent on a course of seduction and the ruination of an innocent young woman. Of course—this explained it all; he had sensed Antonia's attraction to his lordship, yet her unhappiness could only be attributed to cynical attempts in the past by his lordship to seduce her!

Jeremy's hands clenched instinctively at his side, but his natural good sense kept him from a rash demand for a duel. To call his lordship out, as his chivalrous instincts demanded, would be fatal to Antonia's reputation, for it could never be kept quiet. He took a step forward, held out a hand to her and said, in a voice of thunder, "Sir, I demand to know what you are doing here with my fiancée."

Marcus's face showed astonishment, swiftly turning to dark anger as he swung round towards Antonia. "So that was what you were doing here and why Blake was so reticent in his explanations. A tryst, by God! And it appears there are no lengths you would not go to to hide the fact from me, madam. You were most convincing, but no doubt in a few moments you would have discovered a headache and run away home. A pity your lover is less inventive."

"Marcus... I..."

"I bid you both good night. I wish you well of your union—it will, I am certain, bring joy to your friends."

Pausing only to snatch up the rest of his clothing from the river bank, Marcus strode haughtily out of their sight.

There was a moment of stunned silence. Antonia stared blankly at Jeremy who now wore an expression compounded of sheepishness and defiance.

"How dare you!" she stormed, consumed by so many roiling emotions she hit out regardless of who suffered. "How could you say such a thing...to imply that you and I are to be married! Where does that leave me now?"

"In better case than you were in five minutes ago!" he retorted hotly, as confused as she. "You should look to your reputation, Miss Dane, and consider yourself fortunate it was I who discovered you with his lordship. Your name will be better protected as my wife than as Marcus Allington's mistress!"

They glared at each other in the moonlight, then he saw her underlip was quivering and one tear was rolling down her cheek. His hurt pride melted as he realised she was too upset to think clearly. "Really, Antonia, what would you have had me do? I had to think quickly, and it was that or hit the man on the jaw. If I could have managed it," he added with rueful honesty.

"I wish you had," Antonia responded mutinously. Suddenly she felt very, very tired and sat down with an unladylike thump on the river bank.

"No, you do not," Jeremy said firmly, sitting down beside her and putting one arm round her shoulders in a comradely manner. "Fist fights are bloody, unpleasant and rarely achieve anything. Now, tell me what this is all about so we can find a solution to this coil."

"This is not a legal problem you can resolve by consulting a few dusty tomes," Antonia snapped, then relented immediately. "Oh, Jeremy, I am sorry, you are a good friend to tolerate my vapours." She twisted round to meet his eyes. "I did wonder if you had a partiality for me, at first. But you have not, have you? I am right?" she questioned anxiously.

Jeremy smiled. "Mmm…there was a time when I felt fairly sure I was going to fall in love with you. But there is nothing quite as dampening as the discovery that the object of one's interest has her affections fixed firmly elsewhere. That said," he added firmly, "it is no reason why we should not deal very well together, you and I."

Antonia kissed his cheek with real affection. "You are a dear, Jeremy. But I cannot. I love him, you see."

"Then why do you not marry the man, then?" Mr Blake asked with a touch of impatience. "Has he not asked you? He is obviously deeply attracted to you."

Antonia smiled wryly. "Oh, he has asked me to be his wife. But then I discovered that his lordship is a man who is attracted to many women. In my case, the attraction is embellished by the thought of getting his hands on Rye End Hall and its lands.''

Jeremy understood enough of women to ignore the jibe about lands and to focus on the real heart of the matter. ''I assume you are referring to one woman in particular?'' He recalled the expensively gowned figure, the sharply provocative little face, as Claudia Reed lounged at the picnic. ''I can quite see her attraction,'' he added mischievously.

''Mutton dressed as lamb!'' Antonia responded indignantly. ''You are as bad as he is! I wonder what she looks like first thing in the morning…''

''Mmm…'' Mr Blake said speculatively.

''…before her maid and her hairdresser and goodness knows what cosmetics have come to her aid.'' She looked at Jeremy sharply. ''You are teasing me.''

''Of course I am teasing you! Women like that are commonplace in London. She is doubtless an entertaining and compliant mistress—my bet is that there is an elderly complaisant husband somewhere; there usually is. A gentleman like Allington is going to expect his entertainment—he is, after all, not a monk.'' He paused and cast her a doubtful glance. ''You must forgive me being so free spoken, Antonia, I will say no more if I am offending you.''

''No, dear friend, you are telling me nothing that I had not already fathomed for myself: I have had London Seasons, after all. But how could he continue the liaison while he paid court to me?''

''Er…'' Jeremy searched for a tactful way of expressing himself, but Antonia swiftly interrupted him.

''Oh, I know that in arranged marriages these things happen. But I truly believed he had at least respect and affection for me. And to flaunt his mistress so openly…I could not marry a man who was so careless of my feelings."

"Then marry me. I can assure you I would never be careless of how you felt. I can offer you the respect, affection and the companionship you deserve in a marriage which would maintain you in a fitting manner."

"But not love, Jeremy," she said wistfully.

"It will grow. I have the greatest admiration for love matches—after all, look at the example of my aunt and uncle. But very few people begin their married life with such strong feelings…"

"And what would happen if you found the woman for whom you could feel such emotions after we were married?"

"I would not look," he teased, squeezing her shoulder.

"All men look, it is your nature!" Antonia retorted, laughing, feeling surprisingly cheered. "No, Jeremy, I like you too much to marry you. Now come, admit it, I am not breaking your heart, am I?"

"Madam, it is in pieces at your feet." He assumed an expression of anguish. "It will be noon tomorrow, at the very earliest before I have recovered."

"Mountebank! Help me to my feet, we cannot sit out here all night and I am suddenly fatigued. Goodness knows what hour it is."

As they strolled through the silent night, Jeremy asked sombrely, "This is all very well, but what will you do now? You are sure to encounter his lordship again."

"I shall pretend none of this happened. After all, he can say nothing without casting himself in a most unfavourable light. If an engagement between you and me is not announced, he will just see it for what it was, a device to get over the awkwardness of the moment."

They had finally arrived at the back door of the Dower House. Antonia retrieved the big key from under a flower pot and unlocked the door. She turned back to Jeremy. "Good night, dear friend. I am sorry I have embroiled you in such a coil."

Jeremy smiled, then bent to drop a brotherly kiss on her cheek. "Do not give it another thought, my dear…"

"Antonia!" Miss Donaldson's cry of outrage rent the still air. Both Antonia and Jeremy started, presenting a picture of perfect guilt to the quivering figure of the chaperon.

Miss Donaldson, hair in curl papers, her thin body encased in a flannel wrapper of hideous design, stood brandishing the poker she had snatched from the kitchen range on her way to investigate the stealthy footsteps she had heard approaching the house.

"Libertine! Blaggard! Rest assured your uncle shall hear of this you…you…whitened sepulchre, you!" she quavered.

"Donna, please put that poker down and stop abusing poor Mr Blake! He has done nothing to warrant your wrath—he was merely seeing me safely home after my walk."

"Your walk! At three in the morning! A tryst, more like!"

Mr Blake passed his hand wearily over his brow. "Miss Donaldson, madam, I can assure you…"

But Miss Donaldson was well into her stride and was not to be deflected. "And I can assure you, sir, that you will marry this poor child at the earliest moment it may be accomplished without scandal."

"Jeremy—go!" Antonia pushed her much put-upon friend in the direction of the back gate. "Donna, let us go inside and I will explain all before the entire household is awakened.'' She wrested the poker from Donna's grasp and pushed her down on a chair before the flickering light of the kitchen range.

''That it should come to this! I only thank Heaven your poor mother is not alive to see this day,'' Miss Donaldson was wailing.

''Oh, do be quiet, Donna!'' Antonia snapped. ''Poor Mr Blake met me quite by chance by the riverbank. I went for a walk because I could not sleep and he was listening to the nightingales. I had a fright because of…something I thought I saw in the undergrowth and Mr Blake came to my rescue…''

''That's as may be!'' Miss Donaldson said, pursing her thin lips. ''But he took advantage of you—I saw him kiss you!''

''If I had a brother living, he could not have kissed me more chastely, Donna.'' Seeing doubt on Miss Donaldson's face, she pressed on, ''He is my good friend— and only a friend!''

To her alarm and utter astonishment, Donna responded to these bracing words by bursting into tears.

''What is it?'' Antonia fell on her knees beside the chair. ''Were you very frightened because you thought we were burglars?'' She took the thin hands in hers and chafed them gently. ''You were very brave.''

''But we thought, we hoped, you were going to marry him!'' Donna lamented.

''Who? Who is 'we'? You wanted me to marry Mr Blake? Then why make such a hue and cry? Oh, I am so tired I cannot think!''

''Dear Lady Finch and I had such hopes of you and Mr Blake, such a suitable match. And then to think that he was just another heartless philanderer and then to discover you do not wish to marry him, after all!''

"Go to bed, Donna," Antonia said wearily. "We have both had an over-exciting night."

The next morning, both ladies were distinctly heavy eyed and the atmosphere was awkward with remembered embarrassment. Antonia escaped to the drawing-room to con the post. Her interest in a pamphlet on the manuring of roses sent by Sir Josiah waned, however, in competition with the memory of Marcus's hard body, cold from the river, urgent against hers.

She shivered despite the heat, recalling the feel of wet hair crisping under her fingertips as she had entwined her arms around his neck.

With an effort Antonia pulled herself together and opened the next package, which proved to contain a very sprightly missive from Great-Aunt Honoria.

"I find this new doctor most invigorating, my dear," the old lady had written. "He advised changing from that lowering diet to one including red meat, game and Bordeaux and I feel not a day over fifty again! Your cousin Hewitt keeps urging me to rest—sometimes I think he wishes me to remain an invalid—but I find I am enjoying myself too much. And, I confess my dear, that new wife of your cousin Clarence's is such a little peahen that I find myself quite rejuvenated by dislike for her! I know you are much engaged putting the Dower House to rights, but please come and see me soon now that I am returned to my own house. Town is short of company now, but you and I were always able to find some diversion to amuse us…"

Antonia, delighted that her beloved great-aunt was so much better, was indulging in a daydream of escaping from all the heartaches of home to a few weeks in London when the crunch of gravel under carriage wheels penetrated her musings.

"Lady Meredith, Miss Antonia," Anna announced, making her start in her seat and drop the pamphlet on the Turkey rug at her feet.

As Miss Dane sprang up to greet her with a welcoming smile, Anne Meredith's shrewd glance took in the dark shadows under the young woman's eyes and decided that the slim figure was, if anything, even more slender than when she had seen her last.

And as for her brother, stalking around Brightshill like a bear with a sore head with a smile only for the children—why, he was in as bad a case. Oh, she could bang their heads together, really she could!

None of this showed on her calm features as she sank gracefully into a proffered chair and accepted the suggestion of a glass of lemonade with gratitude.

Anne Meredith decided not to beat about the bush. "I will come straight to the point, Miss Dane: this is not a social call. I am in sore need of your help."

"My help?" Antonia looked startled. "Why, of course, any service I can offer I will gladly perform. Is it the children?"

"You are most kind. I am happy to say the children are thriving, for they love the freedom of Brightshill after London. No, it is a certain social awkwardness…" She took a strategic sip of her lemonade. "I felt Lady Reed was not happy: pining for her husband, Sir George, I thought. After all, he has been down at Brighton—doing whatever one does with troops—for months." There was a slight pause before she resumed. "Naturally, I assumed that, if I were to invite him to Brightshill to join our houseparty, this would lift Lady Reed's spirits."

"A natural, and most thoughtful assumption," Antonia said, straightfaced, commendably concealing her bitter amusement at the thought of Claudia pining for anyone but Marcus.

"Well, I thought so! So I wrote to him. But my brother seems most put out…"

"I wonder why."

"I cannot conceive." Both ladies sipped their lemonade thoughtfully. "And as for Claudia, why, she was positively petulant! And the wretched man is arriving tomorrow and Lord Meredith is no help whatsoever, just keeps saying that he cannot see what the problem is!"

"But how can I help?" Antonia queried. This reported reaction only confirmed her belief that Marcus was still hopelessly entangled in Claudia's lures. The husband would be a complication he did not want. Poor man, serving his King and country in the army while behind his back his wife… She shut the picture from her mind.

Lady Meredith smoothed her skirts. "The first dinner will be a very awkward affair, I fear, and I thought to myself, how could I dilute the mood? I felt I could confide in you: you know everyone, and are such delightful company…I know it is a lot to ask, but if you could just help me smooth the path. Sir John and Mr Leigh were only saying over breakfast how long it seemed since you were last at Brightshill…" She broke off, regarding Antonia with a ruefully apologetic smile.

If she were correct in her suspicions, Antonia would desire nothing more than to see Claudia Reed safely under her husband's eye, but equally, Miss Dane was no fool—she must be very careful not to overegg this pudding.

Quite unaware that her guest had any ulterior motive,

Antonia was prey to conflicting emotions. She wanted to see Marcus, be with him, yet she knew it would be painful and humiliating to see him anywhere near that horrible woman. On the other hand, an ignoble spirit of revenge prompted her to witness the lovers' discomfiture when Sir George arrived. And, setting all other considerations aside, she liked Marcus's sister and wanted to help her.

"My dear Lady Meredith, of course, I will help in any way I can. When do you expect Sir George to arrive?"

"Late this afternoon," Anne confessed. "That is probably why Marcus is so cross with me—I did rather spring it upon him. Oh, and I do hope Miss Donaldson will be able to join us."

"I am afraid she will not, for I know she is already engaged this evening at Rye End Hall at a small whist party. Sir Josiah and Lady Finch have an elderly relative staying who is most addicted to the game and Donna is to make up the four."

"What a pity. Never mind, shall I send the carriage for you at seven o'clock?"

Antonia dressed for the evening with great care, knowing that in a display of feminine charms Claudia Reed would win hands down, possessing as she did a wardrobe created expressly to exhibit her lures. Instead, Antonia sought to appear elegant and cool. She chose her newest gown in a shimmering celadon green silk, cut with total simplicity, and ornamented only with a gauze scarf of silver thread that matched her slippers.

Donna, fussing that Antonia was attending a party without her, helped secure her profusion of dark curls high on her head with pearl pins so that the tendrils just brushed the tops of her ears.

"Do not forget your fan." Donna hurried after her down the stairs, for the carriage was waiting at the door. "It is so very close, I fear we will have a storm later tonight." At the front door she admonished, low-voiced, "And do make certain you are never alone with that wicked man!"

Brightshill shone eerily in the purplish light of the approaching storm, lightning already forking through the sky far off over the Vale. The carriage horses shifted uneasily as the coachman reined in at the front steps and steadied them while the footman let down the steps to help Antonia alight.

Her heart beat nervously as she stepped into the hall to be greeted by Mead the butler, but as he opened the double doors and she walked into the brightly lit salon, she felt her apprehension start to dissipate. She supposed, greeting her hostess and Lord Meredith, that it was like soldiers going into battle—once committed to action, it was strangely calming.

Antonia moved gracefully through the salon, exchanging smiles and greetings with Sir John and Mr Leigh, stopping to exchange a few words with Miss Fitch, who blushed prettily at the attention.

At length, her circuit of the room brought her face to face with Marcus, who was standing before the empty grate, one foot on the brass fender rail. He straightened as she approached and bowed over her hand, but not fast enough for Antonia to miss the gleam of appreciation in his dark eyes as he took in the cool elegance of her appearance.

"You are in great beauty tonight, Miss Dane," he observed dispassionately, but not dispassionately enough for Lady Reed sitting nearby, whose eyes narrowed at the overheard compliment.

Antonia looked into his eyes and caught her breath with a shock of love and longing. She wanted to reach out and touch his hair, smooth out the tension that only she could discern in the taut skin over his high cheekbones and caress the lips that had kissed her so thrillingly only the night before.

Instead, she looked at Claudia Reed and hardened her heart. No, she would not let herself be hurt by a man who continued his liaison with such a woman, so blatantly, so cruelly.

''Is Mr Blake not with you?'' Marcus's voice recalled her attention.

''Mr Blake? Why, no, were you expecting him?''

''I expected you to be accompanied by your fiancé.''

''My fiancé? Why, my lord, I am not engaged to be married to anyone.'' She widened her eyes innocently. ''You must have dreamed it—the moonlight has such a strange effect, do you not find?''

Marcus's lips narrowed and his eyes blazed with a sudden fire. Antonia found her wrist gripped none too gently as he pulled her closer to his side. ''Do not toy with me, Antonia. Are you telling me Blake lied to me last night?''

''Last night? I cannot imagine to what you refer, my lord. I was in bed last night…''

She gasped as his fingers tightened and he bent his head so close to hers that she felt his breath on her mouth.

''Last night, madam, you were in my arms on the riverbank and, if that fool Blake had not blundered in, I would have made you mine.'' His eyes glittered and Antonia was seized with the wild thought that he would take her in his arms, stride out into the night and complete his seduction there and then.

"Marcus, do not monopolise Miss Dane, you have all evening to talk to her." Anne Meredith advanced across the Chinese carpet towards them, "And here is Sir George just come down. Antonia, allow me to make him known to you."

Colonel Sir George Reed was a sad disappointment to Antonia who had imagined a distinguished military man of impeccable bearing, nobly sacrificing hearth and home for duty. Instead, the man who took her hand in his damp grasp reminded her of no one more than the Duke of York. Portly, the red veins of his cheeks competing with the scarlet of his dress uniform jacket, and with a lecherous eye to match that of the Prince Regent's brother, he bent over her hand.

For a moment, as he held fast to her fingers, Antonia felt a stab of sympathy for Claudia. Faced with such a husband, who would not turn to another man for consolation—especially if the other man was one such as Marcus?

Sir George's corsets creaked as he straightened up from planting a kiss on Antonia's gloved hand and she had a struggle to repress a giggle. To her alarm, he tucked her hand under his arm and announced, "Now, my dear, you must allow me to take a little promenade up and down the room while I learn all about you."

Antonia shot a glance of startled entreaty towards Lord Allington, which he met with a stony gaze. Claudia, on the other hand, smiled vixen-like from her chaise-longue as her elderly husband, perspiring profusely from the combination of tight stays and the intense heat, passed by.

"Now, do not allow Miss Dane to tire you, Georgie

darling,'' she called sweetly, bringing a flush to Antonia's cheeks.

But Antonia was far more exercised preventing ''Georgie darling's'' straying fingers from inching any further up her arm towards the swell of her breast. It took all her social grace not to shake him off and slap his face. Instead, she drew herself up stiffly and away from him, enquiring in a voice of frigid formality if the drive from Brighton had been free of incident.

''Tiresome, tiresome, my dear, but nothing which cannot be forgotten in the face of your beauty!'' he wheezed enthusiastically. Mercifully, Anne Meredith appeared and begged Sir George to permit her to bear Miss Dane off to admire the new hangings in the study.

The two ladies shut the door of the study behind themselves and gazed at each other. It was difficult to tell which was the more horrified, and almost together they said, ''Beastly man…''

''My dear Miss Dane, I cannot apologise enough… Had I but known what he was like! No wonder Marcus was so angry with me! And the Reeds obviously loathe one another… My dear, you must not leave my side for an instant; fortunately he has shown not the slightest interest in dear Sophia—far too young, thank goodness.'' Lady Meredith subsided into a chair and unfurled her fan to cool her heated cheeks.

''What is the seating plan for dinner?'' Antonia asked, seized with a sudden alarming thought.

''Oh, my heavens!'' Lady Meredith jumped up. ''I must see Mead at once, for I fear I have placed Sir George next to you…'' She hastened from the room, leaving Antonia to divert her thoughts by admiring the handsome cut-velvet draperies at the windows. They changed the aspect of the room somewhat from that cool day in March when she had been dragged unceremoniously into Marcus's presence, accused of poaching.

She ran her fingers over the arm of the carved chair in which she had been sitting when he had kissed her for the first time. Her reverie was rudely interrupted by a kiss of a very different kind: the pressure of wet, rubbery lips on her bare shoulder.

Antonia spun round with a small shriek of outrage to find herself pinned against the desk by the rotund and lascivious figure of Colonel Sir George Reed. "Alone at last!" he announced with undisguised lust.

"No, leave me be!" Antonia gasped, wriggling away.

"No need to pretend now. My wife told me you were a bit of a goer, a game pullet!" He opened his arms as if to envelop her. "Good of our hostess to make this room available, what? Thought she was a bit starched up at first, but I was wrong…"

"Sir George, I believe your wife is looking for you." Marcus's voice dripped ice. Antonia, glimpsing his set face over the gold braid of the Colonel's shoulder, thought she had never been so glad to see him.

Sir George swung round with an oath, failing to read the danger signals in his host's face. "Damn it, my boy, no need to spoil sport! After all, you've got Claudia to amuse you…"

"Sir, if you cannot take a hint, I may be forced to make my meaning more plain. I do not wish to embarrass Lady Reed, a guest in my house, by calling out her husband, but if you persist in annoying Miss Dane, you leave me no choice."

Sir George's face purpled, but he straightened his scarlet coat and barged out of the room without a word.

"Nauseating man!" Antonia felt sick with reaction. "He is really quite beyond the pale!"

"Then why were you foolish enough to permit yourself to be alone with him in here?" Marcus demanded curtly.

Antonia was taken aback by this attack. "I did not invite him here, I came in here to escape from his lecherous pawings, but it appears that his beloved wife had told him that I might welcome his repellent advances!" She stamped her foot with anger. "And if you had been half the man I thought you were, you *would* have called him out! But oh, no! That might embarrass dear Claudia, and we would not want to embarrass her, would we? Tell me, Marcus, just what lengths would he have to go to for you to challenge him?"

Marcus's face was cold, with all the old arrogance back in his eyes. "The man is old enough to be my father, and a guest under my roof…"

"…and his wife is your mistress! And we do not want to upset him, do we? He might stop being quite so complaisant and take her away! You disgust me, the three of you!" Antonia turned her hot face away, wishing she could bury it in the velvet drapes and burst into tears.

"There you both are!" Lady Meredith swept into the room, beaming to see them both together. Her smile froze on her amiable features as she saw the glittering anger in her brother's eyes and the rigid set of Miss Dane's shoulders. "I came to tell you that Mead has announced dinner. Marcus, will you take Miss Dane in?" She met his eyes, daring him to refuse, but instead he said politely,

"Miss Dane?" Antonia, gaze averted, took his proffered arm and allowed herself to be escorted into the glittering dining-room.

Lady Meredith, deprived of a fifth lady by Donna's absence and forced to rearrange her table hastily by Sir

George's behaviour, had none the less managed a reasonable disposition of her guests.

Marcus, at the head of the long board, faced his sister, who was flanked by Sir George and Sir John Ollard. With Mr Leigh on Sir George's right, Anne felt she had safely isolated the Colonel from both his wife and Antonia. Miss Fitch had brightened considerably at finding herself opposite her beloved Mr Leigh and next to the paternal Lord Meredith.

Anne, despite some qualms, felt a certain malicious pleasure at seating Antonia and Claudia either side of her brother. They made a striking trio: her brother in the centre flanked by the two women, one so dark and vital, the other so voluptuosly languid. It was about time Marcus decided where his heart lay, his sister resolved.

Marcus met Anne's eye down the length of the gleaming table, heavy with plate and crystal, and raised his glass in an ironic salute to her. She smiled back, reflecting that her brother was never a poor loser and could be relied upon to rise to a challenge.

Antonia sipped the champagne Mead poured for her, relishing its coolness, the burst of bubbles in her mouth. Normally she would make one glass of wine last all evening, but tonight she scarcely noticed that her glass was being refilled again, and then again as the fish dishes were removed with entrées and roasts.

The long windows had been thrown open to the warm evening air and the scent of beeswax, perfumes and food mingled headily. Marcus was being meticulous in his behaviour towards Claudia, maintaining a polite dialogue about trivialities and showing none of the ennui he would normally display at such chatter. But however attentive, he was not flirting and seemed impervious to her coquettish looks and teasing jibes.

It was obvious to Claudia, if not to Antonia, that his attention was equally fixed on her rival. Antonia chatted easily with Lord Meredith, but when he turned politely to engage Miss Fitch in conversation, she found it difficult to talk to, or even to look at Marcus. She was acutely aware of him, of the Russian Leather cologne he used, of his long fingers as they played on the stem of his glass. She wanted them running up and down her throat, caressing her nape…

Antonia pulled herself together with a start and took a long mouthful of wine. The effect made her blink with the horrified recognition that she had drunk rather too much.

"Lord Allington…" Claudia managed to make the formal title sound like the most intimate endearment. "Please will you help me to just the tiniest morsel more of that lobster; it is so delicious."

"And matches your dress so perfectly," Antonia observed, then giggled, immediately putting her hand over her mouth to suppress the sound.

Marcus bit his lip as he struggled to serve Claudia without bursting into laughter at the sight of her cheeks, flushed with anger, as pink as the boiled crustacean.

Claudia, stung, responded acidly, "How brave of you, Miss Dane, to wear such a very trying shade of green. One so rarely sees it without feeling depressed, although Lady Jersey, I suppose, has the style to carry it off…"

"Well, I wear it a good deal, but I can quite see that on an older woman with a faded complexion it could be difficult to carry off." Antonia took another sip of wine and continued smoothly, "Unless, of course, she used a lot of rouge."

Anne, pausing to send a worried glance down the table, wondered what was being said to amuse Marcus so much. She would swear, if she knew no better, that he was hiding a broad grin behind his napkin.

Claudia had gone so pale with anger that her rouge stood out in circles on her cheeks. She took a deep breath, knowing how it enhanced the spectacular uplift of her breasts in the-low cut gown and reflected that Miss Dane, for all her pert charms, had not the advantage of being Marcus's mistress. Although, as he had not once come to her all the time she had been at Brightshill, she was beginning to panic.

Damn his discretion! In London, she had sensed his attention was wandering after the first few tumultuous weeks of their liaison. That was why she had invited herself down, playing on his sister's good nature to inveigle herself into the houseparty. But Claudia soon discovered that Marcus would not tolerate loose behaviour in his own household with his sister acting as hostess.

Well, she had waited long enough for him to come to her room—tonight she would go to his. Meanwhile, she could give him a gentle reminder of what he had been ignoring. She put her hand lightly on his thigh, her long nails scoring the fine fabric, feeling the hard muscles tense in response.

Marcus turned his head sharply to meet Claudia's hooded gaze as her fingertips ran down, and then dangerously up, his thigh. As they insinuated themselves down between his legs, he grasped her wrist in none-too-gentle fingers and with great deliberation moved her hand back to her own lap.

Antonia saw the edge of the tablecloth move and had no difficulty interpreting the movement of Marcus's arm. Anger and determination ran through her veins like fire.

She was tired of behaving like the well-bred virgin she was. If she wanted Marcus—and with the champagne coursing through her, she knew she wanted nothing more in the world—then she would have to fight for him.

Chapter Twelve

At the end of what seemed to the harassed hostess to be an interminable meal, Lady Meredith at last stood up, gathering the attention of her female guests with a smile. "Ladies, shall we leave the gentlemen to their port?"

As she got somewhat unsteadily to her feet, Antonia bent and whispered in Marcus's ear, "Meet me in the conservatory as soon as may be."

Neither the gesture, nor Marcus's rapidly controlled reaction, was lost on Claudia, whose eyes narrowed in speculation as she swept past Sophia Fitch and into the salon. What was that little provincial miss about? Well, it scarcely made a difference—tonight she would go to Marcus and obliterate everything but the knowing caress of her fingers from his mind.

Claudia sank down on the chaise with a scarcely concealed sigh. Oh, lord! Yet another interminable evening. She gazed at Anne Meredith with dislike; God, she was plain and such a bore, always prating on about the Whigs. And she was responsible for George being here. At least *he* knew better than to come to her bedroom…

Seeing Sophia Fitch perching nervously at the other end of the chaise, Claudia decided to amuse herself by patronising the little mouse. "Tell me, Miss Fitch, when are you going to announce your engagement to Mr Leigh? Such a…worthy young man, I am sure. Does he have a patron? I suppose, coming from such an obscure family, he will need one."

Sophia, normally paralysed when addressed by the exotic Lady Reed, rallied at this attack on her beloved Richard. Her little figure quivered with indignation but her voice was steady as she replied, "Mr Leigh is one of the Hampshire Leighs, and as such need look no further than his uncle the Bishop for advancement. He is going as private secretary to Lord Seymour at the War Office, but hopes before long to stand for Parliament."

"Oh…" Claudia laid one small white hand on her forehead in a weary gesture "…do not talk to me of politics, it is so tedious."

"Well, in that case," Sophia snapped, "I will not bore you any longer." Slightly staggered at her own temerity, she rose to feet, walked across the room to the piano and began to pick out a new ballad.

Claudia shifted her attention to the other two women. Antonia, to her experienced eye, had had rather too much to drink, although she doubted if Anne Meredith had noticed. What was that minx up to? She was plotting something with Marcus, and now she was shifting uneasily in her chair, glancing every few moments at the ormulu clock on the mantelshelf.

Antonia, unable to bear sitting still any longer, bent and whispered in Anne's ear.

"Oh yes, my dear," her hostess whispered back. "Down the corridor on the left, the third door. Marcus has had one of Mr Bramah's flushing water closets installed—such a benefit."

Antonia admired the new-fangled sanitary arrangements, wondering how much it would cost to replace the old earth closets at the Dower House. She glanced in the mirror on the wash stand, tweaking her hair into order and wishing she had a little rice powder to calm her hectic cheeks. That last glass of wine sang in her veins, making her feel quite unaccustomedly reckless. Never mind, it would give her the courage to do what she had to do and drive Claudia out of Marcus's mind for ever.

The conservatory was filled with a damp heat and the heady scent of lilies underlaid with wet moss and earth. A few candelabra had been set on columns amongst the plant stands and beds of ferns, casting mysterious pools of shadow. Moths fluttered in through the open doors, fatally drawn by the voluptuous smell of the hothouse plants towards the candle flames.

Antonia strolled up and down the tiled floor, her gown swishing in the stillness. Would he come to her after that angry scene in the study? She walked on, biting her lip in growing anxiety as the wine-induced courage began to ebb away. No, he was not coming, she had lost...

"Antonia." His voice was husky and very close. Antonia's heart leapt in her bosom, but she turned slowly to face Marcus, the man she loved.

The moonlight burnished his hair, casting strong shadows across his face, veiling his eyes. But she could see his mouth curling with a sensual tenderness and the rise and fall of his shirt, gleaming white against the dark blue cloth of his coat, showed that he was not entirely master of his emotions.

"You wanted to speak to me?"

"No, what I wanted was this." Antonia stepped straight up to him, wound her arms sinuously around his neck and, pulling his head down, fastened her lips full on his.

There was the merest hint of hesitation: she had taken him by surprise, acted as no well-bred young woman would ever dream of acting. But then his instincts took command and Marcus pulled her tighter against his body, deepened the kiss, opening and exploring the softness of her mouth, the scent of her filling his nostrils, sending his senses reeling, even against the backdrop of the lilies.

Without freeing her mouth, he swept her into his arms and carried her effortlessly to where a bench had been set in a bower of fragrant stephanotis. Antonia found herself nestling on his lap, the strength of his thighs supporting her, his arms holding her fast against his chest.

The kiss went on and on druggingly, sweeping away all reason and sensibility. Antonia had prepared a little speech, all about how she was prepared to forgive him if he renounced Claudia, but even if she had been able to free her mouth, she could hardly recollect what she had intended to say.

At last his mouth left hers and she gave a little moan of protest which became a whimper of sheer sensual pleasure as his teeth nibbled gently down her throat, his tongue-tip tracing the sensitive line of her jaw before his lips found the swell of her breast.

His lips were so hot on the satiny cool curves, they seemed to burn where they touched. Antonia's hands pushed under the edges of his coat, her fingers caressing and tasting the firm flesh beneath the fine lawn of his shirt.

Her fingertips found the waistband of his breeches, tugging his shirt free so she could press her palm against the smooth muscled back. Marcus groaned deep in his throat and cupped the swell of her breast in one hand in an answering caress. His thumb stroked against the silk of the bodice, sending such a sensual shock coursing through her that Antonia gasped.

Concerned, he raised his head and gazed into her eyes. For a long moment their eyes held in a wordless communication, then Antonia saw his eyes flicker as his attention was caught by something behind her.

To Antonia's shock she found herself deposited unceremoniously onto the cold ironwork of the bench as Marcus got to his feet, tugging his waistcoat straight over the chaos she had wrought with his shirt. "Marcus…" she protested softly.

"Shh!" he hissed, hard eyes staring into the dark foliage. Leaving her breathless on the bench, he stepped out into a patch of moonlight. "Claudia!" His voice was heavy with sensuality. "So, this is where you are. I was looking for you." He took another long stride; Antonia, peering through the tangle of foliage, saw him reach the side of Claudia Reed, bend his head and claim her lips with a hard kiss.

Antonia was too shocked even to gasp, then too humiliated to risk being seen by the other woman, who was greedily kissing Marcus, her knowing body curving into his.

"Later, Claudia, later," Marcus murmured, leading her towards the door. "We must rejoin the others, or it will cause comment."

White-faced in the moonlight, all intoxication burned away by anger and humiliation, Antonia stared at a moth scorching its wings in the candle flame. Just like me, she thought in desolation, scorched by my passion for Marcus.

She should have known he was not a forgiving man: she had refused his suit, she had tricked him on the riverbank with Jeremy, putting him at a disadvantage in front of the other man. She had let her satisfaction at the trick show too plainly this evening and he had wreaked a terrible revenge on her, guaranteeing she would never dare cross swords with him again.

Bereft, humiliated, stricken to immobility by misery, she sat on, unheeding of time, until Anne Meredith sought her out, concern on her face.

"Antonia, my dear, are you unwell?" Who could doubt it, looking at the pretty face so pinched and pale, the elegant fingers cramped in the folds of her gown?

"No…yes." Words seemed to come from a long way away; it was an enormous effort to squeeze them past her stiff lips. "I think I have caught a chill…forgive me, but I must go home. May I have the carriage?"

"But, of course, my dear." Lady Meredith hurried out, returning some minutes later with Antonia's cloak and reticule. "Let me put this round your shoulders— why, your hands are quite frozen! Mead is sending for the carriage, it will not be long. Would you like me to accompany you back to the Dower House? Miss Donaldson may not have returned…"

"No, no, thank you. You are very kind, but I shall be better by myself. I am so sorry."

"It is I who am sorry," Anne Meredith replied grimly as she helped Antonia to the front door, cursing the stupidity of all men, and her brother in particular. Not for a moment did she believe Antonia's story. When a young girl is found alone in a conservatory in a distressed state and another woman is almost crowing with triumph, it did not take a genius to understand what had passed.

Anne stood looking after the disappearing carriage, anxiety on her face, fury in her heart. She would speak to her brother tonight. What was he about, she fumed as she re-entered the salon, trifling with a lovely young girl who was worth a hundred of that Reed strumpet? To her frustration, Marcus had ordered the card tables to be set up, foiling her desire to get him alone.

Marcus caught his sister's eye as she swept into the room, guessing from the sounds of carriage wheels on gravel that she had just handed Miss Dane into the conveyance to take her home. His mouth set in a grim line, he continued to play, determined to give Anne no opportunity to speak to him that evening. Beside him, Claudia pressed her thigh against his, her breast brushing his arm whenever she leaned across to examine his cards. No, he needed to avoid Anne tonight, he had other plans.

One o'clock was striking as he dismissed his valet from his bedchamber. "I will undress myself, thank you, Dale. And if you see my sister as you leave, tell her I have already retired."

"Very well, my lord." The valet, used to Marcus's ways, bowed himself out, leaving his master staring rather grimly at the big bed.

Marcus shrugged out of his swallow-tailed coat and waistcoat, removed his cravat and pulled on a light silk dressing-gown. He had no doubt that his solitude would soon be interrupted by Claudia, lured by the promise of his kiss in the conservatory. He could not have given her a much clearer signal that the weeks of denial were over—and that tonight he wanted her in his bedchamber.

Restlessly he tugged aside the heavy curtain and looked out over the pleasure grounds, then his focus changed and he found himself regarding his own reflection as though in a looking glass. "You damn fool," he addressed his image dispassionately. "What a coil."

He was still at the window when the door opened quietly and Claudia slipped in. He watched her without turning as she tiptoed across the carpet, her negligee of gold silk gauze moulding her voluptuous body. She pressed her palms flat against his shoulder blades, then ran them insinuatingly down the planes of his back until she reached his waist.

Marcus turned then, catching her wrists in his hard grasp, arresting their knowing progress. "Darling," she pouted, "you are so masterful." She shivered and looked into his face, her tongue-tip running lasciviously round the full curve of her lips. "It has been so long, Marcus…come to bed now."

She started to back towards the fourposter, only to be pulled up short and none too gently by Marcus's immobility. "Mmm…" She smiled wickedly at him. "So you want to do it here?"

"No, Claudia, I do not. And I do not want to take you to my bed, now or in the future. It is over."

Looking into his hard face she could not doubt it, but ever a fighter, she was unwilling to concede defeat. "I do not believe you! The way you kissed me tonight tells me you do not mean it!"

"I had to make sure you would come to me: there is nowhere else in the house we can be certain of being alone."

Ready tears started in the lovely blue eyes. "Marcus, how can you be so cruel? You know you love me, and I have been faithful to you, only to you…"

"Faithful to my fortune, my dear Claudia. I have never had any doubt that you would remain faithful to that while you had any hopes of presents—or until a bigger, richer, fish swam by."

The tears slid decoratively over the pink cheeks, but

a hardening anger was forming in the depths of her eyes. "How could you be so cruel? Inviting me down here only to spurn me when I have done nothing to incur your displeasure. Come, darling, come to bed. You are tired and cross, let Claudia make it better…" She wriggled seductively, sending the gauzy fabric sliding from her shoulders. Only the fact that he was still holding her wrists prevented the entire garment slipping to the floor.

"Yes, Claudia, I could go to bed with you. You are a very beautiful woman. But that beauty is only skin deep; it took me but a few weeks to realise that. You knew it was over, you knew I did not want you here, yet somehow you cozened my sister into inviting you down. Since you arrived, I have done nothing to encourage you, yet you persist."

"But I love you, Marcus," she wheedled.

"You love only yourself. You are vain, self-absorbed, cruel and dismissive of others' feelings. You are redeemed only by your beauty—for so long as that lasts, my lovely. Do not frown so, Claudia, frown lines are so very ageing."

"That did not concern you when you were in my bed taking your pleasure of me," she hissed, two hot spots of colour mottling her cheek bones.

Marcus dropped her wrists and stared down at the spiteful little face that tonight, despite the artful maquillage, had lost every iota of its freshness and appeal. "But then you managed to hide those characteristics from me so well, did you not?"

Claudia reached up one long-nailed finger and ran it scoringly down his chest, exposed by the open shirt neck. "I hid nothing from you, remember…?"

Marcus did, vividly. Then he had been consumed by passion for the sophisticated, available—oh, so very available—Lady Reed. The burning desire had been short-lived; now he felt only distaste that he had surrendered so easily to her lures. A reflection of his thoughts must have shown on his countenance.

Claudia, her wheedling smile vanishing in a second, struck like an adder, the flat of her hand cracking across his face so hard his head snapped back. Beyond touching the stinging weal with his fingertips, Marcus did nothing, but his eyes burned with a cold fire that stopped Claudia's breath. With a sob which was half-petulance, half-apprehension, she ran from the room, her negligee swirling in disorder around her.

Marcus stalked across the room and shut the heavy panelled door behind her, then slumped down into a wing chair before the empty grate. He stuck his legs out, easing the tension from his long frame, then ran his hands through his hair.

Egad, that had been unpleasant! He blamed himself for having become entangled with Claudia in the first place. At first he had admired her spirits and beauty, the courage with which she coped with an empty life married to a corrupt man old enough to be her father.

Society was full of grass widows, game for a fling with any gentleman who was willing. As long as everyone concerned was discreet, no one turned a hair, even when there were some aristocratic households where all a man could be certain of was that his first-born son and heir was his own.

But that sort of life had palled, Marcus realised. It was no longer enough to have passion without attachment—not since he had met Antonia.

A great weariness suddenly overcame him. Marcus shrugged out of his clothes and climbed into the great fourposter. His last thought before he fell asleep was that he must ride over and see Antonia as soon as maybe in the morning. He knew how much he must have hurt her in the conservatory, but he would explain how he had needed to shield her from Claudia's venom, and her vicious, gossiping tongue.

His next conscious act was to blink in the full glare of the morning sunlight as Dale pulled back the drapes at the long casements with their view east over the park. ''Another fine morning, my lord. I trust you slept well, my lord. Shall I direct them to send up your bathwater immediately?''

Dale, an immaculately trained valet, was well used to carrying on a one-sided conversation with his master, who was never talkative much before eleven in the morning. Encouraged by a grunt, he ushered in footmen carrying hot-water cans and began gathering up his lordship's discarded clothing from the day before.

So well schooled was he and so discreet that Dale had been known to retrieve intimate articles of feminine apparel and return them to the wearer's lady's maid perfectly laundered and without even a quirk of an eyebrow.

This morning's tumbled linen revealed no such embarrassments, however, somewhat to Dale's surprise: there was very little in an aristocratic household that escaped the notice of the upper servants. And later, when he noticed the faint bruise on his lordship's cheek, he did not comment, beyond wielding the cutthroat razor with extra care.

Lady Meredith, sweeping downstairs an hour later with every intention of bearding her brother, encountered him in the hall, dressed for riding and pulling on his gloves as he gave orders to Saye, his head groom.

"And tell Welling to come with us, you can both ride over to Sir George Dover's and collect that bay gelding I bought off him last week. It is unbroken and will need both of you to bring it home." Seeing his sister, he paused. "Good morning, Anne. I trust you slept well?"

"Marcus, must you go out now? I particularly wished to speak to you." It was a demand rather than a request.

"I shall be back later, my dear." Marcus bowed over her hand, avoiding her gimlet eye. He had no doubt she intended to lecture him on the subject of Antonia; well, by the time he returned, her lecture would be redundant, and she would be too pleased with his news to scold him.

Anne, fulminating over her brother's escape, was even less pleased at the discovery that her sole breakfast companion was Sir George Reed, making a hearty meal of sirloin, ham and porter.

Marcus, meanwhile, giving the horse its head on the fine cropped downland grass, was in the best of spirits as he cut across the parkland to the Dower House. The sound of the church clock striking ten reached him faintly over the pounding of three sets of hooves. The sun, though warm, was still tempered by the fresh early morning air and the prospect of bringing the smile back to Antonia's face lent urgency to the ride.

The old, twisted chimneys of the Dower House came into view behind a stand of trees and Marcus reined the mount in slightly, slowing him as he entered the lane that ran along the front of the property. At the gate he turned in the saddle. "Wait here, Saye." What instinct prompted him to keep the two grooms he could not say; something perhaps about the unwonted stillness of the normally bustling house.

Surely they were not still abed, he thought, as the

heavy knocker dropped from his hand onto the old oak door. Anna appeared and dropped him a curtsy, her cheeks even pinker than normal.

"Good morning, your lordship."

"Good morning, Anna. Is Miss Dane at home?"

Anna's pretty country complexion grew more rosy. "No, my lord."

"Well, may I speak to Miss Donaldson?" So Antonia was angry with him still. That was not to be wondered at.

"Miss Donaldson is not at home, my lord," Anna recited with the air of a child repeating a lesson.

Marcus's lips tightened. "Do you mean," he enquired with dangerous civility, "that the ladies are not here, or that they are not at home to me?"

This threw the maid servant into even more confusion than he might have expected. "Yes…no…that is…" She took a deep breath and said desperately, "Miss Donaldson said as I was to say, that they aren't at home, your lordship."

For a moment Anna thought his lordship was going to shoulder her aside and stride into the house, there was such a flare of anger in the dark eyes. But instead he nodded curtly, turned on his heel and vaulted into the saddle. Outside in the lane, the waiting grooms were startled to see their master urge his horse into a gallop away from the house.

"What are we supposed to do now?" Welling demanded. "Follow him or go for the gelding?"

Saye, well used to his lordship's sudden starts, dug his heels into the side of his hack. "Follow him—at least, until he rides off that temper."

After the first quarter of a mile, Marcus reined back to a more temperate pace, smiling grimly at his own mood. He was not used to being thwarted, and he was uneasily aware of how hurt Antonia must be feeling, but storming around the Hertfordshire countryside was no remedy. He would go back and write her a note.

He pulled up where the lane crossed the Berkhamsted road and watched the approaching grooms. If he sent the note with Josh Saye, who was courting young Anna, there was a good chance it would reach Antonia, more so than if he took it himself.

The men had just reached him under the shade of the chestnuts when a gig came bowling round the bend from the direction of the town. It was driven by young Jem, whose cheerful demeanour changed into a look of alarm tinged with shiftiness the moment he saw who was at the crossroads.

A sudden suspicion made Marcus snap, "Stop that gig," and the two grooms moved their mounts into the road.

Jem tugged his forelock and shifted uneasily on the bench seat. Marcus, still unsure why he had stopped him, urged his mount alongside the gig, then saw a beribboned hat box on the floor.

"Where have you been, boy?" he demanded sharply.

"Nowhere, sir," Jem responded sullenly.

"You speak proper to his lordship—" Saye lifted a hand threateningly "—or I'll thicken your ear."

"Do not bully the lad," Marcus intervened. "What is your name, boy?"

"Jem...your lordship." Still he would not look up.

"Jem, ah, yes. You work for Miss Dane, do you not?"

"Yessir."

"And have you been driving Miss Dane this morning?"

"Couldn't say, sir...my lord." Jem's face was almost crimson.

"That is all right, Jem, you do not have to tell us anything you do not wish to. What a pity Miss Dane forgot her hat box," Marcus said sympathetically.

"No, she didn't forget it, she said there weren't no room in the ch—" He broke off appalled, one hand clapping itself to his mouth.

"No room in the chaise?" Marcus finished gently. "So your mistress has hired a chaise, has she? And where is she bound?"

Saye advanced to the side of the gig. "You speak up when his lordship asks you a question, boy, or I'll have your ears off."

"You can boil me in oil and I won't tell you nuffin about Miss Dane," stammered Jem, almost in tears now.

"Stop bullying the lad. He is only being loyal to his mistress and no doubt following her instructions. Here, lad." Marcus fished in his waistcoat pocket and sent a half sovereign spinning through the air to the startled boy. "Do not worry, Jem, you have kept your silence well, now be off back to the Dower House."

The lad needed no urging and was off down the road as fast as the elderly horse could go. Marcus used his spurs and sent his mount cantering off towards Berkhamsted.

"What the blazes?" Welling demanded.

"You hold your tongue and follow," Saye growled. He urged his own hack after his master, adding under his breath, "Never seen his lordship in such a taking over a woman before, and that's the truth."

The King's Arms was the only hostelry in the town that hired out carriages, but enquiries there were met with little information. Yes, Miss Dane had hired a chaise and four with two postillions, but no, neither the landlord nor the ostlers could say which direction she had taken.

"We've been very busy, my lord," the landlord explained apologetically, wiping his hands on his apron. "Market day, you see."

Marcus was standing in the inn yard, fists on hips, sizing up the possibilities: east for London or west for Aylesbury, when Mr Todd the curate walked through the arch.

"Oh, good morning, my lord," he beamed, bowing obsequiously. "Why, all local Society seems to be abroad in Berkhamsted today. I was gratified to see Miss Dane earlier. Such a charming young lady, such an ornament to our Society…"

"Mr Todd, good morning to you, I trust I find you well." Marcus regarded his curate with a speculative eye. "Splendid sermon last Sunday, I hope you intend to stimulate us again this week." Marcus had, in fact, dozed through most of Mr Todd's interminable prosing on the subject of the Ephesians, but he did not want to cause gossip by pouncing too readily on the subject of Miss Dane.

"Thank you, my lord, you are too kind. I was, in fact, intending to enlarge upon the theme of the dangers of heathen imagery…"

Marcus allowed him to prate on until he drew breath at last, then slipped in a remark.

"I am glad to hear Miss Dane succeeded in finding a suitable chaise. Now, where was it she was going… London, I think…?"

"Oh no, my lord," said Mr Todd brightly. "She took the Chesham road."

Chesham, Marcus ruminated, why would she go south to Chesham? Unless she had some intention of disguising her destination, for once along that road she could turn off for either London or Aylesbury. Mr Todd was prattling again, but his lordship excused himself brusquely and strode back to his horse, leaving the curate to worry that he had somehow given offence to his patron.

"Saye, you and Welling take the Chesham road until you find which way Miss Dane's chaise has gone. When you are sure, send Welling back to me and you follow until Miss Dane reaches her destination, then send me word. Here—" he tossed a leather purse to the head groom "—this should cover your expenses."

Not waiting to see the two men follow his instructions, Marcus turned back towards Brightshill, a thoughtful expression on his face. He had come to expect spirited behaviour from Antonia, but even by her standards, setting off alone in a hired chaise was extraordinarily daring. When he discovered where she had gone—and London or Bath seemed the most obvious destinations—he would follow. Still, for once in his life Marcus Allington was discovering that events were not following his desires.

This impression was reinforced when, no sooner had he set foot over his own threshold, his sister pounced on him and marched him with scant ceremony into his study.

"Well?" Anne demanded. "Have you been over to speak to Miss Dane?"

Marcus sank into a deep chair and crossed his booted legs negligently. "Yes."

"And? What did she say? Marcus, I do wish you would not sprawl like that!"

"She said nothing." Marcus continued to sprawl, although his rather grim expression showed no desire to tease his sister.

"Nothing? What can you mean? Marcus, you are going about this very badly—did she refuse to speak to you? Although it is not to be wondered at, with that minx Claudia Reed all over you at table last night—"

"Antonia has gone," Marcus stated baldly, cutting his sister off in mid flow.

"Gone! Gone where?" Anne sat down abruptly in the chair opposite.

"I have no idea, although I would hazard either Bath or London."

His sister's colour was high, rising to match her temper. "So you have thrown away the one chance you have of marrying someone who would suit you to perfection—and hurt a sweet girl into the bargain!"

"I offered for her before our first dinner party here, and she turned me down." This was compressing events somewhat, and made no mention of Claudia's role in it all, but Anne was not to be deflected.

"I suppose you thought she would fall into your arms for the asking?" she demanded hotly. "After all, everything else does, does it not, Marcus?"

Startled by this attack, he pulled himself up in the chair and stared at her. "What can you mean?"

"Ever since you were a boy, you have been admired and fêted, for your rank and your fortune and your looks. You have never had to be accountable to anyone for anything, which is no doubt why that sweet girl has refused your suit. No, hear me out," she held up a hand as he opened his mouth to protest.

"You are a good brother and uncle and an excellent employer, but you are aloof, sometimes haughty. I am assuming you love Antonia? Have you told her so, or have you just presumed that the honour of being courted by the great Marcus Allington is sufficient?"

Marcus returned her angry look with one that was thoughtful, weighing what Anne had said, but before he could respond there was a discreet tap at the door and Mead entered apologetically.

"My lord, I regret the intrusion, but Welling is here, saying you required immediate speech with him."

Marcus rose swiftly. "Tell him to wait, Mead, I will be with him directly." Turning to his sister, he added, "Will you be so good as to direct Dale to pack a valise for me; this will be news of Miss Dane and I intend to follow her." He kissed Anne's hot cheek. "Do not fret, my dear, I have taken your strictures to heart. What you say may be true, but I do not despair of rescuing the situation."

In the hall he waited only for three words from Welling, "London, my lord," before ordering the man to bring round his high-perch phaeton within the half-hour.

Lady Meredith hurried out on to the steps as Dale was stowing the valise under the seat of the carriage and preparing to climb up beside his lordship. "Marcus!"

"Give my apologies to our guests, my dear, and tell them I have called away to Town by urgent business."

"So she is in London, then?" Anne asked, keeping her voice low as she looked up into his serious face. "How will you find her?"

Marcus bent down to touch her cheek. "Saye is hot on her trail, he will mark where she is staying and then await me at the town house. I will find her, never fear."

Anne, watching the sporting vehicle sway dangerously

round the curve of the drive, prayed that Marcus would not only find Miss Dane, but that having found her, could prevail upon her to receive him.

As she walked slowly back into the hallway, Anne mused that once she would have been glad to see her haughty brother brought low by love; now all she wanted was for him to be happy. With any other unmarried girl Lady Meredith would have had no fears, but Miss Dane was no ordinary debutante: she had a mind of her own and spirits to match.

Chapter Thirteen

The carriage jolted over the London cobblestones, jerking Antonia's mind back from the miserable circles it had been running round all day. Even in a swift chaise, with no money spared in hiring postillions and making changes whenever the horses faltered, the journey had seemed interminable.

In the country it would still be light at eight o'clock, but here, with tall buildings crowding all around and the press of humanity on the streets, the evening seemed well drawn in.

Antonia had directed the postillions to Half Moon Street, hoping that her great-aunt had suffered no relapse and was therefore at her own home and not at Cousin Hewitt's. To her relief, the knocker was still on the door, a sure sign that her ladyship was in residence, and lights glowed from the windows.

As soon as the carriage steps were let down, Antonia hurried up to the front door, which opened as she reached it as if in greeting. But it was not for her— Hodge, her great-aunt's long-serving butler, was in the process of bowing out a portly young gentleman. Antonia would have recognised her cousin Hewitt Granger anywhere by the expression of smug self-satisfaction playing on his fleshy lips and took some pleasure in seeing his face change at the sight of her.

They had never enjoyed a happy relationship: Hewitt was deeply suspicious of Antonia's position in his grandmother's affections and had been only too pleased to see her depart to Hertfordshire. But at the same time she was uncomfortably aware that Hewitt Granger found her attractive. He never lost the opportunity to touch her, squeeze her hand or stare blatantly at her figure in a manner that left her feeling somehow soiled.

Even as he regarded her now with suspicion and dislike in his pale eyes, Hewitt's tongue ran wetly over his full red lips.

"Antonia! What are you doing here? We did not look to see you in London again. Perhaps you sent a missive which has gone astray?" One gingery brow rose haughtily in an attempt at superiority.

"Good evening, Hewitt." Antonia dismissed him— and his questions—coldly, turning to the elderly butler with warmth. "Good evening, Hodge. I trust I find you well? How is the lumbago? Better, no doubt, in this warm weather."

The old man beamed back, for she had always been a favourite with him and he had missed her sorely these last months. "Much better, thank you, Miss Antonia. And may I say what a pl—"

"Now look here," Hewitt interrupted rudely. "I do not know what you think you are about, Antonia, but you cannot go in there." He moved to block her entrance with his bulky body. "Grandmother has been very ill, she cannot possibly see you and certainly not at this hour. You must go to an hotel."

Antonia glimpsed the expression on Hodge's face, the

almost imperceptible shake of his head. "Fiddlesticks, Hewitt! I am here at Great-Aunt's invitation. Now do step aside and let me past. You have grown so stout since we last met; I cannot but feel it will do you no good, especially in this warm weather." She regarded his empurpling face with cloying sympathy. "You really look rather hot and agitated—quite puce, in fact. Goodnight, I will not detain you any longer."

Hodge curbed the smile that was beginning to dawn on his face and said urbanely, "Your usual chamber is prepared, Miss Antonia. And Cook has your favourite supper all ready."

Antonia, even knowing this was untrue, could detect no falsity in the butler's tone. With a sweet smile at Hewitt, who was gobbling like a turkey cock, she slipped neatly into the hall. Her cousin was further discommoded by two footmen running down the steps to collect Antonia's luggage from the chaise. Thus comprehensively ignored by everyone, he clapped his hat on his head and strode off towards Piccadilly.

Hodge beamed at Antonia. "I will ring for Mrs Hodge and have your chamber prepared directly, Miss Antonia. Do you wish to go in directly to her ladyship?"

Antonia twinkled at him. "You said just now that my room was already prepared, Hodge. Was that an untruth?"

"Merely a slip of the tongue, Miss Antonia," the butler replied blandly. "Her ladyship will be delighted to see you, if I may make so bold. She is in the blue parlour; shall I show you up?"

"Thank you, no, Hodge. I know the way." Antonia whisked upstairs, happy to be back in the reassuring familiarity of her old home. It only lacked Donna to be quite like the old days, but her companion, when Antonia had announced her intention of fleeing to London, had reluctantly agreed to remain behind and supervise the Dower House.

Antonia paused, one hand raised to tap on her great-aunt's door. She remembered the uncharacteristic blaze of fury on Donna's face when she realised the exigencies to which Lord Allington had driven her beloved girl. Antonia had left in the gig with Miss Donaldson's furious instructions to Anna ringing in her ears: ''That man is never—*never*—to be permitted to cross this threshold again! Do you understand?''

Antonia tapped firmly on the door, for Great-Aunt's hearing was not what it was, and peeped round the edge, somewhat concerned that she might give Lady Granger a shock, for the old lady was in her eighties and her health was uncertain, despite the recent improvement.

All that was visible was the top of a most elaborate lace cap showing over the back of a heavily brocaded wing chair. A small fire flickered in the grate despite the warmth of the evening and an embroidery stand and a basket of silks had been pushed to one side.

''Is that you, Hodge?'' Lady Granger's voice was still as strong and commanding as it always had been. ''Has that fool of a grandson of mine gone? Thinks I do not know why he comes round! Sits there prattling on and all the time measuring me for my coffin with those wishy-washy eyes and wondering about my will! Pshaw! Does he think I am a fool?''

Antonia smiled to herself. The old lady was as outspoken as many of her contemporaries brought up in the more robust manners of the reign of the second George. She was quite likely to use intemperate language and could be open in her admiration for a comely young man in a way that caused blushes and giggles amongst younger women.

Antonia adored her great-aunt and was about to call her name when the old lady demanded, "And bring me my brandy, Hodge! Take away the taste of that bloodless sherry wine Hewitt pressed upon me."

Her niece picked up the tray from the side table and carried it round, carefully placing it before her aunt.

"Good Gad! Antonia, my child, is it really you?" Lady Granger held out her arms and Antonia went into them, enveloped in a cloud of rose scent, rice face powder and lace. "It does my heart good to see you."

"I am sorry to come with no warning. I hope it is not a shock, Great-Aunt." Antonia sat on a footstool beside Lady Granger and took her hand. She was shocked at how thin and papery the skin felt, but under her fingers the pulse beat strongly and the old eyes were bright and shrewd.

"Reading your letter, I was so happy that you are feeling better, that I wanted to take up your invitation immediately." It sounded false even to her own ears and Lady Granger was not fooled.

"Now tell me the real reason you are here," she demanded. She tipped up Antonia's chin with a bony fingertip and peered into her face. "Some man has made those shadows under your eyes, I suppose. Who is he?"

Even used as she was to her great-aunt, Antonia was taken aback by her directness and answered honestly, "Marcus Allington."

At that moment Mrs Hodge entered to enquire whether Antonia wished to eat her supper with Lady Granger and, receiving an affirmative answer, gathered up Antonia's pelisse and bonnet and bustled out.

"Allington, eh?" A mischievous glint lit Lady

Granger's eyes. "And is he as handsome a dog as his grandfather, I wonder? Now there was a man with a fine leg in a pair of satin knee breeches. A man with a true damn-your-eyes attitude to life!" She cackled reminiscently. "I nearly married him, but he was too much a rakehell, even for me."

"He is handsome, right enough," Antonia admitted ruefully. "And arrogant, and a rake…"

"And you love him, I suppose?"

"Yes." Antonia raised her face to her great aunt, tears starting in her eyes and her lip trembling.

The old lady held up an admonishing finger. "Do not dare cry, girl! Remember who you are and keep your pride. They are none of them worth a single tear, and I should know."

Antonia bit her lip until the tears stopped and began to believe the rumours she had heard about her great-aunt: that she had been a great beauty, the mistress of powerful men—even, it was hinted, one of the highest in the land.

The bright eyes suddenly froze on her face. "Why have you run away, girl? Has he been playing fast and loose with you? Have you permitted him any liberties?" She remembered Edmund Allington and his winning ways with the ladies. If his grandson had seduced her Antonia, he would find himself down the aisle before the week was out, if she had to take a shotgun to him herself.

"No," Antonia denied, blushing hotly, remembering how close she had come to yielding to the urging of his hard body on the riverbank that night, remembering her responses to his mouth on hers in the conservatory.

"Indeed, miss!" Great-Aunt took a sip of her brandy

and fell silent as Mrs Hodge brought in a light collation, laid the table and departed with a neat curtsy.

She brooded quietly as her great-niece ate hungrily, then, when Antonia finally pushed away the plate, asked, "What is the matter then, that you have come to me?"

"He does not love me and I cannot bear to be near him and his mistress a moment longer," Antonia burst out, getting to her feet and crossing to the window to look out on the street below. It was full dark now, except for the lanterns at each doorway, and she failed to notice the wiry figure in riding clothes standing in the shadows regarding the house. After a few moments, Saye detached himself from the darkness and hurried away in the direction of Grosvenor Square.

"Keeping a mistress, is he? Clumsy fool to let you know! Young men these days are losing their finesse— his grandfather would never have paraded his fancy piece in front of a girl he was courting. Has he made you any sort of declaration?"

"He has proposed marriage and I have refused."

"Glad to hear you have that much spirit, girl! And I am glad you had the sense to come to me although, with the Season over, Town is thin of company." Lady Granger mused on the available men who might take Antonia's mind off her broken heart. Marcus Allington was very eligible, she sighed to herself. She doubted her niece would ever make such a good catch again, but the important thing was that the child be happy.

"Come back and sit by me, child. You may stay as long as you wish, we will be comfortable together." Antonia put her head in the old lady's lap and felt her hair being gently stroked. She shut her eyes and let the wise old voice wash over her. "You will forget him in time, child. You are young and beautiful and there are plenty more fish in the sea.''

The following morning brought Hewitt and his younger brother Clarence, accompanied by his wife of a few months who, Antonia decided, after the briefest of acquaintances, was a total ninny.

The ladies had scarce finished their breakfast when the knocker sounded the arrival of the unwelcome party. Lady Granger was not pleased at the early interruption. ''What I have done to deserve such fools for grandsons I do not know,'' she confided to Antonia, not bothering to keep her voice down. ''Neither of them has a thought in his head, but that does not stop them sticking their beaks into my business at every turn.''

The unbecoming mottling of Hewitt's complexion showed he had heard at least part of this condemnation, but he swallowed his anger, bustling forward to kiss his grandmother's hand and enquire condescendingly after her health. Clarence followed his elder brother. Although two years separated them, they were as alike as twins with their florid complexions and bulky figures.

Clarence turned to his cousin and presented his wife with the air of a man showing off a rare jewel. Emilia Granger was at least ten years younger than her husband. She was blonde and fluffy and simpered up at Clarence, who swelled with pride at the blatant adoration in the shallow blue eyes.

Antonia marvelled that any woman could regard her cousin with adoration until Mrs Granger opened her mouth. ''Have you been in London before, Miss Dane…oh, yes, silly me, I quite forgot… Clarence told me you used to live here. Oh, dear, I am a goose!'' She giggled inanely, a noise not unlike a guinea fowl at its most irritating, and prattled on. "We are just a little early, are we not? But dear brother Hewitt was so set on visiting. He said last night…''

Even a woman as stupid as she could not fail to recognise the fury with which her brother-in-law was regarding her. Emilia flushed unbecomingly and subsided into silence. Hewitt glowered at her until he was certain she would prattle no more and turned his attention once more to Antonia.

Gad! His cousin was a handsome woman! Perhaps her complexion had caught the sun too much for fashion, but with her dark hair and flashing eyes it gave her an exotic look. Hewitt's mind drifted to a dark beauty he had encountered the other night in Vauxhall Gardens and the pleasures that had followed after the exchange of more guineas than he normally expended.

Antonia, catching his eye, shifted uncomfortably and moved closer to her great aunt, who was snapping at her visitors, "Sit down, sit down! Do not hover about like a flock of pigeons! What do you want, Hewitt? You were only here last evening."

Emilia, scared out of her remaining wits by this terrifying old lady, squeaked and dropped her reticule. The contents fell out and she scrabbled at her feet to pick them up, her cheeks scarlet. The two men sat firmly, one at each end of the sofa opposite their grandmother.

"Ha! Like a pair of bookends!" And with no sense between them. Lady Granger snorted, wondering how her stolid but reliable son had produced two such as these. But then, that well-bred goose he had married…

A moment of silence followed. Clarence finally broke it by clearing his throat. "Well, Grandmama—" he fiddled with his neck cloth "—sensible as we all are of your weakened condition and mindful that your doctor has prescribed rest…''

''Poppycock! I have dismissed the old fool, as well you know. Young Dr Hardcastle—does me good just to see his handsome face—stands for none of that nonsense.''

''Be that as it may, Grandmama,'' Clarence continued gamely, ''we were concerned that our cousin's presence might fatigue you. So we have come to offer her accommodation with us. For the week or two you are in London, coz,'' he added, turning to Antonia.

''She stays here,'' the old lady snapped, causing another spasm of fright to course through Emilia's thin frame.

''And I intend to stay for quite some time—months, in fact. So, of course, I could not possibly impose on you in Wimpole Street.'' Antonia smiled sweetly at Emilia. ''And I could not possibly intrude into the household of a newly married couple.'' Mrs Granger, thus addressed, was so discommoded that she dropped her reticule again.

''Fool of a woman,'' Great-Aunt muttered quite audibly, then, raising her voice, added, ''We have all the dress shops to visit—why, Antonia needs a complete change of wardrobe—and I fully intend to buy all the latest novels and volumes of poetry so we may read together. And, of course, we must get out of London soon. Bath, perhaps, or Brighton. What think you, Hewitt? Only a house in the best area, of course, and at this short notice it will no doubt cost a pretty penny. But there, I cannot take it with me, can I?''

Hewitt had raised a hand to cover his eyes and was murmuring gently to himself. Antonia thought she caught the words, ''The money, the money…''

Lady Granger tugged the bell-pull at her side. "Well, you may all remain here if you wish, but we were about to go out. Antonia, did I mention last night that I intend to take my diamond set to Garrard's to be cleaned and reset for you? We can do that on the way to the modiste's." Having thus completed Hewitt's anguish, she smiled benignly on her grandsons and, leaning on Antonia's arm, crossed the room slowly but steadily.

Antonia was surprised to discover, when they sat down later to luncheon, how effective a good shopping spree was in keeping a broken heart at bay. Her mind still flinched from thinking of Marcus, but her spirits were lighter and she found she could look forward to the next few weeks with pleasant anticipation.

"I must go and lie down for a while, my dear," Great-Aunt announced. "No, no, I am not fatigued." She waved aside Antonia's concern. "Dr Hardcastle has told me to conserve my energies. Why not take a walk in the park? Or would you prefer one of the grooms to drive you?"

"Thank you, Great-Aunt, but I think I will walk. I have grown used to walking some distances since I have been in Hertfordshire and I confess I miss the exercise." Antonia dropped a kiss on the dry, papery cheek and went upstairs to put on her bonnet and pelisse.

With one of her great-aunt's maids at her heels, Antonia set off briskly towards Hyde Park. Green Park was closer, but the more open expanses of the larger park beckoned and the afternoon was pleasantly sunny with a light breeze.

Antonia had an enjoyable walk, wandering further than she had intended. She finally turned for home, much to the relief of Julia the maid, who was not used to lengthy excursions of this sort, when she slipped on a tussock and turned her ankle painfully.

"Oh, Miss Antonia, are you all right, miss?" Julia's face was anxious as Antonia grimaced and rubbed the side of her kid boot.

"Oh! That was a nasty wrench, but I do not think it is sprained." She placed her foot gingerly to the ground and winced. "I shall manage well enough if I lean on your arm, Julia."

The two of them had begun their slow progress homewards when there was the sound of carriage wheels behind them and a cry of, "Cousin! What has befallen you?" The two young women turned to see Hewitt in a new conveyance pulled by a somewhat showy bay.

"I have turned my ankle, Hewitt, there is no cause for concern."

Hewitt jumped down from the carriage. "But you must ride back with me, dear cousin, I insist."

Antonia's first instinct was to refuse, but the thought of hobbling conspicuously across the Park was not appealing and her ankle was now throbbing.

"Thank you, Hewitt. Is there room for my girl?"

"No!" Hewitt looked appalled at the thought of having a maidservant in his new carriage.

"Very well. Julia, I am afraid you will have to walk—straight back to Half Moon Street, now!"

"Yes, miss." The girl bobbed a curtsy and watched as the carriage bowled off down the gravelled drive. Humph! She'd rather walk any day than sit squashed up with old frog-face and his wandering hands. And if she hurried there would be time to put her head round the basement door of number twenty and see if Tom the underfootman was about...

"Hewitt, do take care," Antonia remonstrated as

Hewitt took a curve so close the carriage rocked. She suspected that he had chosen both horse and curricle for their showy looks rather than quality, and was not entirely certain as to his abilities to control either.

"Well, if you are nervous I will slow down, one would not wish to frighten a lady." He reined back and leered at Antonia, who placed her parasol firmly on the seat between them.

Antonia averted her gaze from his florid features and began to talk of the magnificence of the shrubberies and the greenness of the grass despite the warm weather.

Her determined horticultural commentary was rudely interrupted by Hewitt's exclamation. "That's a damn fine bit of horseflesh!"

Antonia turned automatically, but she had no need to follow her cousin's pointing whip. The magnificent black stallion emerging at a controlled walk from one of the side paths was turning all heads in the vicinity. But after one glance, Antonia's attention was riveted not on the horse but on the rider.

Marcus Allington was controlling the spirited animal with one hand, the other at his hat brim acknowledging greetings from many of the passers-by.

"Drive on, Hewitt!" she demanded sharply, but her cousin had reined back almost to a standstill and was not listening. "Stop gawping, Hewitt, it is only a horse!"

What was Marcus doing here! It was only two days since that disastrous dinner party at Brightshill—now here he was riding through Hyde Park, as cool as a cucumber. One thing was clear—he had not followed her, for how could he know where she had gone after all the precautions she had taken to cover her steps?

Antonia's heart was thudding in her chest so loudly

she felt sure it would be audible to her cousin sitting alongside her. She could not take her eyes off Marcus, sitting erect in the saddle. His boots were burnished to the black sheen of the animal beneath him, his riding clothes were immaculate. His hair was caught by the slight breeze as he raised his hat and her fingers clenched against the desire to run her fingers through it.

"It is Lord Allington, is it not?" Hewitt demanded. "I wonder if he would tell me where he got that animal?"

"Please, Hewitt, take me home, my ankle is painful and I am sure it is swelling."

"What? Oh, sorry, my dear." Hewitt, recalled by her sharp voice, started and let his hands drop. The bay, feeling the lack of control, broke into a trot and the carriage lurched. Antonia, thrown off balance, gripped Hewitt's arm with both hands and was still in that position when Marcus saw them.

He urged the stallion forward with the pressure of his knees and came alongside the curricle as Hewitt once more gained control.

Hewitt just managed to doff his hat without dropping either it or the reins. "My lord."

"You have the advantage of me, sir, no doubt Miss Dane will introduce us. Miss Dane, your servant, ma'am." He replaced his tall hat and raised one eyebrow. "I had not looked to find you here, Miss Dane."

"And indeed, why should you, sir?" Antonia riposted, chin high and leaving one hand resting on her cousin's arm. "Allow me to make known to you my cousin, Hewitt Granger. Mr Granger, Lord Allington."

The gentlemen exchanged stiff half-bows. Hewitt was conscious that Antonia's hand was still on his arm. His lordship might be astride the best bit of horseflesh in the

Park, but he, Hewitt Granger, was driving the finest-looking woman abroad that day! His chest swelled with self-importance and he patted Antonia's hand proprietorially.

Marcus's face showed nothing but the bland amiability of a gentleman introduced to a new acquaintance but Antonia, knowing him so well, was aware of a watchfulness in his eyes. Some devil in her made her lay her free hand on top of Hewitt's. "You will forgive us, Lord Allington; we have been out some time and I am fatigued. Hewitt dear, take me home now."

Marcus's lip curved in an unpleasantly satirical smile. He did not believe a word of that, and Antonia knew it. "In that case, ma'am, I would not detain you." To her chagrin Marcus tipped his hat once more and cantered off without asking for her direction. Not that she would have given it to him anyway!

Hewitt, meanwhile, was recovering from the shock of finding Antonia so affectionate, given that usually she was at best dismissive to him. He had just enough sense not to press matters in the Park, but resolved to call at Half Moon Street the following day and pursue his advantage.

As they bowled along Piccadilly, he reflected that matters could not have fallen better. Antonia's reappearance had been a severe shock to one who had come to regard his grandmother's money as his by right. He knew how highly the old lady valued her niece: now, if Antonia accepted him, he would have it all: the money and the woman. He did not particularly like Antonia, she was too opinionated for him, but he did desire her.

As they turned into Half Moon Street, he resolved to pay a visit to that little actress he had discovered in Covent Garden. A trifle coarse at close quarters, but she bore a startling resemblance to his cousin and his passions were stirred...

Antonia was glad to descend from the carriage at her great-aunt's house. The footman helped her down with care and she waved Hewitt goodbye as she limped up the steps on James's arm. To her relief, her cousin showed no desire to accompany her into the house; she had been concerned that she had overdone things in the Park and that he would try and follow up her unexpected warmth. But no, she reassured herself, Hewitt was too stupid to notice.

The following morning her ankle was still stiff. Lady Granger, having failed to persuade her niece to allow her physician to examine it, had insisted that she spend the morning resting with it supported on a footstool. The old lady had driven out to visit an ailing acquaintance, promising to return in time for luncheon.

Antonia obediently settled down to read the latest volume of Lord Byron's work. Many ladies would have considered it far too shocking for an unmarried girl to read, but Lady Granger had thoroughly enjoyed it and had no qualms in passing it to her niece.

Despite the disconcerting tendency of Marcus's face to appear in her imagination every time she read a description of the hero, Antonia was engrossed in ''Manfred'' when Hodge threw the door open and announced, ''Mr Granger, miss.''

Antonia groaned inwardly, wishing she had given instructions to Hodge that she was not at home. But then he would have denied all visitors...

Hewitt bustled across the room crying, ''Dear Cousin! How is your afflicted, er...'' he boggled at naming part of a lady's anatomy and finished lamely ''...injury?''

"Much better, thank you, Cousin," Antonia replied coolly. Why was he here? "Please, sit down and allow me to ring for some refreshment." Hewitt showed no inclination to sit, instead striking an attitude which displayed an inordinate amount of crimson silk waistcoat. "What a striking waistcoat," Antonia said weakly, eyeing the garment with horrid fascination. In combination with trousers in an assertive shade of canary yellow the whole ensemble this early in the morning made her feel quite bilious.

"I knew you would admire it," he beamed. "I thought to myself, a woman of taste such as my cousin Antonia will admire this garment. In fact, I would go so far as to say I donned it especially for you." His expression was doubtless supposed to be a roguish twinkle, but it emerged more like a leer.

"Really?" Antonia was lost for words. She was beginning to feel increasingly uncomfortable and wished she could reach the bell-pull to summon Hodge.

Eyeing her even more warmly, Hewitt crashed to her side on one knee and seized her right hand in his fleshy paw. "Miss Dane! Cousin! Antonia! Be mine, I beseech you! Say you will consent to be Mrs Hewitt Granger!"

Antonia stared down appalled at the thinning crown of his head bent over her hand, then struggled to her feet with a painful lurch, attempting at the same time to extricate her hand. Hewitt, misinterpreting her gesture, staggered to his feet and seized her in his arms manfully.

"No!" she cried as his lips descended inexorably towards her face, but the sound was muffled by Hewitt's ample chest.

There was a discreet cough behind them and Hodge's voice announced, "Lord Allington, Miss Dane."

Antonia, scarlet with mortification, attempted to free

herself, but Hewitt clung to her hand until she freed it with a sharp jerk. "My lord, good morning. Please sit down." She was amazed at how calm her voice sounded, for inside she was trembling and, in truth, felt a little queasy. Her ankle throbbed, but that was nothing compared to her utter revulsion at Hewitt's embraces.

Steeling herself, she raised her eyes to Marcus's face, hoping to see some sign of jealousy, some sign that finding her in the arms of another man was painful to him.

Lord Allington stared back, his face a polite mask. Not by one whit did he betray surprise, dismay or the slightest sign of jealousy in finding the woman to whom he had recently proposed in the arms of another man.

"How kind of you to call, my lord," Antonia continued desperately. "May I offer you some refreshment? Hewitt, please ring the bell before you sit down."

"Thank you, Miss Dane." Marcus sat back and crossed his legs, smiling politely at both the cousins. "How pleasant to see you again, Mr Granger. I was wondering where you had acquired the striking animal you were driving yesterday."

So you can avoid the same dealer, no doubt, Antonia thought sourly. She was hoping that Hewitt would leave, but at such flattering attention her cousin settled himself comfortably and began to prose on about his search for the perfect driving horse.

Marcus caught Antonia's eye and allowed one eyelid to drop into an unmistakable wink. Antonia, despite everything, could hardly contain the laugh that bubbled up her throat. Marcus could have asked nothing better calculated to encourage Hewitt into a display of pompous conceit—and now Marcus was inviting her to enjoy it with him.

With a struggle she controlled her expression. Beside

her Hewitt, conscious for the first time that his lordship's attention was not solely on him, ground to a halt. Antonia spoke hurriedly in the sudden silence. "How did you know my direction, my lord?"

"Your direction? Why, I had not come to see you, Miss Dane, but Lady Granger." Marcus smiled. "No, this is merely a pleasant coincidence—did you know, Mr Granger, that Miss Dane and I are neighbours in Hertfordshire?"

"No, I was not aware of that," Hewitt answered rather shortly. "I was also not aware that you were acquainted with my grandmother." He disliked the thought that any of his most wealthy relative's business was not known to him.

"I have never had the pleasure of meeting her ladyship, but she and my grandfather were great friends. When I heard she had risen from her sickbed and was receiving once again, I naturally hastened to pay my respects. I would not have wished to, shall we say, leave it too late."

"I can assure you, my lord," Antonia snapped, "that my great-aunt is in the best of health. Touching though your concern is, there was no need to hasten to her side as though she were on her death bed."

"But she is very frail," Hewitt added hastily, as if to reassure himself.

At that moment the lady herself entered, looking not a day over sixty in a mauve silk creation that combined the latest fashion with great dignity. Both men leapt to their feet, but she ignored her grandson completely, fixing Marcus with a gimlet stare before allowing him her hand.

"Well, well—there was no need for Hodge to tell me who my caller was! Just like your grandfather, another handsome dog. Sit down, can't stand people hovering about! What are you still doing here, Hewitt? Every day you are cluttering the place up, every day. Go to your club, why don't you, if you can't stand to go home to that simpering peahen your brother married.''

Hewitt, deciding that being belittled by his grand-mother in front of Lord Allington was detrimental to his dignity, smiled at Marcus as though to indicate that the old lady was ga-ga and bowed himself out with a mean-ingful stare at Antonia.

Marcus sat under the penetrating stare and smiled back, apparently at his ease, but inwardly reflecting that he had never met such a terrifying old woman in his life. The grey eyes regarded him shrewdly but not unkindly, and the wreck of the very great beauty his grandfather had once described was still there in the fine bones of her face and the spirit that still burned strong.

''So you think I am like my grandfather, ma'am?'' he enquired.

''Cut from the same cloth: I would have known you anywhere as an Allington.''

''And I would have recognised you, ma'am, from his description.''

''Get away with you, boy!'' Lady Granger waved a hand dismissively but Antonia could tell she was pleased. ''I'll wager he did not tell you everything about our acquaintance.''

Antonia blushed at the improper implication, but Mar-cus laughed. ''Enough to make me envious, ma'am.''

The two settled into a conversation that subtly ex-cluded Antonia. She sat to one side, watching Marcus's face, the play of expression, the movement of his hands, listening to the laugh in his voice. She loved him, wanted nothing more than to run across the room to him, bury her face in his chest and hear his heart beat under her ear.

It was so painful to see him here in her old home, talking to her great-aunt but to know that nothing had changed, nor could it. Ruthlessly she reminded herself that she could not ally herself with a man so unprincipled he would flaunt his mistress before her. And if that meant she had to live out her life in spinsterhood, well, so be it. If she could not have Marcus Allington, she did not want second best.

Not that she any longer had the choice. He had made it quite clear that he was not here to see her and his reaction to Hewitt had been one of total indifference.

Antonia became aware that Marcus was on his feet taking his leave. As he bowed over Lady Granger's hand once more, Antonia saw her great-aunt give a decisive little nod as though she had reached a conclusion to a difficult puzzle.

Antonia curtsied slightly. ''Good day, Lord Allington.'' And goodbye for ever, she whispered to herself.

Chapter Fourteen

Antonia discovered, as she dressed for Almack's that evening, that deciding on a life of spinsterhood did not diminish her pleasure in putting on her newest gown. The confection of silver cobweb gauze over a deep jade green underskirt was outrageously becoming, especially when worn with her great-aunt's diamond set, newly returned from the jeweller.

As she waited for the carriage to come round, Great-Aunt Honoria regarded her critically and observed, "You look very beautiful tonight, my dear: that simple Grecian hairstyle becomes you. But you are not in spirits, are you? It is Allington, is it not?" Antonia nodded silently. "Well, I can see why you have fallen for him. Can you not forgive him? Men are but fallible creatures."

"No, never!" Antonia said emphatically. "He flaunted his mistress before me—and besides, he does not love me."

Further conversation was curtailed by the arrival of the carriage with the Granger party. Reluctant as she was to accept Emilia's chaperonage, Antonia knew she had little choice, for Great-Aunt Honoria could not be expected to attend every evening party with her niece.

Emilia thoroughly enjoyed being able to patronise her husband's alarming cousin. Mrs Granger sensed that Antonia was not only more beautiful and better bred than she, but also far more intelligent and at ease in Society.

As soon as Antonia took her place in the carriage, Emilia scanned her appearance, noting with dismay how both her husband and her brother-in-law stared openly at the gentle swell of Miss Dane's breasts in the low-cut gown. What was the old lady about, to let an unmarried girl flaunt herself in such a gown? Something like her own modestly cut bodice would have been more appropriate. Emilia arranged her own lace complacently across her thin chest and basked in an unaccustomed feeling of superiority.

As soon as they reached the exclusive establishment, Antonia accepted an invitation to dance and was not displeased at the end of the measure to find herself on the far side of the room from her relations. She was pleased to see the family of Sir George Dover, another Hertfordshire neighbour, and was soon in conversation with his two pretty daughters.

Miss Kitty fell silent in the middle of a description of the most ravishing silk warehouse she had visited the day before ''…and two dress lengths for scarcely more than you would expect to pay for one…'' and blushed.

Antonia, turning to follow her gaze, saw Marcus Allington enter the room. Few men could carry off the severe evening wear insisted upon by the Patronesses of Almack's to such advantage. Antonia's heart beat wildly and she fanned herself, lest her cheeks were as flushed as Miss Kitty's.

''Is he not the most handsome man in the room, Miss

Dane?'' Kitty Dover whispered in Antonia's ear. ''In fact, I do declare him the most handsome man in Town.''

Antonia could only stare dumbly across the dance floor, lost in hopeless love for Marcus. A lump in her throat prevented her from answering Miss Dover and she could only hope her feelings were not written plain on her face.

''Oh! He is coming over here! Why, I shall just die if he asks me to dance,'' exclaimed Kitty's younger sister Amanda.

Marcus strode across the floor as the next set was forming. Antonia was aware that many pairs of female eyes followed his elegant progress, and when he stopped before the three young women, bowed and then addressed her, she was conscious of several dagger-like looks.

''Miss Dane, Miss Dover, Miss Amanda. Good evening to you. Miss Dane, will you do me the honour of standing up with me for this cotillion?''

''You must forgive me, my lord, I have a headache and cannot dance. Excuse me.'' Without a backward glance, Antonia pulled back a curtain and stepped into one of the small retiring rooms.

The room was deserted, without even the presence of the maidservant who was normally in attendance armed with smelling salts, a pincushion and other essentials for rescuing ladies at a disadvantage.

Antonia laid one hand on her breast in a vain attempt to steady her hectic breathing. It was so foolish to respond so—after all, she told herself with an attempt at lightness, if she came to the most fashionable resort in Town she must expect to find Marcus there. She must accustom herself to the sight of him…

A footfall behind her sent her whirling around. "Marcus!" she gasped. "You should not be in here, it is most improper. Were we to be seen...people might believe...assume..."

"Then they would be correct," he remarked calmly, taking her in his arms in a manner which brooked no argument.

Nevertheless, Antonia tried to break free, but his arms were strong around her waist and when his lips neared hers she stopped struggling. All propriety, all thought of what was correct flew from her mind the moment his teeth nibbled delicately along the sensitive curve of her upper lip.

Antonia gave herself up to the sensation of being kissed by the only man she would ever love and when he deepened the kiss she responded in kind, kissing him so fiercely that she felt rather than heard his answering groan.

At length he freed her mouth, although his arms continued to support her. That, Antonia acknowledged shakily to herself, was a good thing, for her legs were too tremulous to hold her up.

Marcus's eyes as they smiled down into hers were dark with desire, yet sparkling with mischief. "Now confess—that preposterous cousin of yours does not kiss you like that."

Antonia freed herself with an angry shake. "So that was what prompted your kiss, was it? A desire, not for me, but to best my cousin Hewitt? Well, for your information, sir, I have never permitted Mr Granger to embrace me, nor will I ever do so!"

Marcus looked down into the angry eyes, sparkling magnificently in the indignant face, saw the rise and fall of Antonia's bosom and judged the time was right to do what he had intended ever since he came to Town in pursuit of her.

"But you permit me to embrace you. Come, madam, let us end this foolish charade: say you will be my wife and have done with it."

"It is no charade, sir. When I give my hand, it will be to a man whom I can love and respect, not to one seemingly prompted by an unwarranted possessiveness."

"Antonia, enough! Stop behaving like an outraged old maid. After all, you have not always shown such delicacy." Marcus groaned inwardly as soon as the words were out, for there was hurt as well as anger now in her face. Even so, he was not prepared for the stinging rebuttal that followed as her palm met his cheek.

With a sob, Antonia whisked out of the retiring room, carried onto the dance floor by the speed of her exit. A stately measure was in progress with complicated sets moving slowly the length of the ballroom. Her intrusion set several couples out of rhythm, but they were even more discommoded when Marcus strode to her side, seized her hands and forced her into the line.

"What do you think you are doing?" Antonia hissed, sending apologetic glances to the couples on either side.

"I had not finished with you," Marcus ground out, the social smile on his lips at variance with his tone. "And if the only way to stop you boxing my ears again is to converse on the dance floor, then so be it."

They had reached the head of the set. To her horror, this brought them directly under the scrutiny of Lady Jersey. From her raised brows, Antonia gathered that their irregular entrance had not escaped the Patroness's notice. Beside her, Marcus directed a charming smile at her ladyship and was rewarded by a relaxing of her adamantine gaze.

He whirled Antonia around and they took their place in the centre of the circle, Antonia convinced that every eye in the hall was on them. She curtsied and began the complex sequence of steps with her partner while the other couples circled around them. Miss Kitty, brown curls bouncing, was agog with excitement at Miss Dane's unconventional behaviour.

"Will you stop this nonsense and say yes?" Marcus demanded, in an almost conversational tone that was surely audible to those around.

Antonia's cheeks flamed. "Shh!" The steps took them apart and then together again.

"I mean it, Antonia!"

"You cannot force me!" she flashed back, still in a whisper.

Now they were hand in hand, sidestepping down the long row. "You will stay on this dance floor until you give me an answer." Marcus's eyes were hard with determination.

Antonia was conscious that heads were turning and amongst the watchers some women were whispering behind their fans. She half-turned, looking to flee through the throng, but Marcus was too swift for her, seizing her wrists and keeping her to the measure.

"Marry me, Antonia, you know it was meant to be," he insisted as they whirled around.

"Never! Nothing you can do or say will induce me to marry you, Marcus Allington!" The words fell into a sudden silence as the band came to a halt in a flurry of strings.

Aghast, staring wildly about her, Antonia realised her words had been audible in every corner of the room.

The floor failing to open up and swallow her, she picked up her skirts and fled, the crowd parting before her.

Outside, careless of cloak or bonnet, she hailed a passing hackney carriage. The driver seemed startled to find a lone gentlewoman hailing him outside Almack's, but he was polite enough when she stammered out the direction.

Hodge, with the licence of an old family retainer, was frankly scandalised to find her alone. "Miss Antonia! Where's Mrs Clarence? And your cloak…and your bonnet! What is amiss?"

"Oh, never mind! Please pay the driver and send my maid up to me."

Antonia managed to maintain her sang-froid until the maid had helped her into her nightgown, then hastened to dismiss the girl. "Thank you, that will be all. Please make sure Lady Granger knows I am returned, but tell her I have a headache and will see her at breakfast."

Antonia sank down on the bed, put her head in her hands and despaired. Under her fingers her temples throbbed and she could still feel the heat of humiliation burning her cheeks.

The whole of Society would know by tomorrow that she had made an indecorous exhibition of herself at Almack's and humiliatingly rejected Lord Allington into the bargain. He would never forgive her for that very public rebuff, even though it was he who had been to blame.

Antonia groaned. To think she had come to London for sanctuary! Now she would have to retreat once more into Hertfordshire and rusticate until some other scandal arose to titillate Society and she was once more forgotten. And Great-Aunt would never forgive her, broadminded though she was.

At that moment the knocker thudded, audible even through her closed door. Hewitt, no doubt, with Emilia squeaking in his wake, ensuring that no sordid detail of her disgrace remained untold. There were footsteps on the landing and her great-aunt's sitting-room door opened and closed, but strain as she could, Antonia could not hear voices.

The visit lasted half an hour. When carriage wheels rumbled away in the street outside, Antonia sat tensely, awaiting the summons to account for herself. It never came and eventually she fell asleep.

Nervously, Antonia entered the breakfast parlour the next morning to be met by a benign smile from Lady Granger. "Good morning, my dear. I trust you had a pleasant evening last night."

"No, Aunt, I did not." Antonia sat down, gazing miserably at her plate. "Surely you have heard…surely Hewitt told you last night when he came?"

"Oh, Hewitt! I never pay any attention to what he says." Lady Granger fell silent as a footman brought in a fresh jug of chocolate. As he left, she remarked, "I suppose you will be wanting to go out of Town for a while?"

Antonia raised troubled eyes and the old lady saw with a pang the depths of her misery. But years of experience had taught her how to keep her thoughts from her countenance and she merely added, "You may take my travelling carriage and Blake my coachman will, of course, drive you into Hertfordshire."

Antonia accepted gratefully. She was a little surprised that her great-aunt had not offered one of the maids to accompany her, but concluded that, despite her calm, the old lady was displeased with her and so she did not care to ask the favour.

It was only a few hours later that Antonia found herself driving out of London, feeling not unlike an unwanted package being returned to its sender. Great-Aunt Honoria had been affectionate, but somehow distracted. Antonia concluded miserably that the old lady was concerned with limiting the damage to the family's reputation and did not press her to talk.

Blake was a middle-aged man used to driving an elderly lady and so progress was steady and smooth. Arriving at last in the late afternoon at the Saracen's Head in King's Langley for the last change of horses, Antonia declined the landlady's offer of refreshment in a private parlour and sighed to see the coachman lumber down from the box and stride into the taproom.

Antonia picked up a book, resigned to wait at least half an hour, but scarcely had she found her place than she saw the skirts of his great coat as he once more mounted the box. Soon they were bowling through the green countryside with surprising speed. The new horses must have been an excellent pair but, even so, Blake's driving had acquired a verve and flair he had not demonstrated in the previous miles.

She thought little of it, however, grateful to be making such good progress and hopeful of being back at the Dower House by nightfall. Blake made the correct turning in Berkhamsted, wheeled left by the castle and began the long steady climb to the Common. Antonia dozed fitfully, but was woken with a start as the carriage lurched.

Strange, she did not remember the road being quite so rough. Puzzled, Antonia looked out and realised she had no idea where they were. Blake must be lost, and she had given him such careful instructions before they set out from Half Moon Street!

Irritated, she knocked briskly on the carriage roof with the handle of her parasol, but Blake took no notice, nor did the conveyance slow. Antonia's annoyance increased. Was the man deaf? They could end up miles out of their way and the shadows were lengthening. She dropped the window and, clutching her hat firmly, leant out.

"Blake! Stop the carriage. You are going the wrong way!" To her relief she felt the pace ease off and saw a clearing ahead with a barn beside it. At least he could turn the carriage there.

As they drew up, she opened the door without waiting for him to descend and jumped down on to the grass. "Really, Blake, this will not do! Heavens knows where we are."

He had turned and was climbing down from the box. Antonia waited impatiently. "There is no need to get down. Just turn the carriage…" The rest of the sentence died on her lips as the man reached the ground and turned to face her. "Marcus! What are you doing?"

Lord Allington shrugged off the heavy greatcoat and tossed the battered beaver hat up on to the coachman's seat. "Why, I am abducting you, of course." His manner was so matter of fact he might have been offering her a cup of tea.

Antonia stood amazed, robbed of speech and movement by the shock of his outrageous words. Marcus led the horses over to the barn and began to unbuckle the harness. "Will you come and hold their heads for a moment while I drop the shafts?"

Mutely Antonia complied, wondering if it were he or

she who had lost their senses. At length Marcus loosed the animals into a nearby meadow. Taking Antonia by the hand, he led her unresisting into the barn.

It was a small building as barns went, but clean and dry and smelling of hay. The floor was swept clean to the beaten earth and pitchforks were propped against the walls. Only a small pile of hay remained, and that was incongruously heaped with rugs and pillows.

Even more astounding was the sight of a table and two chairs, the board set with a white cloth and various covered dishes laid out. Marcus crossed and struck flint to light the candles which, in their fine candelabra, added the final touch of unreality to the scene.

Antonia put one hand to her brow and pushed back the curls. "Are you run mad? What can you hope to achieve by this?"

Marcus came and untied the ribbons of her bonnet and took it from her head. He undid the buttons of her pelisse and handed her into the nearest chair, then reached for a bottle of wine.

"Here, you must be in sore need of something to eat and drink."

Antonia took a reviving sip of wine and demanded again, "What do you mean to do with me?"

"Why, ruin you, of course." Marcus raised his glass in a toast and drank.

Antonia put down the glass sharply, sending the red liquid splashing on to the white cloth. "Can you be so vindictive, sir? I have thought many things of you over these past months, but not that you would seek revenge for a humiliation last night that was at least as much your fault as mine."

Marcus smiled. His teeth gleamed white, and almost menacing in the shadows. "I can assure you, revenge does not come into it. Admittedly, I do not relish having to apologise to Lady Jersey, and many mamas have had their opinion of me as a rakehell confirmed. On the other hand, the odds on our marriage have shortened in most of the betting books of the clubs: I am glad I placed my bet when I did…''

''You…you…you are no gentleman, sir, to bet on such a thing, to bandy my name…'' She was on her feet now, heading for the door. If she had to walk to Berkhamsted—whichever direction it lay in—she would do so, whatever the risk.

''Come back, Antonia. Where do you think you are going? It is nearly dark. I was only teasing—I have never so much as whispered your name in my club or any other. I cannot resist seeing your eyes flash so, it is most piquant.''

Antonia hesitated. Indeed, it was dark out there, and the woods were pressing in on all sides. She turned from the door and found he had taken off his jacket, tugged his neckcloth loose and was lounging easily in his chair, his long legs stretched out in front of him. The candlelight glanced gold from his hair and shadowed the dangerous, mocking mouth. But his eyes were warm on her; when he stretched out a hand, she walked uncertainly towards him.

As she reached her chair, he caught her hand and pulled her on to his lap, settling her comfortably in the crook of his arm. Knowing the certain outcome of struggling, Antonia yielded to the temptation to sit quietly. ''You do not really intend to ruin me, do you?'' she asked, afraid to hear the answer.

''You are ruined, anyway, by the very act of being alone with me, here, all night. Come, Antonia, let us be hanged for the sheep, not the lamb.'' As he spoke he stood up, lifting her easily in his arms and walked slowly to the hay bed. Antonia found herself laid gently on a rug.

Marcus loomed above her. He seemed very large and all the humour had fled from the dark eyes. "Antonia? One word from you and I will take a rug to the far side of this barn and stay there all night. But, as a result of this night you are ruined in the sight of Society. You must marry me, you have no choice."

She understood him well enough, and believed him. If she told him to, he would take himself off and not trouble her. But she loved him, and if she were never to see him again for the rest of her life, she would at least have this night.

Wordlessly Antonia held up her arms to him and he sank on to the soft bed beside her. Marcus's fingers ran through her hair, tossing aside pins, fanning out the lustrous curls against the blanket. "You are so beautiful, you take my breath away," he murmured, his voice curiously husky. His finger traced the line of her jaw then moved to map the curve of her full upper lip.

Antonia shivered in delicious anticipation, shot through with apprehension. Instinctively her teeth fastened on his fingertip and she saw his eyes close momentarily. Antonia began to unbutton his shirt and, smoothing the linen aside, ran her palms flat across the planes of his chest. The heat of him shocked her, but even more shocking was the realisation of the power that her touch gave her over him.

Her fingers moved, tugging and smoothing until she could push the shirt from his shoulders. It was silent in the barn except for his ragged breathing. To her surprise, he did not kiss her, seemingly willing to let her set the pace.

Exploring, giving way entirely to instinct, Antonia let her mouth trail kisses down his muscular shoulder before hesitating for only a heart beat as her lips moved across to his chest. They fastened on his nipple and she heard him gasp as her tongue flicked out and over the sensitive tip.

Startled by her own temerity and the effect she was having on him, Antonia stopped in confusion, hiding her hot face in his neck. Marcus caressed her neck, then neatly unfastened the row of pearl buttons securing her bodice at the back. The gauzy muslin seemed to float from her shoulders and she felt her naked breast against his bare chest, cool against the hot, muscular planes.

He rolled her gently over on to her back, deftly freeing the rest of the dress from her limbs, leaving her clad only in her stockings and chemise. He got to his feet and Antonia closed her eyes, hearing the rest of his clothes fall to the bed beside her.

Antonia ventured to open her eyes again as she felt his weight dip the hay beside her and found herself looking into his intent, serious face. "Antonia, my darling, are you sure?" For the first time she saw uncertainty in his face.

Apprehension filled her, but was overwhelmed by longing and her love for him. "Yes," she whispered, "but kiss me."

He needed no further bidding, his mouth possessing hers, his tongue invading sweetly so that she was scarcely aware at first of his weight upon her. When that other, totally intimate invasion came, she cried out against his mouth, but then she was carried on a tide of sensation with him. The pleasure alarmed her even more than the momentary pain, but she gave herself up to it, trusting him to guide her.

Then came a moment when he became still above her, his body rigid as he groaned deep in his throat and then he cried out, a shout of triumph as she too arched against him, her cry of ecstasy muffled against his hard shoulder.

Marcus pulled her into the curve of his shoulder as he fell back on to the bed and she let him hold her, holding on to him in turn as though she would never let him go. They slept wrapped in each other's arms, oblivious to the noises of the night.

They awoke at dawn, Antonia blissfully becoming aware of the movement of Marcus's mouth on the swell of her breast.

"Mmm," she murmured, sleepily, rolling over to wrap her arms and legs possessively around his naked body. This time it was she who set the pace, urgent in her need for him, revelling in his strength, his power.

At length he propped himself up on one elbow and gazed down at her flushed face. "And how do you feel this morning, my beauty?" he enquired softly.

"Quite, quite ruined," she confessed, praying that he would not say the words that would destroy this dream of happiness. But it was a futile hope.

"And how long are you going to make me wait until we marry?" Marcus asked, getting up and reaching for his shirt.

Antonia was struck silent by seeing him standing there, naked, so close, so real, so very masculine. Then she too reached for her chemise; somehow she felt the need for clothes before she could continue this.

"I am not going to marry you," she said bluntly as she stood, her back to him for Marcus to fasten the buttons of her bodice.

His lips grazed down her nape. "Tease."

"No, I mean it." She stepped away and turned to face him. "I never said I would marry you."

"But you have no choice!" He gestured to the rumpled hay bed with its eloquent impression of two bodies.

"I will not marry you. If anyone realises that we have been here all night, then yes, I am ruined. But I will have to live with that."

"And if you are with child?" he demanded brutally.

Antonia felt herself grow pale. The thought had never entered her mind, she had been so swept along by her love for him. Her nails bit into her palms as she regained her self-control: she almost capitulated then, but at no time had he told her that he loved her, needed her, could not live without her and she would not marry him without that declaration of love.

All his words of tenderness were occasioned by their lovemaking; none of them had spoken of a shared future. "If that is the case, I shall raise the child myself, as others have done before me."

Suddenly he was in front of her, holding her by the shoulders, impelling her to meet his gaze. But he was not angry as she had thought. His face was curiously gentle as was his voice when he asked her, "Just why, in the face of all this, will you not be my wife?"

Antonia could not meet his eyes or he would see the way she felt about him. She could not bear for him to pretend to love her out of pity.

"This is not about Claudia, is it?" he demanded. "Nor about your feelings for Jeremy Blake, let alone your ludicrous cousin Hewitt?"

She shook her head mutely, her eyes still averted from his.

"You told me there was nothing I could do or say to

make you agree to marry me. Well, I have done all I can, but I have not said all I should.''

Antonia did look at him then; something in the tone of his voice was different, more tender even than it had been last night. She held her breath, waiting.

''I have never told you I love you, Antonia, but I do. I love you, heart and soul and body—and for ever. I have never loved another woman, and I never will. So if you do not marry me, I shall never marry—for no one could ever take your place.''

Antonia gave a little sob and threw herself into his arms, too overcome even to kiss him. All she could do was hold on to him, feeling his heart beat against her cheek, knowing his strength and his love were hers for ever.

''Well?'' he murmured into her hair. ''Will you marry me?''

''Yes, Marcus, my love, of course I will.''

They stood there, holding each other as the rising sun sent a shaft of sunlight spilling across the floor of the barn. At last Antonia freed herself. ''We cannot stand here all day, we must have some breakfast and go home. Thank goodness Donna is not expecting me.''

As she spoke, she moved to the table and began to sort through the hamper with hands that trembled. ''Look, here is bread and ham and a flask of ale. Marcus, how did you manage to contrive all this? And what have you done to my great-aunt's unfortunate coachman?'' Somehow the calm domesticity of preparing food with this man convinced her that this was real, and forever.

He moved to her side and began to cut bread. ''He is on his way back to London, having hired a hack as his mistress instructed him.''

Antonia stared at him. ''You mean, you and she…that

you plotted it and she knew...and permitted it? Last night..." Antonia could not help but blush.

"I had to ask her permission." He laughed at Antonia as he reached for the ham. "When you said there was nothing I could do, I knew I would have to take desperate measures. I could sense Lady Granger approved of me..."

"She remembered your grandfather!" Antonia riposted, but she was smiling.

"I went to her direct from Almack's. She told me to behave like a red-blooded man and all would be well. Then I remembered my sister's advice."

"Anne was in this plot, too?" Now Antonia really was incredulous.

"She told me, when you left for London, that I was arrogant, that I had never felt the need to explain myself or my actions to anyone. I realised I had never told you I loved you, never realised that I needed to. I should have known you would never marry for anything less."

Antonia reached up and kissed him. "And when did you realise you loved me?"

"When I saw you in Pethybridge's office. I knew what it must have cost a gentlewoman to undertake business like that. And despite the reverse you had obviously suffered, you were brave and defiant. Although I was still angry with you about your poachers, yet in that moment all I wanted to do was to protect you."

She stepped into the shelter of his arms. "And now you can," she said softly.

Marcus kissed her gently, all the love he had never spoken until now evident in the embrace. Eventually he released her, with a sigh. "I could stay here for ever, but I suppose we should eat and then make our way home."

When they left, he handed her up onto the seat of the carriage next to him. "Come, ride here beside me until we get closer to the village, there will be no one about at this hour to see you."

Antonia linked her arm through his as he gathered up the reins and asked, in a mock-severe tone, "And you can tell me all about Lady Reed."

Marcus looked down into her laughing face and knew he had never been so happy. "Lady who?"

* * * * *

Modern Romance™
...seduction and
passion guaranteed

Tender Romance™
...love affairs that
last a lifetime

Sensual Romance™
...sassy, sexy and
seductive

Blaze
...sultry days and
steamy nights

Medical Romance™
...medical drama on
the pulse

Historical Romance™
...rich, vivid and
passionate

27 new titles every month.

*With all kinds of Romance for
every kind of mood...*

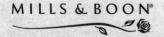

MILLS & BOON®

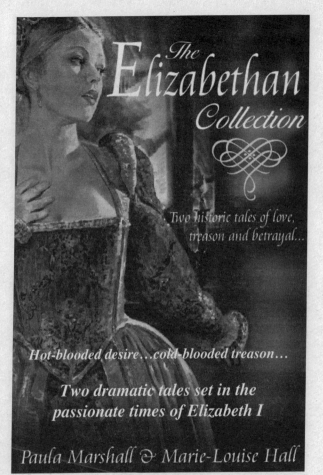

CHRISTMAS
SECRETS

Three Festive Romances

CAROLE MORTIMER   CATHERINE SPENCER
DIANA HAMILTON

Available from 15th November 2002

*Available at most branches of WH Smith,
Tesco, Martins, Borders, Eason, Sainsbury's
and all good paperback bookshops.*

1202/59/MB50

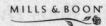